Invasion

Invasion Series I

Jay Allan

Join my email list
at www.jayallanbooks.com

List members get publication announcements and special bonuses throughout the year (email addresses are never shared or used for any other purpose). Please feel free to email me with any questions at jayallanwrites@gmail.com. I answer all reader emails

For all things Sci-Fi,
join my interactive Reader Group here:

facebook.com/groups/JayAllanReaders

Follow me on Twitter @jayallanwrites

Follow my blog at www.jayallanwrites.com

www.jayallanbooks.com
www.crimsonworlds.com

Books by Jay Allan

Invasion Series
Invasion

Flames of Rebellion Series
(Published by Harper Voyager)
Flames of Rebellion
Rebellion's Fury

The Crimson Worlds Series
Marines
The Cost of Victory
A Little Rebellion
The First Imperium
The Line Must Hold
To Hell's Heart
The Shadow Legions
Even Legends Die
The Fall

Crimson Worlds Refugees Series
Into the Darkness
Shadows of the Gods
Revenge of the Ancients
Winds of Vengeance
Storm of Vengeance
Crusade of Vengeance

Crimson Worlds Successors Trilogy
MERCS
The Prisoner of Eldaron
The Black Flag

Crimson Worlds Prequels
Tombstone
Bitter Glory
The Gates of Hell

Red Team Alpha
(A New Crimson Worlds Novel)

Books by Jay Allan

Blood on the Stars Series
Duel in the Dark
Call to Arms
Ruins of Empire
Echoes of Glory
Cauldron of Fire
Dauntless
The White Fleet
Black Dawn
Invasion
Nightfall
The Grand Alliance
The Colossus
The Others
The Last Stand
Empire's Ashes
Attack Plan Alpha
Descent into Darkness

Andromeda Chronicles
(Blood on the Stars Adventure Series)
Andromeda Rising
Wings of Pegasus

The Far Stars Series
Shadow of Empire
Enemy in the Dark
Funeral Games

Far Stars Legends Series
Blackhawk
The Wolf's Claw

Portal Wars Trilogy
Gehenna Dawn
The Ten Thousand
Homefront

Also by Jay Allan – The Dragon's Banner

Characters

Travis McDaniel – A 24 year old graduate of the Marine Academy, a serving lieutenant in the Corps. After graduating from college and attending Officer Candidates School, he was commissioned a 2nd lieutenant, and assigned to service. He is very intelligent, and always got along with his younger brother, Hugh, who often had difficulty with others.

Hugh McDaniel – A 19 year old genius, who completed high school when he was 10, and college when he was 12, he is currently completing his third PhD, and trying to decide which offer to accept for employment.

Lucas Kiley – A 24 year old Marine who went through the course with Travis and became one of his closest friends. Lucas has no close family and has come home with Travis on several occasions.

Sarah Jones – A woman from the neighborhood, and an on-again, off-again love interest of Travis'.

Gavin Sanders – A young man, and Hugh McDaniel's only real friend other than his brother. Gavin is extremely intelligent, though not at Hugh's level.

Janet Howers – A local girl who gets caught up with the survivors.

George McDaniel – Travis and Hugh's father.

Denise McDaniel – Travis and Hugh's mother.

Prologue

Approaching Earth

The planet is perfect, better even than we had expected to find. And, perhaps more importantly, it is teeming with inhabitants…people who are very likely to ideally serve our purposes. Our preliminary scouting, our early efforts, all suggest that the people will be ideally matched to us, perfect for our needs. But we cannot be certain until we take control…and really try.

Our initial fleet will reach position shortly, and then the attack will begin. We will kill many of them, most of them in fact. This will help us in many ways, destroying whatever resistance ability they have quickly, before they can organize and try to strike back. It will also provide us with the survivors, and still in numbers beyond what we need at first. For the future, assuming the tests work, we will breed new ones, see that they are raised from birth with no idea of independence, no recollection of living on their own. The first group will be somewhat difficult to maintain, perhaps, but in the longer term, they will exist only to serve us, in the capacity we require, and nothing else.

As I have stated, our initial assault will be deadly, but it will have the effect of wearing down the morale of those who survive, leaving them battered, shaken, able to be picked up as we require them. We expect to have some trouble with a portion of them, at least at first, and possibly even some quasi-organized resistance, but this is to be expected…and it will be easily quelled.

PART ONE

—

The Invasion

Chapter One

From the Notes of Hugh McDaniel

I find myself writing in this log more often lately than ever before, perhaps even much more. I don't know why, particularly since I do not imagine that anyone else will ever read it. I am intelligent, I know that, very intelligent even, but I don't imagine my life will be so eventful, so intriguing that it will provide interesting reading. I guess I write it for myself, though I don't suppose even I will ever find it all that intriguing. It is just a hobby, I guess, and one I find enjoyable.

I have been edgy recently, disturbed by…something I can't put my finger on. It is almost as though I know a problem is coming, which, of course, is absurd. Perhaps it is just the realization that I have to pick something to do with my life, some field to truly devote myself to. I had always imagined that I would do that eventually, that I would find some subject that truly interested and excited me. But I haven't…not yet at least. There are many I find moderately intriguing, but none I can imagine dedicating my life to. Not yet at least.

I truly do not know if this is something most people find to be easy, or if the majority of them just go about their lives doing whatever presented itself, and not what they loved…but for me it is difficult. I know I am intelligent, far more than the average person, and yet despite my education, and my knowledge, I haven't found anything I find terribly…interesting. It is helpful to imagine that I will one day, though with each passing week, month, year, it seems less and less likely. One of these days—and soon—I will have to choose something to pursue. And right now, I might as well throw a dart at a board to decide.

123-21 7 5th Road
Forest Hills, Queens
D – 3 Days

Hugh McDaniel pressed his face firmly against his telescope. He'd seen something strange, for just a few seconds, perhaps, but he'd swear it was *something*. He couldn't tell what it was, or even be sure it was anything of note…but his brief checkout session on the Internet told him at once that he wasn't the only one who had seen it. Not even close. At least a dozen others had, and probably a lot more than that, and many of them were even then arguing pointlessly that it was everything from a comet to an alien invasion. Hugh avoided such pointless discussions, knowing they were based more on unlikely probabilities than facts. However, he *was* curious…very curious. And the possibility that it *was* something of note, as small a chance that was, clung to him.

Still, he hadn't found anything since, despite hours of efforts, and it was very late now. He knew he should call it quits, go to bed and get a few hours of sleep, but something tugged at him, drove him to remain where he was, for just a few more minutes. He had class the next day, but as with his other intellectual pursuits, he was well ahead of the curve on that, and even the professor. He had learned to hide it somewhat over the years, at least a little, and he didn't put on quite the show he did when he was younger, but still, at

19 he was about to complete his third PhD, and his intellectual capacity was…obvious. It took almost no effort on his part to get straight As in any class he took, and even going, listening to the lectures, was boring. He knew that he was gifted, that his abilities far outranked those of his associates…but it mostly made him uncomfortable.

His thoughts gradually shifted, back to reality, and he decided he would go to bed after all, at least in a couple minutes. He could still get a few hours of sleep, and he felt strange for getting so caught up in something that was probably nothing. But still, he didn't see much he couldn't explain, and what he had witnessed through his telescope was…strange. Despite his best efforts, he couldn't get it out of his mind.

His thoughts wandered, drifting back to college, to his life. He understood that he couldn't go to school forever, that he had to go to work eventually, to do something with his life, but despite a long list of companies—and government agencies—that had expressed interest in him, and sometimes more, nothing had really grabbed his attention, at least not yet. He was a genius, there wasn't much question of that, but he lacked the hardcore interest in any single field to devote enough time to it to make it a career. In truth, for all his intelligence, he hadn't found anything that *truly* interested him. He just didn't know what to do. He was young, at least in comparison to most of the others around him, and he knew he could use that as a good enough excuse to avoid making a decision, at least for another few years. But, in truth, he was ready, intellectually at least…if he could find something that intrigued him. He was concerned that he would end up bored out of his mind, that he would spend his life doing something he didn't really care about. Just like most normal people did.

He looked through the telescope one last time, again not seeing anything abnormal. Then he let out a loud sigh, and he pulled away from it. School, perhaps, wasn't enough to tear him from his efforts, but at least tomorrow offered more than just class. Travis was coming home on a two week leave. His brother was by far the closest to him of anyone, and he hadn't seen him in almost a year. Hugh didn't get excited about much, but he was dying to see his brother. Travis was very intelligent, though by normal standards, and not on Hugh's scale, and also unlike his brother, he had always had a future in mind. He had wanted to be a Marine since childhood, for as long as Hugh could remember, and he had done just that. He'd gone to the Officer Candidates School, and he'd emerged as a 2nd lieutenant. He'd spent the past two years as head of a rifle platoon, and now he was up for a bump to 1st lieutenant, and the second position in the company. Hugh knew his brother's exploits were less than those he might be expected to undertake one day, but he was impressed nevertheless, and very excited at the prospect of seeing him.

That, more than anything else, drove him away. He wanted to get some sleep before Travis arrived, if not for class. He pulled down the telescope, and he shoved it in the storage room where he kept it. Then, he went inside. He could get almost four hours of sleep he figured, and still make it to his class…and then get back home just about the same time Travis was scheduled to walk in.

* * *

"Hey Travis…thanks. I mean it. This is the second time you've had me come home with you, and I really do appreciate it." Lucas Kiley looked over at his friend, and his face was one of pure sincerity. Kiley was universally recognized as a good guy, but also as a shy one, and he didn't say much more than he had to most of the time. But he was different with Travis. He had no family, at least none still alive, and he had clearly enjoyed the experience of his friend's close household. He'd even gotten along with

Hugh, which most people didn't, at least not well...and Hugh had enjoyed his presence too. Still, he'd been surprised when Travis had invited him to come along again.

The train was going around a curve, heading into the city. Travis was excited to be going home, and especially to see his brother. Hugh was difficult for some people to get along with, but Travis had always been very close to him...and he was confident his brother would be glad to see Lucas again as well.

"Are you kidding me, Lucas...I'm thrilled you could come. And so is my family. You got along with all of them...even with Hugh..." He paused for a moment, thinking about his younger brother. He was very close to Hugh, but he realized that even he couldn't truly understand the depth of thought that ran through his brother's brain. He realized Hugh wasn't very...typical...not even for a genius, and he was worried about his brother finding something he was interested in, something that would provide a chance for him to truly use his incredible intelligence. He was very educated, and he had never gotten a grade below an A, but Travis could tell that none of it had truly gained his interest. At least not really.

"Your family is amazing...and your brother is very special." Lucas paused for a moment, but then he continued, "I understand why you've always been close to him. He is brilliant, of course, but he is also very...normal, in ways, at least. I know that may not be obvious, that he is shy, that he has trouble interacting with many people, but once he gets past that, he is really very easy to get along with. Very easy."

Travis nodded, but he didn't respond, at least not right away. He knew his friend was right, at least in the part about Travis not being...typical...for a genius. He dismissed a thought about how stupid that sounded, especially since he knew his brother had few friends, and struggled considerably when dealing with people he didn't know well.

Still, with Lucas, as with a few others, Hugh *was* normal, or at least close to it.

"I'm glad that you get along with him, Lucas…and I'm happy that you understand. I'm afraid most people don't."

"Most people don't understand much, Travis. Your brother is a good soul…and he is as smart as they come. He will rise up to a level we can't even understand, my friend, I'm sure of that, though exactly what and where that will be remains a question."

Travis smiled for an instant, and then he sat quietly, pondering his friend's words. He knew his brother was having trouble finding areas of interest, and though Hugh hadn't really shared them with him, he was sure his brother had been almost buried with offers. His thoughts about Hugh had centered on that, on the question of whether he would discover an area of real interest, one that truly excited him…or if he would end up settling for something lesser. It would be a shame if his brother couldn't find some area that truly excited him, if he ended up doing work he found less than interesting. Even boring.

He'd had a fair number of doubts about that, worried that Hugh would struggle to find something that truly interested him, but his friend sounded sure, so sure that his brother had a future, one hopefully, that truly intrigued him, that he started to believe it more himself. If Hugh did find something that actually excited hum, that allowed him to draw on his knowledge with sincere effort, on his powerful intellect…there was no telling what he could achieve.

"New York Penn Station…ten minutes."

The announcement came over the PA system, and it pushed Travis's deeper thoughts away. Whatever his brother would do, whatever else might lie in the future, he was just excited to go home, to see his family again. A quick ride out to Queens on the subway—he had been clear that no one was to come into Manhattan to meet him, even keeping the specific train he was on a secret to avoid it—and he would be home once again, for the first time in almost a year. He would see his family again.

He would see his brother.

*   *   *

"So, how have you been, Hugh?" Travis spoke, taking advantage of the first time he and his brother had been alone. He had said his hellos and the like earlier, but he realized that this was the first moment when he and Hugh could honestly talk. It was late, very late, and the dinner and everything that followed it was over. Everyone else was in bed, sleeping as far as Travis knew, but he was awake, and he wasn't surprised to find his brother even more alert.

"I've been fine, Travis…really." The last word, and his entire tone told Travis that the statement was true to an extent, but also was not, not on some level at least.

"Hugh…you can be honest with me, you know that. I know Mom and Dad don't really understand you, but I think that I do, at least as well as anyone can. You haven't found anything that really interests you, not yet. Have you?"

Hugh listened to his brother, and he looked as though he was going to deny it, that he was going to claim some kind of interest in something or other. But then he just looked at Travis and said, "No…not really. I've taken a lot of classes, and I should have found something that really intrigues me…but I haven't. I've done well, learned everything I needed, but nothing has really caught my attention. I don't know…maybe I have a warped perception, perhaps I expect to be interested all the time in whatever I am going to do. Maybe that's not normal…perhaps everyone else pursues things they're not really interested in either. Maybe I should just pick…something."

"No, Hugh…you're right that many people do that, certainly, but not all. I am doing what I want to do, what I have desired since childhood. That doesn't mean I enjoy every moment of it, every aspect. Certainly, I miss you all, my family, who I don't get to see nearly as often as I would like. But this is right for me, I know that." He paused, for a moment. "And there is something that you will truly enjoy as well. I don't know what makes things the way they are, what is behind the world…but I am sure almost no one has your abilities, your intelligence. You will find something that uses it all, I am sure of it…just keep looking."

Hugh managed a smile, for a few seconds. "I appreciate your thoughts, I truly do…but I will have to start some kind of career eventually. I can't keep going to school forever."

"Eventually? I know you've been ahead of yourself for a long time, Hugh, in classes with people older than you for most of your life. But you're only 19. There is time. Time to consider what you want to do. Time to decide."

"Perhaps…but I just can't find anything I'm more than a little interested in. Not really. I know I have the ability to do well at whatever I choose, but it all seems…boring…to me. Pointless." He was quiet for a moment, and then he said, "Maybe you're right…maybe it is out there, waiting for me to find it. I just don't know." He looked up at the sky, and his mood changed, his genuine curiosity becoming clear. "I want to set up my telescope," he said, changing the subject. "Last night, I could swear I saw something—something truly different—but then I lost it, and I couldn't get it back. I might say it was just my imagination, but I went on the Internet and at least a dozen others saw it and posted about it. I don't know what it was—probably something routine or pointless—but I wanted to check again tonight. Just to make sure."

Travis looked for a moment as though his brother was just trying to change the subject, but then he realized Hugh was serious. He believed entirely that he had seen something, and probably something significant. Perhaps more amazing, something that had left him in confusion about what it was. "Let's get the telescope then…and see what is up there."

Hugh smiled, and he nodded his head. He turned and walked around the house, to the small out-building where he kept much of his gear. He pulled out the telescope and set it up, and then he started to look. He didn't see anything abnormal, and after a few minutes, he pulled back and let his brother look. He didn't really expect Travis would find anything he hadn't…but he figured his brother might enjoy looking, at least. He was still a little preoccupied, worried about what he knew he had seen but couldn't find again. He was starting to tell himself to let it go, to forget about it, and then…

"Hugh! What is this?" Travis pulled back from the telescope, waving for his brother to take another look. Hugh figured it was just his brother's inexperience, that it was something normal, at least to a frequent stargazer like him…until he looked.

He felt his breath seize up for a moment. He saw what he had the night before, and so much more. There were suddenly dozens of…something…in his view. Just a moment before there had been nothing…and then, a moment later…what? What was it he was seeing? He fought back against the thoughts coming out from his brain, told himself there was no way…but almost immediately, he realized they were right.

Whatever he was looking at was manmade. They were ships, though they had to be massive ones, far bigger than anything that could be constructed on Earth. His mind, as vast and powerful as it was, reeled, thinking it through, realizing what he was looking at. He tried to come up with alternatives, with explanations that could explain it…but he realized almost immediately what it was, what it had to be.

And what it meant.

Man was not alone in the universe. He had already believed that, at least in a sense…but now he realized that the proof was right there, approaching the Earth.

He wasn't sure yet that the beings were hostile, that they had come to attack the Earth...but he realized just how close they were, and that there were dozens of them. If their purpose had been one of exploration, of reaching out, they would have been detected days—weeks perhaps—before. He didn't know what had kept the vessels hidden, what technology they had used, but the size of the force, and the fact that they had apparently deliberately kept themselves from discovery, didn't support many good results. He kept his mind from coming to any stark conclusions, but he couldn't help but come back to the same suspicion.

Earth was about to be attacked. Attacked by aliens.

Chapter Two

From the Log of Captain Jason Wrangle

I don't know what is happening, not really. Everything was quiet, perhaps as calm as I can ever remember, and then suddenly, we were on full alert. I know what caused that, what is happening, though I still find it difficult to believe. The international situation seemed as calm as I can recall just before the news broke, and the status change didn't carry any explanations at all. Just to prepare immediately.

For war. With an enemy from space.

This sounds insane, like some crazy joke. Only it isn't. Every company commander and higher up from the installation was called to a special meeting...immediately. I don't know who this enemy is, or even have a guess. I don't even know for sure it *is* an enemy, except for the general sense that something is very wrong.

In all my thoughts of my career, I have conjured many potential conflicts, considered multiple opponents...but *this* never occurred to me, not really at least, and much less that it could happen so quickly, and without warning. I tried asking my superiors, the couple times I could get a moment's attention, but I don't think they know any more than I do. I think we're all in the same boat...told to prepare for the worst, and nothing else. And the worst is likely going to be pretty damned bad. Any kind of power that can travel through space and reach our world is clearly vastly superior to us technologically. I don't think there can be any doubt about that. My mind already wants to give up, to yield before I even know anything about them…but my Marine training is there, too, telling me to get ready for the greatest fight I have ever imagined. I honestly don't know which will win out, what I will do…and I imagine most of the other officers feel the same way.

The regular Marines, the combat warriors, have not even been told yet, at least not officially. But still, it appears that some word is spreading. I passed at least one barracks that appeared to be…disturbed. In another half hour, the entire place will be consumed, at least by rumors. I know the meeting I am about to go to, the one at which I assume we will be told whatever the higher ups know, was scheduled as quickly as possible, but I wonder if it was fast enough. I feel the urge to get back to my Marines, my own company, quickly, to stop whatever rumors are spreading, and to figure out just how we are going to fight, if we are attacked.

My company—the entire battalion in fact—was on light duty until less than an hour ago. I took the opportunity to allow a large number of my people to take leave, as did the other commanders. In my case, this included my two best platoon leaders. I just sent out the recall notices, to both of them, as well as to all of the Marines currently away from duty, more than thirty percent of my strength. Hopefully, they will return on time, though I doubt it.

I don't know what is worse, learning about what is happening…or passing it on. After the meeting, I must go to my company, and explain to the Marines who are present exactly what is going on. That would be difficult enough in any situation, but since I have no idea what is actually happening, and I doubt the commanders do either, I don't even know what to say. I will just do my best, and no doubt most of those present will assume that I know more than I am saying, that I am in on something they are not.

I am not. I don't know a thing...but there is no way to convince them of that. Perhaps after the meeting, the conference beginning in about 10 minutes, I will know more. But if I had to guess, I'd say the higher ups don't know much more than me...and they will share even less of that.

**Camp Lejuene
North Carolina
D – 1 Days**

The stage had been quickly set up, and the attendees, all captains and higher ranked Marines, sat still, looking occasionally around at each other, as though any of them knew more than the others. But mostly, they just stared straight ahead. They had been called together very suddenly, and that rarely precipitated good news, even when it wasn't joined by the thin but fateful announcement that this summons had been. Everyone present knew there were aliens of some kind, though it will never be certain how many actually believed it at the time. One thing was certain...few if any could figure out just how bad things were, at least not until the general walked out on the stage.

Even before he reached the microphone, anyone who took a good look at him could see he was truly shaken up. Usually a perfect image, without so much as a ripple in his uniform or a crease in his cheeks, this time the general looked used up, his jacket and pants wrinkled, his face covered in creases and wrinkles. Whatever the information he was about to share, it was clear the speaker hadn't made his own peace with it yet...and that shook Wrangle up even more. He was used to the general being calm, knowing what to do...and that was obviously not the case now. It also upset maybe half of the others, the ones who were really paying attention. The rest were already in their own worlds of defeat and despair, their minds buried in a litany of disaster, and they didn't even notice the general particularly.

He walked up to the microphone, but he just stood still for a moment, silent, looking out at the Marines, at the officers present. He clearly knew he had to present something, that he had to tell them what was going on—and what to do—but for a short period, he just stood where he was and stared. Then, he finally cleared his throat and spoke.

"Gentlemen, I will keep this as short as possible. You have all been to many assemblies before, heard announcements that were negative, that suggested difficult times ahead. But you have never listened to anything as significant as what I am about to say." He paused again, clearly struggling to even say what he had come to announce.

Wrangle twitched, his mind racing, trying to think of the specifics he was about to hear. The Russians or the Chinese—they were, of course, the two likely enemies, the only major ones he had ever considered a fight with—would have been bad enough, of course, but at least he and his people were more or less ready for that. He found himself glad at least that he didn't have to make the announcement, that he could sit in his chair and listen while the general struggled to say what he had come to say.

He knew the basis of what the general had come to tell them…but when the man spoke, when Wrangle finally heard the words, he still almost went blank.

"We are facing an apparent invasion, a massive one." The general hesitated again, but only for a few seconds. "Not from a neighboring country, as I assume you already know, but from beyond. Beyond the Earth." The general spoke in a cold, hard tone, looking both like he realized how ridiculous he sounded, but also that he was absolutely serious. Wrangle just looked back, silent, as silent as everyone else in the room. The meeting had been hastily convened and held in the main audience hall. He was surprised at first to be included in something that seemed to be targeted to higher level commanders, but then he realized that time was a major factor, that his force, all the forces, would probably be moving out almost at once. That shook him up more in some ways than the actual facts…which hadn't entirely sunken in yet.

"What I just said is correct…exactly how you are thinking about it. At first, we thought it might be some secret weapon, some development of another nation, even some kind of malfunction in our detection devices." He continued, and his voice changed, became even deeper, more ominous. "But now we are certain. Sure that we face possibly the worst nightmare possible." He paused for a few more seconds, and then he said, "We have apparently tried to contact them in every way possible for some time, with no result. They do not respond, nor even attempt to, at least not in any way we can detect. They just keep moving forward, toward the Earth. We are almost positive now that we are dealing not with an outreach, an exploration…but with an invasion. An attack by a force from another world."

The general stopped once again, half because he probably didn't know what else to say immediately, and half to give those in the hall a chance to catch up, to understand just what he *had* said. Wrangle struggled to do just that, to overcome his doubts…to accept what he had just heard. The setting, the sound of the general's voice—everything— gave him no real chance to doubt any of it, not that he would have anyway, after essentially knowing much of it for half an hour or so. But still, he couldn't believe it, not really. Invasion? By aliens? He had considered it, of course, even assumed that the newcomers were hostile. But this was the first he had heard about it, at least from a source with some credibility. It all seemed absurd. Impossible.

And yet, he knew it was real. That suddenly he—and everyone else, he realized, in the Marines, in any service, and

all those others not in the military, everyone on the planet—
had just moved into a new reality, one that seemed darker
and bleaker with every second that passed.

The general started to speak again, looking upset
certainly, but basically holding his tone steady. "As I speak
here, we are tracking over one hundred vessels, moving into
orbit. They have begun intercepting satellites, destroying
them, disabling most of our long range communications and
other capabilities. As I said previously, they have not
responded to any of our communications attempts, and at
this point, there seems to be little doubt as to their
intentions. By all of our standards, they appear to be hostile.
We have no real information on their specific intentions, at
least I do not, but it seems likely that a full invasion is
planned, that it is about to begin. Whether they plan to
subjugate us, enslave us—or outright destroy us—we don't
know. But we will be assuming the worst. You will deploy
your units immediately to the field, taking position where
you are assigned, and once in position, you will await further
instructions. Our air assault units will engage the enemy
first, striking any craft that attempt to land or conduct any
offensive operations. If they are successful, if they are able
to destroy the aliens, perhaps that will be it." His voice
made clear he didn't allow much for that possibility, and
Wrangle imagined few if any of those present did either.
The aliens had traveled probably lightyears to reach Earth,
and that, coupled with the technology they likely possessed,
meant the forces sent against them—all of Earth's—would
be hard pressed. The chance of the initial planes deployed
just wiping out the enemy seemed almost impossible. Still,
he couldn't argue with the thought, with the plan to attack
as quickly as possible.

"As I said, once you are in position, you will wait. If our
air forces are victorious, if they are able to chase away
the…aliens…then that may be it." He paused, again giving
the impression he didn't believe that, not for a second. "If

the enemy *is* able to land forces, then we will go into action, depending on where they come in. We will engage them, wherever they attack…and we will close on them when possible, launch our own offensives. Forces from this installation will cover an area of approximately two hundred fifty miles in any direction, at least at first. As soon as we have more information on the enemy's intentions, on where they have landed, we will redirect various units to face the invaders. We will be fairly spread out, at least until we get some real information on where the enemy is attacking…but hopefully, we will have the chance to converge before we are engaged." Then he stated, "We will be keeping our military as much out of cities and heavily populated areas as possible." He didn't elaborate or explain…but he didn't have to. The thought of nuclear assaults on the cities was present with every word, but not stated at all.

"I know this news is…strange, that it is extremely unexpected, even unbelievable. But it is true, nevertheless. So, get over your surprise, your concerns…there is no time for them. Our culture, our very reality, has changed in a flash, and the likelihood that we will be facing an enemy more advanced—and possibly, probably, far more advanced—than we are, seems profound. I can only say that you are among the best of our fighters, and if it does indeed come down to a fight, I know you will give the enemy all you've got. This is, without much question, the most serious fight we have ever undertaken, that anyone has. I know you will all do your best to give the enemy one hell of a struggle." He didn't say that they probably didn't have much chance, at least not directly, but his outlook was fairly obvious, despite his efforts to sound confident.

"All I have to do is stop and think about this, about what is happening, and I begin to lose focus." He continued, clearly trying to stay calm, to sound as though he was prepared…with limited success. "I urge all of you to think about your duty, about your obligations, as much as possible…and not about any other part of what is happening. Don't think of home, nor on any other area of the nation or the world. That is the only way I believe we can be ready…ready to do whatever we can to defeat this invasion." He stopped and looked out at the assembly, and for an instant, it was even more deathly quiet than it had been. Then he said, "We have no more time to waste. Go now…to your units and await receipt of your individual commands. And God bless us all…give us the strength we need to face this gravest threat, and to somehow defeat it." He did a fairly good job of sounding positive, but Wrangle knew better. His forces were about to go up against an enemy with technology far beyond anything they had. He knew his side would probably have numbers at least, but from human history, he knew that was usually not enough, not against an enemy with superior technology.

And probably far superior.

He sat still, struggling for a moment to do just as the general had requested, to push back against his wonder, his dread, and to…function. Somehow. He had a company to manage, and soon he would have orders to carry out. In all likelihood, his forces would be engaged, against an enemy they didn't know, one they didn't even understand. For all he knew, they could just press a button, and make all of his troops simply vanish. He didn't have anything informative, nothing at all about the enemy's forces, about their capabilities. And worse, perhaps, he believed that was because no one did. Not yet.

He tried to force his thoughts to focus, on his readiness, on the platoon's. He had to do it. It was all he *could* do. He knew every Marine present was trying the same thing, and it was clear that most of them were not doing any better at it than he was. He knew he would proceed, that he would lead his forces…somehow. But still, he almost lost it, for a moment at least, and one look around told him he was not alone. Somehow, beneath what remained of his professionalism, his Marine drive…he realized that he was almost certainly going to die, that all his people were.

After perhaps a minute, he regained some measure of control over himself. He got up, and he moved slowly towards the door. Perhaps a quarter of those present were doing the same, the others still sitting, trying to absorb what they had just been told. Wrangle wasn't sure if it made sense to try to think it through, or just to proceed as he would in a more normal situation. In the end, his people would fight, he was almost certain of that…most of them at least. They would battle hard…and probably fight until the enemy destroyed them. He wasn't sure if that would be immediately, or if his people would get a chance at least to strike back, to put up a fight.

He had almost no idea what he thought, what he expected.

Except to die. That he was almost sure about, whether it came sooner or a bit later. He was almost positive he was going to die.

But now, he put that all aside, the thoughts, the dark feelings. He had to assemble his men…he had to tell them what he'd just been told, and probably field questions, many of which he didn't have the answers for. He had to tell his people that they had to fight, against an enemy that would likely be brutally overpowering, one that would almost certainly win. And he wasn't sure how to do that.

He walked, picking up his pace as he moved…and somehow, from somewhere, he started to get some basic thoughts, a small start to what he had to say to his people.

Chapter Three

From the Notes of Hugh McDaniel

I have been busy, almost insane for the past 24 hours, with barely enough time to make a few notes and write anything down. I had half expected to find something with my telescope…but what I found went well beyond even my wildest expectations. My brother and I discovered what can only be described as a fleet of massive spaceships, approaching the Earth, and coming down into the atmosphere. It all seems insane, as though I am dreaming and not seeing what is actually occurring. But it *is* happening. I even went online again last night, checked to see that others agreed. For about two hours, there was a growing number of observers who saw the same things I did…and then it exploded. Thousands of people came online, hundreds of thousands, and the systems became overloaded, blocked. Then, the television announcers confirmed what I had come to believe—and what many thousands of others had as well, by then.

There was a fleet of spaceships surrounding the planet…almost certainly alien spacecraft.

I went through every possibility, imagined for a few moments that they were human-operated ships, that the Russians or Chinese had lunged ahead of us, developed some breathtaking new weapons. But that was ridiculous, and I realized it almost immediately.

Still, it seemed impossible that they were aliens, and I struggled to accept it. But it rapidly became apparent, however absurd it seemed, that it was the case, what was actually happening, no matter how insane it sounded. By morning, the word was out everywhere, and the neighborhood was hysterical. People were trying to leave, to stock up on food and other essentials, to do anything at all that they could think of.

This was probably the single most amazing—and terrifying—moment in all of human history, and I wondered who was really taking it seriously, not in terms of their own survival, but rather the overall response. What was the government doing? My brother was home, but what was his unit up to? The rest of the Marines and the army, the navy, and air force? What orders were being given to our military assets…and could they even put up a fight against whatever power the aliens possessed?

That assumed, of course, that the aliens were hostile. Despite the lack of communications, the arrival of an entire fleet, and every other sign that they were indeed here to attack us, to dominate us if not destroy us outright, many people held out the hope that it would actually be a positive, that the new arrivals would open communications, that they would guide us, lead us to a greater level than we could reach on our own. That was an appealing thought, I suppose, but it was not one I shared, not considering the reality, the lack of even an attempt to communicate with us.

I didn't share it at all. The forces, even now entering our atmosphere, *were* hostile. I was almost certain of it…for all the logical reasons I could come up with, and others as well.

Worst of all, I had no idea what we could do about it.

123-21 7 5th Road
Forest Hills, Queens
D – 0 Days

Hugh raced around, trying to do everything he could think of to…prepare. He wasn't at all sure what that meant, what, exactly to do. He didn't have any doubt that the new arrivals were hostile, unlike many of the others, but he wasn't sure just how aggressive they would be. Did they want to seize Earth, destroy the inhabitants and take it for themselves? Or did they want to enslave mankind? That last option didn't sound very good, but at least it meant most people would be left alive, which as far as he was concerned, left some hope. As long as humanity endured, there would be a chance to overcome the invaders…to survive.

And Hugh McDaniel knew only one thing for certain. Whether it was his intellect, or something that burned within him apart from that, he would never yield. Never. He would fight, do anything possible…even die. But he would not surrender.

Not ever.

"Hugh, are you sure we should stay here? Maybe we should get in the car, and try to get out of the city?" It was Denise McDaniel, his mother, asking the same thing she had brought up twice before. He understood, of course, and his mind raced once again, thinking of every aspect of both staying and going. He'd been doing that for hours now, and despite the many superficial urges to run, the answer had always been the same. Stay. At least in the city, if not at home.

He knew any prospect was a gamble under the current situation, that if the enemy wanted to destroy humanity, perhaps staying was a bad option. But so was running. There was no way to escape, at least not from Queens, not in the time they probably had left, not with the horrendous traffic. Besides, if the enemy was dead set on destroying all humanity, he figured they could do it easily enough, regardless of where people went. He hadn't quite come to terms with it yet, but he was beginning to realize that his actions were all based on the enemy having some use for humanity. If they just wanted the planet, devoid of all its inhabitants, he realized they could achieve that, and probably fairly easily.

It was better to stay where they were, or perhaps to find some local shelter. The last he had heard—or even looked outside—the roads were so blocked, it would take twelve hours, and maybe more, perhaps twenty-four, just to get out of the city…to get someplace only infinitesimally safer. It was probably a trip measured in days to get anyplace truly farther out, someplace meaningfully less dangerous. And if the aliens were going to attack, it would probably occur within a matter of hours…or less.

"I am sure, Mom…" He slowed his response, trying to change his tone to one a bit softer. It wasn't realistic perhaps, but he figured it would do his mother some good. "The traffic is horrendous…and honestly, if the enemy is going to attack…" And he was almost sure they would, in one way or another, though he didn't say that. "…we're probably safer around here than tied up on the street." He knew his family was aware of his intellectual capacity, but he just realized that they were now looking to him in many ways, seeking his guidance in matters he wouldn't have expected. He understood, at least a little, why they were doing that, how the current situation overwhelmed them, brought them to the point where they came to him. But as smart as he was, he didn't have any more real idea what to do, perhaps not than his mother did.

"I understand, Mom, I really do…" he continued. "I know that your thoughts are to escape—mine are too." *At least my undisciplined ones.* "But the…enemy…" He had already decided that's just what the aliens were, but he still hesitated a moment before going on. "…is too close. We won't even get out of Queens before they...do whatever they are going to do." His mind was racing, trying to think of the best thing, the course of action that offered the greatest survival chance. However small it may be. Pulling out in the car wasn't right, he was sure of that. But staying where they were, completely exposed...that wasn't it either.

"Get ready...we will go to the subway station." He said it quickly, without thinking about it...but he realized almost immediately, it *was* the best course of action. His mind had been going, almost non-stop for hours now. He realized that staying in the house wasn't the right course of action any more than getting in the car and trying to escape. "We will get underground, as far as we can manage...and stay there." He shut up, realizing that he was making plans for the whole family. He understood that, in part, realized that he *was* the most intelligent member by far...but he was still surprised that everyone was listening to him.

Especially since he knew that even he was just guessing.

Everyone was standing around listening except Travis. He'd been trying all morning to reach his command...to no avail. He'd almost taken one of the cars, tried to head back toward North Carolina with Lucas...but Hugh had talked some sense into him. It would take hours and hours, just to get out of the city...and there was no way of even guessing how long it would take to get all the way back to base. Whatever was going to happen, whatever action the aliens were going to take, it would certainly occur before that.

Travis was still trying to get through to the base...but with no practical way to get there, it didn't seem to matter even if he did get through. Hugh figured he wouldn't anyway, that the destruction of the satellites and the commotion going on everywhere made it extremely unlikely that he would get a line through. But at least it kept him in one place, focused on something...while Hugh continued to think, to try and figure out the best way for his family to survive.

His mother had nodded, and then she said, "You're right, Hugh…let's get going." Then she turned and raced away, to gather all the things the family could need…or at least what they could carry. He could hear her yelling to his father, telling him what to do, and Hugh couldn't help but smile for a moment…perhaps the last one he would enjoy, at least for a long while.

About half an hour later—and Hugh figured his mother was right, if they weren't going to stay at the house, they'd better get going as quickly as possible—he went and talked to Travis. "We've got to go…soon. We're going to the subway, down as far as we can get below the city…and quickly. Whatever is going to happen is going to be soon, I'm almost sure of it." He wasn't "sure" about anything really, but the more he thought about it, the greater his belief became that the aliens—and he didn't see any point in ignoring what were close to facts…they *were* aliens—had hostile intentions. He'd expected his brother to argue, to say he had to find a way back to his unit or he had to keep trying to reach them.

But he just nodded grimly. "You're right, Hugh. We'll never get out of the city in time…but staying here isn't right either." He looked down for a moment, and then back up at his brother. "I'd be inclined to take your advice even if I disagreed…but in this case, I am 100% in agreement. So, let's go!" He stepped aside, revealing a bag behind him. "I've packed, some stuff at least, and Lucas is right behind me."

Hugh was surprised, at least somewhat, but he was also relieved. He knew his choice was the correct one, more with each passing moment, but having his brother's agreement helped him realize it. "Ok…let's pull out of here in fifteen minutes. We will be to the station, and underground, in half an hour." He hoped that would be fast enough, that whatever the aliens had planned, it would take longer than that…but he just didn't know. He didn't say anything about those concerns—there was no cause, nothing that could be done about them. He just nodded to his brother, and then he turned away, off to find his mother and father…and to hurry them along.

*   *   *

"Travis, Hugh…where are you going?" The voice was tired, stretched out with fear and stress. Sarah Jones was a neighbor, and perhaps more importantly, she was the one-time—and off and on again—love interest of Travis. The whole family really liked her. Now, she was clearly struggling to maintain control over herself, and she was all alone.

"We're moving to the subway station." Travis turned toward her. "Where is your family, Sarah? You all should come with us! If there is any kind of attack…" He paused for a moment, and then just said, "Well, we'll be better off there than here."

"I'm alone, Travis…my parents are away on a cruise. I've been sitting in the house, trying to decide whether to run or not. The traffic is so bad…and I couldn't decide what to do." She was definitely edgy, but she was more or less hanging onto her control.

"Come with us, Sarah." Travis was going to say the same thing, but Hugh spun around and said it first. "It's the best option…even if it is a poor one." Hugh had a tendency to be truthful, even when a bit of lying might have been better. In his own mind, he figured there was perhaps a thirty percent chance his family would survive the day…and he didn't even try to go out any farther than that. There was no point. But despite the grim thoughts, he was strangely calm, the threat of death and whatever else might come leaving him largely unaffected. It wasn't that he didn't feel it, but he knew that the more he stayed focused, the better chance they would all have, and that was it.

"Yes, Sarah…come with us. You can't stay behind…"

Travis looked out at the street, full of unmoving cars. "…especially alone. And trying to get anywhere in a car is pointless right now."

She stood for a moment, looking back at them, and then she just nodded her head, a few tears working their way out, but mostly she held things together. "I will go get my stuff."

"Hurry, Sarah…we're leaving in a minute." It was Hugh again, and his voice was strangely calm.

She nodded and then turned and ran back to her house.

Hugh followed the others back inside, and he spun around, even as Lucas and his father raced back toward the front door, carrying several large boxes. He thought for a second, and then he just said, "You've got to cut down on the amount of stuff we're carrying. Just food and medicine, and a few changes of clothes…everything else has to stay behind." He watched as his father and Lucas both paused, and then nodded to him, and began to put down the boxes, and work through the stuff in each of them. It seemed strange that they were listening to him so intently, but then he realized he was the only one acting calmly, rationally. Travis and Lucas were both still split, thinking of themselves and the family…but also about their Marine detachment. The others were all on the verge of breaking down, of bursting into tears or something else equally useless. But Hugh was calm, rational. He was afraid, yes, in a way…but he was also totally in control, working hard despite his full realization that his entire family could—more likely would—be dead by the end of the day.

"Alright…we've got to get going, fast. Honestly, we've waited too long already." He pushed a pair of bags, loaded only with the essentials, into a pile on the front lawn. It was smaller than it had been, but as he calculated what they could carry, he realized it was still too large. He began to go through the bags and boxes, throwing half of their contents onto another pile. He realized he was unpacking things his family had just put together, that he should probably talk to them, involve them in the decision of what to bring and what to leave behind. But he knew there wasn't time.

"We're going in five minutes!" His first comment hadn't gotten any real responses, so he repeated it, this time with a set period…and a quick one. And he meant it. In five minutes, his family would take whatever they could carry, and they would begin walking to the subway station. That was no more than five minutes away. Five more would get them underground—and he intended to continue on, as deeply as he could go, past the station itself, into its underground guts—and then they would just wait. He had a radio, two actually, though the stations were mostly off the air now, only a bit of news programming alternating with mostly dead air. He thought for a moment, realized that the entire world was like this, that all authority was on the verge of disintegrating. He knew that could be as big a problem as whatever was coming from the aliens, that being shot by other humans would make his family just as dead as anything they could face from the invaders. And he realized it was just as likely, and perhaps more, that they would run into a human enemy too.

He looked into his bag, checking to make sure the guns were there. His father had a rifle and a pistol, and he had taken both of them, along with a decent amount of ammunition. He knew his brother and Lucas both had their sidearms, and he was sure they would bring them, along with their rifles. Still, he was troubled, about a lot of things, and as much as anything that his family wasn't particularly well-armed, not really…at least not counting the Marine weapons. But it was as good as he was going to get it, and there was nothing to be gained by thinking further about it. He closed the bag with the guns, and he lifted that one up himself. He saw Sarah emerging from her house, carrying one large bag. He almost smiled at her precision, at the reasonable load she was carrying. Then he turned back

toward his house and yelled to his own family. "Let's
go…it's time."

Chapter Four

From the Log of Captain Jason Wrangle

I wasn't able to reach any of my personnel on leave…not one. The aliens—the enemy, almost certainly—has destroyed all of our satellites. That has thrown our telecommunications into a disastrous mess. Some things are still getting through, at least I've heard rumors that some communications have been successful, but not most of it. Including all of my attempts to reach my troopers.

I had to stop my efforts when we moved out, redirect my attention to the sixty-eight percent of my forces still on duty. That required some changes, some transfers from platoon to platoon to try and even things out. I wouldn't have gone to so much effort…but I imagine that the fight we are about to begin will be the most important one in history. I don't know that, I don't really have any idea what is going on, what is going to happen, but I am confident, nevertheless. And scared to death. I imagine all of my troopers are terrified, uncertain what to expect. I have even seen a few desertions, Marines racing back home, or at least trying. But the majority of my people who were on duty remain with the colors…ready for whatever lays ahead.

However bad that is.

30 Miles South of Camp Lejuene
North Carolina
D – 0 Days

The branches of the trees snapped back as he pushed forward, some of them slapping him hard. He was tired, very tired, but he suspected there would not be much sleep in his future. His Marines were still fairly close to the base, just thirty miles from it—and some other units had gone much farther—but his company, his entire battalion, in fact, had walked the entire way. Thirty miles was a decent distance, but in less than 12 hours, it was a *long* way…especially since at least half of that was through ground that qualified as wilderness.

Still, Jason Wrangle had held on, barely. He had his company to lead, and that was all he tried to think of. He had expected the enemy—he knew others were still speculating on the true purpose of the alien spaceships, but he had decided they were definitely hostile—to attack by now, but twelve hours had passed with nothing but their repositioning ships. He wondered if he could be wrong, if they weren't really hostile…but if they weren't, why hadn't they communicated yet? Even if they spoke a different language, or communicated some other way entirely, surely there was some method of transmitting a lack of hostility…especially since it would be taken as a virtual assurance that the lack of such an effort meant hostility.

He turned and looked out, seeing perhaps ten of his people. His unit was deployed in a spread out fashion, and visibility in the woods was poor. His Marines were ready, as ready as they could be, but he wondered what they could do against an alien attack, against an enemy advanced enough to build ships that could travel across vast distances. He was far from an expert on such things, but he knew light speed was the high end limit on travel, at least as far as human knowledge went. Was the enemy advanced enough that they had found a faster method of travel…or were they *truly* alien, capable of engaging in trips that took years, or even centuries? He didn't know, but he wasn't sure one answer was all that much better than another. He would fight, all his people would, but whenever he thought about the outcome, he realized they probably wouldn't have much of a chance. Any group that could travel so far, bring so much firepower to Earth, could very likely defeat the combined armies of all the nations—and probably ridiculously easily—and they could impose anything they liked on the survivors.

Assuming any humans were left alive.

He tried to force such thoughts from his mind, clear them away and concentrate only on his duty. He was partially successful, his thoughts reverting to the wider—and bleaker—picture occasionally, but most of them remained on his company…and on the orders he had gotten, however sparse they were. His commands so far had been limited, mostly specifying the area he was to occupy. He knew that was because his own commanders had little more information than he did, that they, like almost everyone else, were waiting to see what happened.

To see if humanity was simply vaporized, blown away in a few moments…or if they at least were going to get a chance to fight, however small the possibility of victory.

* * *

"Sir, the enemy has launched what can only be an attack. Over five hundred smaller craft have just separated from their orbiting ships and are now moving into position around the world. There has still been no response of any kind to our communication efforts. These smaller ships are likely to land, or to bombard our cities, and the lack of any form of response to our repeated attempts at contact strongly supports our inference of hostility." The officer was aggressive, angry at the speculative invasion, but also scared. That was obvious. He paused briefly before he continued. "I must request immediate authorization to attack, before the enemy gets too far along. We are very likely at a major disadvantage to begin with, and wasting any more time will only make it worse." The general was upset, clearly, as was everyone else present. They were in a secondary position, away from the White House, but still fairly close to Washington. The president wondered now if they were too close, if one or more of the enemy ships might come down quickly and cut them off. He had no one else to blame…he'd given the orders, abiding by the restriction of the move to the ground as a result of the enemy ships in the air. But now, his thoughts dogged him, putting alternate ideas into his mind before shooting them down with doubts. He was right to stay out of the air, he certainly believed that…but maybe he should have pushed on, moved farther from the capital. He was a veteran himself, with eight years of combat experience, but right now, none of that seemed relevant.

He knew only he could speak, could answer the question. He was the president of the United States, the last word, at least for his forces…and probably for much of the world's. He knew the general was almost certainly correct, that the enemy moves were hostile. But until they had actually attacked—beyond the destruction of the satellites, which was hostile but didn't kill anyone—he was just unsure how to proceed. He had been silent for a time, trying to decide what he was going to say. But before he could open his mouth, the door swung open, and a woman ran inside.

"Mr. President, General…all of you…" The woman rushed into the room, a panicked look on her face as she spoke. "The ships…the ones that separated from the larger craft…they're pausing…over major cities, sir. Over all the big cities in the world." She looked right at the president. "And they are launching…weapons, sir…we believe they are nuclear weapons."

The general had remained silent, just as everyone had when she first ran into the office. They had all, of course, thought about a nuclear bombardment, worried that the aliens just wanted Earth, that humanity was merely in their way, a simple problem to be removed. But they hadn't assumed that to be true. He hadn't, at least. There were just too many other purposes the invaders could have...or maybe it was just his own unfounded hope.

The odds on that possibility, and on the destruction of humanity, however, had just increased dramatically.

The president turned almost immediately, looking at the general. He stared for a few seconds, and then he said, "General...your forces are all authorized to attack. At once." The president's voice sounded surprisingly calm, though he was anything but. "At once," he repeated, even as the general had already nodded and begun turning quickly to the comm unit he held in his hand, to issue the orders.

"All forces...attack at once. Repeat...all forces, attack!" The officer said the words, managing to sound fairly calm himself, though the president figured it was just as fake as his own previous tone was. No one could be truly calm, not now. At least no one sane.

The general turned and looked back at the president, and at the others in the room. He looked like he was trying to decide what to say, and finally he uttered, "Sir...I believe we should get you out of here. If Washington is attacked too aggressively, some of the effects could reach us here. I agree we need to stay on the ground, but we have to get farther from Washington. Now."

The president felt a burst of defiance, an urge to argue, to remain where he was...but he realized that didn't make sense. If the enemy *was* nuking the surface, even part of it, millions of people were about to die. But he had to remain standing, for as long as possible. He was the commander-in-chief, at least of the United States, and he needed to maintain some level of control. And that meant staying alive…or at least not getting killed because of his own foolish decisions.

"Very well, general…let's pull out of here." He struggled for a moment, one instant displaying the kind of courage he knew he needed to, and the next hanging on the verge of despair. "Let's move to Camp David…the entire operation. That will be our command facility." It wasn't the best choice, perhaps, especially if the enemy knew anything specific about them, but it was better than staying where they were. "Let's go!"

He watched as the men and women present scrambled to follow his commands. He knew their minds were awash, wrapped up in dozens of things right now. Where their loved ones were, whether they were ok, or whether they were going to die in a matter of hours, or even minutes. This wasn't that much different from how they had expected things to go if the U.S. and one of its major enemies on Earth really came down to it, but he doubted many of his personnel were really ready for that either. Still, his office functioned, if barely, and his people worked hard, holding the darkness back, or at least struggling to do so. They had snapped into motion, clearing the room of everything that had to go with them…and preparing for the ride to Camp David. He realized the burden, the job of moving the HQ was actually helping his people, pulling at least some of their thoughts away from homes and loved ones. It wouldn't last, of course, but he would take what he could get.

He knew that wasn't going to be enough in the end, probably not even close…but it was the best he could hope for right now.

*   *   *

Jason stood, looking right at one of the trees, but not really seeing it. His com unit was still in his hand, but there was no sound coming from it anymore, nothing except static. He had gotten the last message, and he had acknowledged, but that was it. There had been nothing since. He was still stunned, surprised…and not surprised, too.

The enemy ships had launched some kind of devices, almost certainly weapons. They were even then heading toward many cities, perhaps all of them. Jason's unit was far from any population centers, and almost certainly not a target, at least not yet. But he still felt a cold chill, a dark feeling, knowing that a huge percentage of the population— of the whole world's population—was perhaps minutes away from dying. He thought of his own family, of his mother and father and sister. He wondered about his Marines who were away on leave. Tyler McDaniel, for one, was in New York City, his home. Tyler was one of his best officers, probably *the* best in his company…and he tried to imagine what he was doing now. How he was preparing to die.

"Alright…everybody get ready. Take whatever cover you can." He shook himself, pulled his thoughts away from his family and his officers who weren't there, and back to the matter at hand. He had a hundred people depending on him, and that was where his thoughts needed to be. He knew the attacks were probably all far from his location, that his people, his Marines, would survive, at least the first blasts…but that was only an assumption, and all he could do now was protect his people, however he could. "Focus…dig in and stay where you are." In the end, there wasn't much he could do, he realized. Digging in wasn't going to provide much protection, certainly not if the enemy launched a missile nearby, but it was all his people could do…so they did it.

He checked his watch, tried to calculate when the bombs would start falling. It was a guess, that's all, but he figured it was just a few minutes. Perhaps, even, some of them were coming down now. For all he knew, millions could already be dead, perhaps billions. And if they weren't yet, they would be soon.

"Carlyle, Barret…get down. Now!" Somehow, his attention was focused suddenly. He was worried about his family, about friends who lived all around, about what was going to happen. But he knew there was nothing he could do about any of that. All he could do was keep his hundred men alive…or as many of them as possible. For as long as he could…even if that wasn't very long. And he was determined to do just that.

Whatever it took.

Chapter Five

From the Notes of Hugh McDaniel

I will remember that day perfectly forever, no matter what else happens to me, no matter how many crises I oversee. It will be clear as a bell...until the moment I die. It is impossible to forget the deaths of millions—billions—the unimaginable horror of watching your civilization destroyed, of knowing that the end is very near, that it is probably coming for you. Subsequent to the bombing, to the immediate destruction, I recovered, I realized that I had to fight, with every bit of effort I had...that I had to struggle to preserve myself, to do whatever I could to save anyone within my reach. But for a moment, a brief period of time that seemed unending, I just looked out in horror as my world was erased, as the entire image I had known was wiped away, turned to rubble.

As I was trapped, with a couple hundred others, in the subway station that had now become our sanctuary.

67th Avenue Subway Station
Forest Hills, Queens
D – 0 Days

Hugh pushed open the door, shoving his head through and

looking around. It was dirty—filthy actually—and there were sounds too, beyond the noise coming from the small crowd behind him. Probably rats he told himself. It was a situation that any other time might have scared him to death, and sent him scrambling away...but right now, he knew what was outside, what was coming down, and the passage in front of him was his only chance for survival. The only chance for his whole family, and for the others who had sought protection in the subway station. It would take more than rats to scare him off.

He knew there were missiles coming—he'd heard the confirmation as he was entering the station. He wasn't sure that he or any of the people with him would survive more than a few more minutes...but depending on the number and size of the weapons deployed, they had a chance, and that was a lot better than nothing. Better certainly than all the people stuck in cars, trying to escape but hardly moving. His fear actually subsided, and a strange sort of calm overcame him. He had to try. It was almost as though something fundamental in him was changing, that he was starting to become a leader of sorts. His brother was that already, he knew that for certain, and he was right there, too, also leading the group. But Hugh imagined that Travis was surprised at his standing, at the drive that was pushing him forward. He certainly was...though oddly, he realized, his brother seemed less so, almost as though he'd known Hugh would be a leader someday, at least when forced to shed his shyness.

"Let's go...this way." He turned and shouted, something he rarely did, and then he entered the area. It was large, and partially lit, and it was two levels below the subway track. It looked mostly abandoned, a storage area or something similar, but his eyes quickly told him it was more than large enough to hold everyone. He had come to the station with his family, and a few friends, but there had been others there, too. He hadn't been of a mind to take in everyone, but when he saw them, scared and wandering helplessly, he knew he had to do what he could. There was no way to just hide his family anyway. He was surprised, however, that the others all followed, almost without a word…but they did.

His eyes locked on Travis's for a moment, and unspoken, they shared two thoughts. First, they had to get everyone into the room. And second…quickly. Hugh didn't imagine his brother's thoughts were as disciplined as his own, but he figured they had a minute, perhaps two, before the missiles hit the ground. It couldn't be much more than that.

Perhaps before they were all killed. Or just maybe they survived, at least the initial impact. He knew it could go either way, that it depended on the types of weapons and the exact points of explosion. He was sure his group had a better chance than someone in Manhattan…but even with his mental ability, the best he could do was come down to a rough coin toss. Fifty percent, and his people would be eliminated immediately, incinerated or buried under rubble…and fifty percent, they would survive, for a while at least.

What 'a while' was, he didn't even try to calculate. Not yet. That depended on information he didn't yet have, on the ability of the enemy to launch subsequent attacks…and whether they wanted to completely destroy the native species, or just to cut down on its numbers, to kill half or more of them, and to eliminate their ability to defend themselves. It could be either…and he had no idea which to expect.

He looked as the people were coming forward, listening to his commands almost as though they were somehow official…and not just the rants of a neighborhood kid who had somehow taken charge. He told himself it was Travis they were obeying, that his time in the Marines, issuing orders to his platoon, had built him up. That was true, to a point, and the people *were* listening to Travis, too. But even when he spoke alone, everyone followed.

He waved his arms, encouraging them all to hurry. He knew he very well might die, in just a moment, but the fear was theoretical, submerged beneath the need. He knew he had to remain as calm as possible, in the hopes that it would carry over to the people around him.

He watched as the last of them raced through, and then he slammed the door shut immediately. He turned to see all of the people, standing around, looking up at his brother and him, their terror clear…but mostly silent He glanced over at Travis, then looked back at those he had led so far. He didn't know if they could go any deeper, if there were any other doors available…and he had just started to think about that when the place began to shake hard.

He grabbed onto a railing that was within reach, and for a moment, he almost lost his control, and began to panic. But that only lasted a few seconds, and then he was in command again. The vibration continued, and even grew in severity, and he could hear something in the distance…an explosion. Then another.

The lights went out, leaving the room lit only by a few flashlights, and the shaking continued. He felt some sediment from the roof come down and hit him, and for an instant, he thought the room was about to collapse. But it didn't…it held.

He knew what had happened, at least somewhat. Nuclear weapons had gone off above the ground. He realized now more even than before how much he had expected the explosions to destroy the room where he had led the people, to obliterate all of them. But even as he heard a third explosion, the room still stood. Some more sediment fell, and a few chunks of stone came down. He heard a howl, no two, and he looked around to see two of the people—his people?—had been hurt. He snapped out, almost unconsciously, asking if there were any doctors present, or any nurses. He hadn't really expected any, but then he heard a voice.

"I am a nurse," she said, even as she made her way over to the two injured people, carrying a flashlight with her.

Hugh swallowed hard, relieved that his group had at least some medical assistance. He turned and looked at Travis, and then back again to the room. They had survived, at least the first attack's early hits. Whether there would be a second assault—or a third or fourth—was just a guess now, as was whether his people were as safe from radiation and other effects as they had been from the first impacts.

He realized this was just the very beginning, and of precisely what, he didn't know. But he had survived the first attack, and that was something at least.

* * *

"What should we do?" Travis spoke, his words soft, almost silent. They were intended for the ears of his brother and Lucas as well, but no one else. He had tried to seem assured in front of the others...in control, but Hugh knew he showed something closer to his actual feelings in the tone of this statement.

"I think we should see if there is a way to get farther down, Travis." Hugh spoke quietly, but then he looked around and after a second, he continued even more softly, "We survived the hits—the first ones actually—but that doesn't mean there isn't radiation." He paused, and then he added, "Maybe a lot of radiation." He almost added, *we could all be dead already*, Travis guessed, but he caught himself and held that back. "Not to mention the possibility of additional missile strikes." He paused, and then added, "And the other people are a potential problem, too. We have to remember that the members of our society who survived will behave differently, and we might have to...take some serious steps if we are going to have any real chance at survival." Travis knew exactly what he meant, and a second later, he realized he felt exactly the same way.

Travis nodded, and then he prepared to continue to search. That assumed, of course, that there *was* any way lower, that they weren't already there, at the deepest spot. None of them had any idea what connected to the subway station, what—if anything—might lay down there. They knew the city had a maze of tunnels and rooms under it, but they weren't sure what, if anything, might be right below them. "Alright…let's look around, try to see if there are any doors." He looked around the room, but most of it was black. There were more flashlights now, perhaps thirty, but outside of the meager light each one threw off, there was nothing but darkness.

"I think we should stay together, the three of us. We will work our way around the outer wall, looking for…anything…a door certainly, but really any path to something else. I know we could do it faster individually, but I think we're better off tripling up for now." Hugh looked at his two companions, and each of them agreed with him. Then he reached down, pulled out the large light he'd kept hidden until then. "I knew we would lose the power…so I brought three of these. We'll use them one at a time, since I don't imagine we will be able to find any replacement batteries or bulbs easily." He lit up the flashlight, and it was several times as bright as any of those currently in use. He nodded, and he began walking, heading to the exterior wall, and then proceeding around, looking up and down, from floor to ceiling every couple feet, before exchanging glances with his two companions and then moving on.

The people in the room were mostly silent at first, shaken up and trying to decide whether they were happy to be alive…or sad that their lives, all that they knew of them at least, were gone. About a third of the way through their excursion around the outside wall, Travis could hear that the people were starting to get more restless. They were still scared, no doubt, but they were also beginning to wonder about what was next, about what to do. Some of them were hungry, and most of them were thirsty. It was amazing to Travis, and almost certainly to Hugh as well, how many people had come this way, left behind their homes and almost everything else...and yet didn't bring any food or even a container of water. Hugh and Travis had brought a fair amount, as much as they could carry, but neither of them wanted to take it out...not now. Their outlook was on the whole group, on all the people present, but that only went so far, to decision making, perhaps, but not to sharing their scraps of food. Travis knew that problem would only get worse, and quickly, but he pushed it aside, out of his mind...at least for a few minutes.

They continued their excursion, and four of the others came over, curious about what they were doing. Two were unfamiliar, but the others they knew. Gavin Sanders was a good friend of Travis's. They hadn't seen him in the initial confusion, but the instant they did, Hugh reached out and grabbed him.

Travis was a bit slower, but he hugged him right after. "Gavin...I didn't realize you were here." Travis was more sociable than Hugh, but in truth, he didn't have many friends either, at least not good ones like Sanders.

"Yes...I saw you both a bit earlier, but I didn't want to interrupt. I figured now was a good time, at least to let you know I was here."

"It is...indeed." Travis was...happy was too much of an overstatement, how could anyone be happy then, with the city likely in ruins right above their heads...excited to have a friend present, someone else he could count on.

The other person they knew was Janet Howers. She was younger, around 18, Hugh guessed, and she was also from the neighborhood. She was very shy, but Travis knew she was intelligent. Travis was about to say hello, when Hugh once again beat him to it.

"Janet…I'm so glad you made it here."

"I am, too, Hugh." Her voice was soft, and she was clearly uncomfortable. Everyone was, Travis reminded himself, though he recognized that Janet probably would have been, even if the setting had been less…severe.

"Yes, Janet…it is good that you made it." He paused for a few seconds, and then he asked both of them—really all four of them, though he only really intended to inquire among the two people he knew, "Were your families able to…make it here?"

"Yes…my mother is here, and my sister." Sanders answered first, followed by the other two, whose responses he mostly ignored. Janet was the last one, and he knew as soon as he heard her voice that the answer was not a good one.

"My mother was in the city…she called, but then we got cut off. I waited for a while, hoped she would come back, or at least call. But…" She couldn't finish, but she didn't have to. It would have taken her mother hours to get back home…and that was time they just hadn't had.

"Maybe she is okay, Janet. She may be someplace in Manhattan, just like we are here." It was Hugh again, sounding very believable…though Travis knew the odds were heavily against that being true, and he was sure Hugh knew that even better than he did.

She nodded at him, trying to look like she believed him—and on some level, perhaps, she did—and then she went quiet.

"Okay…Gavin—and Janet—stay with us. The other two of you…" Travis knew they had told him their names, but he couldn't remember. He paused for a second, and then he heard Hugh answer.

"Jack and Dave…can you guys go back and check on the others? Things are going to get bad down here, and probably very quickly. The longer we can hold things together, the better we'll be." He looked at the two, and he acknowledged their nods.

Travis was amazed, shocked at his brother's—his normally bashful brother's—action. He knew the situation was like none he'd ever imagined, but Hugh was taking things far better than he had expected…better even than he was, despite his military training.

He watched as the two individuals moved back, heading toward the others, and then he exchanged a quick glance with his brother. Hugh was clearly concerned and upset…but there was something else there as well, some kind of energy. He knew his brother was smarter than he was, than almost anyone was, but there was something new going on now, too…some kind of inner self emerging. Hugh was coming out of his shell. Everyone was taking the situation hard, working at some fraction of their normal capacity.

Everyone except for Hugh. He was certainly as upset as everyone else…but he was excelling.

He tried to put it out of his mind, to focus on the matter at hand. Was there any place further down, someplace that offered protection from fallout?

And from other humans, too, he thought, those whose choices of survival tactics were more onerous than his own. He knew that would come too, that before his people even had to deal with the aliens, the real villains, they would have to handle other people.

Kill other people.

Chapter Six

From the Log of Captain Jason Wrangle

I only have time for a brief entry. In ten minutes, we are going to continue our march, for God knows how long before we take another break. Reality has exceeded my worst nightmare. Cities have been nuked, perhaps all the cities in the world, though that exceeds my knowledge. I can't imagine the millions dead—the billions—whether my family is still alive, or anything else. All I can do now is lead my company…and fight. And not think about Mom or Dad or my sister…or anything else except the battle. Our purpose is to strike back now, somehow, and while I know we don't have any real chance, I still feel the urge to fight.

We are uncertain of the enemy locations, or whether they have even landed any forces. From what I heard, our cities were nuked with garden variety fission weapons, potent killing machines no doubt, but not the true fusion nightmares we might have expected. I can't imagine the enemy hasn't developed fusion bombs, or perhaps even stronger ones, with antimatter or some unknown, even more powerful type of weapon. Any power that has developed the ability to travel across the stars should have devised fusion bombs centuries, even millennia, ago. So, is there a reason for the use of the smaller yield weapons? Do they want to subjugate us, perhaps not kill us all? That is a great leap, as for that matter is my assumption that they have only used fission bombs. My position, my role as a Marine company commander, hardly makes it essential that I receive all information. Perhaps the enemy is using fusion bombs as well, or perhaps even something stronger. Possibly, they do want to destroy us, to wipe the Earth clean for whatever use they have. I just don't know…and truth be told, I don't care either. I am a Marine, and the current situation makes little difference between being a slave and being dead. Both are unacceptable…and I will fight to prevent either one.

I will battle to the end, with every breath I have…even if that only lasts an hour. Or a minute.

60 Miles South of Camp Lejuene
North Carolina
D + 2 Days

"Cobb, Rechnick…move out fifty yards. Check things out. Carefully." He clung to the ground, as all his other Marines did, issuing the order…and feeling sorry for the two men he was sending out. It had been two days since the enemy attack, two days since many cities—perhaps all of them—had been bombed. For a brief time, he had received some audio of a fight in the air, several squadrons of planes going in against one of the enemy ships. He got excited, at least for a moment, hoping against hope that they would prevail, or at least be able to damage the enemy. Then, he felt the horror, the nightmare of the situation, as the vessel opened fire…and all of the attacking planes were destroyed almost immediately.

That wasn't exactly a true image of the fight worldwide, of course, at least he couldn't be sure all the attacking planes were wiped out everywhere. He hadn't gotten any more direct contacts, at least not with units in action, but he did receive some reports, and they were all the same. Everywhere he knew of that the planes went in, they were destroyed…and as far as he could tell, not one of them had managed to hit an enemy vessel.

That should have broken him, perhaps, sent him running and screaming into the night…and it almost did. But Marine training was heavy, and part of him, at least, believed it would be different on the ground, that once these…whatever they were…landed, his people—and the army and whatever other units were waiting—would tear them apart. It was foolish, and he knew it was, and yet part of him believed it, even as he moved his men out.

"Be careful boys…" The words slipped out of his mouth, partly in answer to the acknowledgement he had received, the confirmation that the two Marines were obeying, that they were moving forward. He knew it was dangerous, or at least that it could be. There had been no contact yet, no combat with the enemy. But there had been a bright flash up ahead, and something told him they had come down…that his force was about to run into them. He wasn't sure whether that was a logical conclusion, or just his own craziness taking hold, but, nevertheless, he was almost sure of it. Sure his people were about to meet up with an enemy from another world. It was almost too much to believe. Almost.

He stayed where he was, low to the ground, but he raised his head a little, tried to keep an eye on his two men…two Marines sent forward to meet with the enemy. Or at least, to see if they were actually there. Perhaps they weren't, maybe he was wrong. But he believed they were…and he was sure that his force was on the verge of combat.

He sucked in a deep breath, watching his two men move forward. He held a rifle in his hands, and he had it extended, covering his patrol. The dozen or so men he could see were doing more or less the same thing, protecting the advancing troops as well as they could. He wondered what would happen, whether there were enemies out there, and if there were, just how well they would fight. The air battle had sapped some of his courage, but not all of it. Whether it was just Marine foolishness, or whether his people truly had a chance, he didn't know. At least not for a few more seconds.

He looked forward, his eyes fixed on his two men. They were crouched, fairly low, but still high enough to see…and be seen. They took another few steps forward…and stopped.

Then, they opened fire.

The shooting only lasted for a second, perhaps two. Then, the two men almost disappeared.

That wasn't true, not exactly. They didn't vanish…they were just torn apart by rapid fire, by a storm of it coming from several places.

Wrangle sat where he was, for perhaps two or three seconds, stunned. Then he pulled the trigger of his gun and opened fire, at the same time, shouting into his comm, "Fire…everyone. Open fire!"

* * *

"Sir…every city has been bombed, and the enemy ships are moving now, taking position over secondary and tertiary targets. It appears that they are, in fact, trying to destroy us, though we cannot explain why many of their weapons seem lesser than they should be. The cities are all destroyed, but in most cases, there are definitely survivors, and possibly considerable numbers of them. I am not sure whether this is deliberate, or whether the enemy will return, and bomb the targets again…and I have no answer why the weapons used were mostly—or all—simple fission bombs." The general spoke, his voice rough, the result of three days spent completely awake, watching the gravest nightmare in human history unfold. Everything that had happened greatly exceeded the president's worst nightmares…everything, perhaps, except the mix of enemy weapons.

The president just shook his head. The past several days had seen nothing except horrible news, stories of bombardments, of wholesale destruction. He had issued orders, moved whatever forces he had left, lined them up to face a ground invasion…if it even came. But every air asset he had sent in was destroyed, and as far as he could tell, none of them had even scored any hits. He had a few planes left, as hidden as he could make them, but he didn't know what to do. If the enemy landed, at least his ground units could fight—and probably die very quickly—but until then, all he could do was watch. And listen to a seemingly endless series of negative reports.

"There is nothing we can do, now, General. If the enemy lands troops, we will see if our ground forces can do any better than our air units." *And if they don't land, if they just remain in position, bombing the Earth until nothing can live here…we are finished.* He thought that last part, but he didn't say it. There was nothing to be gained by bringing the mood level even lower than it already was.

"Mr. President…we have more planes. Perhaps a combined strike force could overcome one of the enemy vessels…"

"To what end, General? There are 500 ships attacking us…and we have what, eight percent of our planes left, maybe ten, if everything can be made flight ready?" He knew, even as he shot down his general's idea that he would be forced to order it himself eventually, no matter how bad the odds were. The planes would eventually be found and destroyed…and even a one in a million chance of taking down an enemy ship was better than just sitting and waiting for ruin.

At least a little better.

The president fought back against fatigue, against all the darkness that was trying to take him. He had been a good president, he was fairly sure of that. At least reasonably good…and coming as he did after a series of poor ones, he had been very popular. He thought back, to a few days ago, though it felt like years now, to a time when his biggest worry was a reelection that seemed assured. That, at least, was off his mind for now. He was the president and would probably be the last one. The election scheduled for next year had become so irrelevant, he couldn't even imagine it anymore.

And anyone who wanted to be president, who wanted to watch over the destruction of the United States, and the entire world, should just show up. He would be glad to trade places with them, allow them to sit and watch what was left of American greatness blown to bits and destroyed.

No…you can't do that. You have to lead…until the end.

He took a deep breath, and he stared at the maps. He had removed himself, and what remained of his team, from Camp David as well—to a small collection of buildings in the Pennsylvania countryside. He didn't know what the aliens knew about the world, but he had decided that Camp David was too connected to the presidency, that he could only be safe—or marginally safer—at a much more remote location. He had ordered the withdrawal, the retreat that had led his staff across the border to rural Pennsylvania. The buildings he now occupied, the handful of old homes now serving as the U.S. headquarters, were the only ones within a mile…and they were unoccupied when his team found them.

He turned and moved toward the window, probably not the best idea, as he saw two of his secret service agents tense up. But he did it anyway. If the enemy wanted to kill him so badly, if they had followed him all this way, they could just as easily blow up the entire building as shoot him through the window.

He stared out, saw the peaceful looking sky, the untouched meadows and small areas of woods all around him. He knew, from endless reports, that his cities were all gone, that they had been bombed to oblivion, that the attackers were moving along, now destroying smaller cities and towns now. But where he was looked untouched…at least for the moment. He imagined for a moment that the reports were wrong, that the rest of the nation looked the same as the area he now inhabited, that the reports he had been getting for two days were somehow incorrect.

But he knew they weren't. And he knew his ground troops would fare no better, that they would fall also, that their hopes would probably quickly pare down from victory to just hurting the enemy before they were eliminated.

He had considered defeat since the enemy assault began, and part of him had realized the chances of any of his armed forces were poor…very poor indeed. But this was the first moment he truly wanted to give up, to try again to contact the aliens, to beg them to allow his people, those that were left at least, to survive. There might not be much hope to that, of course…but there was absolutely none the other way.

He walked over to the small table he was using as a desk, and he waved his arms, signaled to the others present that he wanted to be alone for a few minutes. He wanted to consider surrendering, or at least trying to. It came hard to him, against almost everything he believed in…but he couldn't think of a better option, any other route that offered even the chance of some of his people surviving.

"Mr. President!" His aide came rushing into the room. "We're getting various messages, suddenly, from all across the country. Our ground forces are engaging, Sir…they are fighting the enemy. In at least twenty locations!"

The president could hear the hope in the aide's voice, the pointless—at least to him it seemed pointless—expectation that soon they would get follow ups from the engaged parties, notifications that the enemy had been repelled, that the fight went on. But he was sure, surer even than he'd been a moment before, that his forces would lose, that the enemy was omnipotent, that they would destroy everything that fought against them. He detested himself, tried to believe there was a chance…but that was gone. He knew the only way any of his people could survive was to yield, to beg the enemy for mercy. He detested himself for thinking that way, but that's what he believed.

And he was far from sure that would work.

"Get the comm room going…" He suspected that most of his people assumed that he was about to send out an inspiring message, or something similar, to whoever could read it now. But that wasn't what he had in mind. He was going to try to contact the aliens once again…and he was going to surrender.

He wouldn't have done it just for himself—he would gladly have died in combat—but he knew that there were still people dying across the country, all around the world. The enemy had not responded to early communications, but now he was going to send something very different.

He was going to surrender. They might still ignore him. For all he knew, they couldn't even communicate with the people of Earth. But he had to try. It was the only way he could think of to save at least some of his people.

Whatever they thought of him, however much they hated him, if some of them lived, that was better than watching everyone die.

Chapter Seven

From the Notes of Hugh McDaniel

It's been two days since the attack, and as far as I can tell, there haven't been any follow ups, any further assaults designed to obliterate the survivors. The death toll is almost certainly in the millions, probably in the billions, but there are likely many still alive as well. We have had over a hundred more people come to our haven, find their way to us, through the debris and ruins of the subway station, and down to where we have made our haven. We have accepted them all into our group, as the only choice would probably have been to fight them instead. But now, we have over three hundred fifty people, most of whom I don't know. It was bad enough at close to two hundred, with no one officially in charge, but with almost twice that number, fights are close to breaking out.

Our people are hungry and tired...and scared to death. Many of them had expected, as did I, that follow up attacks would have taken place by now. But there was nothing, no further bombs, no attacks of any kind, at least none that were apparent. Still, that expectation, that belief, bought us two days. I had feared there would be fighting, that our people would be at each other's throats for food. Largely, that did not happen during the first two days. Our people shared, to an extent, and many just went without food. We found water, at least, though how healthy it was to drink I don't know, and we got two days…during which we found multiple underground compartments, and pulled the people deeper down, away from the radiation that was almost certainly penetrating the upper levels.

But that time is now passed. In the last several hours, we have had several fights…and there is talk beginning of who is in charge, who is the leader. I knew this would happen, and in some ways, it actually took a bit longer than I had expected. But now it is here. For two days, we fought only against the deprivation created by the alien attack…but now, we face a closer enemy, our own people.

Deep Beneath 67th Avenue Subway Station
Forest Hills, Queens
D + 2 Days

Hugh looked behind him, checking to see that his small assemblage was still being left alone. There were about a dozen people in his group, mostly those he had come with, plus a few he had met in the last two days and decided he could trust. He had always known he was different in many ways, but now he realized his judgment of people—something he had rarely exercised before—seemed excellent.

They were talking about what to do, how to operate their unit, their small team of people who were still alive. There had been numerous talks of this kind over the past two days, between them, and among the others, too. But those had mostly been directed against the enemy, the aliens who had assaulted Earth. Now, Hugh raised the issue of the others present. He wanted them on his side, working with him, striving to survive, as he knew their purpose should be. But he had also targeted some of those present, marked them as difficult, as troublemakers. He knew what would ultimately come about, that some of them would probably have to die, at least if he wanted the others to survive. He found the very idea downright repulsive, the thought of killing anyone…and yet, he knew it would happen, sooner or later. His mind had driven ahead for two solid days, analyzing the situation, and he had come up with two facts he considered incontrovertible. First, they needed food, and a fair amount of it.

And second, probably up to a third of the people present couldn't be in the final group, *his* group. They were dishonest, or at least they didn't see things the way he did. And he knew he was right…or at least more right than anyone else present. He might argue something with his brother, work through a disagreement…but he wasn't going to waste time fighting with people he knew were wrong. People trying to benefit themselves, at the cost of the others.

His first thoughts were to kick out those he thought were unworthy, and to do so right away…but that wouldn't work. Who would leave? And where would they go? No, no one would set out willingly. They would insist on remaining where they were, and groups would form. Ultimately, fighting would start. He found that idea horrifying, but he knew it was the truth. Worse, perhaps, he was sure the problems would only get worse. Two days…that seemed about as long as people could deal with an external threat, before they started sniping at each other. There hadn't been any murders, not yet—though fourteen had died of natural causes, mostly radiation in the case of the late arrivals—but he knew that was only a matter of time. And probably not much time, either.

"Okay, I think we are all together on what to do…" He spoke softly, intent that no one could hear him save those in his group. He even turned and put his back to the masses, just in case anyone could read lips. "I know you are all shaken up, that you weren't ready for this. Who could be ready? But the cold, hard fact remains, we either do what we have to do…or we all die. In a day, or a week…or even a month, but there is no doubt we *will* die if we do not plan our actions…and plan them well. We may die anyway, but at least if we do things right, we have a chance."

He looked at his companions, hoping they would see things the same way he did. He intended to get more serious, to begin to discuss the true reality of their situation. He had fought off the realizations, the tiny chance he believed his people had of surviving, at least in the longer term, but it was bearing down hard now, and his mind had gone wild, thinking of anything he could do to improve the odds, even a bit. And not coming up with much.

He had considered various options, many in fact, but the first thing, the only important thing until it was addressed, even more crucial than dealing with any rivals, was food. He had to find some, and quickly…or all the groupings, even his, would fall apart in a day or two. If he didn't find food, and quickly, his people would become a nightmare.

And they just might start killing…and even eating each other.

"First, we need food…and the only place we might be able to find that is the surface. All things considered, I would wait another week or two before I returned there, but we don't really have a choice. We need to see if we can find food. Now."

"I agree, completely." Hugh turned to look at his brother, who was now speaking. "I will lead a small team to the surface…and we will see what is what. Maybe we'll get lucky. It is definitely possible, probable even, that some of the stores will still have food…even if it is buried a bit."

Hugh stirred. The plan was basically the same as his…but in his mind, he led it. "Travis…I think you should stay here and watch the others." He was having a bit of trouble, realizing that his brother probably was the better of the two to go, but not accepting it.

"No, Hugh…I should go. And you know it." Travis spoke softly, but his determination was obvious. But Hugh wasn't ready to back down yet.

"Travis…perhaps we can discuss this ourselves…"

* * *

Travis crawled out, from one room out into another. It was all familiar, of course, a room he had been in just a few days before. He and his brother, and their colleagues, had explored, searched for deeper rooms in the complex…and they had found them. They had led the people deeper, into the vast underground rooms that existed beneath the subway. Some of them were fairly obvious in their former use, and others were completely unfamiliar…and all of them were filthy, old and mostly abandoned for years. But they were deeper, farther underground, and that was the only thing he and his brother, and those who showed any signs of leadership ability, had cared about. Then.

Now, food was just as big of a worry…perhaps even worse. He didn't relish going to the surface so soon, but he knew that unless he found food, and soon, the radiation would be the least of his worries. He had come up, with six others, all people he trusted, at least to an extent. They had slipped away, gotten out without setting off the other people present. Most of those were still sitting around, trying to figure out what had happened…what had gone so wrong. But he knew that wouldn't last, that they had almost eaten all of their food. And hunger would quickly displace fear—and anything else. Things would get ugly fast. Unless he managed to find some food.

He had come to that conclusion himself, and he had been somewhat surprised when his brother had agreed completely. Hugh was no happier about going to the surface, searching through debris for food—and risking the still unknown status of the air, of the radiation. But there was no choice. In another day, he would have twenty people insisting on going…and in two, they all would go, whether he liked it or not. He had agreed that they had to go, had to see if there was anything…left…up above.

Hugh had intended to go himself, but that, Travis hadn't agreed with. He understood Hugh was the smartest person present, probably the only hope of long term survival in the entire group…but he was also his little brother, and Travis had to keep him safe. That was a ridiculous goal, he knew. He doubted he would ever again see anyone enjoy what he would call true safety. But he had to do the best he could.

He had expected an argument, and he got one…but Hugh gave in fairly easily in the end, and he agreed to remain with the others, for a while. Travis was surprised, mildly at least. He understood that his brother was special, that his mind allowed him to consider things on a level he couldn't…but he wondered if for the moment, he should just accept success.

He climbed up a pile of debris—the stairway they had taken down had fallen, but there was enough debris in place to climb back up. He turned and looked back at his followers, checking to make sure they could all manage. They had, even his father, who he had argued should remain behind longer than he had fought with Hugh. This argument, however, he'd lost, and George McDaniel had come along. Travis was both happy an unhappy about it, his intention to keep his parents safe clashing with his realization that they were all at grave risk no matter what they did.

He turned and walked up through yet another hole in the wall…and into the subway station itself. He looked around, seeing the track, or what was left of it. He speculated that there was considerably more radiation up here, but generally, though it was fairly badly beaten up, the room still retained its overall shape. He didn't know if more of the people would have died if they had remained up here during the past few days, if they hadn't all descended several levels, where presumably there was less radiation, but he was fairly certain some of them might have survived, the blast that is. Whether they would have received lethal doses, whether they would be dying even now, he didn't know. But there was no one present…not a massive surprise since those who had come had set off for deeper sections just moments before the blasts hit.

He walked across the subway pad, now broken in at least a dozen places. He had to climb down, and then up again, to get across—twice—and he looked back several times, again watching to see that the others had all made it. He paused, and he wiped his hand across his face, removing some perspiration. It was warmer up top, which wasn't surprising. It was June, after all, and whatever the nuclear blasts had done, they probably hadn't seriously affected the weather. He looked around, wondered what he had been thinking, what he had expected to find. Destruction, certainly…but how bad? He had been underground for three days, safeguarded to an extent, but he was sure he would have heard any subsequent blasts…and he hadn't. The enemy had launched their first series of bombs against the city…but they hadn't followed up. Not yet anyway.

He walked to the staircase that led up…to the street. It had collapsed, all of it, broken into several sections. The covering was dark, no light at all coming through. He looked at his watch—he had remembered to bring it when he had first set out, knowing his phone would die quickly—and it was just after noon. There should be light. For an instant, he almost panicked, wondered what could be causing the darkness. But then he climbed a bit of the way up and saw that it was just debris. His view was better, and he could see piles of stone and other materials…and from where he had moved, a tiny patch of light coming from the sky.

He turned and yelled, "I can see the sky!" It was more a

bit of personal excitement than anything else, and despite his worries, his concerns over fallout—and a hundred other things—the thought of looking out on the sun was almost overpowering.

He worked his way up to the hole, trying to peer through it. There was nothing to see, not really. It was a deep cavity, and all he could make out was a tiny bit of light coming through. It hurt his eyes, which for three days had seen nothing but flashlights and darkness, but he ignored that, and he looked at the hole, dying to pull at it, work to expand it, but also aware that all he had to do was pull the wrong bit, start an avalanche, and he would be finished.

He looked for a minute, trying to judge the best place to expand the hole. The light was still bright, and it hurt his eyes, but he kept at it…and finally, he reached up and pulled down a section of the debris. It broke free almost immediately, and despite a small slide of dirt, it came out easily. He looked again, and yanked on another piece, and then again…and the light grew, the size of the hole roughly double what it had been. He felt urgency, and he could hear some of the others gathering around beneath him. He wanted to rush, to hurry his efforts, but he realized any mistakes made now could be catastrophic. He wanted to get outside, badly, despite the fallout and the other dangers…but he realized that he could as easily end up on the concrete below, battered—even dying—from a cave in. He forced himself to remain calm, to ignore the setting, the people down below…and just to pay attention.

He pulled a long piece of steel, slowly at first, and it gave way. Then he removed it entirely, and some gravel began to flow downhill. It was disconcerting, at first, but he realized again that it was only a bit…and the opening was now larger…almost wide enough for him to squeeze through.

It was bright, too, very bright, and his eyes started to tear. He knew the situation was grave, that many—probably most—of the people of the city were dead, that Earth was invaded by aliens…but at that moment, he felt almost nothing but the urge to see the sun. Despite his cautions, his realization that one mistake, one small mistake, could bring his doom, he moved faster, clearing away the rocks and debris. Then, almost without a thought, without the slightest concern for what he might find on the surface, he lunged upwards, through the hole, and out into the light.

Chapter Eight

From the Log of Captain Jason Wrangle

My unit has been engaged for a day now, almost constantly. I think the enemy is going to attack again any minute, and I wanted to get a few words down...in case they are the last ones. Over half my company is gone now, and half of the balance is wounded. We've hardly even seen the enemy. Their weapons are so long ranged, their targeting abilities so advanced...if we were anywhere else save the deep woods, where we have extensive terrain to hide in, I am sure we would all be gone by now.

We will keep fighting, as long as any of us are standing...or even crawling. We are extensively outgunned, and I do not know how much longer we can continue to fight. But we don't have anywhere to go. The enemy has nuked most of our cities, probably all of them, and our families are probably dead. That much was confirmed over our comm, when we still had semi-reliable communications. Everyone we know, our friends and families, is likely gone. That is a bad thing, terrible, but strangely, it does amp up our courage, instill in us the determination to fight...while we have any strength left, any ability to continue in arms. Even just to hurt the enemy before we are all killed.

Assuming someone ultimately picks up this diary,

someone who is on my side, who can read it, know that we fought…that we struggled hard, battling for every inch of terrain that we ultimately gave up. Know that America, and the entire world, will not be defeated, not as long as one of us remains, ready to continue the struggle.

Anywhere.

65 Miles South of Camp Lejuene
North Carolina
D + 3 Days

Wrangle fired again. He was on single shots now, not because he'd had so much success with the heavier use of ammunition, but because he was almost out. He had already completely expended his own ammo, but he'd ordered his survivors to pillage their dead, to take any ammunition they could find…and he had a bit of that left.

The battle had been strange, and as far as he knew, none of his people had actually seen the enemy they'd been fighting. They had ideas of where they were, where their shots came from, but at least in the dense woods, no one had reported actual solid visibility. That hadn't stopped the enemy from scoring hits, from killing his people, and he suspected his forces had managed to take out an enemy or two as well…but that was based mostly on conjecture. For all he truly knew, his company hadn't even killed one of the enemy, but he had decided that was probably not the case, that they had obliterated at least a couple. He wasn't sure if that assumption was based on any reasonable assessment or just some pathetic need to create some positives in a fight that had been woefully negative overall, but he hadn't had much time to think about it either.

Whatever had happened, he knew it was almost over. Besides being low on ammo, he was exhausted, and he knew his men were just as bad. And they were all low on ammo…if anything, as commander, he had fired less than most of his troops, and he was sure his meager total of rounds left was actually well above the average in the unit. The battle had been a running affair, his troops moving—retreating—and stopping to fire as they went. But once they ran out of ammo, once the enemy became aware of that, he suspected his force's time would be measured in minutes…perhaps seconds.

He hadn't heard from his commander in almost two hours. He knew what that probably meant, but he hadn't received any comm from a replacement either. The entire operation was breaking down, a bunch of smaller units deployed, with no real way out…and no upper levels to issue orders, even just a command to remain in place, to fight until the end.

But he knew that was what he had to do. If there was any real way to escape, to get his unit out of there, he might have done it, but besides the lack of any real escape routes, he reminded himself there was probably no place to flee to. He knew there had been nuclear attacks on the cities, and with the enemy's vast superiority in equipment, he suspected that virtually everything had been destroyed by now.

He ran back another fifty feet or so, shouting out to his troopers to do the same thing. He heard on both sides of him, others passing the word down. That, as much as anything, reminded him that he still had a decent number of troopers, that his people had met the enemy—the still largely unknown enemy from another world—and even if they had been badly beaten, they had fought them, even held them back…at least for a couple hours. He didn't know what he had expected, whether he had originally thought his people would do better…or worse. He realized that he hadn't really thought about it, not with any level of seriousness. He'd been too shocked to even consider the specifics of the fight…at least until it had begun.

He could hear the firepower of the enemy. The vast

speed of their shots tearing up the dense woods. It was terrifying. Worse, now there were either more enemies coming into the fight, or they were increasing the rate of fire. He saw two of his people go down, and then a third a few seconds later. He could feel his mood changing, the tense but focused attitude quickly deteriorating, changing at least partially to panic. His mind considered the actual situation, the total hopelessness of it all, and he realized it didn't matter if his people had taken out a couple of the enemy or not. They were going to be destroyed, completely wiped out…and it looked like, at least to his point of view, most—or all—of the world was experiencing the same thing.

The strength he'd shown, the endurance he had fought to display, was fading now. Quickly. He had allowed his mind to truly consider the situation, and he knew civilization was lost, that the fight his people were in was the same as a thousand others probably going on just then around the world. It would be over soon—they all would be—and he realized that his life was, at best, measured in hours now. Whether or not a few of his troopers escaped—ran—and gained a few more days of life, he knew he couldn't leave where he was. He had orders, commands he couldn't see changing, and he knew he had to follow them. He realized he would probably die no matter what happened, and this was as good a place as any other.

He looked around, to each side of him, and now he could only see four others. That didn't mean his unit was down to five, but it did show that a lot of his troopers were gone now, either killed by the enemy, or running. He'd always been a stickler for details, and he had expected to hate the men who broke and ran…but now he just nodded and wished them well. He couldn't see any escape, come up with any reason to run, but he found himself hoping he was wrong…praying that any of his people who ran actually made it. Though where there was to make it anymore, he didn't know.

He heard something ahead of him, coming through the trees—or the remnants of the trees. He leveled his gun and fired, flipping it from single shot back to bursts. He still couldn't see anything at first, and he spread his shots around, hoping to hit something...anything.

Then, suddenly, something became visible, about a hundred yards distant. He saw it, and he angled his weapon, fired what little ammo he had left. It was silver, and almost three yards tall, and it bristled with weapons. His shots hit, some of them at least, but they seemed to bounce off the armor. Was it armor...or was he looking at a robot? He couldn't tell. It was too far away, and there was too much between him and...it?

He fired until his rifle stopped, and he knew he was out of ammunition. The enemy hadn't fired, not yet, and it continued forward. He froze, his eyes fixated on the thing, watching as it advanced. He still couldn't tell whether it was a creature in armor or a robot of some kind.

And he never did figure it out. At about fifty meters, the—whatever it was—stopped, and several barrels pivoted forwards...and opened fire.

Wrangle felt the first impacts, for perhaps a second or two, but he was so riddled with fire, that he was dead almost immediately. He fell to the ground, his body torn to shreds, in several pieces. The enemy stopped, probably staring for a few seconds. Then it continued forward, firing in several directions, taking out the remainder of Wrangle's command.

All those who hadn't turned and run...as fast as they could...were slaughtered.

*   *   *

"Mr. President..."

He had been sitting in his room, alone. He had lost some

of his people on the last run, when the convoy had been attacked, and he had sent others away, to take various messages to his biggest units and to whatever sections of government were still functioning. He still had some of his people left, though, perhaps thirty in total…but he had given up.

He was deep in the center of Pennsylvania now, far from any cities, any decent collections of people. That was why he was still alive, he supposed, throwing a bit of luck into the mix. Whether it was good fortune or bad, he didn't know…nor did he have any idea how long it would last. He couldn't explicitly decide he'd be better off dead, but he couldn't see any real escape either. He was the president, but he could feel that slipping away, its meaning dropping off, almost to nothing. He still had a few units hidden away, a few agencies that still functioned, more or less, and at least some hope of getting messages through…but he had already lost most of his power, and what little remained seemed to be slipping away quickly. In another day or two, if he was even still alive, he figured he'd have maybe eight or ten people left…and no contact at all with the other units, if they even continued to exist.

He looked up at his senior remaining aide, somewhat unnerved by the tone of voice he had heard. But it got worse when he actually made eye contact, and he could see that his assistant was almost ready to lose it. "What is it, Simon?"

The aide looked back, struggling to maintain his hold. "Sir…we have a communication for you."

The president sighed. He'd spent most of the past 24 hours talking to his fighting soldiers, in at least fifty different places. The story was always the same, varying only by whether the commander said he was sure his forces had taken out some of the enemy…or whether he was more honest, and said he acknowledged a lack of certainty. The thought of one more such communication almost broke him. "Isn't there someone else who can manage this one?" He knew he could order that, that for all human law really mattered anymore, he was in total charge. But he was losing control, realizing that at best, his ground units were doing only marginally better than his air command had managed. They would all be destroyed soon, he was sure of that…and then, if he was still alive, he would be a leader with nothing left to lead.

"No, sir…it is not one of the units." He paused and sucked in a deep breath. "It is the enemy."

The president looked up immediately, and he stared at his aide. For several days, his people had tried endlessly to contact the invaders, to try and reach them somehow, anyhow…without any success at all. And now…

"What kind of message? How are they communicating?" He leapt up, his surprise as obvious in his movement as it was in his words.

"They are on the main comm, Sir…speaking English."

The president almost panicked at the sudden realization that he had to speak with the force behind all the destruction, the devastation that had almost wiped out America…and the rest of the world as well. He had ordered his people to try and contact them, any way they could, but he hadn't really expected success. Now, he struggled with himself, tried to steel himself up to…speak…with the aliens, with those who had attacked and killed most of his people. He didn't imagine the communication would be anything he enjoyed…but the mere fact that they were contacting him suggested that perhaps they didn't plan on eradicating all of his people. That thought kept him going, gave him the strength he needed.

He finally nodded, and he walked over to his desk and grabbed the headphones lying there. He looked at Simon for a second, and then he pulled the set over his head, and he said, "This is the president of the United States…" It seemed stupid, but he couldn't think of anything else to say.

At least nothing civil…but he realized that whatever his hatred of the enemy, his only purpose now was to try to carve out some way that some of his people, at least, could live. It was all he had left, his only hope…and he knew it.

"I am calling you to obtain your surrender." The voice was high-pitched, and very cold. There was no emotion, at least none he could perceive. His mind almost went wild, imagining a hundred ways to proceed…but he realized that whatever the aliens were, whatever purpose they had for the Earth, and for the surviving humans, there was almost nothing he could do. It was obvious they could complete whatever they wanted without him, that contacting him was, if not an olive branch, at least a sign that, perhaps, they didn't intend to destroy everyone. Maybe.

"Perhaps we could discuss options. We might be able to…"

"I am calling you to obtain your surrender." The voice sounded almost identical as it repeated the exact same message…but this time it added, "We do not need you to obtain our desired result. Surrender…or die. This is your only chance."

He sat down, almost panic-stricken. He knew what he had to do, the only thing that gave him some hope of survival…for at least some of his people. But the voice was cold and cruel, and he suspected that even if he agreed totally, the future would be bleak. He almost decided to tell the voice 'no,' to challenge the enemy to continue the fight. But he realized that his forces had no chance of victory, none at all.

And then he heard sounds from outside. He couldn't make it out at first, but then he realized they were gunshots, not the kind his people fired, but higher-pitched, and much faster.

The aliens…

He heard a few familiar rounds, his small remaining force of secret service agents firing a few shots…and then going totally silent. He felt the weight of everything that had happened over the last few days close in on him. The enemy knew where he was, he realized…precisely. If it had been just him, he didn't know what he would have done. But it wasn't only him…it was his entire remaining team—minus the agents he didn't doubt had just been killed. He didn't have any choice. He knew that.

"For the last time…surrender at once or be destroyed." The voice was exactly the same, not a touch of emotion.

He closed his eyes, and his hands clenched. He tried, for a moment at least, to think of something he could do. But there was nothing, and he realized it. His few remaining forces would lose the battle, he had known that even before the message came in…but now he realized that the enemy knew where he was, that they had probably known since the attack began.

Whatever thoughts he had harbored, whatever longshot images of survival, disappeared almost immediately. The enemy was utterly dominant, as much as he had known that already, he was even more certain now. He wanted to tell them to drop dead, to declare his peoples' willingness to continue fighting…but he knew that would do no good, that it would only get the rest of them killed.

He knew what he had to do, but still, it took him some time…to truly accept the situation. To do what he had to do.

"I surrender," he said, barely getting the words out of his mouth. "We surrender."

Chapter Nine

From the Notes of Hugh McDaniel

I will always question whether I should have yielded to my brother, allowed him to lead the expedition to the surface instead of me. I wanted to go, no question, but in truth, I had to agree with him. First, he was clearly in better shape than I am, unquestionably more able, physically at least, to return from the trip. Second, and though he didn't say this, I know he thought it, I am probably the most valuable one present, at least in our group. I hate thinking like that, placing myself over others, but I know it is true. I am the smartest in the station, for sure, and possibly now in the whole city. That sounds egotistical, but it is not, not in this case. I would trade if I could, switch places with any of those here...for my intellect is now a burden to me far more than a benefit. I *must* lead these people, even decide which ones should live...and which should die. It is a terrible position, at least in our current situation, and I know the odds are against us, against our survival regardless of what I do. The enemy apparently doesn't intend to destroy us all, that is apparent in their use of smaller nukes, and in the absence of a follow up bombing run, though they are clearly prepared to do away with many of us. Perhaps even most.

Why do they even want any of us? Why would they

destroy our culture, all of our industry, everything that makes us useful to an oppressor, leaving us as little but herds of panicked beasts? It is not difficult to imagine why they would want us gone, extinct, but right now, assuming the other cities were bombed similarly to New York, there are survivors everywhere. What does the enemy intend to do with them? I suspect that anyone would have a bad view of that, of course, but mine is probably worse. The aliens destroyed our culture without even communicating with us, demanding a surrender. That portends something terrible, and it probably means that it is we, the survivors, who will actually have face worse than the billions who died more or less immediately.

Just Above the 67th Avenue Subway Station
Forest Hills, Queens
D + 3 Days

Travis looked up, squinting as the sun beat down on him. He tried to stare steadily, but days of existing in the darkness, of making his way around with flashlights, had affected his eyes. They were half closed, and shielded by his hand, and still, the brightness was almost more than he could bear, at least for the first moments. He stepped forward, making room for his companions to come out, though he wasn't sure that was a good idea. He was smart, but in truth, he didn't know how bad the fallout was, either underground where he'd been for several days, or here, on the surface. Allowing his companions to come up only increased the risk on them...but he knew there was no other way. They wanted to see the surface as he did, to judge for themselves the damage that was done...and he had to allow them to do it.

"God...it's bright up here." Lucas spoke first, even as he shaded his own eyes. "I expected something else, some clouds or...other stuff...hanging all around, something from the bombs."

Travis turned and looked back at his friend. "No…they hit us hard, but not that hard." He started to look around, a bit. The city was a wreck, most of the buildings destroyed, and the few still standing badly damaged. And as his eyes adjusted and he looked closer, he realized that there *was* a gauzy…something…hanging across the sky. It wasn't heavy, though, and it seemed to be dissipating.

Travis turned and looked at Lucas, moving his hand slowly as he did, lessening the cover over his eyes. "They've taken out the city, no question…but they hit us with a large number of small bombs. Small by our standards, much less theirs. I can't quite figure out why." He turned and looked around, at the shattered city…but also at a target that was less battered than he might have expected. "They could have killed everyone, Lucas, that is almost certain…instead, we're alive, and probably thousands of others are, just in the city." He looked around again, finally uncovering his eyes completely. "Maybe tens of thousands."

"What are you saying, Travis…that the enemy wants us after all? Some of us at least? For something?" Lucas put his own hand down from his head, and he turned and looked at Travis.

Travis was silent for a few seconds, and then he answered. "I don't know…at least not definitely. There could be a lot of reasons why we're still alive, why so many likely are. It has only been a few days, after all. Perhaps the enemy simply has far more uranium that we do…and it was just cheaper to use fission weapons instead of fusion ones. The answer to why they have not attacked again, launched more rockets down on us could be as simple as they just haven't done it yet. It's not like we're going anywhere or striking back at them. What difference does it make if they launch a follow up attack in a few days, or a week? They could just be waiting. Perhaps they need to reload, or to bring more weapons forward." He paused, looking around one more time. "It's not like they've got anything to fear from us. I can only assume the military has been as battered as badly as the rest of us."

"So, what can we do, Travis?" Lucas seemed a combination of broken…and stalwart. "We can't give in, no matter what," he added, his stalwart side in control at the moment. "You know the attitude of the Corps."

Travis turned and looked at his friend. "No, Lucas…we won't give up. Never. We might lose…we're probably going to lose…but we will fight, somehow." Even as the words came from his mouth, he wondered just how that was going to be. He didn't know, and he realized that there seemed to be no way to truly fight back. But he knew he would, that his people would. They would fight to find a way to survive…and they would learn how to strike back.

Somehow.

* * *

"I wanted to speak with you all. You—and Travis and Lucas, of course, if they were here—are the ones here I trust, the ones I am willing to bet my life on." Hugh spoke, his eyes moving among those in the small cluster of people present. He wondered if they would have all made that select group if he'd been less desperate, but he knew he had to gamble more than he would in any other circumstance. His mother, of course he trusted, not only because of who she was, but because she clearly recognized his abilities, and was ready to follow him all the way. He looked out, his eyes catching Sarah's, Janet's, and Gavin's. They were the other three that he knew well, and he found it relatively easy to trust them, too. The others present, three men and a woman, were people he didn't know very well—and one he had really just met here—but he recognized that he needed more than just those he knew, and he relied on his thoughts, his gut check on who he could trust and who he couldn't.

"Travis went out, along with several others, to see if they could reach the surface…and to check out the status up there." He was worried, about what his brother would find, about whether he would run into any other groups…about a lot of things. But he struggled to keep his voice calm, to give the impression that he was more in command than he actually was. "He will be back soon, and he will update us when he arrives." Actually, he had expected his brother to return already, and he was beginning to get worried…more worried than he was in general. But he knew it made sense to hide at least some of what he felt, to try and build up his companions…especially since any scenario he envisioned for the next few days was dark.

Actually, any situation he could imagine, short or long term, was pretty damned bad.

He was silent for a moment, trying to decide what he was going to say next. "I need each of you to suggest anyone else out there you trust…*really* trust." He hated allowing all those present to make such recommendations, but there was no choice. He needed more people, and the opinions of those he trusted were more useful than his own wild guesses. "We need a group of people we know will be dependable, because…" He paused, trying again to find the best way to say what he was thinking. But then he realized, there was no good way to put it, and it was best to let them all know exactly what he was expecting. "Because there is going to be trouble…and I don't mean with the enemy, the aliens. Obviously, there is tremendous difficulty with them as well, but long before that likely comes back into play, our group of refugees will turn on itself. There have already been several incidents, and more are coming. We have *got* to identify the people we can trust, the ones who will act like adults…because we're going to have to fight soon, against those who don't." He was silent for a few more seconds, and then he added, "We are probably going to have to kill some of them…if any of us are going to have a chance to survive, to even take the fight to the real enemy." He knew that sounded crazy, that there seemed no way a group of ragged survivors could wage battle, especially against the aliens…but that is just what he intended to do. At least after he dealt with the human problem.

There was a stir among his people, but no one said anything, or argued with him. He was genuinely surprised at the lack of any real debate…just as he was still shocked that everyone more or less seemed willing to follow him, despite his age. He knew that might not last, that it probably wouldn't, but he hoped it would prevail through the next step, at least.

"I know that is a difficult realization." He paused, for just a moment. "First, we will have to identify the people we have to watch. Ideally, we will just wait until they start something, and then finish it quickly. That will be far easier to sell to the others than acting first. We should be more prepared than they are, and if we are able to have the likely problems targeted, we can act abruptly." He paused, unsure about what he was going to say next. But he decided there was no choice. "So, we will prepare, but for the moment we will not move against anyone, not until they take action. Our guesses, our estimates on who is likely to try something, are not sufficient. We must wait until they take action…or until we have more information." He knew that made it far more difficult, that it would be much easier to target the troublemakers, to take them out carefully, before they took any action of their own. But he recognized that even his own opinions were just that…opinions. Anyone he suspected was only under suspicion. Some would no doubt do as he expected…but others wouldn't. And similarly, someone he didn't suspect could try something. He was almost sure of that.

The entire group was silent for a moment. Then, Denise McDaniel, his mother, spoke up. "Hugh…I know you are intelligent, probably the most brilliant person I have ever met. I don't believe I've ever told you that, but of course it is true. We will follow you, do as you suggest…I will, at least." She was clearly upset, shaken by everything that had happened over the past several days. But she held on to say what she wanted to say. "But please…think everything through. Carefully. I agree that there are problems in the group inside…" She gestured toward the broken section of wall and the sixty or so feet that separated their group from some of the others. "…but be careful, please. We can't lose people who will do what we need them to do…and just as crucial, we can't overlook problems. I can guess at a few, pick out a couple who are probably going to cause trouble…but I can't come anywhere close to guessing everyone's intention, and…" She paused again before saying, "…and neither can you."

Hugh heard his mother's words, and he agreed with them. The last bit hurt some, too, but he had to admit it was correct. He was smart, very smart, but his experience in judging people was extremely limited.

"You are right, Mother…but no one forget. We are not in the situation we were in just a few days ago. Every decision, every effort we make now is literally crucial to our survival. I'm sorry to say this, to put things so bluntly, but some of us are probably going to die in the coming days and weeks. Our goal, as a group, has to be for some of us, at least, to survive, to rise up and ultimately to take on the enemy…and to endure whatever comes our way." He paused for a moment, and then he continued, "We have to endure, we have to survive—some of us, at least. We have to do it because…because there is no choice. None at all. Because, if we don't, and if other groups like this one don't…humanity, at least as we know it, is finished."

Chapter Ten

From the Notes of Hugh McDaniel

I am very worried now. I was concerned earlier, but I told myself, they went to explore, they went further than expected. I figured maybe they had traveled a wider distance than we had discussed…but now I am very concerned. It has been a long while, and I want to go up after them, to explore myself, to do something…but we agreed I would remain here. How long must I do that to comply? When should I lead a group to look for the first one? We didn't discuss that, didn't even address the possibility that they wouldn't return. It wasn't that we didn't think of it—of course we both did—it was just that we didn't speak of it. I know one thing, whether they return or not, we will never do that again. We must discuss everything now, evaluate every option based on all the possibilities, no matter how bad they may be…and we have to have contingency plans in place. Always. We cannot make mistakes, not any longer. Our race is hanging on by a thread, and it will take all we can do, all I can do, just to give us a chance. A very small chance.

I just hope Travis returns. I will push forward here for now, strive to do all I can, and hope that they come back. I have many reasons, of course, but to be honest, I just want my brother back. I am ready to press forward, to do what I can to make us survive…but I need Travis. I am smart, but I can't do it alone, I know that. I need him back.

Just Above the 67th Avenue Subway Station
Forest Hills, Queens
D + 4 Days

Travis looked across the street, holding his arm up behind him. He'd thought he had heard something, and he had ordered everyone to hide…just in case. He wasn't even sure at first it was anything, and then, suddenly, he realized it was. He speculated at first that perhaps it was enemy ground forces, but now that it was close, he was sure it was just another group of survivors. He realized suddenly, with even more assurance than he'd had before, that such a group could be a good addition…or a bitter enemy.

He crouched low, barely able to see the street…or at least what had been the street. He could see the people coming along, moving as well as they could amid the fallen buildings and other debris. He wondered about them, and about the radiation, the contamination that they had suffered…that his own people had endured as well. He was hopeful the positioning of his people so far underground had offered them protection, but he still wasn't sure…and he definitely didn't know how bad it still was above ground. He wondered about the approaching group, about how long they had been totally exposed, about how badly contaminated they were.

He hunched down even lower, trying his best to stay unseen, as the people—whether they were friends or enemies was far from clear now—moved down the street. There was a pile of broken buildings stretched across the street, making a fairly high ridge right before they got to his location. They disappeared below it for a moment, and he heard them climbing up and over it. A few seconds later, he saw the first head, and then the second and third.

He gripped his rifle, unslung from his back and ready for action now. He'd brought it home, which in retrospect seemed smart, but he had only brought a few clips with it. He turned and looked at Lucas, who also had his weapon, and the two exchanged glances. He felt sure about the fellow Marine, positive that he was aware that the approaching people could be friends...or enemies...without any discussion.

Travis stared, unmoving, and hoping none of his people moved either. He was ready to fire, if necessary, but he hoped fervently that it wouldn't be. Humanity was blasted to hell, battered down to a small fragment of what it had been. The last thing they needed was to fight each other. Even combined, with every weapon, every device they could put together, they represented a tiny amount of the military fury the world had been able to deliver just days before...a power that appeared to do nothing to stop the enemy. The idea of wasting time and ammunition shooting at other humans turned his stomach...but he was almost sure it would happen. Eventually...and possibly in just a few seconds.

He looked around the edge of the debris where he was hidden...but he looked a bit too far, stayed extended a touch too long.

"Hey...there's somebody over there!" The voice sounded dark, foreboding. "Whoever is over there, come out now." There was a rustling going on, and all of those who had been moving forth ducked down and took cover. Travis watched, and the combination of the voice and the action made him very worried. Still, he wasn't going to start anything...in fact, he was going to do his best to prevent violence from happening.

"My name is Travis...I'm a survivor." Duh, he thought. "I am looking for others." He gripped his rifle quietly, prepared to return any fire that was offered.

"Come on out, Travis…show yourself." The sound of the voice was harsh, burdensome. Travis thought for an instant of going out himself, covered by the others. That would keep the rest of his people defended, but it offered himself up to…whatever.

"I will come out if you do," he said, not moving at all as he did.

"Are you alone?" The voice was trying to sound calmer, even nicer…but it wasn't really succeeding.

"Yes, I'm alone." It was a lie, but Travis was fairly certain things weren't going well. He'd seen three people, barely, but he wasn't sure how many there were in total. All his people were armed, at least with pistols, and if there were only three of the others—and assuming it did come down to a fight—he was fairly competent his people could win. If there were only three…

My God…the first people you've encountered outside of your group, and you're thinking about a fight. To the death.

He wondered about that, considered it for a few seconds. He almost relented, rose up to see what would happen. But something held him back. If the group wasn't a problem, if they were just another collection of survivors, he had nothing to lose by holding back. They would understand. But if these people were…hostile…there was a huge risk to showing himself.

"If you are alone, come out. There are several of us here, and we will expose ourselves as soon as you do."

Travis started to think, to *really* think. First, he had only seen three of the other party, but he didn't know there weren't more. The tone of voice certainly made him suspicious. *There might be more than three*, he thought grimly. That didn't necessarily mean anything. He reminded himself the other side was as uncertain as he was. And, after all, he had already lied about being alone.

"You first," he said, then he continued, "At least one of you. If there are three, let one expose himself…then I will."

In all honestly, Travis wasn't sure whether he would or not...but he was gambling that the other side wouldn't bite.

"I said you come out!" The sound of the voice changed, became even darker, more menacing. "Now, do it...or we will force you out!"

Travis breathed deeply. He was almost certain now that the other side was an enemy, or at least that they would rob his people—and probably kill them—if they got that chance. Now, he just wondered if there were actually only three. In the end, he decided no...there were probably more.

He turned slowly and waved toward Lucas. The others weren't sophisticated, and they would be seen the instant they moved. But his friend was trained as he was...and he had a chance of making it around, of moving carefully enough to get to the other side unnoticed. Lucas nodded back, signifying that he understood.

The enemy...Travis didn't like the thought, but he didn't doubt it any longer...was moving also. He turned and looked back toward the others, holding his hand out, trying to tell them to stay put. He wasn't sure it would be clear, but it was the best he could do. Then, he turned forward, raising his rifle, looking at the mound of debris.

He waited, perhaps a minute, exchanging one more verbal effort with the others, as much to buy time for Lucas to get into position as because he thought it would be successful. "I insist that you come out first," he said, his voice calm, as mellow as he could manage it.

The sound of the other man's voice was increasingly disturbing. To someone less trained than Travis, it might have been upsetting, but for him, it only increased his assurance that whoever it was that they had met didn't mean well. "You come out...now!"

Travis's rifle was already loaded and ready to fire. He turned slowly, and he couldn't see Lance anymore. Whether he had made it around yet or not was still a mystery. He decided to wait another minute...but he only made it to about twenty seconds.

He saw the movement, watched as a few chunks of debris sunk down from the pile. He knew exactly what was happening, and he could feel his heartrate tick up dramatically, even as he held himself in place, watching. For an instant, he didn't see anything. And then...

He saw one of the men, climbing over the broken rubble. He held his fire, for a few seconds...but then the other guys opened fire. He returned it, almost immediately. Three times.

The first shot took the target out, a perfect hit that clipped the tiny visible part of him and sent him rolling down the pile of rubble. Travis wasn't really looking anymore though. He was confident his shots had taken out the man, and he was moving, looking for the next one. He heard the sound of fire from the mound of debris, and he used it to track the shooters. There were three different ones, in addition to the one he'd hit. That meant there had been four of the enemy.

At least.

He moved to his side, changing his position from the one he'd fired from. He shot again...and continued to move. He was doing all he could to target the enemy, but he realized his main purpose was to keep them looking, to draw their attention in...and away from Lucas.

He fired again, half a dozen rapid shots, and he moved quickly, running out of cover and dashing across the open for a second. It was a calculated risk, and it paid off. The enemy fired on that spot, but too late. One of them exposed himself for an instant...and that was enough. He fired, and he was almost certain he had hit. The target jerked backwards, and he slid down out of site. Travis wasn't *sure* he was dead...but he was pretty certain.

Then he heard more fire, the same sound his own gun made...but coming from the other side of the pile of rubble. Lucas was firing too, on full auto, and he directed his targeting around, shooting at three different enemies. Travis struggled to stay where he was, but an instant later he ran, almost unwillingly forward. He knew his companion had made it around, and that he had likely killed all the people he could find. But there was only one way to check and see if there were any more...or if the enemy was completely eliminated.

He moved, changing his direction every couple steps, giving anyone shooting at him a difficult time, at least. But there were no shots, no sounds of any kind. A moment later, he heard Lucas shouting, "I think that's it, Travis." The words were spoken with a tone of finality, Lucas seemingly agreeing their enemies were all dead...but he wasn't exposing himself. Not yet.

"I think so, too, Lucas...but let's be careful." He moved forward, his eyes moving around, checking for any sign of live enemies. He listened, too, but he didn't hear anything either...nothing except the movement of his own people, now slowly coming out of their hiding places. He felt the urge to hold them back, to wait until he was absolutely sure the enemy was wiped out. But he didn't...he decided there were some things you had to learn for yourself. Besides, he was ninety-five percent sure they were alone...at least for now. Their shooting would have been heard over a wide area, of course, and while it wasn't exactly a temptation, he was concerned it might draw others in.

Enemy...the word had come to him very rapidly, but now he thought about it. The men he had shot, the five people he and Lucas had killed, were the same as they were, residents of New York. They had taken on a different point of view, decided quickly to become hostile, to prey on other survivors. He knew that many people, perhaps most, wouldn't make that leap, not so quickly. But he realized how bad things were, and how much worse they were likely to get. More people would make the decisions the dead ones had, they would be battered, hungry, whatever…and they would become hostile. Many of his own people, those deep in the station, would do the same, he realized, as they became more and more desperate.

He thought, contemplating his own situation, even as he climbed up the pile of debris, and looked all around. There were five bodies, strewn all about…but no one else, no one except Lucas and the group he'd left behind. He wondered again whether the shots would bring more people…or scare them away for a bit. He decided he didn't know. It could be either.

"They're all dead." It was Lucas's voice, and a second later, he climbed over the pile and became visible to Travis. "But we'd better keep moving, Trav…there is no telling who else is up here, and we need to find at least some food, if nothing else."

Travis looked at his friend, and then quickly behind him toward the others emerging from cover, mostly slowly. He considered holding back his thoughts, of trying to speak only with Lucas, but he decided there was nothing to be gained. There wasn't one with them who didn't realize they needed to find food, at least…and since that was the most important thing, the only crucial task at present, he knew any problems, any trouble they might encounter, was information the others had to know.

"Alright…this is a reminder that we have to be careful. Any additional survivors we encounter, from outside our group, however many there are, have to be viewed carefully. They won't all be like these few, of course, but some of them will. We've got to be careful…and we have to find out if there is any food around. That is our primary goal now…that and watching out for any other people we run into. So, let's go find something to eat…and let's do it quickly." He paused. He realized he had told Hugh he would turn back as soon as he emerged outside, but he knew the need for food was severe. And if he knew, his brother certainly did. Perhaps Hugh was planning to go on the next trip, which would undoubtedly leave almost immediately after the first one returned. But Travis wasn't going back…not yet. He knew, as well or more than anyone else, just what his brother was capable of. He understood his desire to come along, his curiosity and his urge to be involved…but Travis knew keeping Hugh as safe as possible was the most important job he had.

And that meant looking for food now, before going back. He knew his brother would worry about him…but he guessed he would figure it out. Besides, if all went well, if there was food nearby, it would only increase the time of his mission by a little bit.

He turned and looked at his entire party, including Lucas, who had worked his way back around. "Okay…let's go. We're looking for food, and any other necessities." He paused for a few seconds, and then after a look at the dead bodies, he added, "And be on the lookout every minute…we don't know who we are likely to meet."

Chapter Eleven

From the Notes of the President

I have never been much of a note writer, or a journal keeper. My life has been a tumultuous one, full of ups and downs…and ultimately, the great campaign and my election as president. I imagined all sorts of things I would do, considered negatives, problems that might erupt…but never once did I think of what would actually happen. Did I ever have a thought about aliens, about finding life somewhere else? Probably, but I never actually imagined anything like what happened…not any more than I thought the plot of some grade B movie I watched late at night would materialize.

But it is real…very real…and now, with hundreds of millions of my people dead, with probably billions gone worldwide, I am sitting here, no more than ten or fifteen miles from Washington, from the destroyed city that until a few days before had been my headquarters…and my home.

I am sitting and waiting now…for what I don't know. The enemy can speak English, that much is clear, but who they are, *what* they are, is anything but. They have little respect for our culture, that is already certain. They couldn't have so casually destroyed all that they had without such disregard. But they must want something from us, too…or they could have just finished us off, killed every one of us. Do they want slaves? That seems unlikely, since they have just killed many of us…most of us? My mind seeks to conjure up an explanation, a reason why…and yet I cannot come up with anything.

Why would they reduce us to scattered remnants of starving survivors scattered all around? It would make more sense to just destroy us all, to keep our planet for themselves. And yet, they clearly have a motive.

I am here…coming as I was directed to, alone as ordered, without any protection. I didn't actually see that as a negative. After all, it was apparent the enemy always knew where I was, that they could have destroyed me, disabled the entire U.S. command center, with the greatest of ease. Yet, they held off from taking things quite that far. The many dead speak up to say this was not an act of mercy…which means they have some purpose, some reason for leaving some of us alive.

For contacting me and bringing me here.

I have come, just as I was instructed, despite the complaints of my few surviving secret service officers. It had taken some argument, but I had gotten them to wait in the vehicle, to let me proceed alone, as I was instructed. There was simply no point in resisting, no hope at all. We had two choices, to bow down before our new masters…or to die.

And I wasn't sure which way I was going to go…not yet. I would at least see what the enemy had in mind.

12 Miles from Washington D.C.
D + 4 Days

He had been waiting for about twenty minutes, spending most of that time scribbling in the small notebook he carried. He wasn't much of a writer, he had never been, but at least it kept him busy…too busy to think about what had called him, what he would see…in a minute, or an hour, or a day? As far as he knew, no one had truly witnessed the enemy, certainly not at short range. What they looked like was a mystery…and he was curious to see.

All he really knew about them so far—aside from their obvious technology and power—was that they knew English. They had to have picked that up somehow. He didn't know if they had been on Earth before, if their agents had somehow been preparing for the assault for, perhaps, years. The ability with which the enemy dispatched his forces suggested that was a possibility, but he knew their high technology level could explain that too.

He wrote a bit more, and then he stopped, put his pen aside and just sat where he was. He had fought off the worries, the concerns for what awaited him, but now they were back, working on him again. For all he knew, he had been called here to be killed, perhaps in a terrible manner. But he didn't think so. He believed the enemy wanted something from him, from the remnants of his people.

Strangely, that made him feel worse, not better. The enemy had already killed the majority of the population, perhaps a large majority, and that meant that whatever they had in mind, it was almost certainly not good for the survivors.

He looked back at his notebook, about to write a bit more, but just then, a section of the wall in front of him began to slip to the side. There had been no indentations, no indications of any kind of door a moment before, but now it was there, and the opening lay right in front of him.

"Enter." It was a voice, the same one he'd heard on the phone the day before, he realized. There wasn't emotion in it, not of any kind. It was simple and straightforward, and he knew he had no real choice but to obey. Whether he was walking into captivity—or worse—he didn't know. But he was sure he didn't really have a choice. He had done everything he could to prevail in the fighting—which turned out to be almost nothing. Now, he had to do whatever he could, get the best deal for his people…no matter how bad it was.

He took a deep breath, and wordlessly, he obeyed, entering the black gap in the otherwise perfectly silvery material. As he walked, he could hear the sound of the door closing behind him, and a light coming on ahead.

It struck him suddenly, affected him badly. He knew he was at the enemy's mercy outside, too, but somehow, now, he truly felt it. He almost turned to run back out, but pointless as that effort might have been in any situation, it was impossible with the door closed behind him. He stood, for a few seconds still, but then he once again achieved control, at least a little. He walked forward, down the short hallway…and into the first room he came across.

He walked inside the brightly lit chamber, and he looked straight ahead, at the…thing…that was standing there. He almost said something to it, but nothing came out. His eyes looked at the…creature? It was metallic and shaped relatively like a man. It looked mechanical, like some kind of robot, but of course, he didn't know what to expect. It could be an alien in armor…or just a different kind of creature entirely.

"Greetings." It was the same voice he'd heard several times already, and it came from the…thing…in front of him. It looked like a robot, he actually decided, a very sophisticated one…but then he realized he had no idea what to expect at all. Perhaps it was a creature from elsewhere, inside of some kind of armor…or simply very different in form from him. Or maybe it *was* a servant, a sophisticated robot, or something of the like.

His mind raced, and he considered the possibility that the aliens were all some kind of robots, that they were the descendants of former servants who had destroyed those who created them. He realized there was no point in continuing with his thoughts, which he suspected could go on for days.

Whatever it was, he realized he had to speak with it, to deal with it somehow. Whether it was the enemy…or simply one of their slaves, he didn't know…but he was certain he didn't have any room for making demands.

"Hello," he said, barely forcing the word out. The entire situation was overwhelming. Was this…creature, thing…a member of the race that had assaulted Earth. Or was it a servant, a slave? Was the true enemy even understandable by him? Was it something else entirely?

"You are the former leader, arguably of the most powerful nation on Earth…that is why you are here. You have ordered all of your military forces to stand down, pursuant to this meeting…now you will issue commands for them to yield, to surrender immediately. Then we will discuss the future…and yes, we do see a future for some your people. We want them to endure…for a long time." The metallic—or at least, metallic-looking—creature spoke, but its lips didn't move. It didn't even have lips. It looked very much like a robotic creature, but he struggled not to draw any conclusions.

"I have ordered my forces to stand down, yes…but to yield, to surrender outright? That is more than I can do…more than I will do, at least without guarantees and assurances."

"There will be none of those. You will surrender because you are defeated. You will yield to us because we are stronger, because we have conquered your planet. There will be no further debate. Acquiesce at once, or you will be eliminated…and we will make the offer to your replacement." The tone was exactly the same as it had been, not a hint of anger or emotion. But the president felt a cold chill. He wanted to stand up, to fight back…even if it cost him his life. But he was exhausted, and he knew his people were defeated. Just maybe, if he yielded fully, he could scrape out some kind of life for some of his people. It was very different from what he'd intended when he ran for office, but he realized just how much his position had changed over the past week.

"Your answer…now." No excitement in the words, no difference from anything it had said previously…but he recognized the threat clearly.

He swallowed, or tried to at least, and he looked at the…he still wasn't sure what it was. It had two eyes, or at least something similar, and yet they looked different, too. Somehow, he knew it wasn't kidding around, that unless he agreed in…a minute, ten seconds, whatever…he would be killed. For a very short period, that actually sounded good. Death would likely be quick, and it would free him from whatever lay ahead. He decided that he wouldn't cooperate, that he would endure whatever was to be inflicted on him, that he would show the enemy just how tough humans could be. However, those thoughts only lasted a few seconds. The robot—or whatever it was—would kill him, without doubt, without emotion, he was sure of that. He thought that was okay, that it was probably better than whatever awaited him if he yielded…but he knew they would just seek out his successor, whoever that was, and proceed as planned. He didn't have the choice to keep his people in the fight, to prolong the struggle against the invader. His only decision, the only thing he could truly affect, was whether he died now…or retained a chance to live a bit longer.

He struggled for a moment, but then he gave in, he subordinated his personal preference to what he perceived as his obligation. "Yes," he said, "I will do it. I will do as you command."

He wasn't sure if it was obligation to his office, or fear for himself, that had finally triggered it, and the second he spoke the words, he knew he had sold himself, that whatever scraps of freedom he had once possessed were now gone.

"I will do it," he repeated, even as part of him railed against what he was saying, what it meant. He knew he was going down a dark path…but he couldn't see any other alternative.

Chapter Twelve

From the Notes of Hugh McDaniel

I was worried, very worried. I know Travis, better even than he thinks I do. It had occurred to me, even as I agreed to let him lead the expedition, that he wouldn't turn around once he had emerged, that he would likely look around, at least a bit, for food and other necessities. But still, I am concerned. Just because I know where he likely went doesn't alleviate my worries. It is very likely dangerous outside, between brigands, which I am sure there are, and enemy action, which remains more of a mystery. I can only hope that he is careful, that he stays alert. I feel confident about that, at least…I just don't know if it will be enough.

I spoke to my mother a few minutes ago, and I lied to her. I told her Travis—and my father—and the rest of the party were just searching the station and its immediate surroundings, looking for any further areas we had not yet uncovered. Normally, I figured she wouldn't have believed that, but, strangely, it seemed that the situation made her more, rather than less, likely to accept what I told her.

I looked around at the crowd, at the people all around. Things had held together so far, but even as I looked, I could sense trouble was coming. They were scared, clearly, and at first this had been helpful. It kept most of them controllable. But most of the food they had brought was gone…and hunger would quickly turn things into a nightmare. Even the quietest, the most docile people would quickly become problems.

I suddenly realized that I had known all the while that Travis would go out looking for food, that he would exceed the mandate for his mission…and I had known this when I had backed down, agreed to let him go while I stayed. That only made sense, of course…he was definitely better than I was at that sort of thing…and I was more essential here. That didn't mean I was going to save everyone, or even some of us, but it probably meant that if anyone could, any one of us, it was me. Assuming, of course, at 19 years old, as a skinny boy, barely a man, I could get anyone to listen to me.

And also assuming that there *was* actually a way to save us, that there was any hope at all. The answer to that question was still a total mystery.

67th Avenue Subway Station
Forest Hills, Queens
D + 4 Days

Hugh was looking around, searching for any other rooms or passages in the subway station. He had found nothing, and he was fairly certain there wasn't anything else, but he looked anyway. He realized that he was just wasting time, that he was trying to keep busy until Travis returned…but he did it anyway.

He had ideas, many of them in fact, on how to structure a group of survivors, how to proceed…but none of that mattered if he couldn't feed them. Without food—in a day or two—he would lose whatever marginal control he had over most of them. They would start fighting, those who still had food becoming the targets of those who had run out. He knew it would progress, each step worse than the last one, until they were killing and even eating each other. For all his intellect, for his vast ability to consider alternatives, he had no solution to that one, none except finding food.

He realized, of course, that Travis might be dead, that his party might have been intercepted, or even that the radiation at the surface was far greater than he had expected. His rough calculations told him no, that it wasn't good, but it wasn't fatal either…but he knew that was at least partially a guess. And even though he understood the assumption that his brother was still alive was just that—an assumption—he accepted it as solemn truth. He could only take so much, after all.

He pawed at the wall, looking for anything, a plastered over doorway, or something of the kind. It wasn't there, he knew…his people would have found it by now, but he looked again anyway. It was better than just sitting and worrying. There really wasn't anything else to do, at least not until he had some food to give out.

He was about halfway through the search when he heard something. At first, he just assumed it was the people getting a little louder for some reason. Then, he realized suddenly…Travis was back!

He turned and raced back into the main area…and he spotted his brother immediately. Only then did he realize just how worried he had been. He moved quickly to the middle of the chamber, and as his brother saw him, he also moved fast. They embraced, for only a few seconds, but the feeling was evident. Hugh knew he would make many, probably most of the major decisions going forward…but he needed his brother too.

"Hugh…I am glad to see you." His voice was relatively high pitched, as close to cheerful as he had been in days. He backed away from his brother and realized that behind him lay piles of food. All of the members of his party had brought as much as they could carry. "I know you expected me to come right back, but I decided to explore just a little." Travis sounded somewhat uncertain about how his brother would take it.

Hugh had known, of course, what his brother would do, at least what he would probably do, but he didn't see any reason to bring that up. "That's okay, Travis…I'm just glad you made it back. With some food, no less."

"Yes…we found a grocery store, or at least the ruins of one. The building was collapsed, but it was full of food. We have to get back there, with a lot more people." He paused, and he continued, sounding as if he felt a bit guilty about what he was about to say. "Before anyone else finds it."

"I agree…completely." He turned and faced the crowd, most of the people now gathered around, watching. "Okay…we need as many people as can make it. The store is…" He looked at Travis.

"It's close…maybe a quarter of a mile, or even less." Travis turned and looked at Hugh. "Definitely less…probably only a sixth of a mile."

Hugh listened, and he realized just how many capabilities his people were starting to lose. Travis had an excellent idea of distance, but over broken down streets and shattered buildings, he could only guess at the ranges. "Okay…everybody who can make it, get ready. We're going to leave in ten minutes…and we're going to keep at it, all day if necessary, until we've got everything here. Understand? Every scrap of food we can find." He was uncertain. He didn't have any real power, any control over the people, not even given to him by acclaim. He had just been aggressive, had done what he could to keep them alive…and they had listened to him. So far.

The crowd murmured, and he realized he was going to have to do something soon to make his command more official, accepted by the people. That wasn't going to be any fun, he realized, and though it could go a number of ways, not many of them went far without any bloodshed. The thought of humans, the pitiful survivors of an alien attack, fighting with each other…killing each other…it turned his stomach. But he didn't doubt it was going to happen. In fact, he was almost sure it would.

A few minutes later, he found out that it already had.

Still, for now, he was certain most of those present would cooperate. They were either hungry already, or close to out of whatever food they had brought…and everyone there accepted that they needed more. Quickly. And they would want to grab it, to get it before some other band of refugees found it.

Hugh thought about that, and while he knew there would be useful people in other groups, he also realized that most of those present already at least partially considered their neighbors, those not here now, to be the enemy. Better they starve than anyone here. He hated that thought, and he wanted to argue, to convince them they were wrong. But they weren't…at least not right now. He realized he would have to gather more people eventually, but first he had to ensure the survival of his own group…and then he had to make them *his*. Finding the food, sharing it with everyone, that would help, at least for a while.

As to when he would make the next move, when he would try to actually gain some control over the group…that was tomorrow's problem, and despite his considerable intellect, he honestly had no idea precisely what to do next.

*   *   *

"C'mon…quickly. We're losing the light." Hugh stood on a large rock…actually, it was part of one of the buildings that had lined the block until five days before. He had made fourteen runs, to and from the supermarket…or at least the wreckage of what had been a store before the attack. He was fairly surprised that his people had found it almost completely preserved, if mostly buried. The bombs had wrecked the building, caused it to partially collapse, but almost everything inside was still useful…and perhaps most miraculously, no one else had been there. Not yet, at least.

He turned and looked behind him, out at the sky, and over the streets all around, what was left of them, anyway. He had seen one group earlier, three or four people, he wasn't sure, and he had reacted by keeping his people inside for a few minutes. The sight had filled him with uncertainty. Was the group he saw trouble, like those Travis had encountered? Or were they just refugees looking for food? And which was worse right now? He wanted to expand his group, at some point…but since it wasn't even his yet, he knew it wasn't time. He already had too many people, and he expected a fight to break out at some point. Adding newer, even more unknown people to the mix now only stretched the food farther and weakened whatever grip he had managed to establish over the group.

Fortunately, he managed to hide from this group. They kept walking, and in a few minutes, they were gone. He stayed up for a moment, making sure they had moved on…and then he went back down into the market.

He knew he had to find a way to recruit others, but not yet. That was tomorrow's problem, not today's.

He turned and watched all the people, about half of those that had come in the first run. They were quickly gathering the last of the goods. He tried to recognize everyone present. Those who pushed themselves to the end were definitely more likely to be on his side than those who had taken a trip or two and then stopped. He realized that he wasn't really in command, that the effort was more of a group thing, that the attempt to clear out the store, to secure all the food they possibly could, was obvious. Anyone who bailed, who stopped coming, was suspect, now. He hated himself for recognizing that, for dividing the people into different groups, based on his expectation of their actions…but he did it anyway.

He turned and looked outside again. The sun was almost setting, and despite the fact that he knew there was some radiation, that the entire world he had known just five days before was effectively gone…he noticed that it was pretty. He couldn't remember the last time he had watched a sunset, but this one caught his attention…for a minute or two. Then he turned and shouted again, "We're losing the light…take what you've got and come on." He knew there was a little food left, that there were a couple more trips to make…but he wanted everyone back in the subway station, by nightfall.

He realized he would have to become daring, take stunning chances to lead his people through the nightmare that had descended upon them. But for right now, he didn't want to have them out at night. He would post guards just inside the subway station—he would stay there himself if no one else would agree to do it—but he didn't want anyone out in the darkness.

He just didn't know what was out there at night…and he wasn't ready yet to find out.

Chapter Thirteen

From the Notes of the President

I am surprised that I was set free, allowed to return to my car, and my final headquarters. I know it is just because the enemy is so dominant, that they are fairly certain I will obey their commands…and absolutely confident, if I don't, they could simply kill me and move onto my successor. Still, it felt strange to leave there, to return. I knew I was no longer the president, at least not in any meaningful way. I was the slave of the invader now, obligated to them. I didn't have much to do, if only because our forces were so badly damaged I didn't have many left to command.

I got back to my headquarters, though I realized almost immediately, as I had not before, that the enemy could spy on me. I do not know how, but it was clear that they had tracked me closely since the first day of the invasion. I had given some thought to ways I could still oppose them, things I could do quietly to continue the fight. But I realized they would probably know as soon as I did anything. And they would kill me and replace me. That wasn't so bad, not really…my life is over anyway, at least any part of it that I want to live. What keeps me going now is hope, the smallest shred of it, that one day, perhaps in months or even years, if I survive that long, I may get a chance to strike back against the enemy, to strive to clear my name from what I must do now.

But first, I must command my forces, whatever little bit remains of them, to surrender. It will be difficult, something I never even imagined doing…but I know, with a cold certainty, that continuing the fight will only bring about their final destruction. That, at least, makes it doable…even if I hate myself for every word, every breath I take from now on.

12 Miles from Washington D.C.
D + 7 Days

The president stood in his room, the space that had been his last office, that still was, to the extent that he required one. He looked out the window, noticed that the outside was calm, that the sun was about an hour from setting. From here, from where he was, where the U.S. government had fled to, everything appeared normal. But he knew that was an illusion, that his country, that the world, had been devastated…utterly. There were survivors, certainly, both in the ruins of the cities and in the far off sections like the one he occupied right now. But there was no hope of resistance. He wondered if he'd had time, if he had been given more than a day's warning, if he could have assembled a better fight. Certainly, he would have brought many more people into the military conflict, given enough time. And his forces would have been better deployed, certainly. Perhaps even, the world would have united, met the enemy with a combined force that would have been vastly more effective than the peacetime segments that were tossed at the enemy. Thrown away. But none of that mattered, not anymore. He had only the ruins of his patchwork defense, and he'd had hardly enough time to even speak with foreign heads of state once or twice…before the international lines were cut, and the world was plunged into ruin.

Before he had gone to the enemy. In the few days before he had surrendered, he had been busy, sending orders to remaining units, desperately trying to win a fight he knew now had always been unwinnable. Whether that would have been different if he'd had six months' notice or not, he didn't know...and it didn't matter. But since he had returned from his trip, he had only one goal, only a single order to give to his few remaining units in the field. Surrender.

He had done just that, issued the order several times over the main channel. He had better contact than he'd had before, the enemy jamming gone. Without satellites, it still wasn't perfect, but he was confident he had gotten through to everyone...or almost everyone.

But not everyone had obeyed. He had forty-three units that he knew of that were left still in the fight, all he was aware of that remained of U.S. forces everywhere. Some of those units had no more than fifty or a hundred men left, and the largest perhaps a thousand...but only around half of them had actually yielded. The others ignored his order and kept fighting...and a few bolted, did everything they could to break away from the battle and flee...with their arms intact.

He had no idea if any of them would escape, if they would break free, find someplace to hide and regroup...but he was hoping for them. He had never thought he would react that way to having his commands ignored, but he did. He wished the best to every unit that continued fighting, to every soldier seeking to escape, to pull back and regroup. He didn't think it would matter. He knew his forces were defeated, that they were almost wiped out, but he recognized the appeal of fighting to the end. He told himself he would have done the same thing in his days in the military, that he too would have refused an order to yield. He didn't know, of course, what he would truly have done, but he recognized that the presidency carried other obligations, other considerations. He was responsible for every man and woman remaining alive, at least in the U.S., and he hadn't had a choice. He knew that, as well as he had ever known anything...but the weight of it, the pressure, was almost too much to bear.

He stared out the window, looking on as the remnants of the beautiful day moved on toward night. He closed his eyes, tried to imagine his cities lying in ruins. He thought of the people who had survived, wondered what they were doing now. Probably trying to get food, to survive...one day at a time. He hoped his surrender, the cessation of any resistance, would mean that they would receive help. But he doubted it. He could pray that the enemy had some kind of use for his surviving people, that they would change their position now that a surrender had been obtained. But he couldn't push away the thought that there was something terrible coming. It was hard to imagine something worse than what had already occurred, but as he stood there, his mind wandered...into some pretty dark places.

But not dark enough.

* * *

"Divine One, I have come to report on the takeover of the human world." Estle-Starric stood before the throne, bowed before the Divine One, the ruler of all the Gavicons. He was the official commander of the Earth Attack Force, though, of course, with the Divine One present, that was more of an official title than an actual one. He spoke the human tongue, which had gotten somewhat easier to do over time. The Divine One had commanded all his people to speak the native language, despite its coarseness and the incomplete nature of it, and Estle-Starric had done so. Of course, the human world had possessed several hundred languages, a strange factor no doubt, at least to Estle-Starric...but the invaders had chosen what they had perceived as the dominant one. English.

"Thank-you, Estle-Starric. It appears that the invasion has gone off quite well, that the humans are virtually subdued already." The Divine One spoke, also using English. His tone was different however, as though he was speaking with multiple voices at one time. He was the highest ranking of the Gavicons, the most able of all his people, and his mind was the most capable one known. The Gavicons encountered other societies, on Earth most recently, and they had seen leaders chosen by various means, though, oddly, never by their own simple method of the most capable one taking charge.

"Indeed, Divine One…everything appears to be going quite well. All human powers have surrendered, and most of their combat units have been destroyed or have surrendered."

"Most?"

Estle-Starric hesitated. We have tracked twenty-three units that have attempted to break off from their fights. A minimum of nine of them have been successful, at least temporarily."

"A minimum? Is your tracking not perfect?"

Estle-Starric paused again, for longer this time. "Divine One, the robot forces were extremely effective…in most cases. However…they allowed a small percentage of the defenders to break off. We had the initial positions of all military units, but we believe that a relatively insignificant portion of the native forces managed to escape from us, for the moment."

"That is not part of our plan, Estle-Starric. I am displeased. I urge you to find them all, quickly…is that understood?" His tone changed, slightly…and Estle-Starric understood.

"Yes, Divine One…I will see to it at once." He knew the supreme leader would leave soon, that the full deployment to Earth was just to defeat its military, to occupy the planet.

When he left, along with much of the fleet, he would leave behind an adequate force, both robots and Gavicons...and presumably with Estle-Starric in command. At least, unless something changed his view.

"I expect all of this to be completed...and very quickly."

"Yes, Divine One...understood completely. You can be sure, all of the local military will be eradicated, and our plan will proceed as projected, without further interruption." He meant it, but he was also a bit edgy. The human resistance hadn't put up much of a fight, not exactly, but they had kept at it longer than he'd expected. Some scattered forces were still fighting, despite the surrender. They weren't causing any real damage to the attacking forces, but it was proving far more difficult than expected to completely eradicate the last of their military units.

The Divine One was silent for a moment. Then he just said, "Very well, Estle-Starric...go on with your operation. The humans are the most likely match we have found, far better than any of the others. We can harbor no delays in final testing...and hopefully full operation, as quickly as possible."

Chapter Fourteen

From the Notes of Hugh McDaniel

I have decided, developed a plan, if not yet for vengeance against the invader, at least for the survival of my group…for a while.

I am not in command, of course, and any decisions I make are reliant on enough of my compatriots agreeing with me, and jumping in. I am unclear whether that will happen, but I am almost certain a fair number will be on my side. Whether that will be enough is unknown to me. Honestly, the variables, from just those normally affecting such a situation, to specific ones, are just too great to overcome. I feel my chances are good, and I know that is the best I will do. If I fail, I may die, or I may be expelled from the station, cast out with any survivors on my side. I can't know…but I am certain that my plan offers the best chance, not only for our group to live, but ultimately to strive to regain our place on this planet, to attack the enemy invaders, and ultimately to drive them away. I know that sounds insane, and perhaps it is, but it is also the only path that leads us to some hope of becoming more than slaves or hiding forever in the ruins.

Beyond my own family and our friends, I have been working on identifying those I feel will be most helpful…and bringing them along to my line of thinking, a few at a time. It is a difficult procedure, as I must tell them of the likelihood of combat at some point. The possibility of convincing everyone, of getting them all to voluntarily join me—to follow me—is almost zero, and ultimately, that probably means a fight. I find myself wanting to think that we can simply part, that one group can leave the other and go off on its own. But I recognize that things are far from normal, that even if such an arrangement could happen, the parties would fight over the food, the medicine, everything we have.

Everyone present, whether they fully realize it or not, is extremely tense.

Despite my best efforts to imagine a peaceful resolution, I know it will not happen. I dread that moment, the final confrontation, the likely waste of human lives, whether they are from those who side with me or from the other group...but I know that it is likely necessary. Avoiding bloodshed is usually a good way to go, but not in this case. Those we will move against, and any who side with them, are inevitably going to become enemies, if not now, then tomorrow, or sometime soon. I can feel it now, even, despite the food, despite the slight gains we have made, that the crisis is moving on, going to a new place. People have already begun getting on each other's nerves. The finding of the food, the joy that brought to almost everyone, bought us some time...but not much.

If we do not make our move, and do it quickly, we will end up fighting anyway, countering the enemy's efforts to do what we have failed to do. And people will die, however it begins. At least if I start it, we have a greater chance to prevail, and the killing will open the way for us to grow, to expand, and ultimately to fight back. I know that sounds insane, that battling against the invader who took out all of our military seems crazy...yet it is our only choice, and even a one percent chance of ultimate success is better than none at all. We will find a way, a way to prevail, to win...or we will ultimately die. I don't see any other options, or at least, none I will accept.

67th Avenue Subway Station
Forest Hills, Queens
D + 8 Days

Hugh stood, looking around, making sure he and the group he had assembled was far enough from the others so that what he was about to say wouldn't be heard by anyone else. It had taken a considerable effort to gather those he wanted to speak to, to get them all together and out of earshot of all the others…and he knew he wouldn't have long, that some of those excluded would wander over shortly. The chambers under the subway station were large, far bigger than the people in them currently needed, and that had made it possible for him to hold the meeting out of earshot of the others, for a brief time, at least. But he had to make good use of it…quickly.

"I'm going to say something now…along with several of my companions." He started almost immediately, speaking quickly. He held out his hand, and Travis walked up to stand behind him. His parents followed, along with Sarah, Lucas, Gavin, and Janet. Then, another half dozen or so did the same, people he had already spoken with, those he'd been sure of. That left about seventy percent of those present, people he knew, ones he had selected, but not spoken to yet, at least not about his plans. Having almost a third of those present behind him already was likely to help, he realized, but he knew things could go badly, too, if he hadn't selected all the right people. Just one who decided to tell the others, or even who brought attention to the meeting, could be enough to damage or even destroy all his efforts. But he knew he had to take the chance, that he had to proceed as best he could. It was only the first great risk that would present itself, and he knew he would need more people than he had brought together before he could proceed with a strong hope of success.

"I don't know how long we will have before the others notice and come over, so I will just say what I have to very quickly. Our world was destroyed. I know you all know that, and yet I suspect many of you have not truly considered it, at least not in its entirety. Everything we knew, all of what we loved—and what we hated—is gone now, completely. Our nation, our jobs, our homes…all of it. Our first goal is, of course, to survive, to find food, medicine…but then what? And what are we willing to do for our survival? I tell you now, what I am about to propose is necessary…absolutely *necessary*. It is *vital* to our having any chance, any chance at all for survival, *real survival*, at least in the long term. We must ultimately be prepared to…" He paused for just a few seconds, and then he said, "…fight back." He hesitated for a longer moment, allowing his last words to sink in.

"That is right…to *fight back*. And win. We are humans, and whatever these invaders want, whatever made them kill so many of our people, while leaving us, and some others, still alive—and they did that by choice, never forget that—it is not for us. We cannot become slaves, or whatever else they want. We must maintain our independence, struggle against whatever they throw at us…and do not doubt for an instant that they will do that. There is clearly some reason we have been left alive. And that is precisely what happened…we have been *left alive*. Any thoughts that you may have about a species that can travel among the stars, deploy multiple sophisticated spaceships, but whose weapons are no more powerful than our own of seventy years ago, can be let go. Now. The enemy could have destroyed us, that much we can be certain of. They could have taken out every human being in existence. They didn't, because they chose not to…and there has to be a reason."

He paused, just for a few seconds, and then he

continued, "We must fight back at some point, and until then, we have to organize, to form up. First into some kind of collective that can survive, that can endure, that can gather more food, and ultimately weapons too." Another pause. "Something that can take back our world, one tiny step at a time…and ultimately, if not in our own lives, then in our children's—and yes, we must have children—to drive the enemy away."

He knew he sounded crazy…perhaps he *was* insane, at least in a manner of speaking. But that is what he felt, what he truly believed…and he was as sure he was right about it as he had ever been, about anything. The chance of success, of victory in an ongoing guerrilla war, was pretty poor, he realized that…but the chances of any other activity, of hiding or contacting the enemy and begging for peace, were much worse. His people *had* to fight. They *had* to…or just surrender, and quite possibly die, or worse. There was no other option. He knew most of them had to learn to fight, hell, he had to learn, himself, perhaps even more than most of the others. But there was no other choice, none save giving in to whatever nightmare lay ahead.

"I know I sound crazy, that many of you are thinking that I have lost my mind…but this is the situation we are in, through no fault of our own, maybe, but it is real, nevertheless. Unless you believe that the enemy would bombard our entire world, kill billions of people, and then treat the survivors well, you will realize what I am saying is true. I don't know why we have been allowed to survive, what purpose we are supposed to serve…but I do know, I would rather die with a rifle in my hand than give in to it. I am just a man, one…but I am free, and I will not give that up for anything." He realized he had raised his voice a bit, and he looked through the broken barrier, checking to see if anyone else heard him. It didn't look like it, but he noticed people starting to watch, to wonder what was going on. In a moment, some of them would come over. He had to finish, now, and he had to do a good job.

He had to do a damned great job.

"I won't sugar coat anything to any of you. Our chances of success are pretty damned poor...but they are not nonexistent. We have clearly been left here, I would say deliberately...but we are expected to remain, to search for food, and otherwise to stay where we are, until the enemy comes for us. I say, we don't do that, that we search for guns and ammunition as well as food, that we do whatever is necessary to prepare, whatever that may mean. That we send out people to scout, to begin to gather information we need, to do whatever we have to. I do not pretend to know anything, to have any more idea of what brought this on us than you do...but I will swear to fight to the end, to do whatever I must to resist the enemy, and to regain control of our planet. And I am asking the same of each of you."

He swung his hand into his palm, partially because he thought it looked good, and partially because he had gotten himself excited. He had been much happier before the attack, of course, just as he suspected everyone else had been...but he felt exhilarated in a way he hadn't before. Part of him lived in terror, scared at the prospect of fighting against the enemy, at the thought of almost anything he had to do...but the other side was actually excited. It almost felt as though he had been created for a purpose, and while he knew that was foolish and almost certainly unreal, he felt it, nevertheless. In some ways, he felt alive, more than he ever had. Now it was time to see if he had reached the others, and if he had, to determine if he was successful in gaining control, at least over the closest of the survivors in the 67th Street Station.

"The first thing we need to do is to take over control of this station..." He paused a bit and then continued, "to take out anyone who stands in our way, who will not give in to our purpose." He knew this was the most difficult part, and he understood. The idea of standing up to the enemy, of fighting back against the odds, it was terrifying, but it made sense, at least in a way. There was nothing else to do, no alternate route that promised any success at all. But calling some of the others there, those trapped in the same station with the rest of them, refugees as much as they were, the enemy, which is essentially what he had done, was a huge step. He knew it was right, or at least he was almost sure…but he recognized that it would be difficult to convince everyone. Very difficult.

"I know that's hard to accept, that many of you have considered all of us together, as a single group. I want to agree with you, but I can't. Each of us knows some of the people here, and not others. This group is a collective, assembled by chance, by each person's actions to come down to the subway for protection. And while we have been badly beaten, almost destroyed by the enemy, it has only been just over a week since it happened. The human mind that all of us possess, has trouble accepting reality in such a time. There is a good chance, a very good chance, that when we announce our takeover, some of those present will contest it…that they may even fight us for control. I hate talking about this, but I have to…because in a couple hours, we *are* going to speak to everyone here, and we are going to announce that things will change, that we will cease being a disorganized group of survivors and begin the route to becoming a well ordered unit. And if that causes trouble, if people disagree, if they fight us…then we will fight." He paused again, just a few seconds, and he looked out at the crowd.

"And we will kill anyone who battles with us, who stands in the way of our survival. Because it is our only option."

He looked out again, saw faces that expressed surprise, even shock. But no one said anything, and no one moved. He wasn't sure he had reached everyone, that all those present agreed with what he had said…but he was closer to believing it than he had been. And that was something.

Chapter Fifteen

From the Notes of Hugh McDaniel

It is time…almost. I sit alone, more or less, apart from even my brother. I would have him on stage with me, to share the responsibility of speaking to everyone…but I need him where he is, ready for action. I don't know that there will be trouble, of course, but to be honest, I feel it is likely, at least two chances in three. Several other groups have been speaking with each other and while they may feel they have done it quietly, that they haven't been noticed…they have. There is no guarantee that they will resort to violence, that my words will trigger them.

But if you're going to bet on it…bet that they will.

67th Avenue Subway Station
Forest Hills, Queens
D + 8 Days

Travis looked out at the crowd, at the people in the main room beneath the station. They were relatively content, for now, still excited that the food supply had taken a considerable upturn. There had been fights over certain types of food, and the best items had already been mostly eaten, or at least claimed and set aside. There had been a number of small disputes, but there was so much food, there was enough for most of them to accept what they got. He knew that wouldn't last, that all the food they had brought back from the supermarket would eventually be eaten…and much quicker than people expected. Much of the food that required cold had already been exposed to room temperature for several days, and was, by any normal standards, bad. Still, it hadn't been thrown away, it had been stored in the deepest sections of the station, and except for particularly sensitive items, he was fairly confident it would remain at least marginally edible for a few days. Travis had intervened as little as possible, following Hugh's lead. He had only separated out the items that would last a long time, trying to get people to eat the foods first that would spoil soon. In that, at least, he was aided by the general appeal of the spoilable items compared to those that would endure for longer.

Watching, looking at the situation, at his brother, made him even surer that Hugh was right, that they needed much more organization if they were to survive. He knew the one supermarket wasn't enough, of course, not for the long term…but he realized that if they had been well-run, if the food was managed properly, it would probably have lasted two or three times as long. He had already been about to take a party out, to explore for more food, and some other items, too, but he had put that on hold temporarily. It was time…time to launch the operation that would put his people in control…or would see them all die. If it was a success, if they survived, then they could go out and look for more supplies in a more organized manner.

Things were about to take a turn, and his people were going to make their move. Hugh had done a miraculous job with those they had chosen as close to them. He had excited them, scared them…and convinced every one of them to join in the…what was it? A power grab? An attack? A revolution? He didn't know, and he realized he wouldn't, not until it began. How it would go, whether it would become a success or a failure, depended on a lot of things, not the least of which was how most of the people reacted...whether they were willing to join and accept effective rule by his small group...or whether they would object, even fight.

He had his side as organized as possible, ready for whatever happened. They were as prepared as they could be, and all those he considered truly reliable were armed. As for the others, he just didn't know. He had been aware of some conversations, had noticed some others talking, apparently seriously, but he had no idea what to expect. And despite his intellect, he didn't think Hugh did either. But it didn't matter much anymore. In a few minutes his group would launch its play, and they would prevail...or not.

He moved to the side. He was wearing a long coat, not his own, but given to him by one of those in his group. He needed it to hide his rifle. It was shoved under his arm, and hidden well, though he figured if anyone was really looking, they would have wondered why he was wearing such a heavy coat.

He looked out, across the open space, and he saw Lucas. The other Marine was positioned at the opposite side of things, also wearing a long coat. If the two had been right next to each other, they might have looked even more suspicious, but Travis figured it was likely that no one would notice them, not in the minutes they had left.

He thought about his mission, and his friend's. He couldn't argue with the fact that he and Lucas were probably the two best fighters in the entire group, but he still hated what he had to do. And he was far from sure it would be a success. His place was simple...at first. He was to stand, quietly, watching everyone, but especially six or seven people, those who'd been deemed the likeliest to oppose the move. He was to watch them...and if they made any kind of move, he was to shoot them down immediately. He felt a bit ill, lying in wait, preparing to take out fellow survivors—to *murder* them—but he truly believed that the hope of the group, the chance that they would prevail, and put up some kind of resistance, against the invading aliens and not just other humans, depended on their coup succeeding. And for that, he was prepared to do whatever he had to do…even commit murder.

He looked around, at all the movers in the plan. They had put together a good number of people who were in favor of the general idea, but the exact timing had been kept to a much smaller group, as had the specific nature of the move. That would test many of the people who had agreed to follow them, and he wouldn't be surprised if they lost some, or at least, if a percentage of them were badly shaken by the severity of the operation they had more or less agreed to already. But he had been totally in favor of keeping those in the know to the smallest number possible. It was better to minimize the risks of letting anyone catch on before they moved…and that, at least, seemed to have worked.

Travis didn't have any experience with this kind of situation. No one there did, he supposed. But they would soon, all of them. He knew his life had changed, that all of theirs' had, dramatically, but he also realized that his mind continually went to what it knew, and not what it had to learn. He would get through it all, he believed, learn to accept things he had to, but he was also sure he wasn't there yet, that no one was. That made the results of their actions over the next hour even more unpredictable.

But they were necessary, all of them. He knew that. Every day they waited would just leave the door open for someone else to make a move…and it was essential that they should go first. That they should make their move now. If they ended up as the resistance, fighting against someone else's bid for power, he was sure things would be worse. Much worse.

He gripped his rifle, reaching under his coat to take hold.

It was almost time. He knew, ideally, that he would have been up there with Hugh, that they would have made the speech together…but he was one of the two best shots on his side, and he had to be among those armed, waiting to take control.

"All of you…attention." He heard Hugh's voice, as he expected, but he was still a little surprised. His brother was brilliant, few would doubt that, but he was bashful, too…or at least he had been. Now he spoke with power, firmly, and even Travis found himself listening.

"I said, attention!" He spoke even more harshly than he had, and the noise in the room, dozens of individual conversations, quickly subsided. In a moment, everyone was looking up, listening to him. "Some of you have spoken to me, asked me what we will do, what our future holds. You all understand our situation, the dire consequences we find ourselves in…but perhaps not fully. We have found food, yes, perhaps a month's worth for all of us. Perhaps a bit less. But our civilization is still destroyed, and our planet is occupied by aliens. We must do more than merely hang around a subway station and eat whatever food we are able to find. We must organize, find others…as well as discover more food, and equipment and drugs and anything else that is useful. Our enemy, about which we know almost nothing, is undoubtedly organized, and vastly more powerful than us. We need to be just as efficient as they are, just as ready. Our first week can be ignored, a reasonable time for those of us who have survived to mourn all the lost souls, to adapt to our new reality. But any longer, any more time, will come at a cost, at a lack of our efforts to do what we must. To survive. To prepare. To reclaim territory." He paused a few seconds and then added, "To retake our planet."

The crowd was silent for a moment, taken by surprise by the speech…but then many of them started to complain, even to laugh. The idea of organizing, of expanding, of actually fighting back, had obviously not been seriously considered by most of them. Whether they just planned to sit, perhaps to die eventually, or to be scooped up by the enemy for whatever purpose they had in mind was unclear. Travis assumed, probably rightly, that most of them simply hadn't allowed themselves to think forward that much. He understood, of course, but he realized that whatever chances they had, however small they were, they probably deteriorated with each passing day. He knew most of them didn't understand, not really, but he realized that the time had come, at least to start organizing. He expected that the enemy, the aliens, assumed that the survivors would simply hunt for food, but otherwise remain in place…and he knew they had to do more than that, much more, if they were to have any chance at all. If they organized, if they built up any ability to fight back…that would be an edge. Not much of one, maybe, but a start. A start to regaining control of their world.

"I know what you are all thinking." Hugh raised his voice, spoke over the din of competing conversations. "That guy is insane! How can we fight back, how can we stand up to forces our own army and navy couldn't take? How can we endure against such an advanced enemy?" He looked around for a few seconds. "I will tell you how…by not standing here silently and waiting for whatever the enemy has planned. By taking the field, exploring, building up…and ultimately by striking back. I know that sounds insane, and perhaps it is in a way…but standing here, waiting for the enemy that has almost destroyed us to come in and finish the job—or worse, whatever they have planned for the rest of us—seems even more foolish than taking whatever chance we have to fight back. Maybe we will fail, perhaps we will all die…but I for one would rather do so fighting, with a weapon in my hands. That is much better than being herded off like some kind of livestock…because you can be sure they have nothing better in mind for any of you."

The crowd started to react more, some of them acknowledging his words, others clearly building up to argue, even to fight with him. But that last sentence was the signal, and Travis opened his coat, and pulled out his rifle. He looked all around him, his senses stretched to the limits. He noticed Lucas across the way, holding his own weapon…and Gavin and the others, eight of them in total, stretched around the outside of the group, also armed.

"Alright," Travis shouted, "everybody just remain calm." He held his rifle up, making it as visible as possible, while also keeping it well positioned to fire. He knew many of those present had guns, too, though most of them were amateurs.

Except for Lucas, all we've got are amateurs, too.

"We do not want to hurt anyone, but this group needs to become organized. Now! We need to start to do more than just survive, to eat until we're out of food again. So, please…I know some of you are armed, many of you. But don't draw your weapons, not now. We don't want to hurt anyone." He looked around, scanning the group as much as possible. He knew that he would be lucky to spot anyone pulling a gun from their belt, that the possibility of someone getting off a shot, or a bunch of shots, was very real. He suspected most of those present would be intimidated…but maybe not all.

Probably not all. For a brief moment, he hoped that things would go well, that he wouldn't have to shoot anyone.

But then, he saw a man move. He watched it all happen, almost as though it was in slow motion. He told himself the man wasn't reaching for a gun…but he was. He saw the whole thing happening, and his rifle was positioned while the target was still raising his own weapon. He had only a fraction of a second, but it was enough…enough to decide what to do. His instinct was to take him down non-lethally, to shoot him in the shoulder. But he and Hugh had discussed their actions in detail…and despite his revulsion at the thought of it, he knew anyone who tried to shoot was better off dead. He understood the facts, the lack of hospital facilities, the terrible reality of their situation…and he acknowledged what he had to do. He shot.

He fired three times, though he knew the first one had done the job. The man jerked backwards and fell at once. Most of those present panicked and began to yell in panic…but they didn't draw any weapons. Not most of them.

His eyes darted around, looking for anyone else taking action. For an instant, he thought it was over, that everyone else was pacified. But he knew who he had shot, and he was sure the man was part of a group. Whether they had any real intentions of taking over, or they were just friends, he didn't know. But an instant later he saw one of the others moving, and he knew things were about to get worse. A lot worse.

He spun around, and aimed at the second shooter, but Lucas had seen him, too, and he fired first. Unlike Travis, he fired only a single round…right through the target's head.

Travis prayed that two was the end of it, but it wasn't so. He saw two more people reaching for guns, or at least what he assumed were. To be honest, he wasn't sure, not at first. Most of the people were screaming now, and running, trying to take cover somewhere. But at least six stayed where they were…and he realized that they were all reaching for weapons, preparing to fire. He was halfway to aiming on the first man he'd seen, and then, a half second later, he fired, twice. He dropped his second target, as efficiently as the first. But he realized that he wasn't going to get them all…not in time. Not even with Lucas. As far as he knew, all the others on his side were as inexperienced as he expected everyone else to be. He didn't know whether any of them would even get a shot off…or if they would hit their targets. He just hoped they wouldn't take out any of those running around, without weapons.

He saw one of the others drop...Lucas's work. He had been aiming for the same one, and now he jerked his rifle around, and focused on a different one. He fired, twice again, and he took him down, before he got a shot off. But then the rest of them began to fire.

He and Lucas were shooting carefully, picking out those with weapons exposed. But the other side—and several of his other people—were firing more wildly. He tried his best to pick out the most dangerous enemies, take them down before they could shoot anyone, but it just wasn't possible to get them all. He fired, and even as his shots went off, he was searching, looking for someone else who was trying to shoot. But the entire crowd was now in an uproar, and he found he didn't have any clear shots at his targets. There were screaming people running everywhere, and he couldn't see any more of his attackers...but he knew there were more out there.

He didn't know how many there were, how many were of a mind to fire, as opposed to just those who were armed and pulling out their guns now...but he was careful, very careful. He didn't want to hit anyone who wasn't fighting, though he could see that his adversaries were far less cautious. There were already people uninvolved, who didn't want anything except to be left alone, lying on the ground, screaming and rolling around. Some of them had weapons and some were just standing around, in the wrong places. He had known it would happen, at least if things came to this, but he realized he had put the thought out of his head, convinced himself everything would be okay.

Everything was far from okay.

The entire crowd was moving now, panic streaking around. He had hoped there wouldn't be as many people fighting as there were—at least twelve so far by his count, and quite possibly more—and he could feel some concern, the worry of what would happen if he and his people were defeated, if the other side—and it was clear enough that there was *another side*, and not just a bunch of individuals—prevailed. But he didn't think that was going to happen. At least eight of the enemy were down, and only one of his shooters had been hit. But at least ten more of the people out there, those who probably weren't on either side, who just wanted to be left alone, had been shot, and while he assumed most of them were hit by the others and not his people, he wasn't foolish enough to imagine that most of those present would differentiate. Even if—*when*—they won the fight, they would be blamed by most of those out there, both the wounded, and the others. He knew it was true, and just one more thing they would have to overcome to prevail, to lead with the confidence they needed, and not just the fear.

He turned and fired again, taking out another of the…enemy. That's what they were, he realized, an enemy, as much as the aliens. He didn't want to believe that, but he knew it was true, and more with each passing second.

The firing went on at full for a few more seconds, then it slowed down, and, finally, it stopped. By his quick count, eleven of the enemy shooters were down, and three of his own. The three friendlies included Lucas, and for an instant, he was terrified his friend was dead. But then he saw him getting up, and he realized he had been shot in the arm. It was a nasty hit, or at least it looked like one from where he stood, but he was fairly certain his friend was going to make it, even with the poor state of medicine that currently prevailed.

He turned and looked at three men, all standing close to each other…with their hands up. He knew what he should do, what he doubtless would have done if Lucas had been killed, but he held back, and he shouted to his other armed men to do the same. He looked all around, afraid that any others might pull out weapons, and start shooting. Most of the people were panicking now, screaming and still rushing, trying to get around the others, to find some place to hide.

But he knew any of them could be on the other side, that they could be…enemies. The word seemed strange, the idea that they had been invaded by an enemy from outer space and still ended up fighting other humans and not the invading aliens dug at him. He knew it was wrong, realized that the invaders were going to be more than enough of a problem, without fighting other people. But he couldn't see any other way, any method to truly survive, even to build something that could pretend to stand up to the enemy, to make a play to regain the world. It sounded ridiculous, even as he thought about it…but he knew even if the chance was one percent—or one thousandth of one percent—that was what he had to try to do. It was all he could try, the only route open to them.

He looked up a moment later, toward his brother…and he was amazed. Hugh hadn't moved, not an inch. He had been a clear target for the other side, but he had stayed where he was, silent, unmoving. Travis paused, looking. He was amazed. At first, he wondered if Hugh had frozen, if he hadn't moved out of fear. But he stood looking calm, unmoved. He had always thought well of his brother, but in a room where almost everyone was rushing around or fighting, he had remained where he was, upright and just watching.

Then, when the battle had ended, when the few remaining fighters on the one side had been captured, he spoke again. "Please…everyone, the battle is over…try to remain calm. I am very sorry for the violence, but there was no other way. I had hoped we would be able to proceed calmly…" Not really, Travis thought…he was sure his brother had expected the resistance. And he had been right…almost exactly correct. "I want all of you to try and calm down now, to stop racing around. Please, I know this has been upsetting, but you have to accept our new realities…you just have to."

He looked out at the crowd, part of it at least calming

somewhat. "I am sure there are others out there who look hostilely on our...takeover...but I urge you all now, whatever your thoughts, to accept it. We now have control, of the food, of this station." He looked around, his eyes connecting with each of his gunmen for a second. Travis guessed that his claim of outright control was an exaggeration, but he understood it.

"Please...and I mean this sincerely, accept this, for now at least. See what happens...and don't start another fight. Our goal is for all of us to succeed, for us to rise up to find other people, to grow...in size and power. This station, these ruins are just our first step. We will build something...something that becomes powerful. We will attend to our own basic needs first, to our food and medicine, to setting up medical facilities, to finding people who are experts in different fields." He paused just for a few seconds, mostly to give those listening a chance to catch up. He knew exactly what he was going to say.

"We will seek out others, shelter them, and make use of their knowledge, their trades. We will build facilities, many of them, and we will staff them with our people. We will keep going, pushing...and we will rise up, become powerful...and then we will strike back." He looked out at the crowd, now more or less all fairly calm, and every one of them staring, watching Hugh intently.

"When we begin the fight against the enemy, the true enemy, we will not stop, never...not until our world is ours again."

Travis listened, and he realized just how ridiculous that all sounded...but somehow, he realized he believed it. He wasn't sure if it was Hugh's words, or it was just wishful thinking, but despite his realization that it would be long and terrible, he was somehow, at that very moment, confident that humanity would prevail, that they would rise up and take back their world.

And send the enemy back where they came from.

PART TWO

—

Resistance

Chapter Sixteen

From the Notes of Hugh McDaniel

We are almost half a year out from the attack, from the end of the old world and the beginning of the new, darker one. We have made considerable progress in that time, at least from where we were in the immediate aftermath of the enemy attack. Our total population has grown to over two thousand people, additions coming almost daily as we find other individuals and groups. We have somehow maintained our control over most of them…though we have had several battles with other groups, too. Still, overall, we have increased the general loyalty level significantly. We have gathered food, from dozens of locations, set up medical facilities, done everything possible to provide our people with something at least vaguely approaching comfort. Of course, nothing has been anything like it was before the attack. Our opinions had to change…we had to adjust, learn to accept a vastly lesser situation. But we did it, mostly, and attitudes, which dropped during the first month or two, are actually on the rise. People are strange, and they adapt, far more than you would expect. They learn to be content, more or less, with far lower standards than they would have expected before. We even have two pregnancies now, which are perhaps a bit earlier than I would have liked to see, but ultimately necessary if we are going to survive.

The general attitude among our people has improved...save for me. What we have lived through, the gathering of food and medicine, the establishment of tentative housing of a sort, the development of six different bases located all around Queens and into Brooklyn...that is all the easy part, at least to my view. The hard part comes when we meet the enemy—the *real* enemy—and when we have to begin to fight, to engage in our true effort to begin to retake our planet.

Because that is essential...to me at least. Whether our chance of ultimate success is fifty percent—or point one percent—we *have* to try. We just *have* to.

I had hoped, for a while, that the enemy would leave us alone for long enough, that we would eventually be the ones to strike first, to move out and attack. I didn't really expect it, and I had anticipated that the enemy would show up, probably sooner rather than later. But then they didn't. I was given almost six months to prepare, to pull as much together as I could.

I had expected them almost immediately, but there was nothing, not even any signs that we had been invaded, save of course for the rampant destruction. It almost seemed that there were not any aliens at all. All of our time and effort went to finding what we needed, to rebuilding a small fraction of our past lives. In the end, it was over five months before we heard anything.

But then they appeared.

Even I was caught by surprise. One of our scouting parties was out, looking ever farther for food and other supplies...and they found something else instead, something that reminded us of the true severity of our situation. And only one of them came back.

He was wounded, but he had managed to return, and he told us about the enemy. Not other humans, brigands or troublemakers, but the *real* enemy. They were large, perhaps nine feet tall, and covered in metal. Whether that was armor, or whether he had run into robots, wasn't clear, but one thing was certain. Our struggle had entered a new level.

After that, I doubled the size of every group I sent out...and every one of them was as heavily armed as we could manage. For a week, they found nothing at all. It was almost as though the first attack hadn't happened...and then, suddenly, everything went crazy. In three days, we lost more than fifty people. There were ten sightings in three days, ten battles between our heavily armed groups and the...creatures...they ran into. Every group that we had out at that time met the enemy...and all of them were beaten, driven back from the encounters. They had all fought at first, but none of them had taken out one of the enemy and captured its body. A couple reported possibly doing some damage, but honestly, I just didn't know.

There were only two things that were clear to me. First, we had to send out a more powerful group, make a best effort to take one of their groups out. And second, *I* had to go. I had to see these things for myself...before I could decide on our next move.

67th Avenue Subway Station
Forest Hills, Queens
D + 181 Days

Travis looked out, carefully inspecting the ground out in front of him as he stepped forward. The group was the largest one that had been sent out, and he knew it included most of the true fighters he had...including Lucas, and just about every member of the community who had previously carried a gun. There were a couple of former soldiers and six ex-police among them...and they were armed with the best weapons that had been found in over five months of intensely searching the remains of the city. They were as ready for trouble as they could be...which he knew very possibly was far from enough.

Right behind him, walking quietly, was Hugh. He had shared the leadership responsibilities equally with Travis, but they both knew that one of them was replaceable and one was not. Travis was capable, and well-suited to his position, highly valuable…but he wasn't Hugh…and he knew it.

Travis had always realized his brother was more capable, of course, but he was stunned at how well he had adapted to the situation. Hugh had made many decisions, and all of them seemed to be right. Still, despite his understanding of his brother's enormous capabilities, Travis realized that he, too, had played a significant role. The two brothers complimented each other, and together, they made a potent combo, and so far, able leadership for their growing group of survivors. Able enough that six months into things, they had not faced a serious question to their leadership, despite increasing the size of their group by some eight times.

Still, he realized they had reached the first true test. Chasing down food and drugs, organizing a group of survivors…none of that was easy, but it wasn't really hard either. Facing off against the enemy was far more dangerous than anything they had done to date, and Travis didn't know what to expect. Worse, perhaps, he was almost sure that Hugh was as in the dark as he was, or nearly so. They hadn't had any contact with the enemy at all until now, not since the initial bombing, and what it was, what they would encounter, was still a wild guess.

Travis continued forward, climbing over a mound of rubble that had fallen across the road. He turned to help his brother, but he saw that Hugh didn't need the assistance. Hugh had been frail and fairly weak six months before, but he had been training since, and now he was actually quite strong. Travis knew that, at least in theory, but he still wasn't used to it.

He sighed softly. They had been out for hours now, but they hadn't found anything. At least nothing new. They had stumbled on the remains of a fight, about fifteen dead humans from several days before, and signs that some others had been captured and removed. But so far, there was nothing else.

Travis turned and looked at Hugh. "What do you think? It's at least a couple hours back. Maybe we should turn and start heading that way." He wasn't sure that was the right move, but he figured he would ask.

Hugh returned his brother's gaze, and he paused for a moment, the closest sign that he, too, was undecided. But then he said, "I don't think we should...not yet. All of our recent excursions have been attacked much closer in than we are now, and it is clear others have as well." He jerked his hand backwards, toward the direction of the fight they had seen. "I think we've just been...lucky...so far. Let's go on for another hour and see what happens. Then we'll head back."

Travis nodded almost immediately, and then he turned and began walking again. He continued for about ten minutes, silently, and then he stopped suddenly. He had heard something up ahead, and he put out his hands, signaled for all the others to stop and remain silent. Three or four of the others had obviously also heard what he had, and they were signaling, too. He tilted his head, listening. The sounds repeated themselves, louder this time.

He kept himself from assuming what it was...but, in his gut, he knew. And one quick turn told him Hugh was as aware as he was that they had found the enemy.

He turned and gestured to his people, telling them to prepare. To prepare to fight. That was what his group had come for, he realized...to face off an enemy detachment, and to defeat it. His head filled with all kinds of thoughts now, including considerable doubts that they could win. But none of that slipped into his determination.

He found a spot for himself, one that provided some cover, and he turned to look for Hugh. His brother had also found a location, as good as the one he had, and he had pulled his rifle off his back and started to aim. The enemy wasn't visible yet. As far as Travis could tell, they were just on the other side of the debris mound.

He stood stone still, his rifle extended in what he perceived was the enemy's direction. He felt the urge to move forward, to check out what he was hearing, but he stayed where he was. He knew his people had a better chance as defenders, standing behind whatever cover they had managed to find.

Another minute, perhaps a minute and a half, went by, and each second seemed like an eternity. But then it happened. A figure popped up along the top of the debris mound…and it spoke in a loud and clear voice. In English.

"Attention. Attention. All humans, drop any weapons and remain in place. Repeat…drop all weapons and remain in place."

Travis turned and looked at his brother for a second…and in that time, he understood that they thought alike, that they both agreed exactly what to do. He looked at the figure, almost certain on inspection that it *was* a robot of some kind, and he paused, just for a second.

Then he fired.

All his people opened up as soon as he did, and the sole visible figure was hit at least a hundred times. But it didn't go down, not completely. Travis could see dents in it, some signs of damage at least…but it turned and fired itself. One of his people went down almost immediately, hit at least ten times. Then another.

Travis felt something, an urge to run, a feeling that the situation was hopeless, that the enemy was too strong, and it only intensified when a second bot appeared and joined in the firing. But he held where he was, maintaining his fire on the enemy.

His side had lost at least five people so far, but he continued to fire…and when he looked over at his brother, he could see his fury, too. He had become accustomed to Hugh's intellect, to his growing leadership abilities, but now he could see the warrior emerging in his brother. That was new, something that surprised him. He had always admired Hugh…but he had never seen his brother as a fighter. Until now.

He had seen a third enemy appear up on the rim of the pile, but his focus now was on the first one. It had been hit the most, at least two hundred times, he guessed, and it was clearly damaged. The other two fired at least four weapons, but the first one was down to a single one, and it didn't look like it was firing accurately. But it was still up.

Travis adjusted his weapon, trying to direct his fire against the…thing's…final weapon. He blasted it, at his weapon's full ability…and then he saw that it had stopped firing. The robot was still standing, in a way, but it didn't seem to have any weapons left.

He moved his fire to the second one, now also fairly damaged. He had stopped paying attention to his own group. He knew a fair number had been hit, but he also recognized that the fight they were in was to the end. If there were only three of the enemy, he started to realize that his people just might win. Even if most of them were killed or injured, if at least some of them survived, if they were able to bring back the remains of the enemy, they would help their people.

Regardless of the cost.

The second enemy…robot?…was down now, seemingly totally disabled. Every remaining gun was targeted on the third one now, still the last one he had seen. The fire from his side seemed to be about half the amount it had been at the start, but he didn't think about that, at least not for more than an instant.

The last target put up a fight, but with all the fire concentrated, in a few more seconds, it, too, was silenced, and an instant later, it fell. The gunfire kept up, Travis's along with everyone else's for another ten seconds. Then he heard Hugh calling out to stop shooting. He did it himself, along with about half the others, but it took another two shouts, one from Hugh and one from him, to completely end it.

The third bot was definitely dead, its body almost separated into five or six different sections. The second one appeared to be knocked completely out as well, but Travis stared for an extra second, just to be sure. The first one, however, though all its weapons were gone, was still functional…at least marginally. It was down, unable to stand or walk, and only one of its arms seemed even partially capable of movement. But he could see that it was moving, very slowly, toward his party.

He stared at it for a second, backing away slightly, as the others did. A few of his survivors trained their guns on it, but he held up his hand, signaling for them to hold. The thing was badly shot up, so much so that he was uncertain how it could even remain marginally functional. He looked at it, becoming even more amazed as he judged the amount of damage. The thing was barely able to move, but still, it pressed on…and he had no doubt its intention was to kill his people. The fact that its condition made that seem almost insane didn't seem to affect its actions at all.

He thought about it, about taking one of them…alive. But as he looked down at it, saw its intent, he began to doubt how he could do that. Its sole purpose, such that any remained to it, was to reach his people, to kill them. He turned, suddenly, looking toward his survivors, just as Hugh was yelling for some of them to tend the wounded.

He turned and looked at Hugh, even as the enemy continued to move slowly toward the survivors. He exchanged unspoken communications with his brother, and he realized they agreed. There might be time in the future to capture the enemy, but for now, they would have to do with destroyed remains. He glanced at Lucas, exchanging another silent communication. Then the two of them moved forward, angling their rifles toward the enemy. He took a deep breath, and then he fired, his friend following suit. Their bullets, coming from no more than two meters now, ripped into the enemy, and in a moment it stopped the movement it had been undertaking. Still, they maintained their fire, shooting for at least another ten seconds before they stopped.

The bot—he was virtually certain now that's what it was—had been torn apart, ripped into several sections. He stopped and looked at the remains for a few seconds, but then he turned and looked out at his own people. They came first, at least those who were wounded. He gestured toward Lucas to scout forward, to insure that there *were* only three of the enemy. He was almost sure, but he realized he had to be careful, to check out every possibility. His friend nodded, and he headed up the hillside, looking for more enemies, despite the fact that he was almost sure they were alone…at least for the moment. And a few minutes were all they could spare now. They had remains of the enemy, and they had to get back with it all. They had just long enough to tend briefly to the wounded, and to load up the remains of the enemy. Then they would head back…to learn what they could.

He knew it wasn't the end of the fight…it was just the very beginning, and though he was aware his side had lost more of its people, they had won.

They had won the first battle…at least something close enough to claim victory.

Chapter Seventeen

From the Notes of Hugh McDaniel

We spent a lot of time tearing apart the bots…or rather, what was left of them. They were extremely sophisticated, and even in the condition we got them back in, they created a feeling of doom, even beyond what we had already been experiencing. I have always been ahead of those I knew, able to understand things better, but even to me, most of the circuitry, most of the construction, of the alien bots was beyond anything I could readily understand. They were robots, that much I was sure of, but their design was way beyond anything I had ever seen. I have spent almost every hour analyzing them, trying to come up with an idea of what we are facing…mostly without success. I am fairly close to certain that these bots are controlled by actual aliens, that our enemy is another species like us, and not just a collection of robots. But even that, I realize, is based mostly on supposition. The truth is, I just don't know.

One thing I have realized though, after several days of diligent work in trying to understand the enemy…we don't have the luxury of doing that. We don't have the time. Whoever has come to Earth, they expended a vast amount of resources to do it. They didn't do that for no reason, and they didn't do it *just* to destroy us. They have a goal, a purpose that we—that I—don't understand at all. And it is almost certainly bad for us...perhaps so terrible that the fortunate ones are the billions who died quickly, and not those of us who survived.

I have always planned to lead my people in resistance against the enemy, but now I am fighting the thought that it is hopeless, that we have no chance at all to overcome the forces that invaded us, that destroyed our military, that reduced those of us that survived to crawling around in the debris just to live. And yet, what choice do we have? What hope is there but to strike back, and to win...somehow. It seems impossible, perhaps it *is* impossible. But what else can we do but try?

That means stepping things up. It means not sitting around, looking for food and medicine but otherwise doing nothing. It requires us to step forward, to make our pointless   chatter   about   truly   resisting   into something...something that works.

Or to die trying.

67th Avenue Subway Station
Forest Hills, Queens
D + 183 Days

Travis   stood,   looking   straight   ahead.   He'd   been concerned...about the overall group, about the fact that they'd lost twelve of their best people fighting a heavily outnumbered group of three enemy bots, about a hundred different things. But mostly, he was concerned about his brother. He had spent much of the past few days focused fairly deeply on the enemy wreckage that they had brought back, but Hugh had been positively obsessed with it all. He hadn't slept, he'd barely eaten...if Travis was interested, his brother was borderline obsessed. He had told himself he was going to pull Hugh away from it, distract him with something, but he realized that the situation wasn't normal, that it would likely never be normal again. He had to let his brother push himself. At least he did if he wanted any chance of long term survival.

He was keeping busy—that was never a problem, there was always something to do. But his thoughts kept going back to his brother, not only concern for how hard he was pushing himself, but also curiosity as to whether he had come up with anything.

"Travis..." He had been thinking about his brother almost constantly, but he was still surprised when he ended up calling to him. "...come here for a second."

He turned almost immediately the shock vanishing quickly. Hugh had left the room that housed the alien artifacts, for the first time he had seen in at least two solid days. For an instant, he hoped that his brother had discovered something useful, but when he saw his face, and when he realized the tone of his voice, he knew it wasn't good.

"Hugh...what is it?" He walked toward his brother.

"Travis, I've spent the past few days going over everything I could on what is left of the bots. I'd like to say I've got them all figured out, but the truth of it is, I've made very little progress. The tech is very advanced...very." He went silent for a moment. "But one thing I've come up with...and this isn't a question of how well we are likely to do, but rather just what we must do..." He paused again. "...we must redirect all of our efforts against the enemy. Our fight went poorly by some interpretations...but at least we proved we can hurt the enemy, too. And we must focus on that, on damaging any of them that we can, and on bringing the other groups together, on assembling all the power we possibly can. We have spoken of fighting the enemy, but so far we have spent all our time just...surviving."

Travis stared at his brother, realizing that he was very shaken. He was upset too, of course, at least when he allowed himself to think about his life before, about all that had been lost. But Hugh was troubled by something even deeper, and Travis just stared back, allowing his brother to continue.

Hugh stared at him, his eyes tight and suddenly focused. "We have to strike back…now. Constantly, and in every way we can. We have to fight the enemy, for real and not just by our words. We could spend months trying to research the remains we brought back, or at least as long as we have until the enemy comes for us, but this is a trap. We must battle, immediately, and to the end. We cannot allow ourselves to be distracted, to be intimidated, not for an instant longer. We must accept the reality—the true reality—of the situation, and we must fight, as long as one of us draws breath. Even if our chances are one in a hundred…or one in a million."

Tyler was still looking at his brother. He wanted to argue with him, to push back against the obstinance…but he just remained silent. He realized that Hugh was correct, that whatever chance they had, however small, allowing time to pass only lessened it.

"I understand," he said, after a moment's silence. "And…I agree with you. We have to strike back…somehow. We must fight." The words came out of his mouth, almost without forethought. He looked up as his brother stared back at him and nodded. He knew, as well as Hugh, what they needed to do. And even though he figured they would fail, that they would all die…he knew there was no real choice.

"The first thing we have to do is get the others…the different groups we know of. We have a bit over two thousand people…but there are tens of thousands of survivors, at least. And that is just in the city. We must unite, we must strike together. I realize it will be difficult to convince many of them, that our people have been in competition for finding supplies, for surviving. But we need all the numbers we can get. And the fact that the enemy has been…scouting…is probably known by now to all of them."

Travis stared back, looking doubtful. Finally, he said, "I understand the desire to get the other groups together…but is it feasible? We have managed to maintain a sort of peace between us, most of us at least, but that is about as far as we've gotten. I don't see them agreeing to band together, to fight the enemy with everything they've got. At least not unless we start, score some victories to show them. Do you?"

Hugh just stared back for a moment, as though he was considering how to respond. Then he said, "I agree with you…in all but one area. It will be difficult to convince the others, certainly. But what choice do we have? Our efforts would be bad enough, the odds against our success long indeed…if we are all united. If it is just us, our couple thousand, the odds become even worse, almost incalculable. I will still do it alone, of course, even if our own people decide they won't go along with it, but if there is any way to get the others to join us, to come in now, we just have to do it." He paused a moment, and then added, "We just have to."

Travis stared back at his brother, still wracked by doubts, by questions. But he realized Hugh was right, that whatever chance they had—of true success—it required them to join up with the others. Now.

"I agree," he said. "I can think of a thousand problems…with fighting the enemy, with even convincing the others to join us. But we have to remember our situation…" He paused a moment before continuing. "…how bad it is. We have to find a way to convince the others to join us…now. But I don't know how to do that."

"We'll tell them the truth, Travis…the real, unvarnished truth. I am sure they have all allowed their minds to wander, told themselves things that aren't correct…how else could anyone endure here for long? We will tell them that they have a month, perhaps even a year, but eventually, the aliens will come for them. They will know that this is true, especially now that we have been contacted by the enemy. We can't be sure this will work, but it is the best chance we have. We will have to make it count, make the best effort we can manage…because only if we are able to put together a true alliance, assemble as much strength as possible, will we have a chance…a real one."

Travis listened to his brother, agreeing with everything…and doubting it all, too. He questioned whether they could convince the others, whether even together they had any real chance against the enemy. His answers to those questions would have been negative, but he realized it was still the best chance…the only chance. He wanted to respond, to tell Hugh he agreed, but all he could manage at that moment was a nod, a basic acknowledgement that he was onboard.

It wasn't great, but it was enough.

Chapter Eighteen

From the Notes of Hugh McDaniel

I know I must speak to the others, the "rival" groups we know of, the different packs of survivors scattered all around us. Most of them are just like our group, people who were cut off, who banded together to survive. There were—are—other groups, too, those that have chosen to stalk other humans, those that started aggressively, and have just become worse and worse as the months progressed. We have fought against them, beaten them back from most of our areas, but I never forget that they are out there, that as well as themselves, the enemy has given us another foe, one carved from our own survivors.

But right now, I need to focus on the groups that are reasonable, at least for now. I know that when the food runs out, when the medicines are gone, even the packs of survivors that are reasonable, will revert to savagery, that they will fight against each other, and eventually even among themselves. That is another reason why I must do this now. Time is not on our side. I feel that I have waited too long already, and more time wasted will just add to that. We must begin the effort tomorrow, start the struggle. But whatever chance we have, however small, it is larger if all of the groups join up, if our strength is greater.

I don't know whether that is possible, whether they can be persuaded, but they have all accepted my invitation to a conference, and that is the start. The rest will depend on a lot of things, on their thoughts and concerns, on the exact status of their groups…and on how well I can do this. On whether I can convince them the time is now.

67th Avenue Subway Station
Forest Hills, Queens
D + 185 Days

"It is our only chance…however small that may be. I know that you have different opinions, that you view our situation from various points of view. But we are all cut from the same cloth. We care about our people, and we want them to survive. And I am telling you that this is their only chance, long term, even if it is small. Very small. Whatever thoughts we might have had about being left alone…the recent appearance of the robots destroys that. If we stay here, try to hide, we will just be destroyed—or worse. The enemy has destroyed our government, our military, our civilization. The only reason we are still alive is that they don't consider us a real threat…and probably also because they have some use for some of us." Hugh paused for a second, looking out at the collection of leaders gathered around him. He knew before he had started to collect them that it would be difficult to win them over, but he also knew it was essential. "So, our only option is to *become* a real threat. One that can fight them. One that can defeat them." He knew he sounded crazy. He wasn't sure he wasn't, at least to an extent. But he was certain that his words were right, that resisting fiercely was the only chance of survival his people had.

"How can we fight back? What chance do we have?" Charles Smithers spoke. He was the most critical of the other leaders, Hugh figured, but also the smartest. He guessed that if he could convince him, he could get the others, too. But that was a tall order.

"We fight back any way we can." He was looking right at Smithers. "And I didn't say we had a good chance of success...I said it would be our *only* chance. If we do nothing, we will sit here for another month, or a year, but sooner or later, the enemy will come for us, and they will kill us, or perhaps worse, take us alive, for whatever purposes they have. Do you think that could be good? Tell me...do you? They came here and without a word, destroyed our civilization. They killed billions, without issuing so much as a demand, not even one to surrender. There is no way they have anything to do with us that is good. You all know that."

He stood, straightening out, cutting any bit of slouch from his position. He understood just how important the words he spoke were. His own group, a couple thousand, would never pull off what he was thinking of. He needed the other groups to join him...and he needed it now.

He glared, both at Smithers, and at all the others too, and then he finished his statement. "You all know this is true, every bit of it. So, now is the time to decide. Do you want to crawl around, for a few months, for a year, waiting calmly for your deaths? Or worse? Or do you want to strike back, to hurt the enemy, even if we're unable to win completely. If we are lucky—very lucky—perhaps we can win. But even if we can't, what would you have your final months be? Hiding, skulking around praying for another day...or striking back, fighting the enemy every way we can? They *can* be destroyed, at least their robots. We have proven that...and that is the first step."

He stopped talking, only then realizing how hard he had gone at it, how aggressive he had been. He stared at the others, and mostly at Charles Smithers. He knew Smithers was the key. In addition to being perhaps the most difficult to convince, he was also influential with many of the others.

Hugh was nervous, though he realized he wasn't showing it...but Smithers spoke almost at once, and what he said surprised him.

"You are right, Hugh...I know it. I want to believe we can scrape together some kind of life, start building again...but we can't. The aliens who invaded, who destroyed our civilization, you are right that they must have some kind of plan, and I agree with you completely that it is not good for us. I don't know if we truly have any real chance, but I for one don't want to live as a slave...or worse. So, I am with you, and I will do everything I can to help, to develop a plan." He paused for a few seconds, and then he added, "A plan for fighting...for fighting to the end."

Hugh was surprised, and even more so when he looked at the others. About half of them looked almost enthusiastic, but the others, while doubts were clearly all around, seemed ready to go along. There wasn't one person present arguing. They all knew he was correct...that if they continued as they were, they would end up dead...or worse.

And they still had some fight left in them, and he was going to see that the enemy tasted that...very soon.

* * *

Estle-Starric looked out at the camp. Hell, it was more than a camp now, if not the city he envisioned. He knew he would live on...Earth, it was called by the locals...for a long while, at least if he didn't do anything wrong. Even if he did mess up, the Divine One had left, off to one of the other colonies, to supervise the operations there. The Gavicons were powerful, much more advanced than the humans, or any other race they had taken...but they were also challenged, pushed to the brink of destruction. Their reproduction by natural means had been declining for hundreds of years, and their population had been in sharp decline, but the most recent generation was proving to be utterly incapable of normal reproduction. They were long lived, at least in comparison to those they had conquered, but sooner or later, they would all die, and if they didn't find a species that could aid in their reproduction, the Gavicons would be gone…all of them.

He turned and looked out at the massive construction site. There was a section for his people, but also one for select humans. He hadn't been sure they would cooperate in what he intended to do to most of them, but he was pleased so far at the adaptive qualities, at least of some of them. The president, he wasn't sure about. He seemed tentative, more beaten than loyal…but that didn't matter. If things came down to it, he was expendable. There were plenty to take his place, including a number of people who he was sure had already converted one hundred percent. He even had some people supervising the first round of test subjects, and they were exhibiting a degree of savagery that even surprised him.

He turned toward his…desk, the humans called it, at least the closest match they had. Gavicons weren't like the humans, of course, standing much taller, and having four arms instead of just two. There were other differences as well, considerable ones, but he understood what the scholars had told him, that the humans were the closest match they had yet found. That didn't mean the effort would work, but he was authorized to plow full speed ahead with it. In truth, his people were running out of time. In a few hundred Earth years, they would be reduced too much in population to reverse the slide. They had to do it now.

"Estle-Starric, may I have your attention for a moment?" The voice came through the small speaker on his…desk, he remembered. One thing that had struck him was how loose the humans were in their interactions. His people treasured their alone time, and they always asked a superior for permission to enter his realm. The humans were much more informal.

"Yes," he said, though he was somewhat put out by the request. He had spent much of the early part of the day—short enough in comparison to his home world's 34 hour span, but capable of seeming long enough—with many of his people, and some of the humans as well. He had been hoping for some time alone, now. But… "Enter."

The door slid open, and one of his people came through. Taryn-Kobilic stepped into the room, but he stopped just inside the door, respecting his superior's space. "I apologize for disturbing you, Sir, but I wanted to report that the laboratory is complete, well in advance. Several more days to conduct some tests, and we will be ready to begin operations. I had to ask you…will we use some of the humans that are here, or should we begin harvesting new ones?"

Estle-Starric stood and looked back at his aide—sitting was almost unknown to his people, though they could manage to do it, albeit with considerable discomfort. He wanted to just use the people he had on hand. It wasn't as though he cared much about one human or another, but his people had killed all those who had shown resistance, and the ones that remained were somewhat…valuable. He was better off keeping them in their roles and getting fresh ones for the…process. After all, it was likely to be incredibly uncomfortable, to say the least…not to mention ultimately fatal. "I believe we should use outsiders, new personnel. Give the orders to gather some up…we need 1,000, so let's get double that to start. The ones we already have are too…" He almost said valuable, though his understanding of the English language, which he had compelled his people to use whenever possible, told him that was too strong a word. "…useful."

His aide sank down, the Gavicon method of showing respect. "As you command, Estle-Starric." He turned and left immediately thereafter, leaving his master alone again.

Estle-Starric was cold, especially toward the humans, which he regarded as a barely intelligent race, but for a moment, he felt almost sympathy, at least toward those 1,000, and, of course, the millions more who would follow if the experiment actually worked, if humans proved to be fertile…components…in the revised Gavicon breeding plan. He wasn't one of the experts who ran the program, but he knew it would be staggeringly painful…and ultimately fatal. He didn't care, of course, not really, but he still felt something for the humans who would be so used. It wouldn't stop him, of course, or even cause any hesitation. But it was impossible to use thinking beings in such a way and not feel a bit sorry for them.

He turned back toward the window, looking out at the growing city around him. The project was going well, and he was ahead in almost every area of development. It was very appealing that the humans were the best match yet, the ones likeliest to allow the procedure to continue through, at last to success.

To allow his people to survive.

Chapter Nineteen

From the Log of Gavin Sanders

I have never kept a log, nor written down my feelings, but I understand the purpose of doing it now. Hugh and Travis need to know what I've found, and there is no better way to keep track of everything than to write it all down, anything I think may be useful…and even those things I don't imagine are.

Hugh spoke well, very well, to the other groups, and we now have more than sixteen thousand people united, more or less. That is a tremendous amount, and yet when we consider the old population of the city, it is almost nothing. Still, it was a huge step forward, even if there remain currents of distrust running between the various groups. Hopefully, the merger will solidify, and the people will settle into one solid group. If for no other reason than anything else quite probably results in our deaths.

Of course, even given the best possible results, we will still probably die.

My group has been out for three quarters of a day, the very beginning of our mission. We are heading outside the city, into the remains of Nassau County. Our purpose is twofold, to explore and determine if there are any survivors, and to find any more of the robots. I admit, I am hesitant about the second part. I was with the group that engaged the three bots, and I am very aware how powerful they are. My group is strong, and tough…but if we run into enough of the bots, I know they will overrun us. Our arms are good, at least as good as we possess, and we have no fewer than forty of us, all fit and more or less combat worthy.

But still, I am worried. No…I am scared to death.

Approximately One-Half Mile from Ruins of Prospect Park
Somewhere in Brooklyn
D + 190 Days

"We should be getting fairly close to the park." Gavin Sanders paused for a moment, looking around. He knew the area was familiar, at least before it had been bombed, but he was having some difficulty finding his way around the devastation. Brooklyn had been, if anything, hit even harder than Queens, and the streets he knew were mostly gone, buried under the rubble. "This way." *I think.*

He set off again, leading his whole team off toward the park…or what he hoped was the park. From there, he would turn due east, and hopefully, eventually reach the end of the city. He knew from memory, that was fourteen or fifteen miles, which his people should be able to reach relatively early the next day…or could have before the city was blasted to ruins. His best estimate now was, maybe they would reach it in two days, assuming they didn't run into any real blocks.

Or any robots.

He continued on, trying to accelerate his pace. But every time he tried to move more quickly, he found the rugged terrain and the chunks of battered brick and stone too difficult to pass. He finally accepted that the going would be slow.

He stopped every couple minutes to recheck his

position. He couldn't believe how difficult it was to locate where they were, especially since he knew the area well, at least before the bombing. Then, suddenly, he saw an opening up ahead, an area without much rubble. *The park?*

He tried to speed up, but he almost fell three times before he slowed down again. He was sure it was the park now, and he felt an urge to get there. There was debris scattered around it, but he could see a few sections of brown and burned grass…and he could finally make out where he was. He looked around, behind him and then ahead, and he decided that he was standing in the middle of Prospect Park West. The park was just in front of him, though the sections closest were almost as covered in debris as the streets.

"Let's go into the park, and we will take a break. We have a long way to go after, so make the rest count." He stepped across the street, at least what he thought had been the street, and he climbed into the park. He went another twenty yards, perhaps, looking for a good place to rest his people…and then he heard something.

He froze, moving slowly after a few seconds of not at all. He looked out, and in an instant he saw what he had been afraid he had heard. Enemy bots.

He saw at least two of them, but they were fairly far away, and he realized there could be three or four—or thirty or forty. His stomach was twisted into a knot, and fear threatened to take him. But an instant later, as he howled out to his people, he sounded as calm as he could.

"Quick…hide!" He knew that wasn't a plan, not much of one at least, but he could see that the bots were heading more or less toward his group. He knew they wouldn't be able to hide for long, but the closer the bots got before they realized he was there, the better.

He ducked down behind a large pile of masonry, and then he looked back, making sure all his people had followed his orders. They were all down, and fairly well hidden. It wouldn't last, he knew…in fact, the only reason he had noticed the enemy before they had him was the noise they made. The bots were loud, and he had caught the sound of them before he'd even seen them.

He hunched down, lower even than he had been, valuing the time he had before the enemy found him. If he could stay hidden—not just him, but all his people—until they could open fire, it would be a huge advantage. His command was all under cover, trying to remain out of sight, but there were over forty of them, and the chance that one of them would make a mistake was considerable.

He checked his rifle, even though he knew he had done it a few minutes earlier. Time was moving slowly…very slowly. He could almost feel each second stretch out, seeming to take forever. He peered above the debris in front of him, barely, knowing it increased the odds of the enemy finding him, but also that it was crucial to get an update on their positioning. They had turned, a bit, and they weren't heading right for his group anymore. He thought for a second, wondered about staying put until they had passed. But he realized that wasn't a real possibility. The robots weren't heading right for his command anymore, but they were close enough. The odds of them passing without detecting his people were small…almost nil.

Still, just maybe he could gain an edge, begin the attack more or less on the enemy's flank. That would just last for an instant, but it would be a useful second or two, especially with all his people firing. There were four enemy bots now, and they were close enough that he would see if there were any more. Four wasn't good, certainly, but if his people could get the first shot…

He ducked back down, using his hands to give silent signals to his people. They had trained in the communication technique, but just a bit, and he was far from sure that his people had it down. He wasn't even sure he was proficient. He was telling them to wait, to attack when he did, but as far as he knew, half of them might have thought he was sending them a recipe.

He counted to himself, using the estimate on when the enemy would reach the point where they were closest. He knew his weapons could fire at longer ranges, but he was also sure that most of his people weren't expert marksmen—himself included—and he didn't want to overestimate what they could hit. At the shorter range, he knew most of his people would at least come close, and a lot would score hits.

He counted down, knowing he was just estimating. He didn't want to look again, to expose himself to the bots at close range. He was far from sure his estimates were correct, but he was going with them. And he was almost there.

Three.

He counted down the final numbers, ready to leap up and open fire.

Two.

His hands tightened around his rifle.

One.

He took a deep breath…and he held it.

Then he pulled himself up, over the debris. The bots were there—close—and almost where he had expected. He paused, for a fraction of a second…and he opened fire.

The others—most of them at least—did the same, almost immediately. The level of fire was incredible, forty rifles firing on full auto, delivering hundreds of rounds a second. The bots almost vanished, partially covered by a cloud of dirt and broken bricks and stones. But their response was immediate. They turned and fired, each of them blasting from four weapons, firing at a rate beyond even Sanders' team's heavy guns. They were hit, all of them many times, but they fired nevertheless, blasting his position.

His recruits—and he reminded himself that was just what they all were, himself included—had taken losses in just a few seconds. Three of the team were down, at least, despite being mostly hidden. The enemy aim was relentless, and even as some of their guns were knocked out by the incoming fire, they continued shooting with what remained.

One of them was partially down now. It appeared to have lost a leg, and two of its guns…but it continued to fire with its two remaining ones. There were chunks of metal flying off of all of them, but they continued firing, and now they had hit at least five of his people.

He popped out an empty clip, replacing it quickly, and resuming fire. He knew that his people had a lot of ammo, but also that they were going through it at a very fast pace. But there was no choice, he realized. This fight was to the end, and saving ammo wasn't even a consideration.

He looked up at the enemy. Three of them were badly damaged now, and one of them, at least, appeared to be knocked out entirely. He felt something at the sight of the destroyed bot, something that seemed very much like joy. He had been terrified when the nuclear assault had started, when New York and every other city was destroyed. He had fallen into a confused state, one that surely would have resulted in his death…had it not been for Travis. His friend had saved his life, and the fact that it wasn't direct, that he hadn't been pulled back from some deadly impact, didn't make it any less so, at least to him. But now, his mood had changed. He was still scared, of course. He was sure he would be every day that remained to him. But something else was coming on strong, a taste for destroying the enemy. He was thrilled at the devastation his people were unleashing, at the destroyed enemy bot.

No, two of the enemy were down now.

He kept firing, trying to remind himself to stay as hidden as possible. He knew some of his people had failed at that, had allowed the excitement at the combat to reduce their caution, and now ten of them had been hit. He realized that didn't mean they were all dead, of course, but it was a quarter of his strength. He would have been upset by this, and he would have been if he wasn't so focused on the battle. The fight he was beginning to feel his side was on the verge of winning.

He saw the enemy moving, the two that were still operational, at least. They were trying to get around the debris, to gain better shots at his people. But they were too late. One of them had only two guns left, and the other was down to a single one. They continued to fire, but now all the shots from his group were focused on the two of them. They were badly damaged, and after one particular series of hits, he saw a small explosion of sparks flying around one of their heads. But still, they fired back, one gun each now. Their aim seemed off, but that was only partially helpful, as their weapons fired so rapidly, even without solid targeting, they were dangerous. But both of them were stationary now, and his people were maintaining their own fire. That, too, had been reduced by his losses, but it was still potent, and in another few seconds, there was no return fire at all. He felt satisfaction, but not enough to stop firing, not for a few more seconds. Then he finally held up, and an instant later he turned and waved to his people, shouting out, "Cease fire!"

It took a second and third shout, and considerable hand waving, but finally the fire died down to nothing. He felt his body, only now realizing how tired he was, how battered. But his people had won…and he was happy about that. In truth, he wanted nothing more than to destroy the enemy, their bots—and themselves, too, if there were actual creatures behind the invasion. He forced himself up, and turned toward his people, shouting out to them. "Tend to the wounded…" *And the dead…*

He was concerned about the dead, of course, but he realized that in some way, he was more worried about the wounded, especially the badly injured. They weren't near any of their facilities, not that the hospital provisions there were anything great. All they could do, besides administer first aid, was to wish them well. They could bring a couple with them, at least for a while, but he was starting to realize that he would probably have to leave the wounded—those seriously injured at least—behind. The thought hit him first indirectly, but then he started to really think about it. The idea of leaving injured colleagues behind…to almost certain death…was terrible. But taking them was difficult, and probably impossible.

He truly began to understand the situation, in ways that he hadn't before. He'd known, for months now, that things were truly disastrous, that they would all probably die before long. But now, he realized that he hadn't truly understood, not until right now. Their lives didn't matter. His life didn't matter. All that was important was the mission, the fight against the enemy. The fight that would probably kill most of them, himself included, before it was done. But that didn't matter, not if it was successful in the end.

He looked behind him, watching as his people tended to the wounded. He knew he would have to decide, soon, who got to go on, and who would be left to die. But first, he was going to check out the bots, and make sure they were dead. That was the order of priorities, and he realized that with chilling calm.

Chapter Twenty

From the Notes of Estle-Starric

We have selected the first 1,000 people to use in the facility. That is great, over a month ahead of schedule. Our invasion is going very well, and the projects are underway to begin hunting through the ruins of the cities, to start pulling in the survivors, in the amounts we will need if we are successful with the first batch. I am even optimistic that the initial test subjects will actually succeed, that Earth will prove to be our long-awaited successful match. I know that people have tended to become jaded, to worry that perhaps we will not find a successful culture…but something tells me this will work.

Still, I am edgy, for reasons I can't even express. By every reasonable standard, things are going well…very well. The construction of the city, the initial 1,000 tests, even the indoctrination of the humans we have selected to closely serve us…all of our efforts are on or ahead of the set timetable. But I am concerned anyway. Perhaps it is just the realization that despite my positive expectations, it is very possible that the matches won't work, that this world will be the same as the others. But it feels like more, like there is something here, something I should fear. The people of the planet were certainly not strong. We have had to eliminate a fair number of those we have taken, but we have also found many who are willing to serve us, who grasp at the rewards we have offered, the preferred lives. Some of them have even been advised of our purpose, of the torturous work that is to be done on those used in our purpose…and they have accepted it.

The humans are the most divisive species we have found, the only one with individuals willing to see their kind imprisoned and tortured, as long as they themselves receive superior treatment. That fact only makes our job easier, more likely to succeed. But still, there is something else, a factor I cannot yet understand…but it is one I am sure is there, somehow. In addition to those who are willing to turn on the others, there are also those who seem prepared to fight hard…and aggressively to the end. It is almost as though two races occupy this world.

Gavicon City
Approximately Twenty-Five Miles West of the Ruins of Washington
D + 192 Days

"Proceed, by all means." Estle-Starric stood on the pedestal, looking out over the test room. It was large, big enough to hold 1,000 humans, plus all the equipment each of them would require. But he knew the facility was actually vastly smaller than the ones under construction then, the ones that would hold millions of conscripted people, the ones he would only need if the first batch worked. Still, he had authorized the construction of the first five units. It would be wasted if the initial batch failed, but somehow, he was sure it was going to work. He had no real reason, amid all the failures to date, none save the stats and early studies, which showed the humans were by far the closest, the most aligned group his people had found. He knew that might not be enough…but somehow, he was sure it would be.

"Yes, Estle-Starric, of course." The senior technician spoke calmly, but Estle-Starric knew the process ahead would be severely painful to the humans, all the more because he had ordered no anesthesia at all be used. He knew it wasn't certain that some drugs wouldn't be fine, that they wouldn't interfere with the process, but he didn't have certain knowledge, and at least for the first batch, he had decided none could be risked. The humans would live through a nightmare of pain, he realized that, but he didn't really care. In a vacuum, he would spare them the agony, but not when it might impact the success of the operation. That was the paramount goal.

He stared out, watching his people—and only his people—begin the work on the captive humans. He was amazed at the pliability of many of the humans, but he had decided against allowing any into the room right now. Perhaps later, almost certainly so when there were millions rather than a thousand. But it was too early, and the process too unknown, and probably too painful.

The first twenty of the humans had already been brought in. They were all female, the human breeding type, and they were definitely scared. They had struggled when brought in, tried to escape, but then they were securely fastened to their cots. They had mostly calmed down now, settled to a low-level of moaning...but Estle-Starric knew that would change. His own people expressed verbal complaints when they experienced pain, and from what he had seen, the humans were even more prone to do that. He tried to imagine the room when it was full, the sounds of 1,000 people, tortured almost beyond belief. He told himself he didn't care, that the suffering of humans was not a factor in any decision. That was true, of course, but he had to admit that listening to 1,000 of them, not to mention millions, would be hard to take, even when they were humans and not Gavicons. He didn't exactly care, but he suspected he would spend as little time in the facility as possible.

He watched as his people clustered over the humans, three of them to every Earth resident. The initial phases of the operation were only mildly painful, and still, most of the patients began to shout out. *If this stage is so painful to them, the rest of the procedure will be…*

He stood, looking down attentively, feeling his curiosity consume him. He had been almost sure the process would work, that Earth would prove the be the match his people had searched for hundreds of years to find. But now that it had begun, he found some doubts creeping back in. He still believed in the process, but he knew he would have to wait to discover whether it truly worked or not.

The sounds from the room increased as the technicians took their work farther. They cut incisions into the humans, and then again, below, opening several of their organs. The process would have been immediately fatal to unaided human beings, but each of the subjects was connected to a large machine, Gavicon technology which kept them alive.

Alive and in pain. Almost unimaginable pain. They howled, screaming as loudly as they could. But that was all they could do. They were fastened in place, firmly. The screeching was almost unbelievable, and Estle-Starric was glad that he had forbidden any of the humans to witness this yet.

He stood and looked down, watching as the attendees pulled apart the openings in the bodies of the humans. About forty minutes into the procedure, they turned and opened small metal cylinders. They reached in and pulled out the…fetuses, he realized the closest human word was, though it wasn't entirely accurate…and they carefully placed them inside their humans…

Mothers, he realized the closest term was, though that was even less accurate than fetuses.

He stayed where he was, watching carefully. He didn't want to, not really, but he knew his attention would mean something to those working on the humans. He wouldn't have to remain for the next 980 implants, and certainly not for the millions to follow if the process actually worked, but he realized his presence for the first process would be meaningful.

The shrieking had died down, predominantly because most of the humans had passed out. He knew the surgery was painful, though honestly, he realized it would be worse—possibly far worse—when the next generation started to grow. He hoped the humans would be able to endure it, like none of the others had, at least until they were…born.

He stayed where he was, forcing himself to continue staring, while his people finished the process. They then began to stitch up the humans. For them, the prisoners, he knew it was just the beginning of months of torment. He didn't care, not in any real way, but he couldn't help but feel a sort of sympathy for the lesser creatures. He had no real feelings for them…but he still couldn't shake it off completely. Especially when he thought about what was ahead of them.

"Very well done." He waited until his teams were finished, and then he congratulated them. "I truly believe this will work, that we will be the first ones to achieve success, to save our species." The room was fairly quiet, no more than three or four of the humans conscious, and them barely so. "We will carve out a new future, an escape from the terrible fate that had been ours…and we will repopulate our species, and rule for all time."

He stood for a few moments, as the technicians nodded silently, holding all four of their tentacles skyward, the Gavicon method of cheering. Then he turned and left, glad that was over. Attendance at the first surgery was expected, but fortunately, it was actually not anticipated at subsequent operations. The first one was material, something meaningful. Subsequent ones were less so, at least in the context of his attending.

He was glad to be leaving, but he didn't get far. A few steps out of the facility, he saw his aide moving toward him, rapidly. He stopped and waited for him.

"Estle-Starric…we have received multiple reports from the city the humans called New York. We have lost contact with six different groups of robots, all within a period of three days. We have had losses before, of course, but this is many times the normal rate."

He listened to the aide's words, and his edginess, the feeling he had possessed all along, rose up again. He suspected it was just a particularly effective group of survivors, one that had grown in size and become powerful enough to take on a few bots. He knew four was the maximum size of any party sent out now, that losing several parties wasn't exactly a disaster.

But it wasn't good either, and it was time for it to stop.

"Prepare a larger force…let's say 30 bots, all together." He paused, and then he added, "And send two of us with them. Two Gavicons." He paused a moment. Sending two of his own people off with the bots was an escalation, a significant one, the first use of them since the initial invasion But, he wasn't prepared to allow some resistance group to grow, to use its petty victories to build a meaningful resistance. He realized that his forces were vastly superior, but he also knew that they were much smaller than they would have been a few centuries earlier. And even fewer now that seventy percent of the invasion force had departed for the other planets, the various places his people had taken, where they were engaged in the same process that he was with the native races.

He would destroy them…before they could realize that much of his force had departed. Before the small problem could grow into a more serious one. His concerns were still there, his sense of worry, but realistically, he knew the enemy couldn't defeat him. They couldn't even come close.

Especially if he eliminated the most dangerous of them immediately.

Chapter Twenty-One

From the Log of Gavin Sanders

I am on the way back…back to Queens, to our headquarters. I was sent out just days before, to explore, to go out farther than we had gone and explore. Mine was just one mission, one of seven or eight. We were sent out in every direction, every place where maybe we could find more people. My group did find some, in fact, we were going back with over one hundred, when we had left with just forty-two.

But of that one hundred, only eighteen are originals.

I knew all along, at least in one sense, that we were going to lose many—most?—of us. But I didn't expect it to be this fast. For an instant, I speculated that none of us would return, that our entire expedition would be eliminated. But then we found a few people, and some more after that. The hundred that are with us include representatives of at least two thousand others. They are coming to hear from Hugh, to decide if they will join us. They asked me many questions, tried to discuss joining our group…but I am exhausted, and I have no idea what to say. This whole situation has been almost enough to break me. The one part of it I can offload, the leadership, I gleefully do. Let Hugh and Travis handle that. I will follow orders…that I can do.

And I will get my force the last few miles to home. Yes…it is a just a wrecked subway station in the middle of a destroyed city. But it is my home, at least for now.

Southern Queens
Approximately 2 Miles from Main Base
D + 194 Days

Sanders moved, climbing over the mounds of ruins quickly, despite the fact that he was dead tired. He was getting close to home, at least what passed for it now, and he was anxious. But he had over one hundred people with him now, and he realized that he was leaving most of them behind. Ultimately, he slowed down, forcing himself to wait just a little longer to get back.

His left arm was in a sling. He had taken a round, almost at the end of the third and last battle his people had fought. It wasn't too bad, mostly clean, but it still hurt. He had already given out all the painkillers he had brought, and there were people in the group who still needed them more than him, so he just dealt with it as well as he could.

He looked back at the pack of people he was leading. Less than half of his original group were making it back, and a lot of them were wounded. He wanted to say his mission was pointless, that it had been a waste…but he had eighty members of other groups with him, representing over two thousand survivors in total. If Hugh and Travis managed to convince them to join, even a small percentage of them, he knew it would be worth the twenty-four his group had lost, at least in a cold-blooded sense. Still, the images of his lost people were too great for him to fully embrace it.

He waited for a moment, allowing the others to catch up, and then he continued. He clearly recognized his surroundings now, and he knew he was close to home. He saw two turnoffs, the way to other areas that were now also under the control of his group, but he wanted to go to the remains of the 67th Street subway station. He knew now, with the combination of so many groups, it was probably foolish to call it the main base, or anything of the sort. But that's just what it was to him.

He saw that most of the group had caught up, and he turned and started walking again. He controlled his pace, kept himself from moving too quickly, but he found that every time he stopped concentrating on it, his speed picked up. He realized that he hadn't been prepared for the mission, for the losses he had suffered, but now he understood. He knew they would lose people, that they would lose *him* one day. But his job, the only thing that really mattered anymore, was to do his best until then, to aid in the fight, however little he could give.

He was a bit frustrated at how long the last stretch took. He wasn't an athlete, not really, but he wasn't in bad shape either. He could certainly walk twelve or fifteen miles, or he could have before the bombing. Now, every step he took was through rubble and piles of masonry, and five miles in a day was an excellent pace.

He continued on, recognizing almost everything now. He was very close, and after another few steps, he saw armed men step out into the street. He was surprised…there hadn't been any permanent guards when he had left a few days before. He stopped, and raised his hand, directing all his people to stop as well.

"Gavin Sanders?" One of the guards called out to him. They didn't seem overly hostile, though the other two clutched their rifles in an almost deployed state.

"Yes…I am Gavin Sanders." He stepped forward.

"You have been expected. You had forty-two people with you, but there are more than that here now."

"They are representatives from several other groups of people. They have come to speak with our leadership."

The man was silent for a moment. Then he spoke into some kind of communication device, another new development. Sanders could hear a reply, but he couldn't make it out.

"Okay…you are clear." The man stepped aside, waving for the others to do the same.

"Thank you." Sanders turned and waved to those behind him. Then he moved forward, slowly at first, but picking up his pace as his excitement at being home pushed the concern about the new security temporarily out of his mind.

*　*　*

"I'm sorry, Gavin. I know the new measures must have come as a surprise to you, especially since you were only gone for a few days. But it has been an eventful time. You know we sent multiple scouting parties out…into Manhattan and even New Jersey, as well as Long Island. What you don't know is that every group, not just yours, ran into the enemy. Your team wasn't the only one to lose half its people. In fact, one group dispatched to New Jersey, was completely lost, we think. I sent a larger party to check on them, but I am not optimistic. We knew, at least we should have known, that the enemy came here for a reason, that they had more in mind than just destroying us. Whatever their true purpose, it seems they at least need some of us alive. That is, of course, good…but I doubt whatever use they have for us will be acceptable. Still, if I am right, if they need us for something, and they can't destroy us all…that at least, gives us somewhat of an edge."

Hugh stopped talking for a moment, giving his companion a chance to catch up. Sanders considered everything his friend had said, and he agreed with it all. He was a bit shocked at the volume of robots the people had all encountered, but he realized he shouldn't be. His group ran into three different clusters, so why should he expect less for the others?

Still, the new reality was settling on him slowly. He had

thought the past six months were bad, focusing on food and survival. But he slowly realized that those now seemed like almost the good old days...at least compared to the struggle they were in now. The enemy was clearly putting some kind of pressure on, and that could only mean things were going to get worse. Probably much worse.

"Try to get some rest...as much as you can. I'm afraid we'll need you again, soon. I'm going to go have a discussion with the people you brought back. I already spoke briefly with them, and I ordered some food brought to them. They seem reasonable...if they prove to be, if they agree to join us, that will be great. We've lost over 150 people in the past few days, and we need to keep growing."

Sanders listened to Hugh, surprised at how hard his tone had become in just a couple days. He was always serious, focused on survival, but there was something different now. He could feel it.

He could see it, too...though that hadn't happened in just the past couple of days. He knew Hugh had been working out. He'd even exercised with him a number of times. But suddenly he really noticed the change. The once thin man was now muscular. Six months of exercise had changed him entirely.

"Hugh..." Sanders paused for a few seconds, trying to put together exactly what he wanted to say. "...do we have any chance at all? I mean really?"

He expected an immediate answer, but Hugh just looked back at him for a few seconds. Then he replied, and it was obvious that he was being totally honest. "I just don't know, Gavin. Ask me sometimes, I will say yes, others and I will reply no if I am being honest. But one thing I am sure of, as certain as I can be...I'd rather take my chances, fight the aliens, and die in the process if need be, than give myself over to them, whatever purpose they have in mind for us."

Gavin returned the gaze, and despite the grimness of the prognosis, the darkness of the situation, he actually felt better. "I agree with you, Hugh…one hundred percent." He hesitated, unsure of what he wanted to say next. Then it just came out, automatically. "Victory or death."

* * *

"I know that you are all aware of the robots. The enemy gave us a few months, left us alone, at least around here. Who knows what they were doing…but that is clearly over now. Our group has run into well over one hundred of the bots in total, and in every instance, they have fought to the end. They haven't withdrawn, they haven't retreated…they have just fought until they destroyed all the bots…" He thought about adding, 'or they were taken out by the enemy' but he held that back. He was almost sure that had happened, at least twice, but while he was basically honest, he realized that he *was* trying to convince those present to join his group. The stronger they looked, the better it would be, he realized.

The group just looked on, listening to him, some appearing close to convinced, others less so. But only one of them spoke up.

"Hugh…can I call you that?" The man was strong, but he was polite as well, and he waited until Hugh nodded. "I appreciate what you've accomplished here, Hugh, I really do. The size of your group is truly impressive. But your efforts against the enemy…they seem hopeless. Don't you think it makes more sense to try to hide, to stay out of their way? Even if they want people, for some terrible purpose, they will take the ones that are easier to get. If we moved out, left the city and its surroundings perhaps, maybe we could find some kind of…peace."

Hugh looked at the man, truly evaluating him. He was in outstanding shape…in fact, Hugh was almost certain, from his calm, from his look, that he was ex-military. "I understand that way of thinking, I truly do. There is no way to argue that we have a major chance if we fight, and slipping off, hiding, will probably buy us more time. A little. But I can't believe the enemy has come here to allow any of us to survive in that way for long. You might buy a couple years even, if you're really careful, but in the past week or two, we went from nothing to well over a hundred robots coming here. Do you really feel comfortable that they will just let you be if you slip away, sneak out to the countryside?" Hugh looked at the man—Simon Descartes, he remembered from the intros—and he couldn't tell what he was thinking. He had always been good at figuring out what was on someone's mind, and he had gotten much better at it over the past six months. He could almost always tell what someone was pondering. But not with Descartes.

The man looked back, directly at him, and he had no idea what he was thinking. He was afraid that Descartes was going to be difficult, and he realized that was dangerous, that sort of thing being contagious. But then the man said, "I agree with you...completely. I just wanted to see what your response was, whether you were honest or not." He didn't exactly smile. Somehow, he looked like a man who was rarely happy enough to smile. But he came close, and he said, "I'm with you...and my people as well. We could slip away, hide as you say for a few years, but you are right, the enemy came here, and they started a war." He stared right at Hugh as he spoke. "And, by God, we should finish it!"

Hugh was happy, about Simon's declaration, and about how it was clearly affecting the others. But he was surprised, too, at both the man's statement, and at his ability to hide his attitudes so well. That was good, he realized...both for him to run into someone he couldn't read once in a while, and to have someone with such control in the group. He knew he couldn't trust someone new, not as much as he could someone who'd been with him for six months, but he just liked the man.

"I'm glad to have you, Simon...and you're people." He

looked around, at the others, realizing that Simon's statement had gone a long way toward convincing most of them as well. He realized he was going to get all of them, or at least a huge majority, and that was good. The more groups he took in, the less control he would have, he knew that. But he also realized that if he was to have any chance against the aliens, any at all, he needed as many people as he could get, that assembling a group in the city was only the first step…and a tiny step at that.

But it was the first one, and he intended to do everything he could to take it as far as possible.

Chapter Twenty-Two

From the Notes of Estle-Starric

It took a while to assemble my strike team, longer than I had expected…and in the meanwhile, we received further reports—and the lack thereof—to escalate the matter. The losses are worse than we had anticipated, and I am now sending 200 robots, and five of my own people. That force should be sufficient to destroy whatever form of nascent rebellion is brewing. There have been other reports of greater than expected resistance, of more casualties than expected in several cities, but none as bad as New York. I will attend to the others after we have dealt with the greatest problem.

Meanwhile, I have begun the gathering of people for the next phase, assuming, of course, the one thousand work. I realize this is a considerable effort to make with no guarantee of success, but I am strangely optimistic. Though we have tried and failed on several other worlds, so far, our results here have been the best by far…and that has continued. While the humans have clearly exhibited significant pain, the process itself has gone better than it has anywhere else. That is no guarantee that it will work, that we will, in fact, be the ones to solve our great species problem…but I believe it will. I am very optimistic, more so now than even before, and I intend to crush the resistance the humans are putting up and clear the way for our success.

Gavicon City
Approximately Twenty-Five Miles West of the Ruins of Washington
D + 200 Days

"Go…and take with you our power, and our righteousness. Go to New York, find the enemy…and crush them utterly. Then return, as heroes, with stories of those slain, and with the survivors as captives for the second phase of the breeding program." Estle-Starric spoke, standing on a raised platform, overlooking the entire force. The 200 robots were silent, standing erect and ready, but it wasn't to them he was speaking, not really. At the forefront of the position, lined up and facing him were five of his own people, the leaders of the group. He wasn't taking any chances, and as advanced as the robots were, he knew that sending several of his own people along would greatly enhance the operation.

"Exert caution…the enemy has destroyed many of our bots, and while they have engaged them only in small numbers at a time, never forget that they have at least some destructive force. Send out scouts if you wish but keep most of the force together…and drive the enemy from whatever positions they occupy." He raised his hands in the air, all four of them, and he acknowledged the cheers of the five individuals. He wondered if they were sincere, whether they truly wanted to go, or if they were…scared. He suspected they were mostly sincere, that they wanted to go…but a little bit a fear wouldn't shock him. His people had long allowed the robots to assume most of the risk of their actions, but he wanted some of his people in on this one. Not that the enemy would be able to face two hundred robots…but there was no harm in being sure, in sending the five of his own people as well.

They were the first of his kind to actually go out, among the humans, at least those who were not subservient. He wondered for a moment, if the humans would surprise him, if they wouldn't fold immediately before such an invincible force but would instead put up a serious fight. But despite some small concerns, he pushed back against it all. There was no way a group of humans, already mostly broken by the invasion, would be able to stand against the force he was sending.

He watched as the robots turned to march away, followed by the five Gavicons. The bots would walk, he knew, but his people would ride in small cars. The robots were tireless, they could move non-stop, but he knew his people couldn't. They were biological, and perhaps worse, they were getting older, like all of his personnel. He didn't usually sink into despair, but for a moment, he wondered what he would do if the breeding program failed, if Earth proved no more valuable than any other planet. He would destroy it, that much he knew, killing every living thing on it. But then he would leave, and unless one of the other worlds came through—and they were all rated lower than Earth on their chances—his last people would age, and they would die. And the most advanced society he knew of in all of space would cease to exist.

No, he said to himself. The humans *will* work, they will succeed, and Earth will be the source of his people's survival. He knew he couldn't be sure of that, but he was nevertheless, and he purged the negative thoughts from his psyche.

It will work. It will…

* * *

Hugh sat up, crouched in his chair, working at his desk. It was late, very late, but there was much to do. He had developed an unhealthy pattern, averaging *maybe* three or three and a half hours of sleep a night—and some nights, none at all—but he knew he didn't have a choice. He had tried to remember to give out tasks, to not try to do everything himself, but still, there was a large number of things he had to do. At least that he could do best. Even Travis, whom he trusted implicitly, couldn't match his capability, at least not on some things. He and his brother still worked together, they still shared command responsibilities, but Travis also recognized there were some things only Hugh could do. He had expected that to lead to trouble eventually, for his brother to stand up in opposition to him on some things. But he hadn't, not once. Travis stepped up when dealing with others, when leading the men and women of the group…but he stood down when Hugh came to some calculation or another.

"Hugh…you should go to bed. Do you know what time it is?"

He turned, his eyes focusing on his brother. The room was lit by a pair of candles and was mostly dark. He hadn't known his brother was there—he'd been deeply into the calculations he was running—but he wasn't surprised either. Travis got a little more sleep than he did, he suspected, but not all that much.

"I could say the same thing about you, couldn't I?" He turned, glad for the respite from his work, at least for a few minutes. He wasn't going to leave his chores, not for a couple more hours, at least, but he was appreciative for a short rest.

"You could…but I already got a couple hours sleep tonight. I woke up and noticed you were still out here, and I came to find you." He stepped forward and sat in a chair facing his brother. "What is it? What has you so occupied right now?"

Hugh sighed for a moment. If it had been anyone else, he would have said nothing. But his brother was his sounding board, the one person he would tell anything.

"I've just been trying…" He stopped for a moment, feeling strange about what he was going to say. "…to get into the enemy's head, or whatever they've got. They've lost a lot of robots in the past week or two, probably more than they expected to…and I don't think we can assume that they will maintain the same behavior." He went silent again, and then he said, "I assume they will send a more powerful force, and possibly quite soon."

Travis sat, quiet for a moment as he considered what his brother had said. Then he replied. "I agree completely…and we have to be ready for them. This is our first escalation. We have to deal with it and do it well."

"But how? That is the question. We have a lot of people now…but let's be honest, only a small percentage of them are suitable to act as fighters. And, perhaps worse, we've lost a lot of them in the recent excursions. I estimate we have maybe a hundred people left who have real combat experience, and possibly fewer. Maybe another five hundred are at least suitable for training. Even assuming all of that force is suitable, and we can mobilize it all against the enemy when they come…we've only won battles where we had ten to one odds. That means we can theoretically take on 60 bots, or even doubling our effectiveness, 120 …and that doesn't even try to take into account the changes in force structure between a large number of robots and three or four." He stopped for a moment and drew in a deep breath. "It doesn't factor in multiple enemy forces, or larger groups of robots." He hesitated again, unsure he wanted to add the last thought. If there had been anyone else present, he wouldn't have, but he had promised himself to be open with his brother. "And what if the enemy *is* a lifeform, as we have surmised? They have sent bots alone so far, but at some point, they may dispatch live personnel. That will be good in the sense that it will answer the question for us, tell us that our speculations are correct, and also indicate that we have nudged up the level of alarm…but it will be bad, perhaps very bad, if they are as capable as I suspect they may be."

Travis listened, and he didn't answer right away. Hugh suspected that was because he agreed, and he didn't know what to do about it. But then Travis answered. "I assume you're right...we will get more bots, and very possibly live aliens, and possibly some things we can't even think about. We know this, we've known it all along. Honestly, as much as we've tried to prepare, we haven't done all we can. We need everyone to be able to fight...old folks, kids, everybody. We're struggling for our lives, for all of them, and the odds are against us. I say, tomorrow we start with training...everybody from age 12 and up, and we make it count. We probably don't have long before the first enemy response, but even if we survive that, if we somehow defeat it...you know they will only come at us with something even stronger." He stopped for a few seconds, and Hugh could see a fire in his eyes. He was serious, deadly serious. "And we have to be ready for it, for whatever they can throw at us."

Hugh was surprised at his brother's resolve, at his analysis of the situation, both because of the grim nature of it...and because he realized it was right. He had thought he was doing everything possible, but now he realized that he wasn't. The situation was nothing like anything that had happened before. It was all or nothing...win or be destroyed. And that meant taking it to new levels, beyond anything they had ever known.

Beyond anything anyone had known before.

"You're right, Travis...right about it all. As much as we've done, it hasn't been enough, not nearly so. We need to change everyone's point of view, turn them from victims into predators. And we need to do it quickly." He took a deep breath. "We also need to realize that among our population are people who will not do what is necessary. Whether they are truly bad, or just not up to it...or cowards…we have to be ready." He hesitated again, struggling to say what he knew he had to say. "We have to…kill them if we can't get them to fight. You know that, right? Releasing them, allowing them to roam free, it won't work. Anyone who doesn't do their duty…has to be eliminated." He barely managed to say it all. Hugh wasn't a vicious person, not by nature, and the idea of killing people other than in battle was difficult…but he knew it would be necessary, that he had to increase his level of control over the whole group. The human race was in a final contest, a desperate fight to survive, and there was no room for weakness. None at all.

Travis was silent, for a long moment. Hugh realized his brother had stated that they needed to increase the intensity of their operations…and almost immediately he had not only accepted what Travis had said, but he took it to a new level. His brother was right. For all of his intelligence, for his capability, he hadn't taken things far enough. The instant Travis said that, he realized…and he took it to the extreme.

"Travis," he said after another few seconds, "I know it is difficult, but you are right…and so am I. We are at war, the worst war mankind has ever known, and we can't hold back, not in any way."

Travis remained silent for a few more seconds, but then finally he nodded. "I know you're right, Hugh. But taking things to that level will cause all kinds of dissension in the group, and that will increase the number of…problems we face, not against the enemy, but internally. We could even lose control of the overall group."

Hugh turned and looked right at his brother. "That is a possibility, of course. But what is the point of hanging on to command only to lose the war? Let's be honest, if we do everything we possibly can, everything, our chance of victory is small. If we don't do all we can, if we allow ourselves to be weak in any way, we have no chance at all. You were right, my brother. You saw the situation clearly, but you didn't take it far enough. You know I am right."

Travis turned and looked right at Hugh. "You're right, I do know you are…I just don't know if I…if we…can really do what we have to."

Hugh looked back and, finally, he nodded. "I don't know either, Travis…but we've got to try."

Chapter Twenty-Three

From the Notes of Hugh McDaniel

I could kick myself for not realizing what was truly necessary. I had worked around the clock, done everything I could think of...but I hadn't truly opened my eyes to the darkness, to the horrible reality. Not until Travis spoke, and then it all flooded into place. The hovels we had started to think of as home, the percentage of our people we considered military equivalents—everything—was wrong, and the instant he raised the issue, it all flooded into place for me.

We *must* strike back, with everything we have...and that means everything. We must constantly analyze all aspects, change our plans continuously, keep up the pressure on the enemy one hundred percent. We must defend ourselves...but we must also attack. We must start to take the pressure to our enemy.

First, we must prepare for what I am sure is coming. We can expect a response the enemy feels will be capable of destroying us, and we *must* defeat it. Then, we have to follow that immediately with a strike, an attack of some kind on the enemy. We don't know where they are located, but I think I know how to find that out...and we will proceed with that, along with the training of our people, all of our people.

I am upset with myself…for all my supposed intellect, I spent six months leading my people, gathering large quantities of food and other vital supplies, building up the number of people under my control, and doing all of that well…but I didn't do enough. I didn't prepare my people for their true purpose…to fight. But that will change now.

When the enemy comes, be it tomorrow or six months from now, they will meet an army of thousands, all armed, all ready. I know many of them will not be well trained, that hundreds, even thousands may die, but this is the price we have to pay. We will probably all be killed in this struggle, but we will continue nevertheless, and we will never stop until the enemy has been driven away from our planet.

Or we are all dead.

Just Outside the 67th Avenue Subway Station
Forest Hills, Queens
D + 201 Days

"You have a variety of weapons, based on your skill levels as well as what we have. If you have a lesser weapon, do not worry. Everything that has been handed out is strong enough to hurt the enemy." Travis spoke, standing on a pile of rubble that had been turned into a platform of sorts. He had as many people out in the street as he could get, but he still realized it would take eight or nine sessions to address all the people. He had lost track of the exact number they had managed to assemble, but he knew it was over 20,000. That both amazed him, and also seemed very small. It was more than he could have imagined putting together, but not very many when the job was nothing less than reconquering the world.

He tried not to think much of that. It was too depressing. He focused on simply defeating the next punch by the enemy, and then he could think about striking back, somehow. He knew that last part seemed almost impossible…but it was vital, too.

"Okay, so all of your weapons are loaded. Please, be careful with them." He wasn't used to dealing with a large number of total neophytes, but the more he'd thought about it, the more he agreed that they needed everybody to even have a chance. "We can't all shoot at the same time, so I need you to come up, one hundred at a time. You will each be firing until your gun is empty." He realized some of his people had weapons with clips of 30 or more bullets, while others had six guns, and a variety of other types. He had generally tried to get the best weapons into the hands of those who seemed most likely to make good soldiers, but he acknowledged that he hadn't been able to spend a lot of time on it.

"Let's move out. Form a series of lines from here backwards." He swung his arm generally along a white line he had drawn on the ground. "And just fall into place. There is no advantage to moving up in the line. Everyone will get a chance to fire." He tried to sound cheerful, but inside he was very concerned. He realized that it would take considerable training to get most of his people to even a remote level of competence…but with at least fifteen thousand recruits, he just didn't have enough ammunition to really teach them. His people had found several arsenals, brought back thousands of guns, along with ammunition and other equipment, but now that he was actually using it, what had seemed like a considerable stockpile no longer did. He had sent out a couple groups that morning, out to search ruined police stations and other places that might have weaponry still inside their ruins, but for the moment, he was worried. He had separated out the cream of the weapons, reserved them for those he considered to be the best fighters—and for use against the actual enemy—but still, the supply of guns, which had just seemed so large, felt a lot tighter than they had been the day before. And the amount of ammunition was even worse.

He pushed the doubts aside. He and Hugh had both agreed they had no choice but to arm everyone…and he figured whatever problems he had now, they were likely to get worse when the inexperienced personnel were deployed, when they faced the enemy in actual combat. Far worse. "Alright…first line, get ready to fire." He looked again, checking carefully that no one was anywhere near the shooting zone. Then he paused, just for a few seconds, and he said, "Fire!"

*   *   *

Qualak-Neerie moved forward, walking along with the bots instead of riding in his vehicle. The leader of the expedition, the highest ranked of the live Gavicons present, found the weather to be almost perfect. The day was hot, very hot to the humans, he understood, but it was almost perfect for a Gavicon. Earth wasn't an ideal match for a home, of course, but he was becoming used to it. His breathing felt forced at first, the result of his exercise and a slightly lower oxygen count than his home world, but he had more or less adapted now.

He knew the robots didn't care that he was present, that they would do exactly as they were programmed, whether he was there or not. But he was tired of sitting in the vehicle, moving along at such a slow pace. It could move quickly, of course, but his mission compelled him to remain with the bots, and while they could travel pretty quickly themselves, he had ordered them to move forward at a slower pace. He wanted them in perfect condition when they reached New York. It would take two days to get to the city at the current pace, but a day or two didn't matter. He was confident he had enough power to destroy any group that had likely assembled there and defeat it. The human civilization was obliterated, their militaries destroyed, their populations blasted and reduced to scavengers. From what he had heard, he speculated that those in New York had banded together in larger numbers than expected, and even found some weapons. That was a cause for some concern, but he didn't really think they could hold off against his forces. He was sure of that.

He turned and looked back at the air cars, the four separate vehicles that carried his Gavicon subordinates, five if he counted his own, which was still moving along on automatic. None of them, it appeared, shared his desire to spend some time outside.

He thought about his kind, about the Gavicons. His whole life had been during the decline, the search for a solution to their breeding problem. The population was a small fraction of what it had been in the glory days, the thousands of years when his civilization had been rising. He didn't know what had caused the sudden, and ultimately total, drop off in conventional births. That was still a mystery, despite a truly massive and ongoing effort to determine the problem. Though there was still research going on, he knew that virtually all of the hope—for his species to survive—rested on others, on one of the life forms existing within range of his homeworld being a match.

The Gavicons had been a peaceful race once, unlikely to harm another species, however that had changed. Their problem, the need for a solution, had made them harsher, less sympathetic to alien cultures. He knew that, in a manner of speaking at least, but he didn't really recognize the difference his own culture's problem had made in his civilization's attitudes. His people had changed, they had become obsessed with their own survival. Their love of peace had evaporated, destroyed by the quest to live, and they came to see the other species they were aware of, that lived around their homeworld, as sacrificial, even created for this purpose, to facilitate their own survival.

He understood that all, in a way, but he was mostly a

modern Gavicon, and he couldn't really comprehend the old ways, the kindness that he knew his people had once possessed. The humans, and the other life forms scattered around, might be allowed to live, to grow, even to attain a level of significant power, but not at the cost of his people. If it came down to deciding who would survive, he agreed completely with his people's current viewpoint. It was them.

He looked up, felt the sun hitting his skin. It was very good, and he wondered about the others, about why they remained in their vehicles, rarely coming out. The attacks had been carefully coordinated to maintain the world, to minimize the radiation and other effects. If the experiment worked, if humanity proved to be the working component to their reproductive crisis, this world would become crucial to his people, the home to many of their remaining personnel. Indeed, though it was difficult to imagine, he could even see them abandoning their world, making their new homes here. The total population was so small, they could be moved relatively easily.

Much of the planet was cooler than they liked, but their population was so small now, they could easily abandon the north, and live only in the warmer climes. At least until the breeding program was really accelerated, and there were millions and millions of his people born.

He looked around, seeing debris, the remains of some former moderate collection of humans. There had been survivors there, too, of course, but they had already been swept up, gathered together and placed in pens, waiting for the confirmation that the first thousand had actually worked, that humans could carry Gavicon embryos…that his race was saved.

He stared at his surroundings, looking past the rubble, beyond to the less damaged farmland. Yes, he hoped the experiment would work, that the humans would prove to be useful. He liked the planet, and he could see it as a future home.

* * *

Lucas Kiley stood on top of a pile of wreckage, looking out to the west. He was in Manhattan, pretty close to the Hudson River, looking out over the hills of New Jersey. Of course, he realized all those names, and a thousand others, were mostly things of the past. Whatever happened, even if his people somehow launched a war, and successfully drove the enemy from Earth—something that still seemed downright impossible to him—he doubted anything would be the same as it was before, and that included names.

He was staring, looking for anything, of course, but mostly for the enemy. He fully expected them to respond, to see a force approaching. He had no idea when that would happen, of course, but he had to imagine that the group his friends had assembled to face it, its size and scope, were far more than the enemy had anticipated. That was good, of course, though he realized if they actually managed to succeed, to defeat the alien force, it would just result in an even more powerful response than the one they expected now. That would either destroy their force, eliminate them entirely…or if they did manage to win *again*, result in another, even larger, force being sent. One after the other…until they were wiped out. He couldn't imagine his people enduring that for long.

He liked to think of himself as one of the top people in the group, which he was of course. But he just couldn't see any route that led to overall victory. Sometimes he managed to buy into it, to assume that Hugh knew what he was doing…which, of course, he did…he was simply too outmanned, too outgunned to prevail.

The others, the rest of the people they had assembled, more or less just plodded along, hopeless, but not really wanting to survive in the world as it was now…but not wanting to die either.

His position was the highest one around, and it offered a reasonably distant view across the river. He didn't expect to see anything, nothing beyond maybe another group of refugees, or some surviving animals, but he looked carefully anyway, knowing that one day, probably very soon, someone would see something approaching. He just hoped that the enemy response was a ground force, and not another barrage of nuclear weapons. He agreed that the enemy had some use for surviving humans, probably something bad, but he also realized that New York, as large a city as it was, wasn't a meaningful component of the world. Making themselves enough of a headache, worse than other areas, though of course that was just speculation on his part, carried that as a dark potential reward…a wave of nuclear devastation, one far harder and deadlier than the original.

He stayed up on the mound, looking for a bit longer, just because he found it pleasant to be outside, to be alone, even if that meant standing one hundred feet from his companions. But he knew he had to keep moving. He had a lot of coast to cover, and not that much time until dark.

He turned around, ready to climb back down…but then he froze. A second later, he swung back around and looked out over the coastline he had been covering. He'd seen something, he was sure of it, and a few seconds later, it appeared again.

It was a robot, the same kind his people had been fighting for the past week or two. At first, it was just one, but then, another popped up beside it. For a moment, he wasn't sure if it was another group, three or four of them…or if it was what he'd come in search of.

Then, as he watched, a whole cluster of the bots emerged. They were marching up a hillside, and there were at least fifty of them. He turned and gestured toward his people, yelling to them, "Enemy bots…fifty, at least!" He turned again, and saw more of them, there were now a hundred at minimum…no, more. He was frozen by what he saw, and he just looked as more and more of the bots marched forward. There were around two hundred of them, and they were being followed by five flying vehicles. He wondered about those. Were they supply transports, some kind of support craft for the bots? Or could they contain actual live aliens?

He didn't know, but two things dawned on him suddenly. The first was, he had to get down. The last thing he needed was for the enemy to see him, to be spotted and provoke an even earlier assault than the enemy intended.

And the second was to get back, as quickly as possible, and to warn Travis and Hugh. To warn everyone.

Chapter Twenty-Four

From the Notes of Hugh McDaniel

I knew it was coming, the enemy's attack. I was sure of it, absolutely positive. So, why did Lucas's report shake me up so much?

It was expected—though I have to say, a couple hundred bots is definitely on the higher end of what I was predicting…and that doesn't even take into account the strange vehicles. They could just be support for such a large force, perhaps heavier weapons…but there was another possibility as well.

I understand my mental state, in a manner of speaking. I was ready for this, as prepared as possible…but one can only be so ready for what we are about to begin. The earlier stages, the first months, and the preliminary combats, were all preparatory. This will be our first real battle. And I don't know if we can win it or not against such a force. I just know we have to.

Just Outside the 67th Avenue Subway Station
Forest Hills, Queens
D + 201 Days

"Alright, Lucas…well done. You did exactly the right thing.

You came and warned us, and gave us the chance to
prepare, to get ready." Hugh was appreciative of whatever
warning Lucas's action had given him, but truth be told, he
was neither sure it would be enough time, or even that there
was such a thing as enough. His people had just started
training, and most of them were far from ready for anything
like what was coming.

Ready or not, they'll have to do it…

He knew, immediately, that those he considered ready,
the people he was confident would fight and fight well,
didn't have a chance by themselves, not against two
hundred robots, not to mention whatever was in those
vehicles. He *had* to deploy his people, *all* of them…and he
expected to have losses that numbered into the hundreds,
probably the thousands, even if they ultimately won. He had
no idea how that would affect overall morale going
forward…assuming they came through it at all to go
forward.

His mind was racing, trying to decide how to deploy. He
couldn't put all his people together. They would be an
almost unmissable target for the enemy. No, he had to wear
them down, deploy people all along their line of approach,
hit them again and again, maybe taking out a few bots each
time. That job would best be done by his experienced
personnel, but he realized he just didn't have enough of
them. He would have to assign the people—all of them—to
the groups, and he had to do it now. Lucas had said the
enemy was moving at a fairly slow pace, but even that would
bring them into the city the next morning. And he was sure
they could move faster if they wanted to.

"Thanks, Hugh…" Lucas responded to his comments,
but it was clear that he was somewhat depressed. Hugh felt
the urge to say something, to try to counter it…but in truth,
he felt the same way.

"Okay…we've got to move. Now." Hugh launched into
the whole thing, pushing his own doubts and fears down as

far as he could. It was partly because he knew it was the one way to keep himself going, to ignore all the concerns, at least for a while. And partly because he simply didn't have any choice. The enemy was close, very close, and he could expect them to show up any time. He could be ready or not…but they were coming.

"Lucas…if you feel up to it, I want to give you the forward command. It will mean going back out there, almost immediately…" He hesitated for a second and then he added, "You will be the first to engage the enemy." He knew Lucas well enough to be sure of two things. First, he wouldn't want to do it. He was tired and worn and scared just like everyone else. But, two, he *would* do it, and without complaint."

"Of course, Hugh…I'll be ready to go any time." His answer was clear, and Hugh could barely detect his doubts. But he knew they were there.

"Thank you, Lucas." He looked over at Travis, who had been standing right next to him.

"Be careful, Lucas," Travis said. "We want you to interrupt their movements and start inflicting some losses…not to fight to the finish." Travis glanced at Hugh and then back to Lucas. "Be *very* careful and lose as few people as possible. If we win this fight, it will be hit and run…a dozen small engagements."

Hugh nodded, but he knew Lucas would still suffer significant losses, all the more because he was going to send a large group of inexperienced people with him. He didn't have a choice. He only had so many people who were experts, or even slightly experienced with guns…and he was going to send 500 with Lucas. He knew that was a lot, that there was no way he could manage that many personnel…and that meant more would be killed…but he didn't have a choice. The force approaching was big, perhaps too large to handle no matter what he did. If he sent smaller groups—20 or 50—they would be wiped out almost immediately. He had to focus on fighting the battle the best way, regardless of the losses his force would suffer.

If Lucas made it back with half his force, he would consider it a miracle.

"Don't worry. I'll be careful...you can count on that." Lucas sounded fairly solid, but Hugh realized that they were all shaky right now...and they would be for a long while. If they were still there, that is.

Hugh turned and exchanged glances again with Travis...and then he looked right at Lucas. He held out his hand, and he shook. Travis did the same right after, and then Lucas turned and walked out.

Hugh watched him go. For a moment, it was silent, both he and Travis thinking and not speaking. But they didn't have time for that, not much. They had other groups to deploy, and many of those would have lesser commanders than Lucas...they would need words from Travis and him before being sent out.

He had discussed the strategy with Travis, who was the one of them who actually had military experience, and they agreed completely. There was no way he could deploy twenty thousand people in one area, nothing close to it. They had to be spread out. And one thing he was sure about...everybody was going to fight in this battle.

Designing the plan for twenty thousand people to go into battle, dividing them up into a dozen commands, and directing them, both before and during the fight, was an immense job. It almost overwhelmed Hugh...and it excited him too.

* * *

Lucas prowled forward, about two hundred feet in front of the nearest member of his team. He still had the forty or so that he had before, all sent right back out, after a quick meal and an hour's rest. But he had almost 500 extras as well, mostly inexperienced personnel Hugh had sent with him. When he had been told he would be the first to attack, he'd imagined his forty or so were being sent. But then, he'd gotten word that there would be more. A lot more.

He had almost argued with Hugh and Travis, told them there was no way he could handle so many…but he realized they were right. This fight would be to the end, and anyone not participating would simply be hiding and waiting to see if they would live or die. Or be taken captive. It was much better to fight. He thought that way, and he suspected that after half a year's survival, after thousands had died from radiation poisoning, after all they had endured, most of the people agreed with him.

At least until they faced fire.

His people, those he'd led so far, had been remarkably durable, standing up to the enemy and fighting. But now he had many with him who hadn't fought, not really…and they were coming up against the largest enemy force he had seen, by far. He was sure some of his people would run. He just didn't know what effect that would have on the others.

He had seen this enemy once already. They had been a couple miles away. He'd spotted them from a hillside, atop some wreckage. The two hundred bots, and five ships following them, had almost worn away his own courage and steadfastness at first glance, for a moment at least. He was sure it would have had a bad effect on his people. Better they didn't see what they would be facing until it was time for the fight. That was why he was alone, so far in front.

He waited, knowing the enemy was close. He couldn't see them—they were now in Manhattan and covered by wreckage. He thought he heard something…twice…but there was still nothing visible. Yet. But he waited, stone still, mostly behind a pile of broken concrete pipe. There was no guarantee he wouldn't be spotted by the enemy, but he figured he was doing the best he could. Then, a few seconds later, he saw the lead elements emerge from behind a pile of wreckage. They had been in a decline, but now they rose...and they were close. Very close. He thought it was odd that he mostly hadn't heard them, but he knew sound traveled funnily at times.

The bots were approaching, moving almost directly into his path. It was very nearly time.

He slipped down, moving very slowly, doing everything he could not to give himself away. When he got back to his command, he spoke...softly. "Okay...the enemy is close, less than half a mile away. They're up over the hillside, and they're heading this way. Spread out...you've all got your positions, so go to them and wait." He had specified locations for all of them, as well as he could. "Wait. I will fire the first shot. Anybody else does it, and I swear to God, I will shoot you myself. Understood?" It wasn't exactly a question, but he phrased it that way.

He had already told everyone, six or seven times to be as quiet as they could when they were near the enemy. He realized he was fortunate on the lay of the land. He had a good chance of getting off the first shot. After that...well, he knew his force would only fight for a minute or two. Then he would give the word, and they would scatter. He knew there would be a lot fewer of them then...but so be it. They were all going to die, some just sooner rather than later. He knew there was a good chance his own life was now measured in minutes.

He turned, looking for a spot, one that offered a good firing position as well as some cover. He tried to imagine what the enemy fire would be like, but he couldn't. He'd been almost stunned as the firepower three or four of the bots could lay down...he couldn't even imagine what 200 could do.

He pushed on, turning, getting a decent idea at where he expected the enemy to emerge. If he was right, they would come over the hill, giving his people a shot at a few of them first. That wouldn't last, not long, but if he could take out a few of the bots first, that was good. Because he didn't imagine his line would stand for long once the enemy brought a reasonable amount of its force into play.

He sunk down, hiding behind a large piece of masonry, with just part of his head sticking up. If the enemy moved, if they came a different way—or a hundred other things—his plan would fall apart. He thought about that for perhaps thirty seconds…and then he heard something, and he saw the first robot's head.

He breathed deeply, holding his breath for a few seconds, as the entire first line crested over the ridge, moving forward.

Then, he fired.

Chapter Twenty-Five

From the Notes of Hugh McDaniel

I am looking across the river, waiting for the enemy to become visible. I am uncomfortable with just how much of my plan is based on guesswork. The enemy could come any way, they could travel up or down Manhattan and cross at any point...or multiple ones. But I assume that they were able to ascertain our approximate location, and that they would cross near here. I assigned several groups to the north and south, too, but I put the most firepower here.

In the end, I placed myself here as well, which was, to say the least, controversial. Travis had wanted to go, preferably instead of me, but at the very least along with me. But I had to say 'no,' and that led to an argument between us. I understand that he is protective of me, but I finally told him, there is no safety for anyone, not anymore. And I needed him to remain behind, in charge of the final line. He has more than four thousand armed personnel there, gathered all around the main subway station. His chances of defeating the enemy rely to a considerable extent on what the rest of us do, how badly hurt the bots are by the time they reach him. But whether they are torn to shreds, or hardly hurt, the final battle will be his...as it should be.

But my force will encounter them before he does, at least

if my analysis was correct. And we will hurt them as much
as possible.

Along the East River
Queens, New York
D + 201 Days

"Alright, everybody into position. Take as much cover as
you can get…and be ready." Hugh stood, looking across the
river. He had been wondering whether the enemy would
come the way he expected, and then he heard something.
Sounds.

Gunfire.

He tried to ascertain where it was coming from, where
exactly Lucas's force had engaged the enemy. He knew
that's what it was—there was nothing else it could be—and
he listened, trying to decide how long it would last. Not that
long, he suspected. He knew that Lucas had considered his
force large, far too large, at least for his experience at
command, but five hundred wasn't that many, not really.
Not considering that most of them were raw beginners.
They would open up, and if he had bet well on Lucas, they
would have thirty seconds, perhaps even a minute, where
the fight was theirs, where they were the best. Then, enough
of the enemy would get into the battle to begin gunning
them down. If the struggle lasted for two minutes, that was
about what he expected. Any less than that, and the fight
was going more poorly than he hoped. Any longer, and it
was exceeding his expectations.

He glanced down at his watch, estimating that fifteen
seconds had already passed. He looked back out, not being
able to see anything, though the sounds continued. It was
frustrating listening, but not being able to see anything, but
after a few seconds, he pushed it aside, and focused on his
own team. They were the next ones, a thousand strong,
defending the river line. His force was the only one that had

a real edge of terrain. He knew the enemy would cross without much difficulty, but they would be exposed while doing it, and their ability to fight back would be impaired. He didn't kid himself that his force would stop the attack, but just maybe, between them and Lucas's, and the several thousand he had deployed behind him, in smaller groups on the way to the subway station, they would wear them down enough.

Enough for the main force to finish them off. Travis was commanding by far the largest group they had. They would engage, and he knew many of them would break and run, but hopefully not all of them. He was placing his bets on that group…to destroy the enemy.

Or to be destroyed. He knew some of his people would survive, no matter what happened, but he didn't fool himself. His force, and his and Travis's position as the leaders of the group, depended totally on what happened. If they won, if they held out against such a large enemy attack, they would only reinforce their position, and they would start to build on it. It would only be the beginning, he realized, a tiny fraction of what was necessary.

But it would be a beginning, a true beginning. He just didn't know if it would happen. Even with his intellect, and with six months of hard training thrown into the mix, he had no idea if the rest of the people, *his* people, he reminded himself, would find within themselves the strength they needed to defeat the enemy.

He looked across the river again, realizing that the fight was still going on. It had been two minutes by now, he was sure of that, and he could still hear the sounds of fire. That was a long way from victory, perhaps, but it was a bit less like defeat than he had expected. Next, it would be his turn.

"Alright, everybody in position…the enemy will be here soon!"

* * *

Lucas ducked down…just before a wave of fire came at
him. He dodged it, by how much of a second he didn't even
want to guess. He could feel his heart pounding, even as he
imagined most of his people were worse off than he was.
But they were holding, at least most of them were. He could
only guess how much time had passed since he took the
first shot, but it was more than a minute, he was sure of
that. Hell, it was more than two.

He crawled along, planning to come out on the other
side of a six or seven foot chunk of rubble. It wasn't exactly
a well thought out plan, but at least it was better than
emerging in the same place he'd been, the spot several
enemy bots had just targeted. He didn't know that they
wouldn't be waiting for him on the other side too, but he
figured he'd have a better chance at least. He tried to
channel all his thoughts into the battle, and he realized his
people were definitely doing better than he expected. That
didn't mean they were winning, not even close, but they had
taken down a number of enemy bots already, and a good
number of them were still fighting.

Most of them that were still alive, at least. He'd lost a fair
number already, at least thirty to enemy fire, he figured, and
maybe as many as double that. He couldn't really count his
losses, either to enemy gunshots or to fleeing, but he figured
that at least a quarter of his force was gone one way or
another.

He glanced out a bit, exposing as little of himself as he
could. There were no shots coming in, not yet at least, and
he brought his rifle around. He wanted to fire on full auto,
but he knew he wouldn't have that kind of time. The bots
were very fast, and he had to keep moving or they would
target and kill him. He'd already seen several of his people
pause too long and pay the ultimate price. He could fire one
burst, maybe two, then he had to find another spot. Or he'd
likely end up dead. Part of him imagined that as an almost
certain fate for himself…eventually, in two minutes,

perhaps, or five…but he fought back against it. He had no desire to die today.

He fired…and fired again, pulling back almost immediately, and still nearly too late. The enemy had been surprised initially, at least somewhat, but now they were fully engaged, and that meant his force probably didn't have much time left. He looked around, trying to get some idea of how many of his people were left. The best he could come up with now was somewhat less than half, though he knew that some of those missing had just run. It troubled him that those who ran first were more likely to survive than those who stayed, who fought for longer. But that was always true. The real difference here was that everyone, more or less, was fighting, or at least had fought. Very few, if any, of his people had run initially.

He looked around, even as the barrage where he had been a few seconds ago continued. He was searching, looking for some other place he could take a few shots from before pulling back. Then he saw several of his people, all fairly skilled, two former cops and someone he was sure had been a bad guy before the world had imploded. The fact that they were acting together showed just how much human sensibilities had changed in the past months.

He took a deep breath…and he threw himself out across an opening, perhaps three feet, to the pile of debris his three companions were behind. He half expected to be hit, but he made it across, and he looked at his co-fighters. They were clearly upset, and a bit scared, but they were holding on, not retreating at all. He realized he would have to issue the orders to everyone to pull back soon, or he would just lose all his best warriors. The longer the fight went on, the more people he would lose and the less additional damage they would do to the enemy. But he wanted a bit more, first. It had been three and a half minutes, he guessed, maybe even four, and he was going to try for five. He realized that was really pushing it, and with every second that passed, more of his people were running on their own…and leaving fewer under his command. It wasn't cowardice, certainly not among people who had remained in the fight for so long. But human endurance had its limits.

There were less than a hundred left now, he figured, possibly even fifty or fewer, and the bots were all active now. He guessed that his people had taken out ten of the robots completely, and probably badly damaged another fifteen or twenty. That was far more than he had expected, and amid the turmoil of the battle and his own fear, he felt some satisfaction.

"Thirty more seconds," he said, realizing that he was out of breath. "Thirty seconds more of fighting, and then we all take off." He spoke as loudly as he could, wondering whether it was worth it, whether his people would do much more damage in that time. The robots were fully alert now, and the incoming fire was incredible. Just showing any part of yourself, for more than a second basically meant instant death. He wasn't even sure he could get a shot off, assuming he found someplace new to try.

But he was going to do it. If he failed, if he got shot, he knew his second would take command, and if he, too, died, then the third, fourth, whatever. Six months of life after the attack, after the near-destruction of the planet, had mostly prepared him for death. He hoped it wouldn't come, at least not today, but if it did, he would take it. He just hoped he died well, perhaps taking out the enemy until he closed his eyes once and for all.

He checked his watch, timing the final stretch. The first four minutes were guesstimates—though he knew he had been close—but the final thirty seconds was to be exact. He looked around, searching for a place to fire from, to get a few more shots off before he gave the word…and ran. He could tell the enemy was moving, that they were surrounding his remnant force. In a very short while, they would be in position to fire around the cover. That would be the end of anyone still there.

He climbed up, carefully moving to the top of the berm, getting ready to take one last shot. The time was down to fifteen seconds, and he knew that this would be his final one…whether he survived or not. He sucked in a deep breath, and he nudged up, just a little, bringing his rifle down.

He shot…one burst, two. Three. Then he ducked down. For an instant, he wasn't sure he had done it in time…but after a couple seconds, he realized he had. Just. He never knew how little time he had survived by, how much longer it had been before his former location was covered by incoming fire. It had been less than a second, of that he was sure. He was breathing hard, almost out of control…but he was still alive.

"Alright, everyone…break off. Get away…anyway you can!" He shouted the command, as loudly as he could, still not sure everyone would hear it. But he had done all he could, and now he owed it to himself to run, to do what he could to stay alive.

He climbed down the large pile of debris, and he ran back, away from the enemy. He knew they were moving, that for all his efforts, he might expose himself to their fire. But there was no choice but to run, and to hope for the best.

He stumbled a bit as he slid down the pile, but he caught himself, and he ran. He did what he could to stay behind the mound, to keep the debris between him and his pursuers, but he knew that was a spotty effort. The enemy could get a shot at him anywhere…and the further back he went, the more chance they had. He dodged, mixed up his routine, did everything he could to make himself a tougher target…but he figured he had at best even odds of getting away.

He ran toward another pile of debris, skirting around it, putting it between him and the enemy. He didn't know how fast they could go, or what they would do, whether they would pursue his forces, or whether they would regroup and continue their advance.

All he could do now was run…and hope for the best.

* * *

Qualak-Neerie was in his vehicle, taking advantage of the armor shell as the entire area erupted with fire. He wasn't surprised that the enemy had attacked him, in fact, he'd almost expected it sooner. He had figured the bots would keep a close eye out, but the enemy actually managed to score the first shots. That was lesson one…the robots were top of the line killing machines, but they couldn't handle everything. An enemy who was careful, who was meticulous, could still hurt them.

He was surprised at the duration of the battle as well. His bots were winning—of course—but they were taking losses, too. Pretty serious ones, at least in comparison to his expectations. He didn't really anticipate having a difficult time on his mission, but a few doubts started to cloud his view.

He reached out, adjusted the settings on his monitor. He was just watching the fight, staying out of it, for now, at least. His vehicle was armed, of course, and it could add to the fight, but even as he stared at the battle, he realized it was almost over, for now, at least. All he had to do was decide whether to pursue the enemy, to send the bots out to hunt down all of the survivors…or to reorganize them, and to proceed on to their primary mission. He didn't know where exactly the main base of the humans was, but he was sure it was across the next river. He knew that was the important goal.

Still, he felt something—anger?—and he wanted to hunt down the survivors. But he decided against it. He would reorganize the force, put some of the robots in a wider array. If the enemy decided to come back, to attack again, his bots would be ready…and if they just slipped away, that was fine, too. His mission was to destroy the humans' ability to fight, not to wipe them out. The destruction of one city's population, every individual killed, would hardly impact the purpose of the invasion…but he knew there were problems in other places as well, and he was sure just breaking the will of the people, reducing them to a mob of half-starved animals, was the right thing to do.

He paused, just for a few seconds, and then he began typing, sending orders to the bots. It would be satisfying to hunt down the survivors of the attack, but he realized that wasn't his mission. He had been placed in command of the first major force to be deployed since the initial attack, and he knew he had to do well, that he had to make it work.

And he would…he would see it through, do just what he had been directed to do.

Chapter Twenty-Six

From the Notes of Hugh McDaniel

They're coming. I can hear them, I've seen them, at least twice. They are in a dip right now, no more than a few hundred yards from the point where they will become visible. They will appear at any moment, and our fight will begin.

Wait, I think I hear them now. I think…

Along the East River
Queens, New York
D + 201 Days

Hugh dropped his pen and grabbed his gun. There was already firing going on, the first ten or twelve of his command who had spotted the enemy before he had. He joined them a second later, along with most of the rest.

He was back behind a pile of rubble, though he realized he had enough of him exposed to draw fire. To get hit. The fact that he didn't, that in those few seconds before he reacted, pulled himself back, he wasn't shot—like so many of his people were—was just pure luck. He realized that, a bit then but much more later, when he reconsidered every phase of the fight. but he was mostly taken then by the moment. He wanted to destroy the enemy, to take out as many of the bots as possible, and at that time, for those specific minutes, his intellect, his responsibility, everything, took a backseat to his desire to kill.

He fired, shooting well. For six months he had eaten as well as he could and exercised regularly...and he had practiced endlessly with his rifle. He had done everything possible to prepare himself for the fight he knew was just beginning. He had restricted himself mostly to the same things his other people had, the same food and everything else. Except ammo. He had to reserve the usage, hold his people down to a minimum output to conserve enough for battle. But he had allowed himself extra, deciding that he had to be ready, that his own shooting should be as good as he could make it.

And it was good...very good.

He ducked down, moving over about seven or eight feet before emerging again and firing. He was shooting bursts, three or four, knowing he would have to reduce the time he fired from each position as soon as the enemy was fully engaged. This was one area where, perhaps, he had an actual superiority to his brother. Travis was an experienced military man, with actual combat experience. But that experience was against other men, and Hugh realized that try as much as he might, he couldn't adjust totally to fighting robots. His understanding of war helped him in a dozen ways, but in this one area, Hugh felt he just might have the edge.

He crawled over, positioning himself higher, behind a large pile of debris. He stopped for a moment, breathing deeply, pushing back against the fear...and he jerked himself up, bringing the rifle around. He fired, only two bursts this time, and he came back down, hiding again. This time, there was fire coming over, ripping past his position of a second ago. But he was already moving, scrambling behind the mountain of broken masonry and twisted steel that had once been part of the largest city in the country.

He struggled not to think of all his people he had lost already. That was irrelevant now…it was pointless to even thing about. All he tried to allow into his mind were things that were useful in the current situation. He wasn't totally successful, but he mostly managed to restrict his mind to where it had to be.

He checked his watch—that was something he had never worn before, but with the loss of cell phone service, it became one of the best ways to keep track of time—and he realized that his force had been fighting for over two minutes. That wasn't long, he realized, especially not with the river between his troops and the enemy. But he suspected it wouldn't take long for the bots to cross. It became clear that they were water resistant, that they could simply enter the river…but some of the ones that were damaged badly couldn't, and perhaps six or seven seemed to suffer damage in the waters.

He crawled lower, over to the edge of the mound he was behind. He peered around, pausing just for a moment, not shooting or doing anything to draw attention to himself. He wanted to get a good look at where the enemy was.

And that hit him hard. He had expected that the water would at least slow the enemy, give his people time to fight for longer. But the leading enemy forces were more than halfway across the water, firing as they moved, even those completely submerged. He had hoped his position would be stronger, that he would have more time before they were upon him, but now he realized that the first ones would be there in just seconds. His people were fighting, most of them at least, and that was good. But no matter how he tried to figure it, they weren't going to hold out for long.

He pulled back, moving again, this time looking for a place to shoot from. He had no real idea how many of his people had been hit, but he suspected it was a large number…and growing every minute. But he knew it didn't matter how many were killed, not really. They would just die a minute or an hour…or a month…sooner. It didn't matter how many of his people were killed. It didn't matter whether he was slain either. Not as long as those who were left kept fighting.

He fired, and then he scrambled to a new place to shoot again. He realized that it was foolish, on one level at least, for him to be here, at such risk…but he didn't care. He *had* to be in the fight. He had engaged in arguments a dozen times with his brother, and he hadn't given in, not one bit. He knew it didn't make sense, but he didn't care. He wanted to fight.

He needed to.

He fired again, striking another bot. But as he pulled back again, he realized the target—and at least a dozen others—were now on his side of the river. That meant his fight was almost over, that soon—very soon—his forces would be surrounded. He looked to the right and left, trying to determine how many of his people were left. He realized he couldn't, not with any accuracy, not with his people as hidden as they were, but his gut told him he'd be lucky if a third were still in position.

He crawled along the back of the pile, trying to find the best cover, the spot the enemy would have to come furthest to reach. He picked a location, moving toward it, and he jerked up and fired again. He ducked back, almost immediately, surprised at how close the enemy was. They were *fast*. He realized it was time…time to order his survivors, however many there were, to escape.

He paused, just for a few seconds, but he realized that every delay, even one measured in seconds, was too much. His people needed every instant they could get to have at least a chance to escape. He had no real idea how much damage they had done, but his guess was, a fair amount. The enemy was spread out, deployed in multiple sections…but he had seen a number of bots that appeared to be down, and even more that had various levels of damage. Added to at least half a dozen that seemed not to make it across the river, he figured his forces did fairly well.

"Retreat!" He shouted the command as loudly as he could, and then he repeated it. "Retreat!"

He knew he should go, too, that he had to take off to have any chance at escaping himself. But he found himself moving toward another firing position...and taking another shot. Then he pulled back and moved to a different location, and he fired again. He knew he was taking crazy chances, that the enemy was almost there, but he couldn't help himself. His people were just that...*his* people...and had to do what he could to give the survivors every chance.

Finally, he realized he had pushed things as far as he could. He turned and he ran...and just then, a bot turned the corner. It was badly damaged, and he turned to fire at it, even as he prepared for death. The robot opened fire—with a single gun remaining—and for an instant he knew he was dead. But its targeting was clearly off. He flipped his own weapon to full auto, and he unloaded on it. And as he fired, he realized that two others were still there, too, and also targeting it. He hoped he could take it out...before more enemy arrived. If he could, he just might escape.

And if not, if more enemy bots made it there before he could disappear...he would die.

* * *

Travis stood, watching...and waiting. He had the largest number of defenders, by far. He knew that Lucas had already fought, though he wasn't sure if his friend—or any of his people—had survived yet. They were out there somewhere, probably trying to make their way back.

Or they were dead.

He was certain that Hugh's people were fighting now. He could hear the sounds, some of them at least. He knew that another 500 people, some of the best ones he had, were

positioned between Hugh and him, spread out and ready to
keep the enemy fully occupied as they advanced. The bots
wouldn't have another free moment, not a step they could
take without fighting. He hoped that would be enough.

When they got to him, they would face the bulk of his
people, thousands and thousands. He knew that would be a
horrible fight, that many, if not all, of his combatants would
die. He genuinely wasn't sure whether his people had a
chance or not...but by God, they were going to fight like
they did. He hoped, at least.

Or they were going to run. He had a small number of
experienced fighters, but the vast majority of them were
green, and most of them had just been given their weapons,
perhaps with one or two quick training sessions. The
forward units, the segments his people had deployed up
ahead—under Lucas and Hugh and several others—were
far more experienced on average, but they all had a large
percentage of inexperienced personnel.

Still, he had the numbers. If they realized their only real
chance was winning the fight, if they could truly understand
that anything save fighting to the end meant death...or
worse...perhaps he had a chance. If they didn't, well
depending on how many ran, and how quickly they did it,
the fight could be over quickly.

"Gather around..." He said the words, almost without
thinking about it. He sounded sure, at least he thought he
did, though in reality, he was anything but. He knew all his
people couldn't hear him, that they were scattered out over
half a mile or more. But it was all he could do. "The enemy
will be here, very soon. I know that many of you haven't
really fought yet, but this battle about to begin...it carries
with it our survival. If we win, we live, at least for a while. If
we lose, we are doomed. Whether you die in the fight or you
run, even get away for a time, remember that this is the
moment. Do we win our first real battle against the enemy?
Do we start the actual war and show them who they have

attacked? Or do we get swept up, do those of you who run, who escape, just to live for a few more hours or days, cost us our victory? I say, we will win…we will fight to the end, and we will destroy this force. Whatever that takes!"

He wasn't sure he believed that. Some moments he did and others he didn't, but he definitely sounded sincere. He pulled his rifle out, held it in his hands. He knew most of his people couldn't see him, and that a large number couldn't hear him either. But he hoped his message would be contagious. One person who heard him, communicating with others, pushing the word out, all along his battle line.

He looked out over the ground in front of him. There was a huge wall of debris, actually several, located one behind the other. Some of it was the result of the bombs, but he had his people out, moving debris, building the best defensive network they could. It was just rubble, of course, but he had placed it in the best positions he could…and he had positioned his heavy weapons carefully and trusted them to his most experienced warriors. His mind raced, thinking of everything he had done, everything he could do. But he didn't come up with anything else. He had done all he could think of, and now it was just a question of doing it. He realized that his life could be measured in minutes, that some—perhaps most—of his men might run, and all he really knew was he wouldn't. He understood, perfectly well, and one thing he was sure of was that he didn't want to be a live captive. He had no idea why the enemy had come, but he was sure he had no desire to learn. Drive them away, take Earth back…or die. Those were the only two choices he allowed himself.

He listened, hearing closer shots. The enemy was moving forward, and now they were breaking into smaller detachments. He hoped they had taken losses, terrible losses, in the previous fights, but so far, he just didn't know. But he would soon.

The shots drew closer, the smaller detachments firing,

but not really slowing the enemy's advance. He knew that was their plan, that they were ordered to strike and pull back, to do as much damage as possible before the bots reached the final position.

He looked around, dug in a little. He was in a good position, well-protected with a solid line of fire, at least where he expected the enemy to appear. The shots were still getting closer, and he knew the enemy would show up at any second.

"Get ready…and good luck to each of you!" He yelled as loud as he could…and just a few seconds later, the first of the bots appeared, just where he had expected. He paused, just for a second, but it was long enough for the enemy to open fire.

He returned it…and the battle was on.

Chapter Twenty-Seven

From the Notes of Hugh McDaniel

Our fight was terrible, brutal. I still don't know how many people I have lost, though my estimates have increased almost by the minute. I am sure at least half of my people are dead, or wounded, but it could be more, maybe much more. I am surprised that I made it away. I stayed too long, or almost too long, but fortune was with me.

I am still pulling back, trying to make it to Travis's position...where I will fight again, where, hopefully, everyone will. That is the only option, our only hope for victory. I just hope everyone realizes that. Winning this fight is our only route to survival, at least to real survival. I am sure of that, and I hope the others are as well.

I truly hope they are.

Just Outside the 67th Avenue Subway Station
Forest Hills, Queens
D + 201 Days

Travis fired his weapon, on full auto, staying slightly exposed for longer than he should. He knew better, but he was also aware that his people were in a battle to the end. If they won, they could worry about ammunition, survival, and everything else…but if they lost, everything would be over anyway. If he was killed in the fight, he knew it would hurt his brother, that it would damage the team they had assembled, but it would still be better—far better—than losing the fight.

He looked out for a second, checking the enemy's position. He'd had his people move as much of the debris as they could, making not just covered positions for themselves, but also places where the enemy would be separated, where their forward units would be exposed, but those farther back would still be obscured. It was the only way he could break them up, give his people time to hit a few of them before the others came forward.

And so far, it was working very well.

He was amazed at how the enemy advanced, almost as though they were trying to present themselves a few at a time. They fired, the bots that came into view, and they killed a lot of his people…but they were also blasted themselves. He imagined that, perhaps, his people were doing well, that their efforts exceeded that expected by the enemy. That was good, of course, but he realized that his adversary was very advanced. His bots fired massive amounts, and they killed dozens of his people. Hundreds. If his people somehow managed to win this encounter, their reward, in the near future would probably be a force several times as large coming back. And the next one would not only be more powerful…it would be better run, too.

He pushed those thoughts aside, wrangling around, taking a few shots from each position before continuing on to the next. His last look told him the forward group of the enemy had been heavily battered, that at least half of them were down, and all the rest damaged. But he could feel the losses inflicted on his own people, too…and he was aware that some of his forces were starting to lose it. There were still only a few who were running, but a fair number were just cowering now, hiding behind their cover and not really shooting anymore.

"Come on…fight! It's our only chance!" He yelled toward several people he saw who were hiding, and he spoke as loudly as he could. He wasn't sure it would make any difference—and it was just as much intended for those still fighting who might be about to run—but it couldn't hurt.

He crawled up, almost to the highest point his cover extended to, and he fired again. At least two thirds of the forward robots were down now…but the second group had just become visible. They were marching ahead, firing with all their weapons, and he barely ducked in time, before a shower of shots, far more than there had been just moments before, ripped overhead.

He paused for a moment, drawing in a few breaths, trying to decide where to go next. He didn't really know how the battle as a whole was going, but he was starting to feel like, just possibly, his people could do it, they could win it, defeat the enemy. He held back on that, tried to prevent himself from going too far with it…but he definitely felt it.

He turned, crawling up the embankment, moving to another spot to fire again. He looked around, saw a fair number of people running now, trying to escape. But it wasn't as many as he had expected. Maybe his people did have a chance. Perhaps they could win after all.

* * *

Qualak-Neerie was becoming concerned. His force, the bots at least, had been hit hard, and almost a third of them had already been destroyed or badly damaged. He had assumed he would lose a few, of course, but a third was way beyond anything he had considered. *Way* beyond.

Worse still, the fight wasn't over. His force was still heavily engaged, and it appeared that the number of enemy combatants was many times what it had been in the previous engagements. He suspected he was close to their home base, but he was still surprised that they had so many people. Admittedly, their expertise seemed less than it had in the previous fights, but there were so many of them, over such a wide expanse, it almost didn't matter. For the first time, he wondered whether he had enough strength to win, if his force could prevail…or if it would be eradicated. The enemy certainly had more strength than he had anticipated.

He wasn't prepared for this, for the sheer number of people he faced. There were at least ten thousand of them, and maybe as many as twice that. He had been ready for one thousand, two or three at the very most. He realized that headquarters, that everyone who had looked at the situation, had severely underestimated the severity of the humans' response. At least in this city…and if here, what of other locations?

He reached down, pulled up the communications array. He had to send his people into the fight. He knew they hadn't really expected to engage in combat—no more than he had—but he suddenly realized that he needed everything he could get. The only alternative was to give up, to break off and return to base with his mission unaccomplished. And that was unthinkable.

"All units…we are needed in the battle. Go forward now, and fight!" He suspected the command would be somewhat surprising to the others, though perhaps not if they were truly paying attention. He knew that his people weren't particularly combat capable, perhaps not even the match of a single robot themselves, but they each had a vehicle, and those were heavily armed.

He waited, just for a few seconds. He knew his people had trouble with their ranking system, that they acknowledged his command—sort of—but that they all had their own opinions of what to do. But he received four blips, acknowledgements, and that meant his people more or less agreed with him.

He focused on his own controls, activating his weapons. He wasn't sure he could win the fight, even with his five Gavicons joining in, but he knew he had to try. The Gavicons were many things, difficult to deal with certainly, but they were not cowards. They would fight, and they would die if need be…especially for Earth, since the early word from the first breeding experiments suggested tremendous success.

He brought his ship around, taking control from the computer. He knew his vessel was powerful, that five of them might make a difference in the battle, but he realized also that they were not indestructible. The enemy's weapons didn't match those his forces possessed, but they were decent…much better than he'd have expected. He wondered how they had put together such a force, so large a group with such good guns. It defied all expectations that his people had, and it made him wonder for a moment, if the planet was as secure as his people expected.

He forced his thoughts to the present, pushing aside all other things, all concerns about the enemy, beyond the battle now raging. He had to win this fight, first, take out the enemy.

Or at least do all he could. And hope that he prevailed. That he survived.

*   *   *

Travis was trying to force away his thoughts about the battle's status, about his force's chances of winning, and just focus on the fighting, one second at a time. But he was really starting to fail at that. He wasn't sure how many of the enemy bots were down, and how many were badly damaged, but he was sure it was a lot of them. Despite his best efforts to hold it back, he was beginning to very seriously consider the possibility that his people really had a chance.

Then, he saw the vehicles.

There were five of them, coming up from behind. They had remained back, at first, but now they were moving forward. He wasn't sure what they were, but his guess— educated, but nothing more—gave him the idea that they were aliens, the real ones, not their robots. He knew that was just a guess, that he didn't even know for sure that actual lifeforms even existed. Perhaps their enemy was wholly robotic. But despite his questions, he realized he was almost sure. And that shook him, considerably.

He had been prepared for a large concentration of enemy force, but he found the possible presence of the opposing side, the *real* side, to be intimidating. Very intimidating. He had known about the vehicles, of course, but they had remained back, out of the earlier fights, and for a while, he had allowed himself to imagine his first thoughts had been right, that they were full of supplies. But that was about to change…he was sure of it.

He scrambled around, climbed to another spot and just looked. He knew he should continue firing, that victory, even against only the robots wasn't secured yet, that he and everyone else had to maintain themselves, to keep fighting. But he was too concerned about the flying vehicles…and then, suddenly, he realized he was right.

The first of them opened fire.

He just looked, stunned by the destructive power being unleashed. The weapons were very powerful, much more so than the guns on the robots. There were at least four high powered rifles, blasting larger bullets at an even faster array than the bots…and there was something else, too, an energy weapon firing every few seconds, and cutting through much of the defensive array, taking out multiple defenders with each shot.

He ducked down, just as the other vessels also opened

fire. The sounds of battle, already loud, increased dramatically, and he could see segments of the wall of cover, the first position of his people, blasted to bits. The heavy guns were bad enough, but the energy weapon was enormously powerful, blasting away whole sections of cover, and killing ten or twelve of his people with each shot, regardless of how protected they were.

His stomach tensed, and he knew many of those who had stayed, who had endured the fight and perhaps even come to anticipate victory, would now run. He had to do something, to prove that the ships weren't invincible either. He didn't know what to do, of course, but he realized he had to take at least one of them down, and quickly.

He jumped, moving down the pile, to a spot he figured would offer a shot. But what good was a shot at one of the ships? He realized he needed to organize a large group, to bring in the heaviest weapons he had, to focus all of the destructive power he could on the vessel, even at the cost of letting up on the bots.

He turned, realizing that he had certain weapons he had considered using, but decided not to. They were too large, too slow for effective combat against the bots. But to fight the vehicles, to bring them down, he knew he needed them.

He called out to a group of his people, telling them to follow him. He had kept a dozen of his best close to him, and at least six or seven of them were still up and fighting. They turned and raced back, climbing over the second line's cover—which he knew would become the new front in just a moment—waving for those he had contacted to follow him. "We need to get the heavy weapons," he shouted, realizing that he had kept those guns hidden from most of his people. Few of them would even know what he was talking about. He had considered bringing them out for the fight, but they were difficult to use, and probably not worth the trouble against the enemy bots.

But the ships were a different matter. He wasn't sure

they would be enough against the vessels, that they would work. He just knew he needed everything he could get. Everything. And they just might be enough.

He climbed up, over the third berm and the fourth…right back to the entrance to the subway station. He was moving quickly, but methodically, too. He knew the worst thing he could do was appear to be running. He was heading back, away from the fight, and that was bad enough. But he didn't think he appeared to be fleeing. He hoped not, at least.

He climbed down into the entrance, checking behind him to confirm the others were still coming. The opening was much better than it had been in the early days, easier to access. Most of the work his people had done was based on survival and defense, but they had managed to find some time to make their living area more accessible. More comfortable, at least a little.

He ran down the stairs, another part of the structure that had been replaced. He turned and walked through another chamber, the largest one. It had been a living area, housing almost two thousand, but now it was a makeshift infirmary, a place where wounded troopers could be brought. There were a couple hundred, he guessed, which was fewer than he had expected. That didn't mean there was a smaller number of injured, just that they hadn't been brought back this far, not yet at least. He tried to imagine just how many of his people had been killed or wounded, but then he slammed down, forced it out of his mind again. There would be plenty of time to think about that later, if his people won. And if they didn't…well, it wouldn't really matter.

He spun around, going down again, another set of stairs, also fixed up, though not as well. He ran across a large area that had been turned into a storeroom, full of food and other essentials. He knew that was going to be a problem soon, too. His people had hunted all over the city, searching for any kind of food that could last, but with almost twenty thousand mouths to feed, he knew even the impressive supplies they had assembled wouldn't last that much longer.

He came to another set of stairs, this one rough, barely usable. He took it slow, holding on to the railing, or at least what was left of it. The room he entered was smaller than the one above, but it was still fairly large. There were boxes and crates all around. They were uneven, spread out...a mess from the operations of the past several days when almost every member of the entire group was armed, and most of the ammunition was taken out. They had other arms depots at some of their alternate positions, but the one in the 67th Street station was by far the largest. It had been seriously depleted by the general arming orders, but there was still a large amount of arms left.

He walked to the back of the room, to a large chamber. It was locked, but he reached down and grabbed the keys from his pocket as he approached the door. He had ordered the heavy ordnance, taken from the ruins of National Guard headquarters, stored there. He opened the lock, and stepped inside, looking around as he did. There were a number of heavy weapons stored there. He looked at the guns he had decided against deploying, some bazookas, and some rocket launchers. He wondered whether he could pull them out, get them into the fight soon enough. He glanced behind him, realizing that he had only brought a few people with him. "Gerry...go back and round up some more people. Get the most experienced ones you can find...but do it quickly!" He exchanged glances with the man, and he turned and raced off. "The rest of you...down here. We need to figure out what we can deploy quickly...and we need to do it fast!"

He pawed through the weapons, trying to decide what he could deploy, and how quickly. He knew he didn't have much time, if he even had any. He wondered what was going on up there, what had happened in the few minutes since he had left. He knew he needed to get some potent weapons into the fight…but he had to do it quickly.

Very quickly.

Chapter Twenty-Eight

From the Notes of Hugh McDaniel

I can see the fight up ahead. I have about twenty-five people right with me, though I am sure a lot more survived from my group. Where they are, whether any have already made it back, or are behind us—or still running—I just don't know. One thing I am sure of, however, is that the small group with me probably won't make any real difference, not alone at least. But that doesn't mean we aren't going in. We are— as soon as we can close the distance. This fight will be to the finish, and honestly, if it is lost, I would rather be killed in it than survive for a few days or weeks.

Of that, I am certain.

Just Outside the 67th Avenue Subway Station
Forest Hills, Queens
D + 201 Days

Hugh moved forward, increasing his pace as he neared the battle zone. He was scared, terrified actually, but he managed to push it aside, to focus on what he had to do. He knew a lot more than anyone else in the whole group, but what was in each of his peoples' heads then was a mystery. Whether they were focused on following him, ready to fight to the end, to die if need be…or whether they would break and run at the last second…it was all a question to him. And he knew he couldn't fault them no matter what they did. They had fought bravely before, but he knew all people had a limit, a maximum amount they could take. He would soon see how many of his followers were ready to come with him and throw themselves right back into the fight.

Hell, he realized…he would see how far he could push himself, how much *he* could fight his fear and drive himself forward.

He saw the line, more or less. His people were manning several rows of debris, clearly organized for the fight. They were falling back from the first one, and in places, the second was under attack…but he could see the ruins of a significant number of bots, too. He felt good, almost at least…but only for a moment.

He watched as something crossed over the sky…and a second later, another one. He knew immediately what it was. The ships that had followed the robots were now moving into the fight. He felt his stomach tense up, and he began to worry about whether they would turn the tide, whether they would tear away his side's chance at victory.

The vehicle he saw was firing, heavy shells and some kind of light-based weapon, too. And they *were* changing the fight, making his forces retreat, even as they had seemed on the verge of victory.

He suspected his tiny group of people, those he had led back from the fight on the river, weren't going to make a difference…and neither was he. He understood that his thinking, his mental acuity, was sometimes very valuable…but right now, his force would either win or lose, and that depended more on factors like firepower and courage. The intellect had already been utilized, and now it was down to firepower…and the ability to stand, to hold on.

"Come on…let's move quickly. The fight has reached its

climax, and every man is needed!" As he'd thought, he wasn't sure his small force would actually make a difference, but he certainly sounded like he did. He didn't know, but he suspected that all those who had stuck with him, remained in his group, would now go into the fight again. And if 25 wasn't a significant number, if it didn't make a difference, well so be it. He couldn't speak for anyone else, but he was sure he would prefer death to defeat, to enslavement.

He pulled his rifle around, holding it in front of him as he increased his pace. He wasn't sure his people would follow him, but he guessed they would. They had come this far, and they had all been fully aware that they were heading back to the final engagement, to what they had to realize was a win or die battle. He thought he was ready for it, at least he seemed to be…but for all the others, all he could do was guess.

He angled his approach, trying to keep the barriers between him and the enemy. He knew that wasn't secure, that at any moment, the bots could break through and open fire on his group. But he figured if he ran, if all his people did, they had a chance to join the defenders at the second or third berm.

And if they didn't, then they would die trying.

*   *   *

Qualak-Neerie flew his vehicle, bringing it down across the defensive barricades, blasting the enemy positions hard. The guns, and those on the other four flying craft, were the heaviest ones by far in his force, and they tore into the mounds of debris, cutting through them and taking out the people hiding behind them. He had realized that the battle might be lost, at least without his direct interference, and so he had ordered the five Gavicons forward…and now it appeared they were turning the tide. He was still surprised at the power of the enemy, though, and he wanted to do everything possible to end the fight as quickly as possible.

His ship, all five of those manned by his people, were top quality, even more capable than the robots were. Moving all five of them forward in a great push was a huge risk, he realized, but one very likely to change the result of the battle. He hadn't expected the need to deploy them, in fact, he had at first been annoyed that he was assigned to accompany the robots at all. It had seemed pointless over-exertion. But now he realized that they were necessary, that the bots needed backup. He was surprised at the size of the human force, and the combat abilities they displayed…but he was sure that sending in his entire force of Gavicons in support would be more than enough. It had to be.

He brought his ship around, coming back, against the rear of the human defenses. His weapons were strong enough to bore through the defenses, to hit the enemy from the other side, but from this direction, they didn't even have to. He could see the humans, climbing up on the defenses, turning in panic as they saw him coming…and he gunned them down.

His mind was disciplined, like those of most of his people, but even as he focused on the mission at hand, he found some doubts creeping in. The enemy forces were far larger than even the most outlandish estimates had been, and they were more effective, too. He had expected a mob, with some guns perhaps, but mostly throwing stones. He was astonished at how many weapons the enemy had assembled, and, relatively speaking, how good they were. His bots were tough, definitely, but the enemy had brought down a large number of them, and they threatened to destroy them all. Even his vehicles, he realized, were not indestructible, and he wondered what would happen if one—or more—of them were shot down. Losing bots was one thing, and bad enough…but having casualties among the Gavicons present, that was quite another thing.

He fired again, blasting the enemy positions hard. He

could see that his ships were making a difference. The humans weren't running...not yet, not most of them at least, but their positions were rapidly being torn up. They were weakened, badly, and many of them had turned to flee...and others had turned their fire against the ships. The firepower greatly exceeded expectations, but from the looks of it, the rounds were not strong enough to penetrate the vehicles...and the battle would not be going on that much longer.

He turned his ship again, bringing it around to one end of the human line. He had gone back and forth several times, but now he was changing his angle, bringing his ship around almost 90 degrees. He would go back and forth along the human line now, behind their main defenses. The first position, the initial berm, was almost devoid of live humans now, so he went for the second one. He blasted the area with his weapons, four heavy rifles and a laser turret...and he guessed he hit at least fifty humans in just a matter of seconds. If the others were doing half as well as he was, he guessed the battle would be over in mere minutes, the quasi-army of humans reduced to a sea of bodies and waves of panicked, fleeing personnel.

He was glad about that...and relieved that the enemy seemed to lack weapons heavy enough to seriously threaten his vehicles. In the end, losing more bots than expected was reasonable...but losing actual Gavicons, that would be terrible.

* * *

Travis stared down the sight for several seconds after the shot was fired. It wasn't his first time in combat by any measure, but he recognized just how serious things were, even more so than it had been moments before. The enemy vehicles, the flying craft were very heavily armed, and they were going to turn the tide, he was sure of it. They already had, in fact…unless he could do something about it. This was the last stand, he realized, and his people would win or lose depending on what happened in the next thirty minutes. He knew that, as well as he had known anything. He just wasn't sure what would happen. He had started to believe just maybe they could win…and then the flying vehicles came in, and everything turned around in just a few minutes. Now, he realized, was the chance to take it back again, to draw victory from the maw of defeat.

But he knew he didn't have much time. Most of the people he had left were almost totally raw, their only training being firing a few shots over the past day or two. The truth was, he just wasn't sure they could hold, even for a few more minutes. He had done everything to remind them that however afraid they were, there was no other hope, that ending up as live prisoners of the invader was almost certainly worse than dying in combat. Still, he understood how people's minds worked, how they could be told the truth, even believe it, and still fail in the end to follow through. He had to do whatever he could…and he had to do it now.

He pulled up the rocket launcher. It was the most powerful weapon his side possessed. He only had three, and each of them had only five reloads. He wasn't sure if the rockets would even hurt the enemy ships…but he knew they were the only way. Either they worked, or the battle would be lost.

He looked up, trying to get a shot at one of the enemy craft. He had never fired a rocket launcher before, not one like this, but he knew no one else had either. He doublechecked, made sure the thing was ready to fire. Then he stared back out, trying to look around for one of the flying vehicles, pulling back every few seconds to avoid enemy fire.

He repeated that, at least ten times, but he couldn't find one of the enemy ships, not close enough to fire. He was getting upset, and he could see that his people's morale was really starting to fray. They had stood up, better than he had expected for sure, but the aerial attack was too much for them. They had returned fire, most of them, taking their shooting from the robots to try to hit the aerial vessels. But those shots were incredibly difficult, and it appeared that the outer casing of the flying ships was too strong for a bullet to pierce.

He wondered if a rocket would do it...or if he was just fooling himself. But he had to try.

He looked out at the others all around. The number of them running had increased three or four fold, but, still, a lot of them were still in position, still fighting. He felt a rush of pride in them...but also fear. He knew they wouldn't hold long, and once the bulk of his forces began to flee, it was over.

He looked up again, seeing one of the enemy ships approaching. It was the best shot he had gotten, but it was still difficult. He almost let it go, continued waiting, but then he saw a group of his people start running. He realized that time was almost up, that he had to take down at least one of the enemy ships, to prove to his people it could be done. Or in another few minutes, most of them would be running.

He jerked the rocket launcher up, wobbling slightly until he got it down on his shoulder. He took a deep breath, and he jerked his body up. The ship was moving across the sky, almost perpendicular to him. It was already past the optimum firing position, and he almost thrust himself back down to wait for another. But he didn't.

He stared, trying to get a fix on the ship. He knew he didn't have long, that the vessel was very fast, and that if he exposed himself for too long, he would draw fire. But he waited, for an extra second...and then he pressed the trigger.

Chapter Twenty-Nine

From the Notes of Hugh McDaniel

I am almost back to the fight. I was racing, moving as quickly as I could…and then I saw something that stopped me for a second. The enemy flying craft had attacked, and they looked like they were going to decide the fight, to defeat any chance my people had. I panicked for a moment, devoid of any ideas how to face the ships, how to win the fight regardless of their attack.

And then, something came up toward one of them.

At first, I didn't know what it was, but then I remembered the few heavy weapons, the ones we had stored in the cellar. That was a rocket…I was sure of it now. Travis must have gotten them, that had to be it.

I didn't know if they would work, if they would make a difference…but there was a chance, and any chance right now seemed like a gift to us.

Just Outside the 67th Avenue Subway Station
Forest Hills, Queens
D + 201 Days

Hugh looked up, watching the rocket. For an instant, he thought it was going to hit one of the enemy ships, but at the last second, the vessel turned away. The shot had missed by perhaps half a second, maybe even less, but it had still missed, and he knew they didn't have many of them. Nevertheless, it was close, and he hoped the next shot would be better, that it would score a hit.

Assuming there was a next shot.

"Come on…let's go. We have to get back to the fight!" He truly felt that way, even though he realized that his 25 weren't going to make a real difference. They might win or lose, but that would depend on the thousands of others, not his small group. But he had to get back, to join the fight. He just had to. Win or lose, he had to be a part of it.

He moved forward, almost breaking into a run. He was still getting used to his shape, the fact that he was in, by far, the best condition of his life. He realized that all of his people might not be able to keep up, but they wouldn't fall too far behind. It wasn't that great a distance to the fight.

He jumped over a small dip in the ground, and then he turned sharply, heading for the third berm. He knew he had to get cover, that if he approached out in the open, he would be killed almost immediately. The enemy ships seemed to fire in the direction they were heading, but there were robots, too, and they were shockingly accurate. His people had learned that already, even before today, and as he moved toward the cover, he could see bodies, hundreds of them.

No…thousands.

He was pleased, however, that his people were still holding out despite the losses—and despite the ships attacking—some of them at least. He knew that wouldn't last much longer though…not unless his people scored a hit on one of the ships. And, of course, it was effective. He didn't know anything about the vessels, and he realized the assumption that one could be taken down by a rocket hit was just pure conjecture. But it was the only hope his people had.

He dove behind the edge of the ridge, taking cover from the enemy bots. They were down behind the first and second berms now, those his people had occupied until minutes ago. They were using the cover, just as his people were, and that gave him some excitement. The robots had not been particularly interested in cover in the previous fights, and he realized that they had lost a fair number, that his people had destroyed enough of them to force them into protection. That wasn't all good, he knew…the enemy would almost certainly fire better from cover than his people, and they would use it better than his mostly green soldiers. But one step at a time, and it was good at least that they had decided they needed it.

He pulled out his rifle and peered up around the pile of rubble. It was made of everything, concrete, bricks, metal…anything his people could pile into a large mound. He was lying on a large chunk of stone, looking out through a small gap in front of him. It was a good spot, a very good one, though he realized that was just luck. He'd just thrown himself behind the pile of rubble.

He aimed and he fired, on full auto, shooting for several seconds. It was dicey he knew, a long time to fire, but his position was very good, and he figured it was worthwhile. He knew he might get shot, that he could die at any time, but he was strangely upbeat. He was aware he had no reason, that his people were fighting for their lives, that they could lose at any time. And that the rockets being fired at the enemy vessels required the greatest luck…both to hit and to cause serious damage. But somehow, part of him at least, felt good…felt excited.

He turned to check on his people. About half of them were still with him, scattered around. The others were probably just out of sight, taking positions elsewhere, but he knew some of them—hell, all of them—could be dead, too. He just didn't know.

He crawled along, looking for another small gap, a place

to fire from. He found a spot, and he brought his rifle up. He hadn't seen or heard another rocket yet. He couldn't see his brother or anyone else with one of the launchers from where he was, and he was becoming concerned. Had Travis been hit? Had all their people with the rockets been taken out? He didn't know, but as important as it was, he realized there was nothing he could do about it.

Nothing except hope…and take his next shot.

* * *

"Goddammit!" Travis hauled back the rocket, checking it out, trying to decide why it hadn't fired. He knew how to use the launcher, he had fired it twice already, but this one didn't shoot. He checked it for a few seconds, but then he realized he didn't have time. More and more of his people were running, and those who were staying were being killed, very quickly. He dropped the rocket and drew another one. He knew he didn't have any to spare, but he knew he had to score a hit, at least one. He had to take out one of the enemy ships. He realized that might be impossible, but he also realized it was his best chance. His only chance.

He checked the new rocket. It looked exactly the same as the other one…but he hoped for the best. He brought it down, staring all around, looking for one of the enemy ships. For a second, there was nothing…and then one scooted out into view. It was moving, very quickly. He knew it would take a perfect shot, even better than the first one, which he had thought for a second was dead on.

He brought up the rocket launcher, looked through the sight. He was breathing regularly, doing everything he could to remain calm, to take the best shot he could. He stared at the ship, moving almost directly toward him. That was good…the closer it got, the better shot he had.

Assuming it didn't spot him and shoot him before he fired.

He watched as it approached. He wanted to shoot, but he didn't. Not yet.

He waited, for probably a second, perhaps even less, and the ship was *close* now. He pulled the trigger, doing all he could to hold steady, to make the shot perfect. And this time, it was.

He wasn't sure if the shot was any better than the first, or it was just the closeness of the target, but the rocket went right for the ship. The whole thing took a fraction of a second, and the explosion was bright, and terrifyingly close. He turned away, pulling down, wondering if the rocket had damaged the enemy vessel or not.

He wanted to look up, but he realized that was dangerous. He crawled along, losing his step for a moment, as he scrambled to another spot. He poked his head up, staring out at the enemy ship.

The explosion had subsided, and the ship was still there. It was farther down from where he was now, and for a moment, he thought it wasn't damaged. But then he saw a trail of smoke behind it…and he realized it was losing altitude.

He wasn't sure he had taken out the vessel, but he had at least damaged it. That filled him with excitement, with the renewed hope that perhaps his people could win the fight. He knew that was a long way, that there were five of the enemy vessels, that the likelihood was still strong that the enemy would win the fight.

But as he watched, the ship went down farther…and it crashed just behind the seconds berm. It didn't explode, at least it didn't look like that to him, but it was definitely down. And that filled him with satisfaction.

He turned toward the others around him, and he saw that they were also excited. He realized the fight was still going on, that it was far from won by either side. He felt satisfaction as he realized he had shot down one of the enemy…possibly one of the *real* enemy.

He shook his head and reached out, grabbing another rocket launcher. He moved over, waving for the others with him to come. He had given himself a few seconds of celebration, but now it was time to get back to work.

To take out another enemy ship.

* * *

"Kilar-Sephola, respond. Kilar-Sephola...respond!" Qualak-Neerie was upset now, perhaps truly unnerved for the first time in a long while. He had known, of course, that his people were at risk, sort of, that one or more of them could be killed, but that had been a theoretical assumption. He had believed that he could lose some robots, certainly, but the idea that any of his actual people could be killed seemed...strange. He had served on a prior expedition, another planet that had failed in its breeding program and despite the fact that it hadn't succeeded, he had to say that the residents, those who lived there, had definitely been *as* advanced than the humans...and probably a bit more, even. Yet, they hadn't killed any of his people. He was truly amazed at some of the weapons the humans possessed. They weren't the equal of his own people's—not quite at least—but they were far better than any of the others his race had fought. The humans were only semi-sophisticated in most ways, but they were very well equipped with weaponry.

There was no response at first, but then he heard a reply. "Yes...I am here." He could tell from the tone that Kilar-Sephola was wounded, perhaps badly. But he was alive.

He brought his ship around, back toward the damaged vessel. He planned to land next to it, to recover Kilar-Sephola, but before he could reach it, he saw humans crawling all around, trying to get to it. His fired his guns, cutting down at least twenty of the people who were out in the open, but then he saw something, out of the corner of his eye.

It was a rocket, launching from behind one of the mounds of debris. And it was targeting him!

He jerked his controls suddenly, pulling his ship away from it. He accelerated harshly, bringing his vessel up higher, even as the rocket ripped through the sky toward him. He jerked hard on his controls, bringing his vessel up, first higher, and then down. The rocket ripped by him, missing by a short distance, and crashing into the second pile of debris. The explosion was severe, and his ship shook from it…but he had survived.

There was no question, though. The enemy had weapons powerful enough to bring down his ships. He knew they had such things, of course, in the early stages of the fighting, but he was stunned at just how much power they still maintained. The forces his people had encountered in the early stages of the operation were considerable, but they enjoyed massive surprise over the enemy, and they had won every fight, quickly. Now, assuming the enemy's ability to seriously resist was gone, much of their forces had gone away, toward the other worlds, leaving a smaller detachment behind.

One that was more than enough to take out any remaining enemy forces. Or at least, should be.

The first shot, perhaps, had been a random event, but his own ship was also almost shot down a few moments later. He was shaken, stunned at the humans, at the weapons they seemed to still possess. He had been surprised enough at what their military had months earlier, but he hadn't expected the civilians to have such ordnance, too.

He realized at once that he had to pull out, that he had to report this to the supreme command. If he stayed, he might get shot down, too…all of his people might. He had no idea how many of the rockets the enemy had, or what else. But he realized that the human militaries had been caught by surprise, destroyed before they could properly mount a real defensive effort. If they still had this type of weaponry, even among their survivors, however…

If the enemy could use the time they had, gather and utilize weapons in significant numbers, assuming, of course that New York wasn't just a major exception…then they could mount a real defense if they were given the chance.

He knew his people's population was small, and that many of them had departed, headed off to the other worlds. The situation wasn't ideal, of course, but he knew they had to do everything possible to find a match, a species that worked…and they were running out of time. The humans were the most likely, perhaps, but they weren't the only ones, and his people didn't have the time to wait.

He knew the Gavicons left on Earth were only a portion of that remaining, and that the overall total was far less than it had been years before. It was enough, he was sure of that, even facing the enemy's resurgence, but he suddenly realized his people had to pay attention, to really pay attention. If they identified the spots where the foe was strong and they hit them hard, *really hard*, they could still defeat them soundly.

He looked back at the crashed ship. There were hundreds of humans there now, scouring all around it. He wondered whether Kilar-Sephola has still alive…and he hoped not. It was a somber occasion when any of his people were killed, but he imagined it would be even worse if one was captured alive.

He thought about taking another run, coming in at him, targeting him. It was upsetting to consider killing one of his own people…but perhaps even more so letting him be captured. But just as he reached out and grabbed the controls, he picked up another rocket, coming for him. He couldn't stay any longer. He had to break off…and if the enemy followed up, chased down the bots, he would have to abandon them all, and take off with his three remaining companions.

Run. He would have to run. And come back with enough force to truly crush the enemy.

Chapter Thirty

From the Notes of Hugh McDaniel

I can't believe it! The enemy is actually pulling back, retreating! It was what I had hoped for, what I had spoken of when I talked to the others…but only now, I have come to realize how little I had expected it. In actual fact, it seems I was sure we were going to lose, that we were going to die, even if I told myself other things.

Now comes the difficult part. I have to get everyone charged up, send them after the enemy. I know this will not be popular, that they will want to stop, to fall to their knees and give thanks. But as long as the enemy is still there, we *have* to follow them. Our fight is not this one, nor the next…our goal is nothing less than to save the world. And to win, in the end, to truly *win*, we have to destroy them all…every one of them.

Starting with those that are still here, running away now, but still standing.

Just Outside the 67th Avenue Subway Station
Forest Hills, Queens
D + 201 Days

"Travis…we have to pursue them. We have to take out as

many as we can before they escape. Anything we allow out of here will only be back, with more strength next time." Hugh had just found his brother. He hadn't even said hello to him yet, not really, though he was glad he had survived…very glad. So far at least.

"Hugh, I'm glad you made it." His brother was almost as serious as he was, that was clear…but his first words were of joy that Hugh had survived.

Hugh stopped for a moment, aware of his oversight. "I'm sorry, Travis, you know I am thrilled you are alive…but we *have* to destroy as many of those bots as we can, right now, before they get too far away. We have to fight *every* day, *every* hour, *every* minute…until we have won…or we are all destroyed. There is no alternative…none." He paused just for a few seconds, and then he said, "I am glad you made it though. Truly, I am. More than I can express." He was sincere, totally, but then he turned and looked out toward the crashed enemy ship, and almost immediately returned to his former topic. "Right now, though, the most important thing we need to know is what is in that ship." He jerked his arm over toward the vessel's ruins. It was surrounded by his people, but no one had advanced yet to try to investigate it further. He understood some concern, but that was going to end now.

"I agree with you, Hugh…totally." Travis turned toward the ship, staring out at it for a few seconds. "Let's get over there and see what it is."

Hugh nodded. He had an idea what it might be—and he assumed Travis shared that opinion—but he didn't really know, not yet at least. He was determined to correct that.

The two of them headed over, cautiously but quickly, shouting out commands for everyone they encountered to keep fighting. There were already a large number of his people around the ship, and more coming every second. But then he saw something else, another of the vehicles closing from above. That was a good sign, at least that the damaged ship *was* valuable…but it was also bad. He knew at once that some more of his people were going to die. He just wondered if enough would survive, if they would hold out, or if the other ship would destroy them all, and rescue the damaged vessel.

And the pilot he guessed was inside.

He moved over, accelerating his pace. He glanced at his brother, realizing that he was doing the same thing. It occurred to him, for a moment, that they were right next to each other, that one shot could kill them both in a second. He knew they should separate, that they should come in from different headings…but he didn't do anything. He understood, but he wanted his brother close to him then, even at the expense of what made sense.

He looked up at the enemy ship, the live one coming in. No, there were four coming in…three behind the first one. Then he saw the enemy fire. At least twenty friendlies went down almost immediately, and more seconds later as the other ships went through. For an instant, he feared his people would run, that they would flee…even though he knew that likely meant death for them. But despite the fact that some did run, many remained, and more came forward. He felt something, not joy exactly, but satisfaction…and he raced forward, knowing that at any time he could be killed—that both of them could be killed. But he didn't care, not at that moment.

He just wanted to reach the ship, to confirm that it indeed held one of the enemy, the true enemy.

And he wanted to see if—he, she, it?—was still alive.

*   *   *

Qualak-Neerie brought his ship up to full speed, the other three of them following fairly close behind. He realized he was leaving the bots behind, that they would make it or not, depending largely on what the humans did. But that didn't matter, not anywhere near as much as losing any more of his people would.

He realized that Kilar-Sephola was lost. He had tried to reach him again, but his radio seemed to have given out. He flew by, one last time, and he saw that the ship was surrounded, by hundreds of the enemy. If they had been less well equipped, if he wasn't concerned that he, or another of his people, would also be shot down, he would never have given up on his subordinate.

But he *was* worried. He was afraid...and he knew that he had to get back, to report on the nature of the enemy and its weapons. And hopefully, to lead back a force strong enough to utterly obliterate the human defenses.

He looked behind him, toward the crashed ship, and he found himself hoping that Kilar-Sephola was dead, that he wouldn't be captured alive. But whatever the situation was, he realized he didn't have any way to get to him. He felt strange about leaving him, but he realized that he didn't have any choice. If he went back in, if his other four ships attacked again, they could all end up shot down...and he had to report back, of that much he was certain.

He glanced at the robots, now showing only on his instruments. They had fallen far behind, but they could keep up all day and night, if the enemy allowed them to get away. But if they didn't, if they pursued relentlessly, he suspected the robots, all that was left of 200, would all be destroyed.

He blasted his thrusters, pulling up away from the enemy. He could see some missiles launched after him, but they were too far back now, and they fell further behind every second. He turned and stared ahead. He was moving at high speed right now, and he would be back to base in an hour. He didn't have any real idea whether Kilar-Sephola was dead or not...but he knew what he would report.

And he was sure everyone else present would confirm the same thing.

* * *

Hugh ran across the last few meters, slowing down slightly as he approached, but not much. He understood that the enemy—if that's even what was in there—could have impressive weaponry, but he had also not seen anything active since it had crashed. That wasn't certain, perhaps, but he decided it was good enough.

He had hundreds of people surrounding the vehicle now, but still, none had advanced the final few feet. That seemed strange to him, since he perceived any danger as being just as great from ten or twenty feet away, but he also understood it…more or less.

He didn't share it though, and he raced right to the vehicle, his rifle in his hands, ready to fire. He knew that the enemy—if there was one, and he was alive—was possibly the most dangerous thing he had ever encountered, but he told himself if the alien was truly deadly, he would know that by now. The other enemy ships had killed hundreds of his people, but he hadn't seen a single shot from the one that had crashed.

He climbed up, not really sure whether he was confident or cocky, but a quick look behind him told him Travis and several others were right behind. He spun back around and stared at the ship that was now under his legs. He was partly ready to die at any second, but he pushed that aside and he scoured the craft, looking for a way in. It looked very much like what he assumed it was would. It wasn't exactly like anything he had seen before, but it wasn't all that different either. And then his eyes found a spot that looked like it was split open slightly.

He reached out for it, realizing what a chance he was taking, but doing it anyway. He could tell that at least six of his people had come up on the craft now, all pointing their guns toward it. He paused for just a second, and then he set his own gun down. If he was going to do it, now was the time.

He reached out, touched the split open area. He put his fingers inside, half expecting to lose them, and he pulled hard. At first, nothing moved. But Travis leaned in next to him, and he moved his own hands down. With two of the pulling—hard—it began to sway. At first, it moved just a little, but then, suddenly, it swung open. Hugh and Travis both stumbled backwards, and they fell off of the ship. They careened down and landed hard. Hugh wasn't sure if they were badly hurt or not, but his first instinct was to call out to the others still on the ship, to remind them to try and take any occupant alive.

"Alive…anything in there, we need it alive!"

Then he turned, and he tried to rise. He was injured, of that he was sure, but he managed to get up, and he did his best to ignore the pain. He turned and looked around for his brother. He was also getting up, and while he, too, looked battered, he seemed to be in decent condition. Hugh was grateful they both seemed more or less okay, and he turned his attention back to the ship. He reached up, trying to pull himself back, and he realized that while he didn't think he was *badly* injured, he was fairly scuffed up. There was pain just about everywhere, and he had trouble pulling himself up. He turned toward Travis, who was also having a difficult time…but then he suddenly, he managed to haul himself up. He climbed up—barely—and he turned back toward Hugh, trying to figure a way to help his brother up…when things went crazy.

Hugh heard it first, and he scrambled again to climb the rest of the way up. He just made it up in time to see what was going on.

First, there was no doubt. There *was* an enemy in the ship…and a *live* one. It appeared to be injured, perhaps badly. But it *was* alive…and armed.

And it was firing. It shot two of his people, then a third.

By then, he had at least ten of them up on the ship, and he was almost sure they would fire. But they didn't. Three of his people jumped on the…creature…and tried to take it down. One of them was thrown clear, falling off the vessel as Hugh and Travis had, and another stumbled across the ship, but managed to hang on. Meanwhile, three others had jumped on top, and were struggling to hold on.

Hugh was sore, still not sure just how injured he was…but he lunged forward, throwing himself into the fight. He reached in and grabbed the enemy's gun, at least what appeared to be it, and he wrestled it, trying to take it from the creature. He wasn't able to, not quite, but he managed to keep its angle pointed away from any of his people…until Travis grabbed ahold as well, and the two of them finally tore it from the alien's grip.

He tossed the thing, and he leapt back into the fight, with Travis at his side. The alien—there was no doubt that's what it was—was messy. There was liquid all around. Was it blood, or something like it? Or was it just something he just didn't understand. He thought the thing was badly wounded, but he wasn't entirely sure. It was still strong…there were at least five of them on it, and they were barely holding it down.

The thing was screeching, making some kind of noise that seemed very…alien. But then, as two more of his people came into the fight and grabbed on, it started to weaken. Hugh didn't know what condition it was in, or what language it was speaking. He didn't know much…except that his people were struggling to take a prisoner, the first one anyone had taken.

And then it said, in more or less clear English, "Release me!"

Hugh had expected that the enemy could communicate with humans in some manner, that they had one method or another of…speaking. But the almost perfect sound of its voice took him by surprise.

"If you can understand us, you surrender! Stop resisting!" The words came from his mouth, almost without forethought. He was still struggling to hold the creature, and it was weakening, slightly. "Your people have left you behind. You're outnumbered, thousands to one. Surrender or die!" He wasn't certain that it understood him, but somehow he expected that it did.

It twitched again, putting forth another great effort to break free…and it almost worked. But Hugh and the others held on, and then, suddenly, most of the creature's effort drained away. Hugh realized that the soupy mixture was indeed from a wound, and it was getting worse. The creature lunged again in a few seconds, but its effort was much slower, and it was shorter, too.

"Surrender!" Hugh spat out the word, and then he did it again. "Surrender!" But he got no response, and in a few seconds, the alien stopped all of its efforts and dropped to the floor of his ship.

For an instant, Hugh was concerned that it was a trick, and effort to fool them into releasing it. But he quickly realized that wasn't the case…and then he began to worry that the creature had died.

Chapter Thirty-One

From the Notes of Estle-Starric

I can't believe it, not really. And yet I must. I sent 200 robots and five Gavicons to eradicate the human cell of strength. I anticipated losing some of the bots, of course, perhaps even forty or fifty by the time it was all done. But I lost *all of them*, every one…and one of my own people, too.

That is unfathomable, far greater than our losses in any of the fights against the enemy's combat units. Admittedly, those were a bit different, and we did have incredible surprise on our side. But still…to lose all of the bots, and one of my own people as well? It was unimaginable…and yet true.

I must put intense effort into this, do whatever is necessary to crush this before it goes any farther. It will take a bit of time, several weeks, perhaps. We have sufficient forces, of that I am certain, but we don't have them all in one place, not enough to assemble the force I will send.

I am certain that a week or two will not be a problem, and it is far more important that we strike hard and eliminate this force of humans as thoroughly as possible. There are other signs of problems in different places, but nothing as severe as in New York. Once that force is destroyed, we will move on to the others…and we will bring this planet truly under control.

Gavicon City
Approximately Twenty-Five Miles West of the Ruins of Washington
D + 204 Days

"Qualak-Neerie, I mean what I am about to say most profoundly. I accept what you have told me, and I do not blame you for the occurrences on the mission. But I expect you to be absolutely honest with me in every way. In *every* way." Estle-Starric spoke slowly and clearly. He was being totally honest. He didn't know if his subordinate was at all to blame for what happened, but he was willing to let it go, as long as Qualak-Neerie devoted himself completely to the return mission. Because he was going to send him back again, in command of a much larger force, one powerful enough to take out the enemy completely.

"I have been utterly honest with you, Estle-Starric. I swear." Qualak-Neerie did sound honest—and a bit upset, too, even confused. Estle-Starric had known that his subordinate hadn't considered the mission to be a big deal. In fact, he had thought he hadn't considered it worthy of his talents and ability. Not at the start at least.

Now, of course, his opinions had changed significantly.

"I believe that, Qualak-Neerie, and for that reason, I intend to send you back, at the head this time of a truly large force. We underestimated the enemy...we will not do that again. You will lead the force there once it is assembled, and you will crush the humans, throughout the city. You will break all resistance, and you will bring the survivors back...for use in the second phase of the plan. The initial segment is working so far, very well indeed, and I am becoming ever more confident that we will be ultimately successful. We must crush any resistance now...so we can expand the effort if it is successful."

"Yes, Estle-Starric. I thank you for your confidence…and I promise there will be no foul ups this time. I will destroy all of their resistance, and I will bring the survivors back…in chains." He sounded sincere, and Estle-Starric nodded. He wasn't sure about his subordinate's initial efforts, but he was sure that he wanted to clear his name. That was an opportunity he was being given. If he was successful, if the mission went well, the preliminary operation would be forgotten. He had almost decided to go himself, to gain that glory for his own…but it wasn't appropriate. He was the planetary director, and he had to remain in the city and supervise the breeding operation. The glory of the New York effort—and the other, smaller ones that would follow—would have to go to his subordinates.

"Go now…rest. Tomorrow we will begin organizing your force. We will send enough to New York to eliminate everything there…I can promise you that."

Oh yes…he would send a truly massive force, one the enemy couldn't hope to withstand. He would crush them, completely.

*   *   *

Hugh stared through the screen, looking at the alien creature. He was still amazed his people had taken it alive—and kept it living, so far, at least. It had taken some effort to figure out the alien's make up and chemistry. Actually, most of that was still a mystery, as were its wounds. Hugh hadn't really expected to take a living—and wounded—enemy captive. He realized now, he hadn't even anticipated surviving the battle. But his people had won, and they had taken a prisoner.

For now, at least. Its condition seemed to be worsening, and he was very concerned it would die. He had thought about trying to help it in some way, but every time anyone entered the small compartment where they had imprisoned it, it fought back. It hadn't spoken to them since they had taken it, hadn't slept…it just sat in its cell, staring back, and attacking anyone who entered. They finally had it restrained, all four of its…arms, he guessed…chained, and its legs restrained. He wasn't sure its restraint wasn't making its injuries even worse, but it was the only way they could keep it in place.

He had come back to try again, to try and communicate with it. He hated the creature, of course, as he assumed all his people did, but if there was any way to resolve the issue, to make some kind of peaceful resolution—as unlikely as that seemed—he had to try.

"I know you understand me. And I will not lie. I despise you, all of you, as do all of my people. But if we can resolve this somehow, come up with some kind of resolution, I am prepared to discuss it with you. And I will also offer you medical assistance once again. You must stop resisting…and assist us in helping you. You are quite a bit like my people in some ways, but vastly different in others. I'm afraid we do not have the ability to help you without your aid, or at least without you attacking anyone who comes to try." Hugh despised the alien, blamed it for the virtual destruction of his race…but he knew his options were severely limited. His people had won the recent battle, yes, but they had lost over 2,500 people killed, and more than 1,500 wounded, many of whom he knew would die, especially with his general lack of medical supplies. It galled him even offering medical assistance to the enemy when so many of his own people were virtually doing without, but he knew he had no choice. If there was a chance—any chance—of reaching some kind of resolution, he knew he had to do it.

But as he looked at the enemy, silent, apparently staring back at him, but not communicating in any way, that hope, however vague, vanished entirely. He suddenly knew there wasn't any outcome, save his people's utter slavery…or somehow winning the conflict, however unlikely that seemed. And there was no chance that the enemy was going to tell him anything.

That realization stiffened him...it made him want to kill the alien. He stood where he was for perhaps fifteen seconds, feeling hostility take over his body, a desire to open the door, to attack his prisoner. But just for a moment. He regained control over himself, and he remained where he was, staring at the alien. After another thirty seconds, he stared again at his prisoner, aware that he was badly injured, that he was probably going to die...and he said, simply, "I know you won't believe this, that you will think I am crazy...but I wanted to tell you, while you're still alive, that my people are going to endure. We're going to fight your people to the end, and we're going to destroy you...whatever it takes." He realized how insane he was, how crazy his assertion must be. But he meant it. Whatever it took, whatever he had to do, he was going to see it done. Somehow.

He stared at the alien, his eyes locked on his enemy's, at least what he assumed were the eyes. He looked for a long while...and then he started laughing. He wondered if the alien knew what he was doing, or if even he did. He never answered that question, but he kept it up, for a long while. Then he turned and looked away from the enemy. He knew somehow that the alien wasn't going to tell them anything, that he would die first.

And if he wanted to die, let him die.

He stared at his enemy for another few seconds...and then he turned and walked away.

*   *   *

"I wanted to have all of you here, to discuss our next options." Hugh spoke somberly. It had been a day since he had last seen the alien prisoner. He knew the captive wasn't going to give in, wasn't going to yield at all. He had come to understand that he couldn't really use his perceptions of humanity to judge the aliens. In truth, he knew almost nothing about them. But he had one bit of knowledge that he was certain about now. There was no hope of any resolution, of any type of satisfactory solution with them. It was either find a way, somehow, to destroy them…or else accept the fact that mankind would be enslaved forever.

He knew he, at least, would never accept that, not while he was alive.

The alien seemed to be worse, at least according to the reports he had received. He had thought about trying to force some aid to him, to try to save his life, but between his continued resistance and the general lack of knowledge his people had on the enemy's anatomy, he suspected it wouldn't work, even if he did. He was fairly certain the alien would die, if not from his injuries, then probably from a lack of food or water. He had seen that both were provided—at least what his people considered food—but the alien hadn't touched any of it. He could only assume that he needed them, but again, he didn't really know.

"We won the last battle, though 'won' is a difficult statement to make when we have lost as many people as we have. We can draw some satisfaction from it, surely, but we also have to accept the reality that the enemy is obviously much stronger than us. They lost only because we managed to assemble a greater force than they had expected…and I believe we can be certain they will come back, soon and with much larger strength. Much larger. And I will state right now that I do not know how we can defeat that. I just know we must."

Hugh had thought about what to say, about how to stir his people into truly focusing, into accepting that the battle they had won, was nothing but a starting point, an almost irrelevant blip to the enemy. No doubt they had expected to win, and his people had scored an unanticipated victory…but he knew for a fact the result would be a new assault, and one far deadlier. He had thought about how to deal with that, how to defeat them, but he had come up blank. He didn't really expect his people to come up with anything, either, but he figured it was worth an effort.

"There's something else I think we need to consider." It was Lucas, which took him by surprise. He had been dedicated and reliable since the beginning, but he hadn't expressed much in the way of an opinion...until now. "I agree we need to figure a way to survive here...but we also need to reach out, to connect with people in other locations, and perhaps most of all, to find the enemy. If we simply remain on the defensive, we will definitely lose, eventually if not the next time. However outclassed we are, we have to begin attacking the enemy, or at least, getting some real knowledge on them. We have a single prisoner, who it seems is dying. And we haven't been able to get anything from him beyond the obvious fact that there is a living enemy force. That is definitely worthwhile knowledge, but now we need to take it further. I'm not saying we have much of a chance, but let's be honest...we already know that, all of us do. But whatever chance we can cobble together, it involves more than just staying here and trying to fend off ever greater assaults."

Hugh looked back toward Travis, and then he stared at Lucas. "You're right, Lucas...absolutely right. We do need to take the effort to the enemy, to try to fight them, somehow." He felt strange, aware he should have said that, realized that he had to think of some way to strike at the enemy and not just repulse their assaults. "And we need to come up with another way to face the next enemy assault, too. If we stand as we did, if we face them the way we have, they will destroy us...and whatever we send out to attack the enemy will be alone."

Travis had been silent, but now he spoke up. "You're both right. We can't even consider staying as we did, fighting the same way, even if we manage to recruit more people. If I was the enemy, I would send a truly massive force next time…and we need to come up with some way to defend against it…and no, I don't have any real ideas. But I also agree that we need to reach out, to extend the fight beyond New York, somehow."

Hugh sat and listened, agreeing with all of it. He wasn't sure what he could do, for either of them truly, but he recognized that was the effect of being in the position they were in. He had to stop thinking about the chance of success, which was never going to be good. He just had to come up with the best options, whatever they were.

"We don't know where the enemy is, at least not with any level of assurance, but the approach trajectory of the attackers, and the retreat direction as well, at least as far as we could follow it, suggests they are located to the south, possibly in the general area of the ruins of Washington. So, I suggest that we form a group, a fairly large one, to move out, down in that direction, to find the enemy. We are just working on a purely speculative assumption about their location, and it may take a considerable time to find any real signs of them. If they are near Washington, of course, it will go more quickly, and if they are farther away it will take longer, but I don't see any other way."

He looked up, exchanging glances with Travis and Lucas and a number of others as well. They all nodded, more or less, though everyone seemed uncomfortable. The ferocity of the battle of a few days prior combined with the hard reality of what was likely to come, and it drained away at the largely made up nature of their hope. Pursuing a nearly hopeless battle was difficult enough when one leaned on largely made up chances, but now his people, those present in the room at least, were receiving a healthy dose of reality.

"I agree, Hugh. Maybe 500 total in the group. It will be difficult, no doubt, and dangerous, but I agree the Washington area is the correct place to start looking. But what do we do with the rest of our people? How do we get them ready for...whatever is coming?" Travis looked around at the entire group, but Hugh could tell the question was mostly directed at him.

He was silent for a moment, trying to think of something—anything—to say. Finally, he looked up and said, "I don't know, Travis. We will send out groups to search the city, more even than we have before, really tear it apart, for any weapons, and any additional people we can find. We will spend all the time we have, however much that is building up, getting ready. We will connect as many subway stations as we can, expand the areas where we can come out and go back in, do everything possible to give them a hellish fight." *And quite probably, die.* He didn't say that part, but he thought it.

Travis nodded. "Yes, I guess that's all we can do. Maybe...just maybe...it will be enough." He didn't sound like he believed it, but Hugh saw no reason to challenge it. He didn't believe it either...but he didn't have any other options.

Chapter Thirty-Two

From the Notes of Estle-Starric

I have just made a decision, one that will delay the attack on the enemy for at least a week, possibly as much as two. I could have sent over one thousand bots—and twenty of my people—out, as early as tomorrow, but I want even more to go, two thousand robots and at least fifty of our people. Honestly, I realize that this is likely far more than is needed, but the more we send, the greater the size of the force, the quicker will come the victory…and the lower our losses will be. And, honestly, I don't have enough forces to keep this entire planet under control, certainly not if I lose too many of them. Better to crush them utterly, and put this sorry episode behind us, in the other cities where there are problems right after New York. We will end the entire problem, and we will do it now.

That shouldn't be too difficult. The enemy was definitely superior to what I expected, but a continued review of the documentation confirmed that we did inflict significant damage on them. For a few moments, I was prepared to send the smaller force, to take immediate advantage of the enemy's condition, but then I decided that a week would not make that much difference…to the enemy at least. But for us, that small delay will allow a more than doubling of the force we send. Better to wait for the greater force, to completely crush them.

There is another reason as well. The test cases are coming along very well. Very well, indeed. In another week or two, if the fetuses survive, they will have reached the longest period we have seen on any planet. And they are in by far the best condition they have on any world. I was always optimistic, but now I am truly hopeful. I am also far more determined to do what I must to ensure that we retain control over this planet, and these people.

Gavicon City
Approximately Twenty-Five Miles West of the Ruins of Washington
D + 208 Days

"Qualak-Neerie, your force will be ready to depart in approximately one and a half weeks. I know that is later than you had expected, but I want to send the largest force possible with you. To that end, I have sent for both robots and more of our people from other areas of the planet. You will command a truly large force, Qualak-Neerie, at least two thousand-five hundred robots, as well as nearly fifty of our own people. That is truly enough—far more than enough—for you to crush enemy resistance, and to bring back the survivors en masse. I am entrusting this immense force to you, greater even than any of those that were deployed against the enemy military. I am confident you will handle everything well…and that you will take the opportunity to crush any opinions about you from the last operation that are less than…perfect."

In point of fact, Estle-Starric wasn't entirely certain about his subordinate's performance in the disastrous operation, and he had almost replaced him, especially when he had increased the size of the force so much. But he knew Qualak-Neerie well, and he was sure of his ability. To be brutally honest with himself, he wasn't sure he would have done any better with anyone else, and quite probably worse. Despite his calm demeanor about the brutal defeat, he had to admit to himself that he would have been just as shocked as Qualak-Neerie at the events that had unfolded...and very possibly just as defeated.

"Thank you, Estle-Starric, for your great and sustained confidence." Qualak-Neerie's voice was clear, and despite the fact that Estle-Starric suspected his subordinate believed only some of his confidence, he knew he had no choice but to express thanks. Indeed, whatever inner thoughts Qualak-Neerie had, Estle-Starric was sure there *was* some sincere appreciation there. Qualak-Neerie was very aware he could have been replaced, and that would have only increased the shame from it all. "I will make every effort to lead the mission well, and I will not allow the enemy to...escape."

Estle-Starric nodded. He had no doubt that his subordinate had learned a lesson the first time. He certainly had. The humans were weaker than they were—much—but they were apparently a race that was significantly more violent than any of the others his people had engaged. He, himself, acknowledged that, which was one reason why he was sending so much force.

"Go, prepare yourself, Qualak-Neerie. Consider all you learned from the first effort, and prepare to lead the larger force." It was a true statement, but it was also a way to make his subordinate leave. He was concerned about New York, about the operation that he had planned, but he was even more focused on the breeding program. It was going well, far better than it had on any other planet where it was tried. He wasn't quite ready to accept that it would work, that his people's effort that had gone on now for centuries, was actually going to be successful...but he was very close.

He returned Qualak-Neerie's salute, and he stood still while his subordinate left the room. Then, he followed him out...heading to the facility that housed the humans, 1,000 of them, each containing a Gavicon fetus. They were the first of his race that had reached this far in over two hundred years, and they were strong and healthy.

They are the first that would actually be born, he told himself. And he almost believed it.

* * *

"Okay…okay, but you have to promise me you will take care, that you will do all you can to stay alive." Hugh and Travis had been arguing for days about who should go with the forces heading south, and who should remain with the rest of their people, most of their people, actually. They had both wanted to go with the smaller force, to head south and just maybe find the enemy. But they knew one of them had to remain. Keeping their people alive was the most important job they had, and probably the most difficult. Hugh had known that Travis was the better prepared for the journey south, but he had still argued, for a while at least. But finally, he had given in.

"Thank you, Hugh. You really are the best one to remain. Honestly, if only one of us survives, it is far better it's you. We both know that. And if our main group doesn't survive, the expeditionary force will likely be lost as well…if not immediately, then very soon."

Hugh felt the urge to argue, but he didn't. Travis was hugely important, he was aware of that, but both of them knew that if it came down to a choice, he was the most valuable. That kind of thought made him uncomfortable for sure, but he realized the situation was too desperate for anything but absolute truth.

What he wasn't sure about was whether staying was any safer—or even as much. Going to the enemy's base, at least what they thought might be, seemed the most dangerous, but he had some idea what he expected the enemy to throw at his people back home, too. In truth, he knew the odds were bad everywhere, but he was also aware that he couldn't think of anything better to do.

"I want you to take the best crew you can with you, though. I mean the *best*. I will have more people here, *many* more, but if you run into anything, you will need the most capable fighters you can get." That was mostly true, but what he didn't say was he wanted his brother to have as strong a force as possible, in case he survived and the main grouping, the one he himself would command, didn't. He was far from certain that wouldn't happen.

Far from certain.

"I will select a fair number of experienced fighters, but I will leave a good number as well." Travis paused for a moment, and then he continued. "Not that we have that many left anyway."

He paused a moment, and Hugh knew he was thinking about those they had already lost.

Travis continued, "I will leave tomorrow, or at the worst case, the day after." Unspoken, but known to both of them was the fact that if his people didn't leave before the enemy came back, they would get caught up in the battle…and they had to begin doing something besides sitting in place and trying to deflect the enemy's push. They had to strike out themselves.

"Travis…I just want you to know, this whole thing has been almost unbearable, and having you here has been a large part of what has made it endurable." Hugh was generally calm, almost mysteriously so most of the time, but right now he was very close to losing control. He knew, as he suspected Travis did as well, that the chances of them seeing each other again, of both surviving the coming days, were not good.

"I agree, Hugh. I could never have made it this far without you. I know things don't look good, but please, don't give up, not as long as you draw breath into your lungs. There is always a chance…for both of us."

Hugh nodded, knowing what his brother said was true...even if it didn't feel that way. Finally, he just said, "You should start selecting your team now...that way you might get some sleep tonight."

Travis nodded, and then he reached out and embraced Hugh. They would see each other again before he left, of course, but it was possible this would be the last time they were alone together.

Perhaps forever.

* * *

"Let's check this out. It looks like something might have...landed...here." Gavin Sanders spoke quietly, but he was clearly intrigued. He was leading out one group, one of the first sent out to inspect for, well, anything. He was looking mostly for weaponry, he knew, but he was willing to bring just about anything back. He had already found food, some of it probably still at least edible, and he'd sent back a messenger to let the people know about it.

He was close enough to the command structure to know that the food supply was getting dangerously low, and any more of it would be useful. But he was aware enough of the enemy threat, of the probability that they would be back very soon to understand that weapons were the most important thing.

And he hadn't found much of that yet...just a couple of pistols and a few knives.

"Roger, Gavin...you heard him. Let's go down into there and search." Mike Timmons was one of his best people...his very best actually, probably even a better fighter than he was. Most of the others were average. In all honesty, between the losses in the recent battle and those selected for Travis's expedition, the quality of their forces had declined considerably. But he knew that didn't matter, that all of their people would have to perform...if they were to have any chance at all.

Gavin stood atop the entrance to the building, watching his people climb inside. It took a while, but all twenty of them made it down. Then he turned, looking behind him out onto the street for a moment before he followed them down.

He looked around, realizing that the ruins were different from most of the others. He was out to the east of the city, in Yonkers he thought, and most of the buildings, while badly damaged, were in moderately better shape than those in the city.

Except the few he was climbing down into. These were all torn to the ground, and the insides were ripped to shreds. They were in much worse shape than the others all around. It occurred to him that something had hit them, a plane perhaps. He knew that probably meant that nothing useful had survived there, but he decided to check anyway.

He worked his way forward, back toward the front of his group, and he stared ahead. He realized he was right. It was a plane, at least the ruins of one. He reached down and scooped up a piece of shiny silver metal, and he could see more of them just ahead. He stumbled and almost fell, but he caught himself at the last minute.

"Stay back…all of you. It's really torn up in here." He turned toward Mike and he said, "Let's see if we can work our way down, just the two of us. We have to see what is in here if we can." He knew there was probably nothing of value down there, just the shattered remnants of the plane, and the building it had crashed into, but he was curious. And despite the broken down nature of the building and the bits and pieces of what appeared to be plane fuselage, he noted it didn't look like there had been any kind of explosion. That didn't mean that anything the plane had carried necessarily endured, but he wanted to see. He suddenly had a strange feeling, and he realized it was a military vehicle.

He turned toward Mike, who nodded and began to move. He started down himself. The floor was torn apart just ahead, and there was a huge hole in the floor. He pressed his foot down hard, checking every step for its security before continuing on. He could see his companion doing the same. They made it forward about fifteen feet, and then they reached an opening. The entire floor ahead was gone, and as he looked down, he could see metal, and a lot of it.

It was about fifteen feet below his level, and he called back, asking for a rope. One of his people came forward with it and handed it to him. He took it and gestured for the man to go back. Then he turned toward Mike and nodded. He looked around, finding a solid place to hang the rope, and he tied it tightly. It was firmly in place, at least as far as he could tell, and after one more look at Mike, he grabbed it and began to drop.

Before the attack, he doubted he would have been able to lower himself so far, but the past six months had been brutal, and he was much stronger than he had been. It wasn't exactly easy, but it wasn't all that difficult either. When he landed, he looked up to Mike and gestured, and his companion lowered himself even more easily.

He turned around, looking at what was now, clearly, a damaged plane. He realized almost at once that it *was* a warplane, a large one. It had crashed but hadn't exploded. It was badly damaged, but it was still more or less together. He looked at Mike again, and then back at the plane. He walked over to it, having more trouble than he expected. The ground was badly beaten up, and there were several weak spots, areas that felt as though they might give away. But he made it to the side of the hull.

He reached up and touched it, feeling along the side. It was cold, of course, and there were several holes open in it. He went over to one and extended his hand inside. He felt around, and then he pulled it free and moved to the next one. He did that four times, but on the fifth, the metal creaked, and a large section of the hull broke away, almost the instant he touched it, falling down loudly.

"It's alright," he yelled, mostly to his people upstairs. Then he turned and looked at it. There was a hole now, about three feet square, and beyond it an open area. He ducked down and extended his body inside, just a bit. He reached out and felt all around, trying to ensure that the plane was secure. A few small bits of hull fell off, but most of it seemed to be fairly solid.

He took a deep breath, and he continued inside. He reached out in front of him, but as he worked his way into the plane, he pulled out a brighter light from his belt. He lit it up, and he could see better.

And suddenly, he yelled and jerked back.

"Gavin!" Mike was behind him, just preparing to work his way into the plane.

"It's nothing," he said, feeling foolish for his reaction. "One of the pilots...no surprise." *At least it shouldn't have been.*

"I understand...take a minute if you need it."

"No...I'm okay." Not entirely true, but close enough. He moved himself to the side, avoiding the body as much as he could. A few seconds later, he saw another one, farther to the front. It was no surprise, of course, and now that he took a closer look, he saw just how damaged the bodies were, skeletons, really, with some flesh still stuck to them. That made sense, of course...they were almost seven months old, but it was upsetting, nevertheless.

He pushed forward, shoving aside several large chunks of metal as he made his way inward. He turned around for a second and saw Mike right behind him. The two exchanged stares, and then he began forward again. The interior of the plane was battered in places, and it took a few minutes for him to get much farther.

Then, he reached an open area. There was something

there sitting at an angle. It had slipped a little from the cradle that had held it, and it had slid down a couple feet. Still, despite the general mess, he knew immediately what it was.

He turned toward Mike, and the instant he looked at his friend he could tell that he, too, was totally aware of what they had found. They were silent for a moment, and he turned and looked back at it. He had to get it out of here, take it back somehow to headquarters. He wasn't sure if he had enough people or equipment, or if he needed to send someone back to get more. It was heavy, of that he was sure, and he didn't even know how he was going to move it.

But he was sure of one thing. He was going to get it back, one way or another.

He didn't know if it was operable, or even repairable…but he recognized that it was a nuclear weapon.

PART THREE

The Response

Chapter Thirty-Three

From the Notes of Hugh McDaniel

I am standing here, watching my brother's force pull away. No, that's not really true. It was, perhaps an hour ago, but now I have no view of them at all. They have gone out of sight, and all of those who had been gathered around watching have wandered off, all except me. Even my parents have stepped away, leaving me alone.

I know I may see my brother again, but I am also completely aware of just how dangerous both of our operations are, how much chance there is that one of us, or more likely both of us, will not live more than a few more days. The most difficult part of it is perhaps trying to decide who is in the worst position, him or me. It is easy to say him, setting off across hundreds of miles with five hundred followers, exposed the entire time to…whatever is out there. But if he is able to hide, to travel often at night, perhaps he can make it. Can I do the same? I rather doubt it. Despite the fact that I have more than twenty thousand people again, our new volunteers actually outnumbering the vast quantity that we lost, many of them—most, in fact—are not well trained. Even most of those who fought in the first battle are barely accomplished. And what the enemy is sending, any time now, is likely to be vastly larger than the first force. Unbeatable…almost.

I am here for another reason as well. I know when I go back, I must appear to be ready, to be fully prepared for what the enemy is sending. I owe that much to my people, to seem as though I truly believe we can win. But while I am dedicated to the battle, to fighting to the end, I can't say I really believe we have much chance. All I can do is flip my opinion on who is likelier to survive, my brother or me, and try to ignore the fact that the true answer is probably that we will both die, and soon.

Just Outside the 67th Avenue Subway Station
Forest Hills, Queens
D + 209 Days

"Let's go…move it. We need to get all of this area in shape, and soon. The enemy could be back at any time, and we've got to be ready." Hugh had shaken his earlier malaise. It wasn't that his expectations had changed, but he was determined to do everything he could. He might not expect to win—to even survive—but he was damned sure going to do everything he possibly could to fight back.

He jumped down from the chunk of stone he was standing on, rushing into the crowd of people he had there, extending his arms against the large girder. "Now, all of you…pull!" He gritted his teeth and put all his effort into the mix, shoving as hard as he could. At first, it still didn't move, but then after a few seconds, it jerked forward, and came up. It was still heavy, but now it was loose, and in another ten seconds they had it out. He jerked his head to the side, saying, "Here…drop it here!" A few seconds later, he let go, along with all of the others. The girder fell down, hard, and crashed, tumbling to the side. It was far from neat, but it was good enough.

He stepped back and looked at the whole section. It was about a hundred and fifty feet long so far, and at least ten feet up in the front. He looked out and saw other sections, farther along the line. If he had time, if the enemy gave him another week, he would have all of it connected. It might not be exactly a perfect fortification, but it would be pretty damned good, and stretching all the way around the station, three hundred sixty degrees of non-stop fortification. Perhaps, if they were fortunate enough, they *could* hold out, but whatever happened, he was sure at least that his people would put up a good fight.

If they got sufficient time to complete their work.

He stood where he was and watched for a moment, and then he turned and walked away. He had a hundred things to do.

No, a thousand.

But then he stopped right where he was, staring at three men. It took him a second to place them, but then he realized they were from Gavin Sander's group.

"Yes…what is it?" Sander's team wasn't expected back until tomorrow or the next day, which meant either they had run into some kind of problem, or they had found something useful.

"Sir…we found something. We were sent back to advise you…and to request another hundred or so men to bring it back." The man was edgy, nervous.

"A hundred? What the hell did they find?" Hugh stared back, at first assuming it was something exaggerated, more the excitement of the man in front of him than anything. But then he realized…it *was* something.

"A bomb, Sir." The man barely managed to say it. Then he stood for a moment before he spoke again. "An atomic bomb."

Hugh listened, hearing the words, questioning them at first. But then he realized the report came from Gavin Sanders, who he'd known for most of his life. Sanders wasn't one he'd necessarily have expected to become as capable as he had, but he'd never have doubted him.

"Seriously? An atomic bomb?"

"Yes, Sir. We found a bomber crashed…just outside the city. From the state of things, it looks like it was shot down during the invasion. The bomb appears to be lightly damaged, but it looks like it just might be made serviceable."

The words hit Hugh hard, making his mind go crazy. An atomic bomb…one that might be functional? His mind was racing, thinking about what he might do with the bomb…assuming it was true and that they could make it work. "Okay, let's go. Let's take two hundred people with us." He had decided to go himself, which shocked the man who had told him.

"Sir…are you sure you want to come? It is outside of the city, in Yonkers."

Hugh's mind was already going, thinking of the bomb in every possible way. He still didn't know for sure it even existed—though he was fairly certain it did. But whether it was workable, whether it could be repaired, and actually used, he just didn't know. But there was nowhere else for him to be now, nowhere but checking out the bomb.

"Oh yes…I'm sure," he said.

* * *

Travis continued along his path, tired as hell, but determined to keep on moving. He had been walking all day, and half the night, but he knew that moving mostly under cover of darkness offered the greatest chance of success. That meant continuing until it was almost morning, and then finding a place to rest.

It also meant it was probably foolish to leave early in the day. He had known that he would have to travel under cover of night, but he hadn't really considered it. That was stupid, he realized, and he was determined to get his people some rest, but after they had adjusted their schedule, gotten to moving at night and sleeping during the day. That meant a full twenty-four hours of travel to start.

He was worried, too, very worried. He had tried to maintain as sure a façade as he could around his brother and the others, but in truth, he didn't know what to do not really. He understood what the mission's purpose was, what he hoped to find, but he really didn't know what to expect. He wasn't even sure that he was heading toward the enemy, though he believed he was. Traveling under cover of darkness would help him stay hidden, as would the wide swing he was taking, trying to avoid running into the enemy he was sure would be marching toward the city any time now. But realistically, he knew it would take a lot of luck for his force to make it all the way to the foe's headquarters, or even find it…assuming he was even going in approximately the right direction. And even if they did survive the journey, if they did find the enemy…how could they possibly explore the region and return with information. The whole thing seemed ridiculous, something that was impossible, but then when he thought of Hugh's position, of his brother's responsibilities, they were just as insane.

He wondered what else his people could have done, if anything. Could they have resisted better if the world had been one force, and not many countries, with their own rivalries and arguments? If they had warning, would it have made a difference? He didn't know anything about the aliens, not really, but they seemed to be united, at least, acting as one force. He didn't even know the condition of the people in other areas of the world. He had given some thought to other cities in the U.S. at least, but what about Europe and Africa and Asia? Were there people there fighting as well? He assumed so, but he had to admit, he didn't know.

He looked up toward the sky. It was dark, but the moon was about two-thirds full, giving some light to his path. He wished it was waxing, but he knew it was waning. That meant he would actually have better cover coming…but it also made positioning more difficult.

He looked up again, trying to figure out how much time he had before daylight. It wasn't much, he figured, perhaps half an hour. It was definitely time to look for someplace to hide, somewhere for his people to sleep until it was dark again. He knew that was a shaky plan, that for all he was aware, the enemy could see in the evening as well as during the day. But it was all he had.

He looked out, as far as he could, which wasn't far. There were mostly ruins around them, sections of New Jersey that had been bombed, reduced to ruins. He had assumed the entire world had been so attacked, but again, he realized, that was just an assumption. But so far that seemed to be the case…even the smaller towns out in New Jersey had all been bombed, blasted to utter ruins.

The wreckage offered him a good place to hide his people, at least for now. He knew his route extended out into areas that had been much less developed, that might actually be more difficult places to hide his people. But he had decided to take one problem at a time. And right now, finding a place for his people to sleep was number one.

Number one of about two thousand, he thought for a moment, and then he pushed it out of his mind.

* * *

Hugh stood still, staring at the large item. At the nuclear weapon. He had believed the report, in a manner of speaking, but he realized as he saw it that only *that* made it truly real. Perhaps even more surprising, it was not only an atomic weapon…but a big one. A very big one.

Hugh wasn't an expert on nuclear bombs, but his knowledge on them was still considerable. As he looked, he realized the bomb was several megatons probably, and possibly even larger. He knew there had been a renewed race between several of the nations on Earth in recent years, one that had resulted in larger bombs being created, and he wasn't surprised that some of them had been utilized in the latter stages of the conflict.

Still, finding one in reasonable condition...that was extraordinary.

He moved over to it, crawling through the plane. It was damaged, that he could tell almost immediately. It didn't look as though the radioactive elements were harmed, but he wasn't sure the shielding was holding. He knew there could be radiation leaking, possibly a lot of it, and he thought for a moment of clearing everyone away, of withdrawing, just in case.

But he couldn't. There were a ton of questions, about whether the bomb was repairable with what he had available, about whether he could get it fixed and deploy it in time, about how he could use it...he just couldn't pull away from it. He realized there were a large number of problems, not the least of which was just getting it out of the mauled bomber and carting it all the way back, through the battered streets...using mostly human hands.

But he knew he had to try. The bomb was a device from near the peak of human technology, far beyond anything else he had. And far beyond whatever the enemy thought of his technology. His mind already had a working bomb, and he was considering how to use it. Perhaps if Travis did find an enemy base...

But he realized he was getting way ahead of himself. He wasn't even sure he could get the bomb back and fix it...but he knew that was first.

"Chuck, Dave, Carl...come on down here. First things first...we've got to remove this thing from its moorings and find some way to get it out of here. It'll be hard enough to move it in the open, when we can get more people around it, but it's going to be really tough to get it out of here." Even as he spoke, he began to realize it was impossible to move the thing out the way it currently was lodged in. They would have to dismantle the entire plane around it, and the building, too. It would be a massive job, one that would require hundreds of his people. And it was far from certain they would get anything out of it.

But maybe, just maybe they would manage to make the nuke operational. He didn't know how or where he would use it, not yet…but he knew it would be incredibly useful, however he employed it.

Assuming he could retrieve it and move it and get it to work.

Chapter Thirty-Four

From the Notes of Estle-Starric

It is time, time for the expedition to leave. Three thousand robots and fifty of my people, by far the largest force we have ever deployed on Earth, far greater than any we utilized in the initial attack. I had to draw robots from virtually everywhere, to put the force together, but I am confident it will prove worthwhile. The enemy will be utterly obliterated, and then I will redirect the force to the other hotspots, the areas where enemy forces have been…difficult. One at a time, they will be utterly destroyed…and their survivors will be brought back to serve our great purpose.

We made an error on our initial attack. We vastly underestimated the militarism of the enemy, the strange ability they seem to have to fight. That will now be corrected, beginning with the biggest problem. New York.

Gavicon City
Approximately Twenty-Five Miles West of the Ruins of Washington
D + 216 Days

"Qualak-Neerie, go now, lead this force, this awesomely

powerful attack. Meet the enemy, destroy their willingness to fight, and then bring back the survivors, those who are utterly defeated…to serve as the next group for the breeding program." Estle-Starric stood on the parapet, speaking to both Qualak-Neerie and his people, and to the several hundred others of his kind he had gathered around. He had been too casual before, too lackluster, but this time he would be certain to do everything necessary.

"Thank-you, Estle-Starric…your efforts are greatly appreciated. We will carry out the mission, completely and utterly, and we will return, with prisoners for the program." Qualak-Neerie held up one of his hands in salute. Then he turned toward his forces, and he said, "Forward now…to New York!"

Estle-Starric stood and watched, for quite some time as the force marched off. He was not entirely confident in Qualak-Neerie, but neither would he have been in anyone else, save himself…and he had to remain here. If things went as well as he expected, in a short time, perhaps a week, he would see the first successful breeding program conducted on any planet concluded. It was unbelievable, success in an operation that had gone on with none for well over two hundred years. It meant his race would survive, that they wouldn't die out. It hadn't happened yet, of course, but now he truly believed it would.

He turned after a while and walked back into the building. He had something else to do, something he didn't overly enjoy, but he knew he had to. He found humans uncomfortable to be around, particularly when they were being treated as functional creatures. But he knew he would need them. His people had diminished considerably in the past century, and while they could conduct the initial testing alone, if it worked, if it went on to mass employment, they would need help.

He had been doubtful about that, about turning some of the humans into…masters…over the others, but he had to admit, many of them seemed promising. He wondered about a species that could both fight back as severely as those in New York and in many other cities had and also have many people who would turn on their own, for relatively simple rewards. It didn't make sense, not really…and yet it seemed to be true.

He walked over to the section of the city that had been built for humans. They were isolated—imprisoned really—but they were treated fairly well. Two of his own people, guards, went with him as he walked inside. He stood for a moment while the gate was closed behind him, and then he walked inside.

He knew the president was still in command of his people, but he wasn't sure he would remain so. Many of his personnel, former politicians and government types, had proven more than willing to cooperate…but Estle-Starric was far from sure about the president. He had thought more than once about simply killing him, replacing him with another. But he had decided to wait.

To wait until now, when he shared the true purpose of his peoples' invasion with him.

He walked another fifteen or twenty feet, but then the president came running out. He looked at Estle-Starric, clearly disgusted by what he saw, though trying to hide it.

Don't worry, you are as revolting to us…

"Estle-Starric…welcome. We are very glad to see you." That was a lie, he knew that, though it didn't really surprise him. He couldn't expect his conquered people *not* to dislike his own.

"I wanted to have a discussion with you. I know your people have been here for some time, but now I am going to explain to you the true purpose of our trip here, the reason we came…and the way that some of you can join us, find a way to continue your enhanced quality of life." He paused a moment, and then he added, "I will tell you now, working your way into true usefulness, into the purpose we

have for you, will not be a reachable goal for all of you."
Including you? "But I am confident that some of your people
will be able to do it."

The president looked back, seeming nervous, but he just
nodded. "I understand, Sir." He spoke the words fairly well,
but Estle-Starric was fairly certain he had picked up some
hesitation. He considered again for a moment having the
president shot and selecting a more…appropriate…leader
for the humans. But he didn't entirely understand the aliens,
and he wasn't sure how many of the captive people liked
their leader. He decided to give him a chance.

"Come with me now," he said, turning abruptly, and
walking back through the gate.

* * *

The president walked slowly behind Estle-Starric, trying to
look as respectful as possible. That was difficult, as he
despised the aliens, and he longed to strike back at them, to
take them out. But he knew that was impossible. He'd
wondered for a time after his ignominious surrender, if
some of the military commands had survived, if there was
still some resistance going on somewhere. Perhaps there
was, but what chance could they have had when the whole
military had failed so utterly? No, as much as his insides
wanted to rebel, he realized his people were defeated, that
their only chance was to make themselves useful to their
conquerors.

Or die…which was what he would have chosen for
himself. But killing his whole race was something different
again. Whatever the situation, he was still the president—at
least as far as he saw it—and that carried with it an
obligation to do whatever he could for his people. However
little that may be.

He slowly followed Estle-Starric, reminding himself that
he had two guards at his back—*live* guards, as well as

countless robots. He was certain any questionable move would be his last.

"I am going to explain to you now, why we have come here, what our purpose is. You will have two choices…to accept it, or to die." There was nothing hostile in Estle-Starric's voice, but in a strange way, that made his threat even more credible.

"I understand." The president said the words, not entirely sure they would come out until they did. He was scared, of course, but he was also ready to die. But he figured as long as he lived, he had at least some chance of striking back.

"My people became the victims several hundred years ago of a virus, one that gradually—and ultimately totally—destroyed our ability to breed. We faced a difficult choice, to accept that and disappear forever, or to go out, to explore other worlds and try to find a race that was…compatible."

The president felt something, some kind of edginess. He had never expected the enemy had attacked his world for any reason he would consider good…but now he was truly nervous.

"We explored for almost two hundred years, and we found a number of other races in our section of the galaxy, but none of them worked, not in full…"

The president suddenly knew what was coming. He wanted to vomit, to scream, to reach out and try to attack the alien…but somehow, miraculously, he did nothing.

"…not until we came here. Our success is not certain, not yet, but it has gone far beyond what we have achieved anywhere else. And in a matter of days, I believe we will at last achieve success."

Estle-Starric nodded, and one of his people opened the door. He walked inside, and the president followed him in…and he stopped, looking out with absolute horror on his face.

The room was large, with hundreds of stations inside of

it. And at each of them, there was a woman lying down, her face covered and her stomach large.

Pregnant?

He struggled, reached for all he could to maintain himself. He knew if he struck at Estle-Starric, if he even tried to resist, he would die at once. And as attractive as that was in a way, he knew he had to find some way to resist.

Some way to strike back.

It was worse than anything he had imagined. He had railed against thoughts that the enemy had come to take resources, to enslave his people. But he hadn't even imagined anything like this.

And it only got worse.

As he looked out, as his eyes focused, he could see the women were awake, that they were suffering, moaning softly…and he could see men now, too, also alive, some of them at least, and being…*eaten*?

Everything he saw battered at him, driving him to resist, somehow. But he knew he couldn't, not yet at least. His hope—his only hope—was to buy time, to try to find some way to stop this.

"I appreciate that this is probably rather upsetting to you, but I will explain. What you are witnessing is the fate of your people…some of them, at least. Most of them, in fact. But there is room for another group, a collection of people to help us. I understand that this will take considerable changes in your point of view, but it is time to consider your future. Some of your people can survive, truly survive, even live moderately well…but the cost is the rest of your race. Consider this, and give me an answer…will you engage in this with us, will you lead the higher level of your race, at the cost of the lower ones?"

The president listened, trying his best to maintain control…and barely succeeding.

"Or will you die and yield your position to another of your people."

Chapter Thirty-Five

From the Notes of Hugh McDaniel

I am tired. No, that understates it. I am exhausted. It has been a week since I've had more than an hour's sleep, and the drain is starting to get to me. But I have no time for rest.

It took almost a week to get the bomb back to our main lair, and every moment of that time, I expected to hear from one of our scouting teams that the enemy was approaching. But that didn't happen, and finally, through combined efforts I can't really believe, we finally managed to get the bomb to the station. It took over a thousand people, working on dismantling the ship, on moving the bomb, on preparing the room where we would work on it, try to make it functional again. That all seemed impossible at first, but now I realize it was the easy part. The difficult effort will be to make the thing work.

It is mostly intact, at least more or less, but there are several sections that have minor damage. That would not be a problem on a simpler device, but on a massive nuclear weapon, everything has to function to make it work. And right now, not everything did function.

We have some power at least. One of the projects I had given the go ahead to a while back was a small dynamo. I would have pushed it farther, made a major effort to develop more of them, only we didn't have the fuel for them anyway, not much at least.

But we did have a little, and it wasn't hard to recognize that the bomb, any chance of making it functional, was our greatest opportunity.

One other thing occurred to me very quickly. If the bomb did work, if we were able to completely restore it, we would have to detonate it here. Moving it was too difficult when we weren't under attack…it would be impossible once the enemy was on the move. That meant somehow getting our people out of here—and by "here" I mean the entire city. If I am right about the size of the bomb, it will obliterate the whole city's remnants, kill anyone who remains. It may even go farther, tear into the surrounding areas.

Can we really do it? Can we evacuate all of our people…and wait for the enemy to arrive? Can we set a trap, and destroy their entire force, whatever they send? It seems impossible. I don't know if we can even make the thing work, much less getting everyone far enough away. But the thought of it, of suckering in a large force of the enemy, of destroying them all…it is incredibly appealing.

If we are to do it, to make it work, I will have to start evacuating our people…in fact I probably should have been already. I allowed myself to get very buried in the restoration of the bomb, which of course is also vital, but now I have to decide…will we manage to make the thing functional in time, or is this a waste of resources? Will it work, or will we have no other way to face the enemy except a conventional fight, one that will become ever more difficult with everyone we ship out before.

67th Avenue Subway Station
Forest Hills, Queens
D + 216 Days

"Let's try taking this off…" Hugh was nervous. He wasn't sure of the exact design of the bomb, and while he was fairly certain there had been no radiation leaks yet, he figured there was a chance that some could escape if they removed the piece he was talking about. But he also suspected that one of the problems they were dealing with was there, too. "Let's clear out as many people as we can, first…just in case." He looked down at the bomb for a few seconds, and then back up. "That means most of you, too. Horace, I'm sorry…I need you. The rest of you, all of you…get on out of here. Now."

He looked at Horace, half expecting him to object. But the group's only physicist just nodded his ascent. Horace wasn't an expert in nuclear weapons, far from it actually, but he was the best they had available. Between his knowledge and Hugh's, they had managed so far. Whether they would succeed totally, get the bomb to true functionality, was still a large question.

As was, would they survive…or would they kill themselves with radiation?

Hugh looked up and repeated his assertion. "I mean it…none of you can do anything here, so it's a waste. And we have no room now for waste." He stared at the others present, as they stood still for another moment, and then started to walk away. It was clear they didn't want to, that they didn't like the idea of leaving Hugh and Horace behind…but just as evident that Hugh's statement was correct. There was nothing they could do except stand around and watch…and the situation didn't allow for that kind of foolishness.

Hugh waited a few seconds, until the room was empty save for him and Horace…and then he placed his hand on the piece of the bomb. He hesitated, just for perhaps another ten seconds, and then he started removing it. The first part of it went well, but then he realized that several of the screws holding it in place were damaged. They were stuck firmly in place, and he couldn't turn them. He stopped for a moment, rested, and then both he and Horace grabbed the screwdriver the best they could. They struggled for a moment, but then it moved a bit. They continued, straining as much as possible, and finally, the screw came out. They rested a moment and then continued with the next one. Then the third and final one.

The piece came totally loose, and Hugh removed it, leaving an opening in the bomb's casing. He couldn't feel anything, but he knew that was no guarantee that there wasn't radiation escaping. Hell, he didn't know there wasn't radiation when they found it, though it had now been a week, and he hadn't seen any damage.

He reached inside the bomb, feeling his way around. He didn't know its specifics, but between him and Horace, they had some idea of what to expect. He knew it would take a while, especially since he had to move slowly and carefully, but he figured he had at least a chance of getting the bomb functional.

What to do with it, how to use it, was another question…one he had been considering for the entire week. The bomb was a terrible weapon, one of massive power. If he decided to use it in the city, which he realized, given its size, was just about his only option, he had to do whatever he could to evacuate everyone he could reach, his own people and all of the others…and he had to accept that he would never manage to get to all the survivors and convince them to leave, that in addition to hopefully destroying his enemies, he would also certainly kill humans as well, and perhaps a large number.

He pushed back on that, shoved the thoughts aside, telling himself it was only relevant IF he was able to make the bomb functional. Or at least if he believed he was. He knew that he couldn't be certain until the bomb actually exploded…and he realized he would have to be miles away when that happened. If he believed it was functional, but it wasn't—for any one of a hundred reasons—he would not only have removed his people from the city's ruins and disorganized his entire group…he would have left the bomb behind. It would be a disaster, one which probably ended with the aliens chasing his people and engaging them in a far less prepped area than they might have.

He tried not to think about that any more than he had to. He knew it would only become relevant if he was able to make the bomb work, or rather, convince himself that he had…and that was definitely still a question.

He turned toward the bomb, but before he got back to work, one of his people came running in.

"I'm sorry to interrupt you, Sir…but he is dead. The prisoner is dead." The man sounded upset, and perhaps more, afraid Hugh would get angry.

But he just nodded, and then he said, "Very well…pack his body up the best you can. We didn't have any use for him alive, maybe we'll have some for him dead." He waved for the man to leave, and he held his head up for few seconds, thinking about the alien. Then he put his head down and went back to working on the bomb. The prisoner had been of no value, he had decided that already. But the bomb, if he could somehow get it to work, just might be. It might be insanely valuable.

*   *   *

Travis walked, much as he had been doing for a week. His force was smaller now, by at least sixty people who had not been able to keep up the almost non-stop pace he had set, and now straggled along over at least a hundred miles behind. His force had slept about three hours a night and spent almost all the rest of its time walking. It was a brutal pace, and it got worse the longer it went on, but Travis knew the enemy was going to strike the city. He understood just what his brother and most of their people were going to face, and he was determined to succeed…to make their fight worthwhile. To at least answer some questions about the enemy and its capabilities. He told himself he would then return to the city, that he would reunite with his brother…but he wasn't sure he believed it. Hugh had a large group of people, but most of them weren't expert fighters, and he was almost certain that the enemy would send a significantly larger force this time. And his people had barely won the first fight.

He hadn't even known he was heading anywhere useful, that he wasn't going off in a pointless direction, searching for something he wasn't going to find…until this morning.

One of his scouting parties had come upon a device…one clearly not produced by humans. It was a detector of some kind, he was almost sure, probably on the outskirts of alien-occupied territory. His scouts believed they had managed to back off, undetected. He was less certain of that, but he didn't have any choice except to go on that assumption. At least it was an indicator that some of the aliens were in the area.

He had directed his people to try and move around the location, to avoid the known position of enemy surveillance. But he was sure there would be more, and he tripled the number of scouts sent ahead. He picked them carefully, sending his best people out with explicit instructions to be careful looking for enemy detectors. To be very careful.

He knew his own path was behind his scouts, but he couldn't help but look everywhere he went, too. The enemy was close, he was sure of that, and he knew it was almost time for him to deploy, to hide his troops and send them forward only in small groups. He was far from certain he hadn't been detected yet, but he knew all he could do was hope that was true.

He continued on, tired but determined to proceed. It was almost dark, but he wanted to keep on going, at least a couple more hours. But barely fifteen minutes later, a pair of scouts came running back to the main group carrying news…incredible news.

They had found the enemy…the real enemy. And in what looked like a small city.

* * *

The president sat, alone, trying to overcome what he had done. He had been repulsed by what he had seen, what Estle-Starric had shown him and what the alien had explained. Inside, he raged, he called on himself to fight back, to desperately struggle, even for the seconds he would have left. But instead, he had remained silent for a long while.

And then he had consented.

He was disgusted with himself, appalled at what he had done. He knew there was no way he could stop it, no way he could really fight back…but he had to admit, he had acted mostly out of fear, out of his own desire to live.

There were others in his group who would accept their fate more openly, some even who would come to enjoy it. That thought disgusted him, but he had long known that there were some people who were, at their base level, grotesque. He'd never considered himself one of them…until now. How had he maintained his calm when he had seen the true horrors of the alien plot? He understood why he had, and yet the mere fact that he could, that he hadn't thrown himself instantly at the enemy, trading his death for a one in a million chance of hurting him, tore at him.

No…you have to think. If you threw your life away, they would simply kill you, and replace you, probably with one who wouldn't think twice about doing what so horrifies you.

He knew he had to strike back in some way…but it had to be in a manner that truly accomplished something. Those people he'd seen in the complex—and every moment since, whenever he'd closed his eyes—were beyond his ability to reclaim. He had no idea if they could survive the process, though he doubted it, but he was sure their fates were beyond any human abilities to save.

But if the experiment was truly successful, if the aliens could actually create more of their kind from humans…he had to find a way to stop it, perhaps not to save the thousand or so in the facility now, but the millions that would follow.

He had accepted the enemy's proposition out of fear, but now as he sat down, the luxury of more time and thought descended on him. He was almost certain he would die, that the enemy would kill him within minutes of whatever action he took, if not seconds. But if he could accomplish something, anything, it would be worth it. He had been the president during the greatest disaster ever to strike mankind, and there was no way he could undo it. But he could strike back, perhaps just a bit. Perhaps not enough to accomplish anything significant…but maybe it would leave a message behind, something some of his people at least could follow.

He regretted so much of what he had done, of how badly he had fought the aliens, and of what he had just seen. He was ruined, distraught, and he realized all he truly wanted was death. But he wanted to strike back first, to lash out at the enemy.

To accomplish something, at least, before he was killed.

* * *

Estle-Starric stood in his study, contemplating multiple issues. First, he wondered about the human president, whether he could truly trust him. He just didn't know. He had almost ordered him killed outright, selected another more—flexible—one to take his place, but he had decided against that, for now at least. He was definitely uncertain of the president's feelings, of how he would react…but he was sure of his ability to lead. And he knew his own job would be much easier if he had a human leader who was capable. Amazingly, despite the utter disaster that had fallen on the humans, he had developed a viewpoint that it was the surprise more than anything that had seen them so quickly crushed. If they had been warned, given some notice of the pending attack, he was sure they would have put up a much harder fight. And on one level, he wondered if they still had such a capacity, if they could organize and strike back, especially now since a good number of his people had departed.

He had decided to give the president a chance. He could be useful…as long as he was also obedient. He was doubtful in some ways that would come to pass, but he decided to give him a chance. If he gave any signs of trouble, he would have him killed at once.

His second topic, of course, was the attack on the humans in New York. He had poured all he could into the force he had sent, and he couldn't see any way the battle could be anything but a total victory. Still, there was something eating at him, some little bit of uncertainty that he couldn't really explain. On the one hand, the force he had sent was large, certainly big enough to overwhelm the enemy forces. But something was troubling him, nevertheless.

He looked out at the display, checking all the areas of the planet that contained his establishments. He had bases in different areas of the world, and he would conduct breeding operations in all of them, but he had chosen the Washington-area facility as the starting point. The test was located there, the operation that would prove that humanity was in fact the race that would allow his own to breed—to survive. He was going to hold the second phase there as well. Only with the third operation, with the expansion to produce literally millions of his people, to the wholesale repopulation of his homeworld, would he expand to the other locations.

He had to keep the people under control, and in the US more than anyplace else. He had taken all the action that he could, put together a force larger than any of his people had expected, one large enough to take out the enemy almost certainly.

But something was still bothering him. He just wasn't sure what it was.

He wasn't sure at all…

Chapter Thirty-Six

From the Notes of Hugh McDaniel

I have been working on the bomb for days now, and for the last three neither Horace nor I have stepped away for more than a few moments. I am tired, exhausted really, but I can't allow myself to sleep, or even to eat anything but whatever my people bring to me…and barely that. We are close, I am sure of that, close to getting this bomb working. At least I think so.

The bomb is actually a very complex item, one that has a variety of systems inside it. This is one of our most complex weapons, one of the newest entries into our nuclear arsenal. If it had been deployed against humanity, it would have killed millions. I know, if I am able to make it function, if we decide to detonate it here, it will utterly destroy the ruins of New York City, virtually all of it, as well as much of eastern New Jersey. If I am able to make it work, if I plan to trap the enemy in the city, to destroy them, I will need to get my people out of here as much as two days before the detonation.

I would have sent them away already, but I am just too uncertain that we can make the bomb functional, and without it, while I do not feel my people have much of a chance, I do believe their best ability is right here, in the city.

That is why I have not sent most of them away, why my mind is not made up yet. If I could reach a point where I could truly believe the bomb would work, that I would in fact be able to lay a trap for the enemy, I would send them away.

But so far, I am just not certain, and my people are still working, still building the best set of defenses they can.

Just Outside the 67th Avenue Subway Station
Forest Hills, Queens
D + 217 Days

"Horace…take a look at this." Hugh's voice had something in it that hadn't been there for the entire week. Excitement.

Horace pulled his attention away from his own work, for the first time in at least six hours, and looked.

Hugh realized that his co-worker…and now, he would say, friend…had become more depressed, even as he had, as the days went by. They had both been working nonstop on the bomb, but they hadn't completed it. Not yet.

But right now, Hugh was energized. "I think if we fix this here…then just maybe the whole thing will work. We've checked out every other system in it, and they should all be functional. If we can correct this one and put it all back together…just *maybe* this thing will work."

He wasn't used to being so uncertain about, well, anything, at least not before the alien attack. But he had reviewed every area of the bomb, checked and rechecked every circuit. Once he made the repairs he was talking about, it *should* work. But it was a complex mechanism, and not one he had any real idea of before it was dragged before him several days ago. He would gladly take another week, or a month…but he was far from sure he had more than a couple days left. If he had that.

He would test the bomb, but there was only one way to *really* test it, and that was to use it. That meant evacuating the entire city, including as many of those in different groups from his own as he could. Everyone present, or as close as he could get to that as possible, had to be taken out. Worse, it had to be done very quietly, not taking any chance on being noticed by the enemy.

That would be difficult, if not downright impossible. He had to convince them all to leave what had been their only home for more than half a year, to set off carrying what they could, to go to a place where food and other necessities were even more uncertain…and to do it all under enough control that it wasn't obvious. Then, he had to lure the enemy in and keep them there until the bomb went off.

But he was beginning to realize that almost certainly meant leaving a group behind, a good number, to fight, to hold the attention of the enemy forces.

And then to die, most of them, perhaps all of them, at least if the bomb worked. He tried not to think about that too much, but he knew it was true. People would die no matter how he proceeded, of course, and if he could pull this off, make the bomb work, his losses would almost certainly be lower than if everyone stayed to fight. They would also be from his best people, those he trusted the most.

Again. That was always the part of the group that truly sacrificed.

And what if he evacuated most of his people, and put up a sacrificial group…and the bomb didn't work? That was the worst possibility of all, and it could easily happen.

"As I said, it looks to me like the bomb should work when we've finished this. But…I just don't know." His mind was moving at full speed. "That, of course, assumes we've gotten everything else fixed. If we decide it is workable, if we put it into operation, we will have to come up with a way to get most of the people out of here in time." He realized even Horace understood that some of their people would have to stay behind to fight. To die. "But if it doesn't work, if we're wrong, and the bomb doesn't blow, we won't be in our prepared positions when we meet the enemy. Not most of us. We'll be out in the open. They will almost certainly be able to track where we went, after they have wiped out our forward forces, and while there will likely be debris all around us to hide in, we won't have any truly fixed areas. Nor will we have any plans, any real preparations. I know you believe, as I do, that the enemy is sending a large force, large enough to probably blow us out of our fixed positions here…the ones we've been working on around the clock. We'll be utterly slaughtered if they come on us, out in New Jersey or anywhere else, running, not much surer where we are than they are. If we decide to try and blow this bomb instead of fighting it out here, we're taking a terrible risk. Not only on its working, but on catching the whole enemy force, or most of it at least, here. It's a wild gamble, and there are all kinds of ways it can go wrong…but…"

"But…it is a legitimate chance…" Horace said. "…and not the almost hopeless effort we've got here."

Horace's statement shook Hugh, brought him more clearly to the resolution that at least some of his people—besides himself—had a clear view, and knew their chances were, at best, poor. He had known that all along, at least on one level, but he had allowed his mind to wander, to tell himself maybe they could win in a straight up fight, that perhaps the enemy force wouldn't be invincible. But now he realized, the bomb wasn't just one of many options. It was really the only one he had. And he was fortunate to have it.

He *had* to use it, if possible, take the chance that it exploded, and that it caught all or most of the enemy when it did. He wondered for a moment exactly what kind of response that would provoke. If he exploded it, if it worked, he could find himself in an even worse situation eventually. It might even prompt the enemy to launch its own superweapons, at least at the New York/New Jersey area.

But he pushed that aside. He couldn't think very far ahead…not now.

"You hit the reality of the situation right on the head, Horace. Actually, it is even worse. This bomb may not work, and even if it does, it will cost us our home. We will try to reach the others, those who have not joined our group, of course…but even if they all listen—and that is extremely unlikely—we know there are others, perhaps thousands of survivors, that we haven't even communicated with. If the bomb works, they will die. This weapon that we're working so hard to make functional…it is a disaster for us, too, even in the best scenario." He paused for a few seconds and continued, "But having it is still a far better option than not having it. If we're truly going to survive, to have any chance of really fighting against the enemy, we have to accept the true nature of the struggle. It is a fight to the death. Nothing less. All of us must be willing to die, most of us probably will…but maybe, just maybe, a few of us will endure, and see the enemy driven away forever."

He turned and looked down at the bomb, ready to resume his work. No, almost ready. He realized he had to decide then what to do, right then, whether he could make the bomb function or not. If he could, he had to start organizing the group's departure…now. He had to send people out to the other groups, prepare as much food and medicine—and weapons—as they could possibly move. And he had to get them started, as soon as possible.

"Horace, try to start on this section. I believe it *is* the final piece. I'll be back as soon as I can to help." He got up. He still wasn't sure he was correct, that it would work. But he'd decided it was time.

Time to get his people moving. Time to assume the bomb would work…and to act accordingly.

* * *

Travis stared through his binoculars, checking out the area. He was amazed that the enemy was able to build so much so quickly. It wasn't exactly a city, not yet at least, but it was a massive construction, stretching over several miles. He could see several robots on patrol, and two of the aliens themselves moving about, conducting some sort of business. It was only the second time he had seen the enemy—the true enemy—and he stayed focused for a considerable time. He was partially buried, trying not to move in any way that would draw attention. Still, he was amazed that it appeared his people hadn't been detected yet. The enemy had some security around their facility, but it was clear that they didn't really expect any significant activity from the surviving humans.

That was foolish, he realized, but then he wondered whether he would be any different in their situation. They had obliterated the world's military forces in a matter of days and assumed what appeared to be total control over the world. He had been living in the ruins for more than half a year, and everything he had managed to accomplish, that any of his people had, was the result of the enemy allowing it. They wanted some of his people alive, of that he was almost certain, but more than that he didn't really know. Not yet anyway.

He could only see a portion of the…city…from where he was, but even as he looked, he began to feel more depressed. He had expected—at least hoped—to find some of the aliens, of course, but what he was looking at now was far more than he'd imagined in the time that had elapsed. It was huge, and he couldn't see how he and his slightly more than four hundred people could do anything about it.

For the moment, at least, he had managed to remain hidden, both he and his scouts who had made contact. At least he hoped they had. The alien city was in the middle of a cleared out bit of land just beyond where he was, and he'd gone as close as he could without becoming extremely visible. He was just about to give up, thinking the only thing he could do was to go back to New York. It was far too massive to consider any kind of attack, certainly with his four hundred people.

Then he saw it.

A human being. No…three of them. They were walking along, *next to one of the aliens.* They were much cleaner than any of his people. They were obviously prisoners, he decided, but they were kept at a much different level than his people were. He was far away, but it was clear they had showers and their clothing was washed. He couldn't understand it. Had he made some mistake? Was the enemy less burdensome than he, than all of his people, had assumed? Was it possible to reach some kind of peace with them, perhaps even learn to live together, to share the Earth? He wouldn't have thought that way six months earlier, but now he realized that, alongside the growth of his resistance, there had also been, unseen but real nevertheless, a side of him that would accept less than total victory in return for peace. If the invaders, the conquerors, were prepared to share the planet, in some way that gave his people a reasonable standard of living, part of him wanted to accept immediately, put the effort that would go into an almost hopeless battle against the enemy into rebuilding something of a life for the survivors.

The rest of him, however, swore never. The enemy had killed billions of his people, and there was no way to come back from that. The fight was to the end…the bitter end.

The humans, however…if he could reach them, perhaps they could give him at least some information…on what the enemy wanted, on the size and scope of their forces, on any weaknesses they displayed.

But he stopped, wondered about whether he could trust the humans. For more than half a year, his own people had been stuck on their own, struggling to survive, even before the enemy bots started coming. They had changed, dramatically, and even those least suited to fighting, to carrying weapons and engaging in battle, had become reasonably proficient. What could more than half a year, as prisoners—or whatever they considered themselves—have done to their perspectives? He found it difficult to believe any humans could actually support the aliens who had invaded their world and killed billions of their people. Maybe they were captured, he told himself, and forced into their current positions. That was understandable, though at the same time, he found himself swearing he would never be taken alive himself. But he realized he could never know for sure what he would do if the choice was simple…surrender or death. He could say he would die, swear it to heaven, but he knew he couldn't be sure until and unless it happened.

He had to think about it, about what to do. And in the meanwhile, he had to keep his people hidden. Most of them were back, well out of sight of the enemy base…but some were around him. He had to keep them hidden. If any of them were detected, even one, it could result in an immediate attack by the enemy…and *that* he knew his force couldn't withstand.

He looked up again at the structures for a moment. Then he turned toward his companions, and he started to issue orders to withdraw…*cautiously*. He had to think about the next move, but first, he had to get his people back, out of imminent range. And he had to do that very carefully.

* * *

The president sat for a long while, alone. He still had a few of his people around him—a gesture from his captors, he imagined, and they were performing their tasks as well as they could. Not that they had that much to do. They were all prisoners, nothing more, he realized, and it appeared they would remain that way, certainly for the foreseeable future.

He had decided that he wouldn't, though, not forever. He planned to strike back, even if it was irrelevant, to at least make a statement, if nothing else. He knew that would cost him his life, and that it would likely result in one of his more—willing—subordinates taking his role, but it was the only thing he could think to do. He could pretend for a while, until he had the chance to strike somehow, but he knew that would only last for a time. He told himself seeing the president do something rebellious might resonate with the people, some of them, at least...that witnessing his death might generate some rebelliousness. He wasn't sure it would work, that anyone would even notice, but he told himself they would. It was all he could do.

He had already accepted Estle-Starric's offer, told the alien that he would do what he could to help assemble the group of his people who would continue to be preferenced, who would live at least reasonable lives...in return for conducting whatever services their captors demanded. And he would, at least at first. He would place as many of his people who felt the way that he did in positions of...not authority, he reminded himself, but as close to that as he could come. Sadly, as he ran his thoughts over the roster of available personnel, he realized there were few he truly trusted. Best guess—most of his people would accept the offer, they would turn on the greater population to secure a better life for themselves.

In the end, he only came up with two others he truly trusted, and another three he considered reasonably reliable. He wanted all five of them, but he knew he couldn't take any chances. Dennis was his head of security, and he had remained at his post despite the drop-off of any real ability to protect him. And Carolyn was his senior secretary, who had been with him for two decades, long before he'd been elected president.

The two of them would have to be enough. He felt confident they would go along with his efforts, or at least that they wouldn't tell the enemy. He was a bit less certain they would both be willing to die, as he was. He would just have to see as he went along.

But first, he had to decide what he could do, whether he could make an effort that would truly leave a message…or whether he would just die, leaving little behind, save for his absence, which would soon be forgotten.

He wasn't sure which of those would be closer to accurate, but he was sure, either way, he was going to go forward. Even if his plan was a complete failure, if he didn't make a bit of difference, he was sure of one thing.

He didn't want to live to see what was coming.

Chapter Thirty-Seven

From the Notes of Hugh McDaniel

I started moving our people yesterday. Most of them were surprised, even stunned at my command…yet they obeyed it. I was still amazed, as I usually am, that they took my commands, accepted me as their leader, mostly without question. For most of my life, I was highly capable, but never in a "leadership" kind of way. The alien attack had changed everyone—and everything. Some people, a small minority perhaps, it had made capable in ways they weren't before, and I was one of those. I can't say I am happy that the invasion took place—of course I am not, and I realize that ultimately, everyone around me is far more likely to die than to achieve success—but still, I have adapted very well. I have gotten used to having less sleep. I am in the best shape of my life…and even on some level, though part of me doesn't really believe it, I know I have excelled. I have managed to assemble a large group, over 20,000, with my brother, of course, and a few others, and I have maintained my place at their head for more than six months. Considering the circumstances, that is a very good result.

I have always known, of course, that my mind is different from most people's, that I think differently than others. Still, I am surprised at what we have achieved. We have assembled a large number of people, scoured the city for more food and drugs than I even imagined at first, and kept our numbers growing despite the situation, and the losses we have suffered. We face enormous problems, I know, even excepting the enemy…not the least of which is growing new food to replace the quickly waning supplies we have been able to secure from the city's destroyed stores and restaurants. It wasn't easy to salvage as much as we did, and I was surprised at just how long we have been able to make that last, but any long term solution means actually producing food, and not just finding existing items. We've done everything possible to extend the life of the food we've found…and we have eaten things well past their expiration dates, even rotten items. But even with all of that, what we have found will be gone fairly soon. That would have been our number one problem…if the enemy hadn't started coming to the city and bringing the fight to us.

I don't know if the bomb will work…and if it does, and if we are able to take out the entire force the enemy is sending, I have no idea what their response will be. I am fairly certain, however, that it will send a message, that the use of so powerful a weapon, and the destruction of a large force of theirs' will definitely tell them that our world is far from pacified, that humanity still has the willingness and the ability to fight back.

They may simply lash out aggressively and perhaps they will kill us all…but I am going on the assumption that they do want us—some of us, at least—for something. That is only an assumption, but from the types of bombs they used to the stoppage of bombardment, to their recent operations with small groups of robots, it seems to be a good guess. With luck, Travis and his people will return, and just maybe with some additional information.

And with a little more luck, there will be some of us left—here or in New Jersey—when he does return.

67th Avenue Subway Station
Forest Hills, Queens
D + 218 Days

"Horace…you've done a tremendous job on this. I realize how tired you are…but I think it will work." Hugh spoke with genuine sincerity in his voice. He had been in and out for the past day, splitting his time between working on the bomb and getting his people moving, but Horace had been at it the entire time, no sleep, no rest, not even a meal outside of eating while working. Hugh had become impressed with his co-worker already, but the past day had taken it even farther. From everything he could see, all he was able to check, the bomb looked ready to go.

Of course, he wouldn't know that for sure until it exploded…and if it didn't, it would be too late to bring his people back to occupy their old positions. They would be stuck, in the process of abandoning the city—most of them gone already, scattered around in positions in New Jersey that might be defensible, but would be vastly inferior to their prepared lines in Queens.

They would also only have the amount they could carry of what they had found in six months…food, drugs, equipment. Even if they escaped, if the bomb went off and utterly wiped out the enemy force, they would have maybe a week's or ten day's work of food before they had to search out and find what they could. The rest of what they had worked for six months to find and gather would be gone, obliterated by the nuclear blast.

There was no time for that kind of thinking, though. He had made the decision yesterday, started the evacuation…and now the only thing he could do was make as sure as possible that it wasn't for nothing, that the bomb worked, and his people were far enough away…most of his people, at least. And that they caught the enemy force by surprise…and destroyed it.

"Thank you, Hugh…though you've done as much as me in the time you've been here. My best guess is that the bomb is ready, that it is functional. Still, that is only my opinion, and I could be wrong. There are a hundred small details that could ruin its functionality."

"Yes, Horace…there are. But you have not found one, and neither have I. And the enemy is approaching. We've gotten three different signals from our scouts…and the last one gives us some idea of what is coming. It is large, just as we suspected, more than a thousand, perhaps two or three thousand of their robots…and as many as fifty of their ships. That's *fifty* of them. If we can lure that entire force into the city and destroy them all with the bomb…we will make a true statement. We will truly show them the war is not over. The *real* war…because the enemy response will be…there is no way to know what it will be, except to assume it will be harsher than we can imagine." He thought about his people, thrown back in many ways to their situations right at the start of the crisis, hunting for food with extreme urgency, while also fighting off the next enemy attack. Even a great victory, the utter destruction of the enemy force now approaching, carried with it a massive danger of enemy escalation. But there wasn't time to worry about any of that now…and he forced it aside.

"What if it doesn't work?" Horace's question was obvious and to the point. And there was no answer.

"We have to assume it will work. We have both checked it a number of times, and we haven't found anything wrong with it. It *will* work." He sounded definitive when he said that, surprisingly so…but his mind was full of doubts.

"It will work," he said again.

*   *   *

"You good?" Travis asked the question, knowing what the answer would be. His friend, his former, and present co-

combatant, would say he was fine…but Travis knew that was bullshit. He knew that because he himself wasn't fine either. But he would do it, and he was almost certain Lucas would go as well.

"Yeah…I'm good. How about you?"

Travis was taken by surprise, not by his friend's willingness to go, but by the return of the question he had asked. He was, more or less, ready to go, but he found it easier to ask about it than to answer. "Yes," he managed to say after a pause of several seconds. "Yes, I am ready," he repeated.

He looked out from the patch of woods, carefully inspecting what he could see of the ground. That wasn't much. It was 2am, and while the moon wasn't new, it was far from full, just a thin sliver casting a scant bit of light. That, he realized was just luck. It was a bit brighter than a new moon would have been perhaps, but far better than a bright full moon. "It is as dark as it's going to get…let's go." He turned and looked again toward his friend. He had originally planned to bring a larger group in with him, but then he had decided to limit the excursion to just two people. It made sense, he told himself, though he knew he should send in someone else, and not risk the mission commander—him—on the first effort. If he was caught, he knew the enemy would probably come looking and find the rest of his people…but he also realized there was nothing he could do, even if he stayed back. It was better, he convinced himself, to exert all care on the first mission, to go in cautiously and see if there was any way to reach the humans, to check if perhaps they were prisoners and would cooperate with him. The alternative to that, the idea that some people had yielded to the enemy, made some kind of deal with them, was almost too difficult for him to imagine.

Almost.

He did his best to close his mind to all of the thinking, the doubts and the fear. He had to…it was the only way to proceed, and he was sure that he and Lucas were the two best for the job out of everyone he had brought. He waited another thirty seconds, perhaps a minute…and then he headed forward, doing his best to stay hidden.

He walked for a while, but then, as he got closer, he got down on his hands and knees and crawled. He could hear Lucas behind him doing the same thing. He almost turned to say something to his colleague, but he realized silence was the best tactic right then. There was nothing he could say about the mission that his friend didn't already know…and while the enemy surveillance didn't *look* particularly effective, he reminded himself that they could have any technology, even one he had no idea of. Better to be as quiet as possible.

He looked forward, seeing mostly some lights inside the fortress. He wondered what kind of technology he was up against, how powerful the aliens truly were. Clearly, their ability to travel interstellar distances and their very quick defeat of Earth's military forces told him they were advanced…but how advanced? They didn't seem to be able to simply push a button and prevail, at least. Their weapons, both the nuclear warheads they had dropped all around and the weapons the robots had, seemed more or less comparable to Earth's. The guns were, perhaps, a bit more advanced, but not extraordinarily, and the nukes were actually less complex than those he knew his people had possessed. He had assumed that was because the enemy wanted to reduce them without destroying them utterly, but in fact, he didn't have any real idea. Still, the aliens' mere presence on Earth spoke of a capability that was still mostly science fiction to his people.

He crawled forward, coming to a stop every time he saw any movement by the enemy. He had scanned the fortress while it was still daylight, getting as good a look as he could without making himself visible. As best he could determine, there was only one real guard post, at least with a view this way. But that didn't affect what other forms of monitoring the enemy possessed. For all he knew, they were watching his every move, ready to destroy him at the push of a button. But he didn't think so. Still, he reminded himself that he was dealing with an enemy that was superior to him, at least in most ways. He couldn't make assumptions based on their abilities, because he didn't really know what those were, and how far they went.

He continued on, stopping three more times, and doing everything he could to avoid detection. He realized, or at least he thought based on what he had seen, that the enemy didn't really expect any of his people to come there, to threaten them in any way. That seemed strange to him, and he knew that if he was in the enemy's position, that would be his first concern.

Still, it was good…at least it meant that he could expect a lesser level of being watched than the enemy was capable of, perhaps even that he might reach one of the humans and communicate with him.

If it was true that the enemy was overconfident, he was sure it would be the last time. Whatever level of cockiness the aliens had, he was sure his mission would be the end of it. Even if his forces ended up being wiped out, if they accomplished nothing at all, the mere effort would send a sign to the enemy.

He worked his way around, more to the side that housed—or at least seemed to house—the humans. The prisoners—at least he *hoped* they were prisoners—were his target. Conflict was all he could expect from running into any of the aliens or their bots, but maybe, just maybe, he could get some real intel from the people. He was worried about that, too, especially since the ones he had seen looked fairly relaxed when he had spotted them earlier with one of the aliens. But he told himself, uncertain whether he truly believed it or not, that anyone who had been spared would look no different. He wasn't surprised that, given the chance to survive, and lacking any realistic option, people would make do.

But would they help their own kind, and risk their lives to do it? He didn't know.

The real question was, how would they react when they found out there was resistance out there, still going on, even if without a large chance of eventual success. Would they want to join up, or at least help them? Or would they call in the aliens, shout out the interlopers—in this case, him. He didn't know, and no matter how much he thought about it, he couldn't come up with an answer. His best guess was that some people would never do it, would not abandon their own people to aid some invaders…and others would.

That was far from satisfying, but it was all he had. He knew he had to go, to try to reach some of his people, but he also realized the level of danger he was in, how quickly his life could end. He might not even know it was coming. If the enemy saw him, targeted him…his first indication might be death.

He continued, maintaining his slow pace, checking every ten or fifteen seconds to see if he had been spotted. It was imperfect, all of it, but it was all he had, all he could do. After about twenty minutes, maybe half an hour, he realized he had gone around the corner, outside of the view of the guard tower. That didn't mean the enemy wasn't watching on their scanners, laughing as he moved toward their designated kill zone, but it was the best he could do. And that was that. There was no point in allowing all the things that could go wrong to shuffle through his thoughts.

He stopped for a minute, laying low and catching his breath…and then he continued.

Chapter Thirty-Eight

From the Notes of Hugh McDaniel

I have kept quite a record since the alien attack, and I have tried to make a journal entry at least once a day. I am not sure what I expect from it. Do I perceive that we will find a way to someday win this war that was forced on us, that in the future children may be reading my words, my account of our resistance? Or is it more likely that it will become the possession of the enemy, an amusing story of the doomed rebellion…or more likely, just ruined debris, burned or otherwise destroyed?

It is most likely of all that my words will be lost, that I will be killed along with all of those who are determined to win or die, and my notes will lie for a short while in the blood and gore…and then they will slowly disintegrate, lost forever along with the bodies of those who refused to yield.

Just Outside the 67th Avenue Subway Station
Forest Hills, Queens
D + 219 Days

"Alright, Horace…it's time to set this thing and get moving." Hugh had already tried to get Horace to go the night before, but he had refused. He would go when the bomb was set, and not before.

Horace just nodded. He sat still, staring at both Hugh and the bomb. He looked tired, and if he was anything close to as exhausted as Hugh was, he was *really* tired, but he remained in place, unwilling to move until the bomb was active.

Hugh turned toward the bomb, and he put his hands on the timer they had made. That alone had proven to be difficult, both in terms of connecting it to the bomb, and just in making the damned thing to run long enough. They had found a number of kitchen timers, over the past seven months, but they only ran an hour, which was not sufficient, not if he wanted any chance of getting away. He had finally managed to put something together using a watch and some other items, and now he set it at 8 hours. He looked up at Horace for a moment, silent. Then he flipped the switch.

He looked at the watch. 7:59, 7:58, 7:57…

"Okay, Horace, let's go." He turned and moved up, grabbing the bag he had packed earlier. He went quickly, not quite running, but almost. The bomb was in the deepest part of the station, the last place the enemy would search. He continued, looking behind a couple times to see that Horace was still there. It took about eight minutes for him to reach the top level of the station. It seemed odd to see no one else there. For more than six months, it had been full of people, the whole subway station and all of the connected segments had been turned into a home for thousands.

And now, they were all gone. On their way out of the city…save for the relatively few volunteers who remained to fight the enemy.

He came to the exit, the path that led to the street. He remembered the early days, the way it looked then. In the intervening months, his people had worked on it, building new stairs inside, and smoothing the outside. It was still tougher than it was before the attack, perhaps, but a lot of work had been done.

"I'm going to check on the defense force…you go, Horace. Don't waste time."

Horace stopped and he looked at Hugh. "You've got to come, Hugh. I know the defenders, some of them at least, are probably doomed, but you can't be. The way your mind works…it's too valuable. You're the most important one of all of us."

Hugh looked at Horace. He wanted to argue, but he couldn't. All his life he had known he was different, and now he realized that whatever chance his people had, it was better with him alive. It was better with all of his gifted people, those knowledgeable and capable, but especially with him.

"I understand, Horace. I am coming, I promise. But at least some—and quite possibly all—of those who volunteered to remain, to fight off the enemy, will die. I can't leave without seeing them one last time. I just can't." He paused for a moment, and then added, "Go…don't waste any more time. I will come, I promise." He stared at his companion for a few seconds. Then he turned and left…moving toward the massive fortifications they had built, which would now be occupied by a small force…a force which had to hold off the enemy for 8 hours.

*   *   *

The president stood, looking out quietly, as the morning slowly came, and for quite some time afterwards. It looked like it would be a fairly nice day, which had become rarer in the aftermath of the massive nuclear attack. He remembered, vaguely, his life when he had any desire to live it. His childhood had been pleasant enough, and notwithstanding the troublesome parts of it, his days in the service were mostly pretty good, too. He had known, of course, that running for president, assuming that level of responsibility, would carry its negatives, and probably a fair number of them…and it had, even before the stunning catastrophe that had happened. But he had never imagined once just how bad it would be.

If he hadn't run for president, if he had pursued something in the private sector, odds were he'd be dead now. At least 90% of the population had been killed in the initial assault, and in the days and weeks after. And if he had survived, he would likely be hidden somewhere with a number of survivors, eating whatever he could find and wondering if he would live to see the next week or month. That was the situation that most of the survivors found themselves in…of that he was sure. Even worse, he knew why the enemy had come, what they planned for the survivors, and it was terrible, worse than he'd even imagined. He found it difficult to think this way, but he considered those killed to be the fortunate ones. He realized he would be considered to have presided over the worst crisis in U.S. history, by far…that no one else, not Lincoln nor Roosevelt, had led the nation into a worse disaster than he had. His only salvation was, he couldn't see any way he was particularly at fault…it was just bad luck. But that didn't help much.

Not that anyone would really remember it…or him.

He wished he had been killed in the initial attack, spared from even knowing what he did…but he had sworn at least, not to give up. He didn't really believe there was a way to win the war of course, but just maybe he could find a way to strike at the enemy, to teach them that the battle they considered over was not…not yet at least. Not quite.

He was out near the fence, the barrier that kept his people penned in. The enemy spoke of working together, of cooperation…but by that, they meant essentially for the humans to act as their slaves, and to engage in unspeakable action against their own kind. And to them—whom he suspected would amount to many of his people—the offer of escaping what was in store for most of the people would seem like a good idea. He understood how it would work at first. It would attract those who had no real loyalty to the other people, those who had always been self-centered. The targets of their goals would shift, of course, and they would learn to be happy with less than they would have. Their children, assuming the enemy allowed them to reproduce, would probably follow in their parent's footsteps, just as most of the others born planetwide would grow up to serve their own roles, as breeding implements for their masters. He realized that he was taking his thoughts far, and yet he was almost certain he was correct. Earth would become a breeding ground for the aliens…for all time. And his people would serve them, forever.

One thing he was sure of…he wouldn't live to see it. He had already promised himself that. But he wanted to die for a purpose. He felt his entire presidency had been a disaster, and he wanted his final act, his last moments, to exist in some kind of victory. He wasn't sure what that could be, or when…only that it would be soon. He wasn't foolish enough to believe he could maintain the illusion that he was going along with the alien plan…and he was sure that some of his people would ultimately bring doubt upon him, looking to advance their own positions.

He didn't care about much anymore, but it meant a lot to him to strike, to hurt the enemy somehow. He felt in many ways, that his life had been a failure…he wanted his death to be a success.

He began to move, to turn away from the fence…but then he saw something in the distance. He froze, at first sure it had to be something belonging to the aliens. But then he caught a good glimpse, and he saw a human. No, there were two of them, he was pretty sure of that…and they were close. They were approaching the fence very cautiously.

He felt a wave of excitement. At first he tried to let it pass, to ignore them. They were probably just a couple of loose survivors, perhaps looking for food or something. But then he realized how close they had gotten. He didn't know, of course, but his military days called out to him, told him he was looking at professionals. He knew he couldn't be sure, and yet he was. A pair of scavengers wouldn't come right toward the alien construct.

He turned and looked behind him, checking to make sure no one was watching. There were none of the aliens, at least that he could see, but there were two or three humans…and though it made him sad to realize, he didn't trust most of them either.

He watched for a few more seconds, waiting for a moment when no one was looking. And then it came.

"Out there, I can see you…if you can hear me, listen. This is an alien base…the lead alien base. If you're out scavenging, go somewhere else." He spoke as quietly as he thought he could and still be heard, and he turned around and looked behind him every few seconds to ensure that no one there had picked up what he had said. His heartbeat was accelerated, and he was starting to sweat profusely. He realized that anything, one of the aliens seeing or hearing him, or even one of the less trustworthy members of his own race, could bring everything to a terrible close in seconds. He turned again and said, "Wait…wait where you are."

He looked behind him again, trying not to appear suspicious…and failing at that, he assumed. But the early morning hour, combined with his being in the least travelled spot in the entire installation meant there weren't a lot of people—or aliens—around.

He saw that the figures had heard him…but that they were still approaching, and now they were heading right for him. He felt some panic, and also some excitement. The failure of the two to turn and run told him they were more than scavengers. Was it possible that there were groups of people gathered together, perhaps even that they were still fighting? It seemed amazing to him, almost unthinkable, but then he realized that he had been a prisoner since almost the beginning, that he truly had no idea what the remnant of his people had been doing. There had been some urgency in the alien camp a couple days before, and a group had set out. He had figured it was some mission, part of their general operations…but what if it was a response? What if somewhere, his people were still resisting, still putting up a fight? Was that possible? That some random group could still be fighting when his military, the world's military, was put down in a few days?

He looked behind him again, then out in front. He waved his arms, directed the two people to come closer to him. He didn't know what to do…he couldn't bring them inside, he knew that. The fence surrounding the facility had some sort of sensor built into it. He didn't know much about it, but he was sure it wouldn't allow the two people to sneak in. No, he would have to talk to them quickly…and then send them back, hoping they escaped. He suspected his time had come, that whatever he could tell the two men, and what he could do inside, perhaps to facilitate their escape, might very well end in his demise. He knew that, but it didn't stop him, or even slow him down. He was sure his end was close, much closer than he had anticipated…but he felt good, the best he had in a long time.

"Hey…what is this place?" It was one of the men outside, now close. He had to make a decision, now. Did he speak to them right away? Or should he tell them to come back that night? He didn't know what to do, but his subconscious took control.

"Come back here…right here…tonight after dark." He knew he wasn't supposed to be out at night, but he was also aware that the enemy had sent a decent number of its guards away. He felt it was possible that he could sneak to the wall and communicate with the two men, at least for a few minutes. He didn't know what he would be able to do, if anything, but he was definitely curious where the men had come from. The first intelligence he would have, if you could call it that, in more than six months. And he had about fourteen hours to figure out what to tell them…and just maybe how he could help them.

Chapter Thirty-Nine

From the Notes of Hugh McDaniel

All of you, hear me. The enemy is approaching in vast numbers. You cannot win…so don't try. Just keep the enemy occupied for a few hours. And then pull back, one unit at a time, as slowly as you can. Remember, the bomb is set to explode in seven and a half hours, and even moving at full speed, you will need *at least* several hours to reach even moderate safety. Break off, slip into the subway system to hide your route…but I want to see you again…as many of you as possible. Please…

Just Outside the 67th Avenue Subway Station
Forest Hills, Queens
D + 219 Days

Hugh ran…almost at least. He was tired, and the stress was almost insurmountable. The best possible result for the day was the explosion of the bomb, the destruction of the alien force…and probably most or all of his rearward forces, too. That would leave him without what had been his home for over six months—hell, the area that had always been his home—with almost twenty thousand people scattered around, with no place to rest, no real idea what was around.

And out of the nearly one thousand people he was leaving behind, the volunteers that had stunned him with their courage and their numbers, he wondered if any would survive. Despite his last message to them, he didn't really expect to see many of them—if any—again. It felt terrible to leave people behind on what could only be called a suicide mission, and worse to depart himself, wishing them well and then moving to a position of relative safety. He bounced around, sometimes hoping at least some would escape as his final words to them had stated. But the other side of him, the part that coldly analyzed data, told him that was unlikely...that they would all die, that those who survived combat with the approaching aliens, would be swept up in the nuclear blast and destroyed utterly. He could only hope the enemy was, too.

Maybe, though, a handful would escape. Perhaps they would get down to the subway, find the path that the others had cleared, and get far enough away from the blast to survive. Whether they would be poisoned by radiation, live just to die after a week or two's agony, he just didn't know. The bomb was large—very large—and he knew the blast would be huge. But beyond that, he had no specifics.

Unless none of his plan worked. If the bomb had a flaw that he didn't find, or if his forces fell more quickly than he hoped, and the enemy somehow found it and disarmed it in time, then, all he would have managed to do was separate his people, leaving a thousand behind to be overrun...and the rest to be caught up with and destroyed over the next few days, away from the positions they had worked so hard to build up. He had checked the bomb again and again, and he was as confident that it would work as he could be, but he just wouldn't know for sure until it blew.

Or until another six hours and fifteen minutes passed, and it didn't.

He looked up, saw the crowd around him. They were the tail end of his people, the last group to leave save the one thousand remaining behind. That made them one of the better groups, more or less on par with the first team he'd sent to lead the withdrawal and those left behind to fight for the time they needed. He saw the space up ahead, the tunnel, what had been a train route before the attack, opening up into another station. The route his people had to take was open, he was sure of that. It was open because he had sent parties to make sure it was, and to dig out wherever they had to…but also, he had to acknowledge, out of pure luck. The fact that none of the underwater passages had been breached, that the tunnels, while many sections had been caved in, had been clearable, from Queens through Manhattan, and then through to the tunnels leading to New Jersey was almost amazing. He knew that was because of the types of bombs the enemy had used, their lack of deploying any truly large nukes, and he was truly grateful. The ability to move his people out of the city underground was incredibly helpful. It allowed him to do so quietly, to hide it from the enemy, and to make the small group left behind to fight appear to be everyone.

And he would see how successful that was soon…whether his people escaped, and how his one thousand heroes did.

*   *   *

Travis moved forward, slowly—very slowly. He had been lying in a small scrub of bushes for hours now, waiting until nightfall to return to the wall, to see if the mysterious figure actually returned. The day had seemed to take forever to pass, and he had stayed pretty much unmoving, beside Lucas for hours. Now, it was time…time to see what was happening, possibly to die, or just maybe to learn what was going on. What was really going on.

He was suspicious of the people inside the facility, but he told himself, if the man who gave him the instructions really wanted to expose him, he could have done it last night. There was nothing the two of them could have done, no way they could have avoided a sudden attack. But nothing had happened. That, at least, gave their contact some version of credibility, enough at least for him to lie still all day, to wait until the nighttime and see just what happened. Perhaps they would just walk into being captured—which, in his case, and he was sure Lucas's as well, meant dying—but he didn't think so. Something about the man they communicated with struck him as genuine. He didn't know if that was just his mind drawing what it wanted from the contact or not, but he believed it.

The day had been long, longer than anything Travis could easily recount, but now it was dark again. It was time. He had slipped out of the cover that had held him for hours and hours and kept him hidden. He moved slowly toward the fence, looking all around for any movement. Once, about halfway back, he spotted some, and he froze, extending his hand to Lucas as well. He stared, watching one of the aliens walk by, and staying as still as possible, praying not to be noticed. He had been deathly afraid the alien race had some kind of special ability—seeing in the dark, sensing a threat—but as he watched, the creature continued on its way until it was out of sight.

He waited for a good bit more, perhaps two minutes, and then he continued forward slowly. He began looking, checking in the sparse light from the fortress for the human figure he had seen early that morning. There was nothing at first, only the outer fence surrounding the…fortress? Prison? But then, just as his spirits began to fall, he saw something.

He froze, putting his arm out to stop Lucas as well. At first, he wasn't sure if it was their contact, or just someone else, but the figure moved almost directly toward them, and after a few more seconds, he realized it was him. He was still scared, nervous that the contact would turn out to be hostile or that they would be caught by someone else, perhaps one of the aliens. But the man walked slowly toward the exact same spot in the gate where they had spoken this morning.

He stayed where he was, still for another fifteen seconds or so, but then he decided that he would trust the contact. He had already had more than enough chance to call in help to take them prisoner, and he hadn't.

He still moved slowly, trying to show as little of himself as he could. The last twenty feet or so to the wall was almost completely barren, and he stopped again for a few seconds. *This is it...what you came down here for.*

He looked again, seeing no one but the same man he had seen that morning. He sucked in a deep breath, and he moved out, closing the rest of the distance to the wall.

"Hello," he said. "My name is Travis, and I am from...a small group of locals." That wasn't true, of course, but while he was prepared to bet his own life on his contact, he wasn't ready to put the rest of them at risk...not the 500 that had come with him, nor the 20,000 that remained behind. If he was going to die, to fall into the hands of an enemy, he was going to do it alone...or just with Lucas, that much he had promised himself.

"Hello, Travis." The man's voice sounded familiar, as though he had heard it before. That made him pause, but just for a few seconds.

He edged forward, perhaps another six inches, and the man looked nervous. "Stay back," he said. "I'm guessing the fence is monitored. Don't touch it, and don't move any more than you have to. Just talk...and listen."

"Okay," Travis answered. "Who are you?" He was silent for a few seconds, and then he added, "You look familiar...and you sound it, too."

"I...I worked for the government. Before the aliens came. But there's no time for that. We've got maybe a few minutes before someone comes along, so let's use it well. Listen to me! The aliens came here for a reason, a very specific reason…and you have to know about it. They want to…they want to use us, our women to be specific, as breeding modules. They have some kind of malady, some sort of affliction that interferes with their normal birthing process. They can't have their own children anymore. I know their birthrate has been declining for some time, but I'm pretty sure it is zero now. They've got a thousand women in this complex, even now, as a test phase. If it works, they plan to expand it to millions. Do you understand? They want to use us as a breeding system. I've seen it, the women…it is horrific. I can't imagine they will survive it. I don't know that there is any way out, any way to defeat them…but whatever there is, we have to try. Do you understand?"

Travis was silent at first, shocked. He had known that the enemy couldn't have planned anything good for his race…but he was still trying to understand what the man was saying. And then it struck him.

"Oh my God…you're the president…" He was shocked, dumbfounded. Was it possible?

"Yes…I am…was…but that is not relevant. My time is almost over. I am a prisoner…but that is almost through. I wondered what I could do, how I could strike back one last time. Perhaps this is it…and perhaps I will get another chance. But you have to go now that you know…go back now. Do whatever you can to survive. The enemy is here for a reason, and it is absolute disaster for our people. Tell everyone you can. As soon as the first thousand of their spawn are…born…they will expand the program greatly, condemn millions of women to serve as incubators for their…*children*." He turned and looked around behind him, then he spun around again, turning to face Travis and Lucas. "You *have* to go, while you still have a chance to get away from here. Spread the word. I don't know who will believe you, but I swear it is true. I swear to God it is true.

Now, go…please. Every extra minute you spend here is dangerous."

Travis stared back at…the president. *The president!* He was still trying just to process what he had heard, and to accept who he was speaking to. The whole thing seemed almost impossible…but he realized it wasn't, it was happening. And what the president had told him, his words about the true plot of the aliens, it hadn't sunken in yet, at least not completely, but it was beyond the worst things he had imagined.

He hadn't anticipated any good news, of course, but this was worse, even, than the enemy simply eradicating every human being, and taking over Earth for their own inhabitation. That, at least, he would understand. He wouldn't approve, of course, and he would fight to the last to resist, but this?

He wondered for a moment if he could trust the information, if it was true. But it had come from the president! The government might not be relevant anymore, it might not even exist…but to him, it still did. At least in a manner of speaking. He was a lieutenant in the Marine Corps…and this was his Commander-in-Chief. "Sir…I am an officer in the Marines. Actually, we both are." His arm moved to his forehead…an almost unconscious salute. He could feel the movement behind him, and he knew Lucas doing the same thing. "We will go back to our people…and we will resist, as long as one of us can still stand. We promise that, Sir."

Chapter Forty

From Carl Delvus to…whomever…

My hands are shaking. Hell, my whole body is. I have multiple reasons to be sure the enemy is almost here…numerous scouting reports among them. My watch is not set to the actual time, as the time is immaterial. It says 4:37…and it is counting down. When it hits zero, either the bomb will go off, destroying everything within miles, both any of us who remain and the enemy…or it won't. I don't really know, myself, what will happen. My skills as a New York police officer are many and varied, but nuclear weapons are not on that list, I'm afraid. But I do have one thing, my faith in Hugh, and that is very strong. I expect the bomb will work, and I know I have two things to do…and just maybe three.

First, I have to fight the enemy, keep them occupied until the explosion.

Second, I have to hold the subway station. I can't risk allowing any of them to get inside, to find the bomb before it blows up, and possibly disarm it.

And third, if my lines are holding, if I decide that fewer of my people than I have can keep the enemy occupied, I can start sending some of them away. I know that command came from Hugh's good side, from the part that compelled him to give my people some kind of chance. But does it really? Can an hour or two truly help someone? Or less than that? Is there any point continuing to send off people right near the end, with half an hour left or fifteen minutes? Can they possibly get far enough away to dodge the murderous intensity of the explosion, especially traveling over the difficult ground they would have to?

I don't believe it, didn't think that any of my people will survive...but I am still going to send them if possible, give anyone I can do without whatever chance they have...even if I believe there is no hope.

But I will die here...and I will consider it a massive victory if the explosion takes me, if I am able to endure the hours of combat against the enemy until then.

Just Outside the 67th Avenue Subway Station
Forest Hills, Queens
D + 219 Days

Carl was looking up, staring west when the first shots erupted. He looked at his watch, noted the time. 4:16. That was how long he had until the bomb went off...at least until it was supposed to go off. But now, he put all thoughts of that out of his mind. The bomb wasn't his job, his responsibility...but keeping the enemy occupied, getting them to deploy as much as possible of their force right here, and holding them in place for just over four hours, were all his. And he realized he had never held a more important position. He wasn't sure if he could succeed, if he could pin the enemy down until the bomb went off, hold them there until they were destroyed.

He was in deep cover...all of his people were. They had positions that were intended for thousands of defenders, but there were only 943 of them. He would have cut down on the front, reduced the length of their lines, but he was afraid that might telegraph to the enemy that they were facing only a rearguard. So, instead, his people were spread out loosely, all except the force right in the middle. Around the 67th Street subway station, the place which had been their main base, and his home for seven months…and now, deep within, held the bomb. That was his only priority…keeping the enemy out of there for 4:14 now.

He mostly kept hidden, trying to stay alive. He would have better shots than he did now, and soon, and he found his tactics somewhat different than they would have been. He was generally very aggressive, but now he waited, allowing more of the enemy to advance. He realized that the most important thing—the only crucial part of the operation—was the bomb…and buying the 4:13 until it hopefully went off. He had to keep the enemy away from it and occupied enough that they deployed all or most of their forces right here…and stayed in place until the explosion.

He waited for another minute, perhaps two, and then he raised his head slightly. He could only see a small section of the debris strewn battlefield, but even that was completely filled with enemy bots. He started counting the ones he could see, but he realized after a moment there were just too many.

He ducked down again, breathing hard, trying to center himself, to prepare for a fight he knew would be his last. But, while he fully expected to die, he knew he couldn't let it happen too soon.

Preferably, not for 4:11. He had to keep the enemy occupied for that long, and he wanted to survive, to be killed by the explosion and not by the enemy. It didn't seem like much, but to him it would be victory.

He sucked in a deep breath and popped up, firing his rifle on full auto for a couple seconds, and then dropping back down, as the enemy responded with an amount of fire that seemed almost impossible. He was lying on his back, looking up at what almost seemed to be a solid wall of incoming projectiles, and he slid to the side, moving to a

different spot so he could take another shot. He was
normally rock solid in combat, utterly unshakable, but now
he realized he had lost some of that. He wasn't sure if it was
the size of the enemy force, the severity of the attack…or
just the fact that he was truly realizing that his life was
measured in hours, if not minutes.

He forced in a breath, told himself he had volunteered,
more so, he had insisted he would stay, and he had accepted
the position as leader from Hugh himself, promising that he
would do everything he could to hold until the bomb went
off. For a few seconds, he felt himself fading on that, and
feeling the urge to run, to get as far away as possible. But
that only lasted for perhaps half a minute. Then he found
his courage again, and he accepted his role. He would die
today, but he swore it wouldn't be until the bomb went
off…4:06 from now.

He sat for a few seconds, and then he leapt up again,
opening fire on the enemy.

* * *

Hugh stopped for a moment, both to take a rest, and even
more to allow the group that was with him to catch a breath.
The underground route they were taking had been cleaned
up, as much as his people had been able to do in the short
time they had, but it was still fairly messy. He was in very
good shape now, and he was still tired. He knew that many
of his people were ready to drop without at least a brief rest.
They didn't have long, of course, but he figured a ten
minute break would fit into their schedule.

He sat down on a piece of broken masonry, off a little
from the crowd. His thoughts were still back in the 67th
Street Station, with the people he had left behind. To fight
while the others fled.

To die.

He had discussed their options with them for sending

some of the people away, of perhaps a few at least having a chance at survival. But he knew that wasn't very likely. The most important job they had was to defend the station, and the bomb. Even if that battle went well at first, and the commander decided to begin withdrawing some of his people, he knew that was unlikely to lead to their escape…at least if the bomb went off. He tried to imagine what would happen to the tunnels he had passed through when that detonation happened, how many would cave in…possibly with some of his people inside. He had stubbornly maintained the view that some of those he had left behind could escape, but now he realized how likely it was that none would. Almost a thousand people left behind, and the fact that they had all volunteered didn't make it much better. He wondered how they were doing, both in their fight, and with their choice. He respected every one of them profoundly, but he suspected that some at least would waver. They would question their decisions. Would they break and run? Try to escape, even though it was too late? He didn't imagine most of them would in the end, but he wondered what even a few would do to the other's morale.

He stood up abruptly, trying to push his thoughts from those left behind, who he knew he could regret later, to those with him now, those who could make it the rest of the way, escape from the explosion. There was nothing more he could do, not for those he had left behind, nor to make the bomb work. But he could get those in here to safety, at least from the explosion. He guessed it had been less than ten minutes since they stopped, perhaps seven or eight. But that was enough.

"Come on…all of you." He could see that the others weren't really ready, that they were all tired. But everyone got up, more or less upon his command "We don't have a lot of time left, and we have to finish,"

Then he looked forward, down the rugged but partially cleared tunnel, and he started moving once again.

*   *   *

Travis made it back, while it was still dark. He had proceeded through the night, moving very slowly, with Lucas right behind him. They had been utterly silent, struck by what they had found…both the president, and what he had told them. The thought of the alien's true purpose, their use for humans, was worse than anything he had even considered. He had been determined to fight to the end already, but now he was driven. He became focused now, more even than he was before, to find a way to win…to stop the aliens and drive them off.

He had tried to get the president to come with them, though he didn't know how they would get him out, not without giving up their presence. Fortunately, perhaps, the president had a better grasp on things than he did. He had told them again to go, and go quickly, before they were discovered. Then he had stepped back from the perimeter, away from the fence and after exchanging a final extended glance with them, he walked back toward one of the buildings, without even looking back. Travis and Lucas watched until he went inside, and then they began to make their way back, slowly, still aware that at any time they could be detected.

When they had finally entered the small camp where the most forward of their people were deployed, Travis was finally able to speak. Barely. He turned toward Lucas, and he said, "That was…" But he didn't finish, he didn't know what to say, to his friend who had been there with him, and even more, to the others.

Lucas's eyes were fixed on Travis's, and he just said, "Yeah." His tone was very somber. The two of them had come, had brought their group to do…what? What had he expected to do with 500 people, or even the smaller number who had made it the entire way? He didn't know, not really…and yet he had discovered something beyond what he had hoped to find. The president. Still alive…but not for long, he suspected.

He had been working as the co-head of his group, doing everything he could think of with his brother to lead them all…but now he had seen, and spoken with, the leader of the entire nation. He had been defeated, that much was clear, but still, there was defiance that ran within him. Travis had never expected to meet the president, and he still couldn't believe he had. It felt almost like a dream, but it was real.

"What did you find?" The question came from one of his people. There were about ten or twelve of them around, and honestly, he didn't know who had asked the question.

"We found…" He wasn't sure what to say, how to explain what the aliens were up to…or who they had met, who they had gotten the information from. "…we found a lot. The aliens, we know why they are here, and it is terrible, worse than anything we had even considered. We *have* to win. We have to find a way to destroy them, to chase them off our planet. But first, we have to return now. This base is too strong for 400 of us to take…and we have to tell the others what we found. We need to spread the word. The aliens have not come to use the planet for food production or for colonization…they are here to use us as breeding stock, to help them continue their species." He said the words, but even as they came out, he found himself struggling to understand them. He believed the president, utterly, but he still couldn't quite bring himself to accept what was truly going on…or what it meant, to their next action and to the future in general.

He looked out at the people standing around him, about twenty now, mostly silent, just staring back in shock. One of them started to say something, to ask a question, but before he got it out, there were shouts from beyond, from the guard post off to the side of the camp.

"Enemy approaching…enemy approa…"

Travis heard the sounds of enemy fire blasting as the warning stopped suddenly. He saw his people standing around for a couple seconds…and then they started running, and the robots appeared on the ridge above, and they opened fire.

Chapter Forty-One

From the Notes of Hugh McDaniel

Less than two hours…that is how long we have, how long until the bomb explodes, or it doesn't. Until we find out whether we will survive, at least until the enemy sends another force, or if we will face this assault, in the ruins of Northern New Jersey instead of our prepared lines in the city, with our people disorganized and spread out.

I have a lot to worry about, the enemy, food, my brother and how his expedition is going are the top three for sure, but they are not the only ones. Though right now, leading my group, the last one to flee from the city, requires all my attention. They are ready now to step out into New Jersey. I had figured we would be farther by now, but the underground passages were rougher than I had expected, especially for a large group. We made it, at least this far, but I wasn't sure we could get far enough. Ground Zero would be the 67th Street subway station, our home for seven months…but how far the destruction would reach was, at best, a guess. I figured that being ten miles from the city would be safe, at least from the blast itself, but now I knew we were not going to get that far. Most of the people were, at least, but our group would be fortunate to put four or five miles behind them. That would probably be far enough

342

to protect them from the blast, at least if we managed to take some cover, but the radiation was another question. That was going to affect everyone, even our people who got the farthest away. But there was nothing I could do about that, so I tried to stop thinking about it. Mostly without success.

Tunnels Under Manhattan
D + 219 Days

"Alright, c'mon…all of you. I know you're tired, but we don't have time to rest. Go out, through the tunnels, and into New Jersey. Then, just start walking. Every mile we put between us and the city will help. And stay within hearing distance of the people in front of and behind you. When we get to within ten minutes of the explosion, we'll announce it…and everybody will pass it on. Then you've got one mission. Find and grab whatever cover you can get." *Assuming the bomb works.* That was still a huge uncertainty in his mind.

He looked around, watching his people climb out of what had once been the entrance into the tunnel leading to Penn Station. Once—not all that long ago—thousands of people had come through here every day, he realized. They had taken the trains from stations all over New Jersey and come into the city. That seemed like it had been years and years before, but he realized it had been less than eight months.

He stood and watched his crowd, as they raced through the opening and out into the cloud strewn day. He could see the outside from where he was, but he had told himself he would be the final one to step outside. That was foolish, he knew. He ought to be at the very front of the escape, doing everything he could to save himself. But some things he just couldn't do…and that was one of them. He might be, in one way of thinking, the most vital person his side had, but they had trusted him as their leader—something he still considered miraculous—and he was going to behave the way he thought a leader should. And that meant going last.

Except for the almost one thousand people he had left behind. He still harbored thoughts that some of them might escape, but he knew that was mostly a way of salving his mentality, of pushing off the overbearing view that he had basically sentenced them all to die. He knew that they had volunteered, and he was equally aware that most of those who had escaped with him would probably die, too…in another day, a month, a year. But he still couldn't get those he'd left behind—many of whom were likely already dead, he realized—out of his mind.

He looked outside for a moment, his vision still tender to all the light. The day wasn't exactly nice, it was cloudy and humid, but it was vastly brighter out there than it had been in the tunnels he'd been in for almost six hours.

He could see his people gathering around, not moving forward as quickly as he wanted them to. "Go," he shouted. "We've got less than two hours left, and we want to be as far west as we can get." He turned toward the handful of people still in the tunnel, waving with his arms. "C'mon…all of you. Keep moving. When you get outside, continue on, as quickly as you can. I know it seems bright, but you will adjust to that quickly. I understand that you're tired, but there is no time to rest. Not yet. In two hours, you can stop and take a break…but not before." He knew that was mostly a lie, of course. Even if the bomb went off, and assuming it took out the entire enemy force and left his people there unscathed—a pair of huge ifs—he knew that the situation would only have gotten worse. He would have nearly as many people as he'd had, with no homes, no place to even rest. He would have gone from perhaps two months of food, to, if he was lucky, two weeks…and no idea where he might find more. And his people…he had to admit that they had mostly risen to do what he'd needed, fought bravely and stubbornly…but he suspected the worst was still ahead.

Still, he knew many of them were near the breaking point. Perhaps, the destruction of the enemy forces would buy him some time…but how much? The obliteration of their entire force—and that was more than he could bring himself to anticipate—would certainly communicate to them in a way they couldn't possibly ignore, that his people still had some fight left in them, that however much they felt they had Earth conquered, they didn't yet. Not quite, at least. But what would that result in? Perhaps just an even larger response, and possibly one that happened very soon. And this time he wouldn't have a surprise nuclear weapon waiting.

He looked at his people racing outside, and he tore his thoughts away from everything else. All that mattered now was getting them all far enough away from the blast that they could survive it. The other problems would come after that, and there was no point in considering them right now.

He watched as the last of his people moved out of the tunnel, and into the light of the day. He turned to face the opening, and he started to walk. He got about two thirds of the way, into the light trickling in from outside…and then he heard shooting. For an instant, he hoped it was his own people, perhaps just a mistake of some kind. But in a few seconds, he realized that the gunfire wasn't from any of his weapons.

It was the enemy.

* * *

Travis realized his survival of the first few seconds was just luck. About half of those gathered around him were hit, mostly several times. He had frozen for a second or two, which he knew was the worst thing he could do, but now he was moving, bringing his own rifle up to fire back, even as he dove behind a pile of rocks, seeking at least some cover.

He saw that Lucas had made it too, at least through the first moment. He was also diving for cover and bringing his weapon around.

Travis's mind raced, and he realized he should have been more careful. The enemy had obviously spotted him, somewhere on the way back...and now they were fighting his people. He wondered, for an instant, if he hadn't been wrong about the president, if perhaps it was him who had given them up. But he couldn't bring himself to believe that. Not only did the president have his loyalty, but he was sure the man had been telling the truth about the enemy.

That didn't mean they hadn't been surveilled, that it hadn't been his meeting with him that had given them away. But it could have been a number of other things as well, and it didn't really matter what. He had to endure, to beat back the attack, and to make it back home, to the others. They all deserved to know what was truly at stake...what this fight was really about.

He peered over the rocks for a second, looking out to see how many robots there were. He only saw three. If that was all there were, perhaps they had just been found by a scouting party. But even if that was the case, he knew now the enemy was aware of their presence. They would be sending more, and they could be there any time.

He ducked down, his mind racing, trying to decide what to do. He could hear more of his people racing forward, coming into the fight. He guessed he had a least a hundred combatants fighting on his side now, and, still, all he could see were three enemies.

Two enemies. One of them appeared to be down now, not firing at all, and not moving either. The other two had serious damage, but they were still fighting...and all he had of his own casualties was a wild guess. He knew they were severe, though. Maybe 40.

Whatever the situation, he knew he had to get his people

moving as soon as the other two bots were silenced, that staying there was just waiting for the enemy to appear in greater strength. They would probably be chased even if they moved out, but staying where they were was begging for death. First, however, he had to neutralize the two remaining bots.

He called out, trying to get some command over the situation. "Everybody, fire. We need to take out these two bots. Now!" He brought his own gun up, and he blasted away, shooting for far longer than he had before. He knew that was dangerous, that the bots could target him very quickly, but he was also aware that his own force was up to maybe a hundred and twenty now…and that was after perhaps forty who were taken down already. The two surviving bots had been riddled with shots, and he had seen before that their targeting was often affected. Between that and the number of targets they had to fire at, he decided it was better to stay put and fire away.

He blasted one of them, holding his rifle, and emptying the clip. Only then did he duck back down to reload. The enemy fired back, but it was down to one gun, and its aim did seem to be off. He had managed to duck without taking a hit, and he slammed another cartridge into place. Then he moved over a few feet, and he popped up again, firing as he did. He blasted the same robot, along with at least seven or eight others. It stopped firing and stood there for a few more seconds. Then it fell down hard and stayed still.

He turned to the other one and leveled his rifle. But before he could even get a shot off, it fell too. The shooting from his side continued for another few seconds, but gradually, it stopped.

"Alright, everybody…check around for the wounded. We've got to get moving fast!" He knew that there would be more robots coming, and probably soon. He would try to take the injured with him, but he knew he would have to leave those too badly hurt behind. It tore at him to abandon the seriously wounded, but he knew he didn't have a choice. He had to do everything he could to get the word back to the others, to tell them what they were truly fighting for. Not even Hugh had imagined what was actually going on.

"We're leaving in three minutes! Get everyone who can walk on their feet now." He didn't say anything else. He couldn't. But he knew his people would understand. For a few seconds, he thought about shooting them, the seriously wounded, finishing them off quickly. But then he just repeated, "Three minutes…everyone be ready!"

He looked out over the carnage, seeing dead everywhere…and a few wounded he knew wouldn't survive much longer. He stepped up to one, and he looked at him. The injured man stared back, his eyes full of fear, and he just nodded, gritting his teeth. Travis tried to steel himself, and he brought his weapon around to fire, to put the man out of his misery. But the resolve to do it, to shoot his own combatant wasn't there. He tried, for perhaps a minute, but he just couldn't pull the trigger. He stared at the man for a few more seconds, his eyes locked on his comrade's, the one he knew was dying, but couldn't bring himself to shoot. His expression was a silent apology, a call for forgiveness…and then he turned away, calling out again to the others.

"Alright…let's get moving."

Chapter Forty-Two

From the Notes of Estle-Starric

The past moments have been very troublesome. First, I had a report that the president, the human leader, had not been sincere with me when he had sworn to do as I commanded. That wasn't all that was surprising, of course. I had already distrusted him and planned to watch him carefully. What shocked me was that the tip came not from one of my guards, but from one of his closest people. It was the smart thing for one of them to do, of course, but the idea of betraying their own leader? It was bizarre. We have many personal thoughts, and we disagree about all sorts of things...but the idea of going against your commander, of pursuing your own course of action against your orders? That was unique to the humans.

I was just about to act on that, to deal with the president once and for all...but then one of our scouting parties reported in. They had found a group of the enemy...and even worse, the reporting ceased a few minutes later. That meant that the bots had been destroyed, or at least severely damaged, and it indicated they had found a fairly large and well-armed group of humans.

The whole thing seemed impossible to me. How were these humans still fighting so well, here as well as New York and several other cities, and how were they so heavily armed? Perhaps, some scattered remnants of their armed forces escaped from us during the initial invasion, but how many could that be? And how much ammunition and other equipment could they have carried away with them? It was strange…very strange…and it came at a difficult time for me. The strength I have here is currently severely depleted, many of my bots assigned to the group moving even now against New York. My first urge was to put together another large group, send it out after the humans here, however many there are…but I decided that I cannot significantly weaken the defenses of the city. Not now, not knowing how many humans are out there, and whether they could pose a threat to us. Instead, I have sent out a small force, an effort to strike at the enemy, to see if they are a small and manageable group, and to destroy them if they are.

And if they are not, if they are a large group, it will give us warning, and time to prepare to repel any assault they may attempt.

Gavicon City
Approximately Twenty-Five Miles West of the Ruins of Washington
D + 216 Days

Estle-Starric stood out in the center of the main common area, directing both his bots and his Gavicons. He knew he was being conservative, that his forces were more than enough to take on anything that might attack, but he was not going to take any chances. He had ordered all of the humans to assemble, and he had assigned a number of guards to watch over them all. If there was a fight, if the force outside was large enough to defeat the second detachment he had sent out and attack the main city, he wanted to be ready. The complex was not only the largest and most important one his people had on Earth, it was also the home of the first round of the breeding program, the one that would show whether the planet was yet another failure, or if he had been right all along, if it would witness the first successful births his people had seen in more than one hundred years. He couldn't take any chances. Not now.

He watched as robots moved around, taking up position on the walls. He had Gavicons out there, too, all heavily armed…just in case. He didn't really expect the enemy to have sufficient force to mount an assault, but he had decided that he wasn't going to take any chances. If his decision to keep back most of his forces resulted in some of the humans escaping, so be it. It was far more important to ensure that the base remained secure, that nothing interfered with the breeding program's test phase, now nearing its completion.

He moved around, checking the walls, making sure there were bots defending every portion. Even as he did it, he told himself there was no point, that the enemy might have a force outside, but it was nowhere near powerful enough to attack his city. Still, he realized he had been wrong before, and he just wasn't willing to take any chances.

Carlik-Goosevel, you take command in this area. I know there isn't much chance of the enemy mounting a credible assault on us, but prepare, nevertheless. We're not taking any chances."

His subordinate looked back at him, and he acknowledged. "Understood, Commander." Then he turned and started yelling out specific orders to the bots, adjusting their positions along the wall.

Estle-Starric stood where he was for a moment, watching. Then he moved on, heading to other sections of the wall to ensure that his fortress was well defended from every angle.

* * *

Hugh dove out of the old railroad tunnel, out into the broken sunshine and down behind a large chunk of stone. His mind was racing, wondering what his people had run into. Had he been wrong, had the enemy discovered what he was doing and reacted? Or had they just left a small force behind their attack?

It didn't matter, at least not to his next action. He had to lead his force, get as many of them as possible into the fight as quickly as he could. If there were only a few bots out there, he could possibly defeat them. And if he had miscalculated, if the enemy did have a sizable force present, he knew he would die, that all of those in his group would. But his actions in either situation were the same, to fight as hard as he could…for as long as possible.

He dropped the large knapsack he was carrying, and he pulled out his rifle. It was loaded already, and he took a deep breath and then rolled around, poking his head above the stone in front of him. He looked around for a few seconds, and then he ducked down again, before any enemy fire came in. He hadn't shot, not yet, but he'd only seen four bots. That was far from comprehensive, but it certainly improved the odds that he had just come out on an enemy scouting force, perhaps guarding the advance of their main body.

Still, he realized that the bots he faced were dangerous, especially to his detachment, all armed, but surprised and unprepared for combat. He could hear shooting, some number of his people engaging, but most of the fire so far was from the enemy. He knew that too many of his people had been distracted, worried about the sudden move, about the bomb that hopefully would go off in well under two hours…and about whether they would be far enough away. They would engage, but not all as quickly as they would in better circumstances…and that meant a lot of them would be killed first.

He rolled around and brought his own weapon up again, aiming for one of the bots. He fired, on full auto, for a couple seconds, and then he ducked back down. He was pretty sure he scored at least a few hits, but the bots still seemed to be fully functional. They had taken some damage, but not all that much yet.

He moved over, crawling along the back of a debris pile, and then he popped up again. He was aiming for the same target, but it had moved. He zeroed in on it, but that took perhaps a second, and it left less time to fire. He let off one blast from his gun, and he ducked down again.

He crawled a few more feet, and then he found another spot to fire. He popped up and shot, staying there for a long time, maybe three seconds, and then ducking, *just* before the bots returned his fire. He could hear more of his own side's guns firing now, and the enemy shooting had declined a bit. But there was still a lot of fire coming in, and he knew his force, perhaps two hundred in total, would suffer badly, even if there were only four enemy bots present. And he was certain they would have already transmitted to the main party that they were under attack. Would they send back more bots to aid them? Or would they pull back the entire group? He knew they would be engaged now with the forces he had left behind…but would they realize that there weren't enough of his people there to be the whole group? Would they figure out it was a trap?

He crawled along, finding another spot and popping up. He blasted away…and now there were only three of the enemy visible. He could see some of his people from where he was, too, and at least four who were down. There were more than that in total, he realized, probably a lot more. But he ignored it. All that mattered now was destroying the three remaining enemy bots…and quickly. He *had* to get his people farther, and he didn't have much time left.

He climbed up the large pile of rubble, and he prepared to fire again. He stopped for a second, took in a deep breath, and he lunged up again, taking aim.

But this time, before he could fire, he felt something. It

was hot, and he dropped his gun almost immediately. He realized he'd been hit, but for another second, he didn't feel any pain, just an intense warmth. He ducked down and began looking, checking himself, trying to ascertain whether he was badly wounded or not.

And then the pain came, suddenly and intensely. He moaned, an uncontrollable shriek...and then he stumbled over, rolling down the debris pile toward the ground.

*   *   *

"Alright...listen to me. We've got to get this message back to the others. It's the most important thing we can do. The only truly crucial operation. These aliens want to use us to reproduce...and I have it on good authority it is terribly painful, and probably fatal. Some of us *have* to get back, in spite of any alien pursuit. So, we split up, in ten groups...and we all go a different way back. Some of will have to get through and deliver the message." Travis was looking all around. He was edgy, nervous...afraid that more of the enemy would come at any time. He knew he had to get his groups moving as quickly as possible, but he was also aware that first he had to make sure they all knew what the enemy's true purpose was. It was terrible, and even though he hadn't actually seen it, he knew he would never forget it. He didn't know if he would make it back, but he wanted to be sure if *anyone* did, the word would get through.

Never again, not in another moment in his life...whether that lasted an hour, or he lived to be 100...would he be carrying a more important message. Though he figured there wasn't much chance of making it to old age...not for him, or any other human, for that matter.

"Okay, let's break up into ten groups. I've picked out the leaders, and they each have their routes ready. They're here..." He pointed to a small group of people standing just next to him. "Just break down, into roughly equal groups.

We've got to get moving right now. Every hour—every minute—we spend here is just begging for the enemy to come at us." He stopped talking for a moment, just standing there and looking out at his people. They just stood, looking back at him, no one saying a word or moving.

Finally, he said, "Now! Move into groups…we're leaving in two minutes!"

The people started moving, stumbling around behind the ten leaders. They weren't organized, and some of the groups were larger than others. He was about to interfere, to tell some people to switch, but then he noticed them doing it themselves. In another minute, he didn't have ten exactly equal groups, but it was close enough.

"Alright…let's get going. Remember, follow your leader. Every group is going a different way. If you run into the enemy, it is *your* problem…even if another group is close enough, there will be no interaction. The only thing that is crucial to us is *someone* getting back and telling the main group exactly what we have found out." He was silent for a moment, but then he added, "I am proud of all of you, and I hope every party makes it back. But we don't know what enemy forces we will encounter, so all I can say is, do whatever you can to ensure that someone makes it." He stared at the group for a moment, torn that he didn't know who he would see again, and who would be killed trying to get back.

He felt like he should say something else, but he didn't. Every minute they stayed so close to the enemy was a risk. He turned to his own group, and to the roughly ten percent of his people lined up behind him. "Come on," he said, softer than he had spoken before. "Let's go…let's get moving."

* * *

Qualak-Neerie stared out from his ship, watching the waves

of robots moving forward, blasting away at the human defense forces. He had known his force was invincible, that 3,000 bots would overwhelm and destroy any possible human resistance. But now, it was the level of his success that was bothering him, or more specifically, the amount of defensive fire. It was considerable and constant...but it was definitely lighter than it had been. Considerably lighter...and that concerned him.

His bots had advanced, blowing through the first two lines of human resistance. He'd expected that, of course, but he had anticipated that it would take considerably longer than it did. He knew he could view that as a good thing, as better then expected results usually were. But he had been too pompous once in facing this enemy, and he had sworn that would never happen again.

He looked down at his controls, and he pulled back several units from his attack line. They weren't needed, not now...but if the enemy had hidden some of its forces, if they came out in surprise attack, he would be ready for it. He still didn't think much of the humans, but he had come to accept that they *were* a violent species, by far the most aggressive his people had yet encountered. The mission's focus was the breeding program, literally about saving his race, but he wondered now if the current invasion had served another purpose. What would have happened if the humans had been allowed to advance, if they had been given another five or ten centuries to improve their technology...and to move out to the stars. He was torn between his dislike for them, and the realization that facing a truly advanced human society could possibly have been very challenging, especially for his race, dying out as they were. It only fed his desire to destroy them, to crush their resistance.

And to make Earth what it was to be...a breeding center for his people.

But first, he had to see that the current battle was

won…and won decisively. That appeared to be well underway, but he wanted to make certain, to not leave anything to chance. He stared at his scanner, checking for any readings, signs that there were people trying to move around, to take his force in flank. But there was nothing…nothing save the seemingly very weak force in front of him. His robots were pushing that back steadily…but the whole thing worried him. He had expected a fairly quick and decisive victory, but what he saw now was too one-sided, too complete.

What could the enemy be planning?

Chapter Forty-Three

From the Notes of Hugh McDaniel

I was wounded...shot in the battle we just finished. It is fairly bad...but it won't be fatal, at least it won't be by itself. Though if it prevents me from walking fast enough, from getting away in time...

The fight itself was nasty, and a lot of my people were killed or wounded. But it turned out we were just facing a guard post of four bots. We could likely have done better had we not been so surprised, something I take responsibility for. I have a lot on my mind, those we left behind, the bomb and whether it would work, Travis and his expedition. I have never before had this much to worry about all at once.

Or this little time for it. I have to get my detachment on the move, put at least a few more miles between us and the explosion. Or if there is none, if we weren't able to correctly repair and use the bomb, then it will be a bit more distance between us and our pursuers, the thousands of bots currently attacking our rearward group.

Just Outside the NJ Transit Tunnel
Weehawken, New Jersey
D + 219 Days

"Let's go...help anybody who can move, but do it quickly. We're leaving in two minutes." Hugh managed to get out the words, and he even thought they sounded pretty good. But the pain was bad, enough that after he finished, he put his face down for a minute and yelled into his jacket.

He had been hit, and he knew it wasn't that bad, at least that it wouldn't be fatal...at least he didn't think so. But that didn't mean there wasn't pain, and a fair amount of it at that. He had decided to hide it, as much as possible, and he wrapped up a shirt from his pack and placed it firmly against the injury. He wasn't sure it completely stopped the bleeding, but it did a fairly good job, at least at the moment. He knew he could use some help, that given fifteen or twenty minutes, he could probably get it in at least somewhat better shape.

But he didn't have fifteen or twenty minutes. He wasn't even sure his people had time to get far enough away. But he was damned sure going to try.

He stood up completely, and he stared at his watch before he started to walk. Fifty-five minutes. He was way behind where he had hoped to be. The travel time had been longer than he'd expected...and then he'd lost another 45 minutes or so right here, fighting with the enemy and cleaning up the mess after. In less than an hour, the bomb would go off...and when it did, he knew his people would be closer than he was sure was safe. He'd make certain they were positioned as carefully as he could, and he would hope for the best.

That was the best, he realized, far better than the alternative. If an hour passed without an explosion, that would mean that either he hadn't gotten the bomb properly set up...or that the enemy had sliced through his defenders and found it in time to disarm it. Either one of those two things meant disaster. He had a range of calculations on how long it would take the enemy to track him down, to bring the fight to the rest of his people...but the best possible result he could come up with was tomorrow. He knew his people's only real chance was for the bomb to blow up, to take out the enemy, or most of them. Anything else almost certainly ended up with the total destruction of his force. They might not all die, of course. Many might just be battered into surrendering. He wasn't sure the enemy would accept that, of course, but he was fairly certain they did have some uses for live humans. Otherwise, they would all be dead, he realized. While he didn't know what the enemy was going to do to any captives, something told him those who were killed would be the lucky ones.

"Let's go," he shouted, trying to sound as demanding as possible. He knew they would be leaving behind seriously wounded colleagues, and likely that others would fall out as they raced for safety. That cut at him, made him feel terrible, but he knew the only alternative was for everyone to remain. And that he wouldn't do. Those who were too badly injured to keep up would just have to stay here and take the risk of being closer to the bomb. If it exploded, he would send some volunteers back to check on them, to help them to safety. Or whoever took over from him would do it...assuming he didn't make it.

If the bomb didn't go off, those left behind would be easy targets for the robots making their way west...to the final battle to finish his entire force.

He stood up, holding himself as straight as he could. The terrain was bad, all chopped up, with fallen buildings everywhere. It wasn't ideal for making time, for moving very quickly, but that is just what he had to do. He put one foot in front of the other, and he maintained a fast walk...despite the sharp pain he felt with every step.

*   *   *

Carl Delvus lay on his back, down behind the large pile of debris. He was gasping for air, feeling the pain from two small wounds, but he was still planning on continuing the fight. He was proud to say that most of his people who were left—who were still alive—remained in the line. But that was less than half of those he had started with. The rest were all dead, except for those who were seriously wounded, and waiting to die.

Of course, the others, even those uninjured…were also more or less waiting to die.

He understood now, the difference between an initial urge to volunteer, to accept a position that would lead to almost certain death, and the reality of how one would really feel, when the end was very near. He tried to tell himself he would still consent to lead the group even now, that he would accept his doom as clearly as he had before…but he knew it wasn't true. If he could be with the others now, running across New Jersey, if he could have left someone else behind, he would do it. His stomach ached and he was fighting to hold back the panic that was trying to take him. He had less than twenty minutes to go until the bomb went off, a third of an hour to live, assuming he made it that long, that one of the bots didn't finish him even sooner. But somehow, some part of him held on, kept himself where he was, fighting until the end.

He heard the sound of the enemy, louder than it had been so far in the fight. He knew they were coming, planning to assault his final position. He had held out, his forces enduring almost the amount of time he had to. Perhaps they could hang on long enough. The enemy might break through with a few minutes left, but would they really have time to get to the station and search it well enough to find the bomb and disable it? He didn't think so, but then there was the question about whether it would work at all. He wanted to survive long enough to find out.

But as he listened to the volume of the enemy fire, something told him that wasn't in the cards. He realized the bots would be to his location in a matter of seconds, and he couldn't imagine holding them off for almost eighteen minutes. That was a small amount of time, and yet now it seemed large. He still didn't think it was enough time for them to find the bomb and disable it...but now he wasn't sure. He had to do everything he could to eat up more time, to stretch the battle out a bit more.

He could hear screaming now, the troops on his right. They were running, trying to escape. He could see some of them, and he knew others were just on the far side of a pile of masonry. He heard yelps, and the sounds of people going down under fire...and then the people who had come to his side of the berm began to fall. He gritted his teeth, prepared for a final conflict with the forces coming that way.

But they didn't get there first, not from that side. His distraction was terminated almost at once as a bot emerged at the top of the pile of debris right in front of him. He pulled up his rifle, almost on instinct, and he fired, blasting the thing, hitting it at least a dozen times. But it brought one of its own guns down on him, and it fired.

The large rounds impacted hard. He knew he was shot, badly shot, at least six or eight times, but for an instant he didn't feel it. Then he realized his leg had been completely shot off. An instant later, lying there, his body torn apart, his life draining away, he watched as a dozen robots came up over the crest. He saw them shooting, gunning down those who were running toward him. He used his last bit of energy to move his arm, to look at his watch.

14:20. Fourteen minutes and twenty seconds. He told himself it would work, that there wasn't enough time to find and disarm it. And for a few seconds, he believed it. Long enough, at least, to take him through the rest of his life.

His arm fell, and the watch hit the hard ground and smashed. But it didn't matter, not anymore.

Carl Delvus was dead.

* * *

Estle-Starric looked out at the manned parapets of his city. He had been waiting for the enemy to attack, even though he hadn't really expected it. And he had been correct...so far there had been no assault, not even any forces noticed approaching. He considered sending some of his guards out after them, hunting them down, but his forces were already smaller than he was comfortable with, even more so now that the enemy showed that they could mount, at the very least, substantial scouting missions. He realized that he needed a new attitude toward the humans, that true success would require more aggressive methods.

He also needed captives, millions of them ultimately, if the breeding program worked, if humanity proved to be the species that could carry their children to term. So, mass executions weren't possible. They had already destroyed most of them in the initial attacks, and supposedly left the survivors broken, ruined, struggling just to find food and the like. They had expected some resistance, perhaps, but not as much as they had gotten...not even close. He had lost hundreds of robots in small groups, most heavily in New York, but also in many other cities...and then his first mission to silence the resistance in New York resulted in a massive defeat, with all 200 bots destroyed, and one of his own people lost as well.

Now, he had sent a truly huge force, 3,000 bots and 50 of his own people. That had required him drawing from a number of his other bases on the planet. He couldn't imagine any result except total victory, and that with relatively small losses. But still, it upset his plans elsewhere, and left him with sufficient defenders for the city, perhaps.

but not enough to send out a true killing force to hunt down the enemy.

He wasn't really concerned that the humans had sufficient forces to threaten his overall control, but he was worried that they were more powerful than he had expected at this point...and particularly anxious that they appeared to be sufficiently organized to launch a force, even one too small to seriously threaten his complex. Sending a group out suggested a command structure of sorts, and a level of commitment and organization he hadn't thought possible.

He was tempted again to hunt down the humans who had come, but he decided to wait. He had a huge force in New York, even then fighting to crush the forces there. They were the most powerful, at least that he had seen, and while he had no idea if the people who had come close to his city were related to them, or from somewhere else entirely, he realized the destruction of those forces, and the reclaiming of New York City, would be a large step forward.

He turned, and he saw one of his aides coming toward him. He stopped and waited. It was obvious the officer had something to tell him.

"Estle-Starric, I have a report, something I feel you may find interesting."

He gestured for the man to continue.

"As you know, we have many surveillance systems in the complex. We review all the tapes, of course, but not in real time. There are just too many for that."

"I know all of this. So, what did you find?" He was impatient. It wasn't the aide's fault, but he bore the brunt of it anyway.

"Sir, we have...well, we only have video of it, and not audio, but we found it highly concerning. I have taken the liberty of directing it to your viewer. I suggest you watch it at once."

Estle-Starric sighed. Between the attack on New York, the appearance of enemies here, and the—hopefully—

imminent birth of the first of his species in more than a hundred years, he couldn't help but think that this could have waited. At least until he looked.

He saw a figure, bent over inside the outer fence. For a few seconds, he couldn't tell who it was. But then, he realized.

It was the human president.

He was now completely interested. The president was talking to…someone. He couldn't really see who he was speaking with, but whoever it was, he was on the other side of the fence. Outside!

His mind began to race. Whoever the humans in the vicinity were, they had come closer than he'd expected, even to the walls of the city!

And they had spoken with the president!

The level of resistance, the aggressive nature of the humans, of some of them at least, shocked him. As far as he knew, none of the other targeted populations had shown such an ongoing determination. They had all been battered by nuclear bombardment and reduced to easily manipulated groups of survivors. Except the humans. Some of them had been beaten beyond resistance too, of course, but an alarming number showed an amazing will to fight, even when their civilization was destroyed, when they were reduced to living in rubble.

It was strange. He was sure some of the humans were prepared to work with him, even to turn on their own kind…and yet others were ready to fight on. It didn't make sense to him. It was almost like there were two totally different groups among the humans…and that was utterly unlike any of the other species his people had encountered.

He knew one thing though. The president had lied to him…or at least he had withheld information. And that was intolerable.

"Go and get the human president, and bring him to me at once."

Chapter Forty-Four

From the Notes of Hugh McDaniel

I have done all I can, raced as fast as I could force myself to, and most of my group has kept up with me. I'm sure some of them could have travelled even faster, gotten farther, but no one did. They wouldn't leave me, or any of the other injured parties, alone, not if they could move forward.

My wound is bad, but I think it will be okay. The pain has been awful, but I've started to get used to it. I'm fairly certain there is no bullet or fragment inside, that it went completely through. I'm not sure what that means for my recovery, but I have to admit, I am glad to escape the eventual surgery I would need to remove anything that was in there, especially since I am fairly certain there won't be any morphine or anything else left, not once the more serious cases are treated.

I have stopped our flight and issued commands to all of our people to find the best cover they can. The area around us has a significant amount of debris, enough to provide reasonable shelter from the bomb. I don't know if it will explode…and if it does, I am not sure what the effect will be here. Most of my people are farther away, thank goodness, but this last group is closer to the city than I would like.

But there are less than ten minutes now, and it is time to find the best cover, to hunker down and endure the explosion…or to realize that the time has come, and the bomb hasn't blown.

If that happens, if it doesn't blow, I know I will have to get our people, all of them, as organized as possible for the fight I know will be coming.

The battle I am almost certain we will lose, but the one we will fight if we have to…to the end.

Somewhere in Northern New Jersey
3 or 4 Miles from the Railroad Tunnel
D + 219 Days

"Dig in…deeper!" Hugh was exhausted, his fatigue even worse due to his wound. But he had decided that he had ten more minutes, and that he would use that to do everything he could to make sure his people were ready. He had abandoned badly injured comrades, done all sorts of things he would never have believed himself capable of, but now he was acting the way he felt he should. He realized that he might save a couple of his people—or maybe none at all—that it would pale beside the number of dead he had already prevailed over, but he had to do what he could.

He stumbled, almost falling, but he caught himself. He wondered for a moment about Travis. Was his brother still alive, would he return? And if he did, would he still be here? He just didn't know. He didn't even know if he would survive the next few minutes, though his best guess was radiation would be the main problem for those as far from ground zero as he was, at least those with some protection to their east, like the piles of smashed concrete and rock his people were behind.

"Down…get lower. Nothing exposed to the east, nothing at all!" He stumbled forward. It was about the best he could do, and he vowed to continue it until he was forced to find his own spot to try and endure. "All of you, check your positions. Make sure there is no loose debris, anything that can fall on you...and be certain that whatever is between you and the city, to the east, is as solid as possible."

His mind raced, wondering what would happen if the bomb did blow. Would the enemy be wiped out? Perhaps they would simply send another force, an even larger one. It was possible the gains, even of destroying the entire attacking force, wouldn't be that significant...but he told himself that it would be meaningful, that at least it would transmit to the enemy that his people weren't defeated. Not yet.

"Not ever," he said quietly. He couldn't speak for everyone, but he was sure that he would never surrender, never yield. Either he would free his planet, chase the enemy away, or he would die. There was no in between, not for him.

He gasped hard. Between fatigue and his wound, he could barely continue. But somehow, he found the strength. Then, his watch went below one minute, and he ducked down himself, finding what looked like a good spot. There, he curled up, checking to make sure he wasn't exposed in any way to the east and that there was no loose debris around. Then, he waited.

* * *

Qualak-Neerie looked out at the battlefield. There were still a few occasional shots being fired by an enemy survivor, but mostly, it seemed the fight was over. He wanted to be happy, to enjoy his victory...but it had come too easily. He'd lost well under 50 robots, and perhaps another 50 were significantly damaged...and none of his Gavicons had even advanced into combat. It had gone much better than he'd expected, and he realized that a couple weeks ago, he would have accepted it entirely. But he had fought the humans before, and he'd come to expect better from them. There was no question that those who fought had fought hard...but it seemed there were fewer of them than he'd expected. Far fewer. And that worried him.

What was it? Where could the rest of them be? Were they hidden somewhere, planning a surprise attack...or had they fled? That certainly seemed to be the most likely option, especially considering the size of his own force. He understood why they would flee, but where would they have gone?

He looked at his screen, pulling up the maps of the area. They could have gone in three directions...or they could be hidden in the city, waiting for the moment to attack. He just didn't know. His details on other cultures, on the civilizations his people had attacked and conquered couldn't explain it. He'd never encountered—his people hadn't—a society that would still be fighting. But he believed the humans would be.

He pressed the controls in his ship, scanned all the areas around his forces. He could tell that the whole area had been set up to resist his assault, that it seemed ready for thousands and thousands of defenders. But as he scanned the area, he couldn't come up with anywhere near that many bodies.

He turned and pressed the button, opened up his ship. He knew he was taking a chance, that if there was a human anywhere nearby, he was offering him a shot. But, wherever the humans were, and he had no idea where that was, he was fairly certain it wasn't here.

He climbed out of his ship, and he walked over to one of the supervisor robots. "Report," he said.

"The area is secure. We have just reached some type of significant underground facility. I have sent several robots in to check it out. So, far they have reported no contact."

"Very well...send in another ten bots...and double all of

the patrols. There are more humans in this group…somewhere. Find them!"

"Yes, Sir!" The bot was silent for a few seconds, as it forwarded his commands. Then, suddenly it turned toward him. It was a robot, and it didn't have emotion…but it came close. "Qualak-Neerie…I have just received a signal from one of the units in the facility. They have found what they believe to be an atomic bomb…and they believe it is activated."

Qualak-Neerie heard the words, and for a few seconds, he was shocked by them. Then, it all made sense. He blurted out, "Disarm the bomb!" But he knew the command was unnecessary, that the bots would already be doing that.

How was it possible? How could the humans, just a group of refugees, even if they were better fighters than he could have expected, turn up with that kind of weapon? He stood still for a moment, and then he raced back to his ship. He couldn't believe the danger, the possibility of losing most of his bots, but he had 50 Gavicons as well, and they were just as exposed. He didn't know the status, the amount of time until the bomb would explode, but he knew the supervisor would communicate to him as soon as the data came in. He was sure that the bots would disarm it, but now he wondered if there were others. The humans had proven to be *far* deadlier than he had expected, even after the last fight.

He energized his ship, and while it was charging, he activated his comm to the others. "Attention all Gavicons…get your ships lifted off at once! Get out of the city…now! There is an atomic bomb, and it is live!" He cut off the comm and he reached out, grabbing the controls of his ship. When the bot communicated with him, told him the bomb was disarmed, he could come right back. But just in case…

His ship rose, reaching a height of twenty feet. Fifty feet. But that was all.

The ground rumbled, and an instant later, a wave blew out, dust and dirt and heat…and his ship flew to the side. He had time—barely—to recognize what was going on, and then his ship was bathed in heat. The vessel itself melted down to nothing, and almost vanished.

But by then, Qualak-Neerie was already dead.

* * *

Hugh was behind a large pile of debris, the heaviest he had been able to find. He was huddled there, keeping his head low, doing everything he could to protect himself…which he realized wasn't much. He was both desperate for the bomb to explode…and panic stricken about the effects. His people were mostly safe from the immediate damage, at least if they stayed behind the heavy wreckage and nothing fell on them. But the radiation…he didn't know about that, how much of an effect it would have out this far.

30 seconds. He checked again, making certain that his position was good, that it offered protection against any portion of the blast that could make it this far.

20 seconds. He took a deep breath, and he thought about Travis and his people, about all of those he had sent on ahead of him, even of the enemy he hoped were all inside the city, in the weapon's kill zone.

10 seconds. He felt himself tightening up, crouching and waiting to see if the explosion occurred, or if his whole operation, the removal of all his people, everything had been for nothing.

Zero. For an instant, there was nothing, and he began to feel that the bomb hadn't worked, that everything he had done had only decreased his people's already tiny chance of surviving. But then he felt it.

The flash was first. The pile of debris blocked his direct view, but it was still almost overwhelming. He closed his eyes tightly and buried his face into his arms, and still, it was almost blinding.

Then, the ground began to shake hard, and the wall of debris, too. Chunks of stone began to fall on him. They hurt, some of them badly, but he endured, remained fixed in his position. Until a large portion of the wall of debris began to fall. It hadn't been loose before, but now it was. It came down on him, and he slid lower, becoming half buried by the debris. His wound was torn back open, and he had what felt like a hundred bruises and cuts. For a couple minutes, he laid still, and he thought he was dead, but then, he could feel something moving. Not crashing down on him but sliding away. He tried to raise his head, to see what was going on, but for a moment, he couldn't. He just laid there, as something—someone, he realized—pulled the debris off of him. Then, all of a sudden, he could move. He was in pain, terrible pain, at least a dozen small wounds adding to the larger one he'd already had. But as he slowly came back to his senses, he realized he had escaped any critical injuries. He was battered, badly…but he was able to get up. Slowly.

He looked around, his vision blurry…but improving. He could see the light above the giant mound of debris that was still mostly sheltering him. And his vision improved enough that he could see who had helped him. It was Gavin Sanders.

"How are you, Hugh…anything really bad?"

He looked up at his friend, not sure for a few seconds what to say. Practically every inch of him hurt, and some of it badly…but he was fairly sure none of it would kill him. "I'm okay," he finally said. It was an overstatement, he knew, but mostly accurate. He started to come back to his senses more, and he reached out to his friend, grabbing his offered hand. He got up, slowly and painfully, but he made it to his feet. He brushed off the debris that was stuck to him, and he looked up the hill, to the top, to the bright, shimmering light beyond.

He looked at Gavin, and he knew at once that his friend agreed…he wanted to see too. They turned together and began climbing. That wasn't easy, especially not for Hugh, but somehow, he managed to do it. They reached the top and looked out to the east.

There was a huge cloud of dust. It expanded high into the sky, but it was still rising higher. He couldn't see the city very well, not from where they were, not with all the dust, but he could tell at once that the bomb had exploded, that it had torn the entire place apart.

His mind went at once to those who were left behind. First, his defenders, almost 1,000 of them. And second, all the other survivors of the city's first bombing. He had reached as many as he could, tried to convince them to leave. But as with everything of the sort, he knew there were some that wouldn't listen, who just stayed in place…and others he never even knew about. They were dead now, all of them. He was sure of it.

He just wondered if the invaders had all been there, if they had been close enough to the bomb that they, too, were all destroyed. If they were, if their forces were attacking his volunteer defenders, they would have been almost at ground zero. He didn't know many things about the enemy or their power, not really, but he was sure a multi-megaton atomic bomb was enough to destroy them utterly, particularly near ground zero. Amid the sorrow, the feelings of loss he faced for his own people—and for the others, too—he was excited about destroying the enemy, about possibly taking out a massive force of them.

He stood for a moment, looking mostly away, taking only a few scattered glances back toward the city. Then he turned around. He didn't have any hard data on the enemy positions, whether they were all in the city or not. He knew it was possible that he could run into further detachments…but somehow, even though there was no way to be sure, he believed that most of them, the vast force that had come to destroy his people, had been themselves destroyed.

"Alright, everybody…watch out for that fireball. Don't look at it…at least not for more than a few seconds. Let's make sure no one was injured by the blast, and then, let's go. We've still got to march for hours. We have to catch up to the others."

He turned and glanced once more in the direction he had just warned his people to avoid…and he couldn't help himself. Despite more problems, more things to worry about than he could clearly visualize, his lips broke out into something he hadn't done for a long while now.

He smiled.

Chapter Forty-Five

From the Notes of Hugh McDaniel

Three days. It has been three days since we blew up the bomb. Hell, since we utterly destroyed the ruins of New York City. Three days since we killed everyone who insisted on remaining there.

Three days since we destroyed all the robots, and quite probably a number of aliens as well. My emotions have jerked around, one minute feeling devastation for the people who were unquestionably killed too, and the next joy for the pain we have inflicted on the invaders.

Then the next minute, Travis and his people enter my mind. I have survived, for a little while at least, but I don't know what happened to my brother. Or to Lucas...or any of the others he took with him. All I can do it wait. I have sent groups out all around, to find them, to prevent them from trying to go back to the city...but as far as I know, none of them have been found yet. I have not given up yet, but with each day that passes it becomes harder to maintain some hope that he survived.

My wounds, at least, have all been treated. I am sore, so much so that I can't really express it adequately, but I am going to be fine. Or, more specifically, I am going to endure my current injuries. What the enemy will do, their response to our bombing of New York, remains to be seen.

I should be worried about that, and of course I am, but I find myself thinking mostly about my brother...and hoping against hope that he returns.

Northwestern New Jersey
Approximately 30 Miles from the Ruins of New York City
D + 225 Days

"That's very good, but we need more. We've got almost thirty thousand of us, and we're going to need to defend ourselves...and probably sooner rather than later." Hugh was watching a group of more than 200, who were moving wreckage around, trying to use it to build fortifications. Everything out here was destroyed, as battered as the city was, but the ruins were far sparser. It was more difficult to build defenses, especially of the size his people needed, but he knew they would be needed, eventually.

They had won a great victory, destroyed an enemy force that was monstrously more powerful than they were...but he knew that had been the result of several strokes of luck. Finding the atomic bomb, getting it to work, and managing to blow it up when the enemy were all in range...he knew that a dozen things could have gone wrong, and while he was glad it all worked, he was well aware that it was not repeatable.

Still, there were a couple new factors in play.

First, he didn't have another bomb, and second, he was almost sure that his enemy would be concerned that he did and conduct their operations accordingly. That was good, in a way, as they would have to be much more meticulous, and that probably meant slow. Unless, of course, they resorted to just bombing the hell out of him. They didn't know exactly where he was, at least he didn't think they did, but he realized that he couldn't mass all his people together, not anymore. The enemy would find him, if they didn't already know where he was, and they would act. He guessed that the losses he had inflicted on them might buy him some time, weeks or even a month...but when the enemy came, he knew they would be serious.

Very serious. And he had to be ready.

He knew his people had to be spread apart...just in case the enemy decided to use their own nukes. That wasn't a good solution, he realized, but it was the best he could come up with, and he had his followers spread out even now, all across Northwestern New Jersey. If the enemy came as they had before, he was sure they'd be more spread out, too, also concerned for more nukes. And if they decided to use their own nuclear arsenal, at least they couldn't take out all of his people with a few bombs.

He turned and looked out, over the ground to the south. He had been to Northern New Jersey before, a number of times in fact, but the devastation had been so complete, he couldn't recognize anything. Still, he realized that, for the moment at least, it was his new home. He turned and walked up a hill, to a spot he knew had a view that reached Manhattan. Once, the view had been full of buildings, a city of eight million people, but now it was just ruins. It had been ruins for almost eight months of course, but now it was utterly lifeless, and the skyline it had once shown was completely gone.

He looked out, but he couldn't see anything. The skyline was gone, the buildings that reached for the sky were all destroyed. And the people, he realized, apart from those who had come with him, were dead. He didn't know how many he had killed, and the fact that at least he had saved them from whatever purpose the enemy had for them gave him little comfort. He knew he would carry their ghosts with him everywhere he went. Forever.

"Hugh!"

The call shook him from his thoughts. He turned,

expecting one problem or another, just as the past three days had gone.

But when he stared down, he saw something he had wished for, that he had held out some hope to see, even while he didn't really expect it.

"Travis!" He had hardened considerably, throughout the past eight months certainly, and especially over the last few days, but now he felt his control slipping away. He raced down the hillside, running toward his brother, ignoring the pain in his wounds.

"Hugh…my God, I figured you'd put up a hell of a fight against the enemy, but seriously?" Travis smiled, and he moved forward, toward Hugh with his arms open. The two of them came together and embraced. They held each other for a while, not saying anything else for perhaps thirty seconds. Then Travis backed away, and his expression of joy faded away. "We found an enemy base, Hugh, a big one, and I know now why they are here."

Hugh stepped back. He could tell from his brother's face that the news wasn't good, that it was worse than he expected. But even that didn't prepare him for the truth.

* * *

Estle-Starric stood in his study, alone, thinking about what had transpired. He had been prepared for a variety of outcomes, but the total destruction of the force he had sent, so large and powerful, wasn't one of them. He had adapted to humans being more violent than the other species, even them having better weaponry than expected…but the civilians, and by and large, that's what they were, having access to nuclear weapons? And worse, large ones, powerful enough to totally destroy the ruins of the city?

He couldn't believe it, in fact he hadn't at first. He'd even flown up there himself, witnessed the total devastation. He had lost 3,000 robots, and 50 of his people. It was almost unbelievable. He wanted to respond with his own nukes, big ones this time. He was furious, and part of him wanted to depopulate the planet, to utterly destroy every human being, wherever they were hiding. But he couldn't. Amid the disastrous news of three days before, there had been some tremendous developments as well. The breeding program, its pace greatly accelerated from natural birth, was almost complete…and everything was still going according to plan. In fact, he expected the first "birth" to occur imminently, and if everything went according to plan, if the human specimens proved capable of bearing Gavicon children to live deliveries, they would become almost priceless. They would save his race, and they would also save their own, at least to breed and grow and live to serve as future delivery vehicles. That wasn't a pleasant future from their point of view, perhaps, but his focus was solely on his own race's needs.

He turned and looked at the item on his desk. It was strange, he realized, to keep it there, but he somehow enjoyed it. The president's head was already starting to rot, but he had vowed to hold onto it, to maintain it for a long while. He told himself that the president couldn't have known about the bomb in New York, that he had been a prisoner since the very beginning. But that didn't stop his anger. He had interrogated the president after he had seen the video of him speaking to…someone. But the moment he had returned from his trip to New York, his anger got the better of him. He went right to the cell where the president had been imprisoned, and without a word, he took off his head. He didn't know that he had anything to do with events in New York, but he had decided he didn't have time for those he couldn't trust, and there were other humans in the facility, people he could rely on far more than the president. There were also some he wasn't sure about…some who had been close to the president. They would also die.

He heard his communicator crackle, and then...

"Estle-Starric...it is time. It is time for the first births!" The voice calling to him was excited, and he was too. The enemy resistance was a terrible problem, but it could wait until after this. If the program succeeded, if a live birth actually occurred, he knew it would be a moment that would be cherished in his peoples' history. They would have come close to extinction, and now they could repopulate their planet, and grow to become what they should be.

And if it didn't work? If none of the children were born alive? That would be terrible, and it would tear at him badly. But at least he would enjoy the final step...cleansing this planet of its human occupants. Yes, he would truly enjoy that.

But now, it was time...time to go and see if he'd been right, if Earth and humanity were the match his people had been looking for.

*   *   *

Hugh stared at his brother, almost not believing what he had just said to him.

Almost.

He had assumed that the aliens wanted humanity as slaves, to work in mines or factories or something of the sort. But what his brother spoke of was...almost unimaginable. They had come to Earth to use its people in some kind of breeding plan? That was the entire purpose? Of the invasion? For the survivors? It was almost too much to believe, but then Travis had told him who he'd heard it from.

The whole thing seemed almost unbelievable, and yet he realized that his own story—finding the nuke, fixing it up to work, catching the entire force of the enemy in its kill zone—was fairly unbelievable as well. For that matter, having the Earth invaded by aliens had been pretty damned unexpected too. But his brother finding the president, speaking with him…it was almost impossible to accept.

And yet, he did accept it…and somehow he knew it was all true.

He was silent, for a long while, trying to make sense of it all. He had detested the aliens already, as invaders, as the destroyers of human civilization…but the fury inside him now was almost unimaginable. The aliens had come, they had devastated Earth and killed billions of his people, but now it somehow had gotten even worse. He swore to himself that he would *never* stop fighting, that he would not let anything stand in his way until every one of the invaders was off the Earth.

And preferably…dead.

He looked at his brother, and he saw at once that he agreed totally. Their eyes locked, two hard expressions on their faces, and he was sure they were both in union. They would fight like hell, do whatever they had to do…but somehow, however ridiculous it seemed, the two of them agreed silently.

They would drive the aliens from the Earth…whatever it took.

*   *   *

Estle-Starric stood, watching. He was excited, as all those present were. In a few minutes, he might see the first live Gavicon born in over a hundred years. The sight was truly amazing, the tremendous efforts his culture had made, expending almost all of its remaining productivity on the need to find another race, one that could carry its children to the point where they could live on their own. Nothing else had worked, no test tube efforts, no artificial constructs, not even any of the other species his people had conquered and tried to utilize. Not until this moment.

He stared, ignoring the howling of the human surrogate.

The birth would kill her, he was fairly certain of that, but until then, any kind of painkiller was out of the question. She had to be fully alert…for the child.

The Gavicon crew was around her now, preparing to deliver the child. He wasn't really paying attention to the human, but then she yelled out, so loud he couldn't ignore it. She tensed up for a few seconds, and then, suddenly, she fell to the matt, and she lay still. For a moment, Estle-Starric almost panicked, afraid that the experiment that had come so close to success had failed at the last minute. He knew they wouldn't give up on Earth over one failure, that they would move on to the next, and then to the one after that. But he also realized that each effort after the first would be made at decreasing chances of success.

Then, he heard the sounds. He had never heard them before, save perhaps as a child, but he knew what they were immediately. The sounds of a newborn.

A live child!

He felt his excitement return, and almost at once he realized that everyone else there was just as thrilled as he was. He saw the crew working, hunched over the body of the human surrogate, and then the lead technician turned to face him. In his hands he held something that hadn't been seen in over a century.

A newborn Gavicon!

Estle-Starric looked down at him, realizing that despite his optimism, his assurance that Earth would prove to be the planet that produced what his people had searched everywhere for, he was actually stunned. He realized that much of his prior confidence had been manufactured, designed to keep him pushing forward. Now, it had worked…Earth was proving to be the planet his people had sought, the world that would allow them to regrow their society, to build back up in numbers, to millions, and eventually billions.

He realized there was still the chance that there would be

problems, that the child he was looking at could be stricken with some type of illness, that he could die. But as he stared at him, he could see that he was strong.

"Congratulations, all! To the medical staff, you have done it. You have saved our race, nothing less. There are no words, no statements to make, except thank you. Thank you very much. To all of you, the humans have proven to be more difficult than we expected, but they are also priceless. We will have to accelerate our pacification methods, and drive away this rebelliousness, but without significantly reducing their remaining population. Our initial assaults were intended to destroy all resistance, as they have with all the other races, and we had calculated that enough of them would survive worldwide to serve our breeding program. What we did not take into account was such a level of continued resistance, and sadly, several days ago, we saw the true nature of this, and we lost a very large number of our robots…and 50 of our Gavicons as well. I will plan the retribution, the response against the dangerous elements of humanity, even as we begin sweeping up the more docile ones to expand the breeding program. Always remember, the humans have given us problems, more than any other species, but they have also provided us with our goal…the only thing we have searched for as a race. Now, it is on us, to expand the program, and to destroy the human resistance. Utterly."

He looked out at his people, and he saw in them joy, excitement. The problem that had existed all of their lives, that had threatened the very existence of the species, was solved! And that seemed to wash away even the consternation of the news of several days ago. He realized it had helped him as well. He might have faced the loss of his position when their leader returned, as surely he would when he heard of the great success. But now, he was far more than the commander who had lost a large force to the enemy…he was the Gavicon who had supervised the greatest success in their history.

"Estle-Starric…what of him." The head of the team that had produced the first birth in more than a century stood still. The human female was dead, there was no question of that. But the technician stood beside a man. He had been restrained, under the table, connected to the woman by a series of tubes. The birthing process required both the humans, but the man had survived it…barely.

He stared for a second, looking at the human's face, uncertain whether he had anything left of who he had been, or if enduring the procedure had left him a vegetable. But after a brief look, Estle-Starric realized he didn't care. The human had served his purpose, and he had done it well. He served no future purpose.

"Kill him. And dispose of both the woman and the man."

He looked at the child one more time, realizing what he owed to it. He knew he had been saved from disaster, that the debacle that had happened under his command was nothing compared to this success. That the birth of the child would effectively wash away the blame for the military disaster.

He turned and walked out of the room, making his way back to his quarters…and swearing one thing to himself.

He would make the enemy pay for what they had done, for the destruction of more than 50 of his people, for almost bringing him down. He would make them pay dearly.

Epilogue

Somewhere in Central Ohio
D+365 Days

Hugh stood on the plain, looking out at those gathered around him. All of those of his usual retinue were there. Travis, of course, and Lucas. Gavin Sanders was there, too, as were Sarah Jones and Janet Howers. And Horace, too, the physicist who had become his friend working for days on end on the bomb. His parents, too, though he knew that was more the reason for their presence than anything else. All told, he had twenty-four people gathered together. They had come in from various elements of the population that had sworn allegiance to Gavin and him. There were over 40,000 of them now, situated in terrain that used to be Pennsylvania and Ohio.

They had spent the past few months fighting in several spots, and they had been driven out of New Jersey. He had been concerned the enemy would use nuclear weapons in response, but since his brother had returned and told him of their true purpose, he understood why they didn't, too. That didn't mean they wouldn't, if they could gather enough of their enemy within a blast zone, but they couldn't use a lot of them. They had utilized a nuclear bombardment to cripple to planet, to beat the survivors down into a helpless lot of battered survivors, and they couldn't do it again, not when they needed fairly large numbers of humans…for their other purpose.

He had thought about their mission, about what the enemy would do, almost every day. He realized that they would have to capture people, pen them into large camps, use some for their purposes, and others to produce future humans, to sustain their breeding program…forever? He didn't know that for sure, but he couldn't guess at anything else. That meant that as long as he could keep people fighting, struggling against them, they would have problems. But he would have to spread it out, extend the fight. If it was just his people, sooner or later the enemy would wipe them out, either with nukes, or just with conventional assaults. They had already launched a bunch of attacks, all much smaller than the one he had destroyed, but now he lacked any atomic weapons to fight back. At least five thousand of his people had been killed, and while he had managed to add more than he had lost as he moved farther west, he knew that wasn't the route to success. Not in the long term.

"Hello, all…I'm glad you could come. It seemed to me like we should spend our first anniversary together…and I have a surprise. Several actually." He smiled. The situation was still dire, and they were impossibly far from any kind of victory, but he had finally managed to make contact with some others…people who had raised their own groups in other areas, just as determined as he was to resist…to the end.

"So, without further delay, allow me to introduce Brian Kelleher, Daphne Smith, and Jon Mallachek. They are from the Midwest, and they have assembled groups of their own, much like ours." He knew they were smaller, but together they had almost fifteen thousand, and added to his own forty, that was getting large. "When I sent out scouts, they ran into their people, and I invited them to come and meet